# Hand of Destiny

Book I

## The Appointed

Pen Press Publishers Ltd

First published in Great Britain by
Pen Press Publishers Ltd
25 Eastern Place
Brighton
BN2 1GJ

ISBN13: 978-1-906206-29-1

Printed and bound in the UK

A catalogue record of this book is available from
the British Library

Cover design by Jacqueline Abromeit

# Dedication

This book is dedicated with love to my parents, for their endless patience and support, but most of all for their faith.

# Prologue

The bottle trembled in Tobias's hand as he tilted it over the goblet. He clenched his fingers around its smooth surface in an effort to still the tremor and up-ended the bottle. In no time at all, the goblet was full of what appeared to be simply water, and to an unpractised eye it was impossible to tell the difference. Tobias set the bottle down and threw back his head. Now was the moment, the one he'd been preparing for ever since he first discovered the truth. No one was given the gift if they weren't fated to use it.

The sound of a baby crying drifted into him from the next room, and tears started in his eyes. He longed to go to her, to cradle her against his breast one final time, but he had to hurry. They would come for him soon. He only hoped Ivan had received his message.

He took several deep breaths to steady himself and, in a clear voice, he recited the words he had hoped he would never have to say. As he spoke, he fixed his gaze intently on the book lying open on the table beside the now empty bottle. It lay open at the page in the exact centre, which, like all the pages, was completely blank. The baby's cries grew louder, and his voice rose too as he strove to drown her out. He could not permit his concentration to lapse.

He could feel it working. The air had become taut, an invisible thread between his body and the open book. He could hardly bear the tension. He needed to be free. Tobias uttered the last word in a desperate shout, then he brought the goblet to his lips and drained its contents in a single gulp.

The effect of the poison was instantaneous. The goblet fell to the floor and shattered as every muscle in his body went into spasm and his skin began to feel as if it might burst into flames. He fell backwards and collapsed, writhing on the floor.

At that moment the door flew open and Ivan almost fell through in his haste. "My god! Tobias, are you alright? What has happened?" He rushed to the bedside and seized Tobias's hand. "You're burning up! You need a healer at once!"

"Ivan!" Tobias's voice was a harsh whisper. His breathing came hard and shallow. "Listen to me, old friend. I have not much time left. You must take the book and my daughter, and go directly to Jeremiah. He will tell you what to do."

"But I cannot leave you here!" Ivan protested. "They come for you. I barely managed to give them the slip. They will pick up my trail soon enough."

Tobias attempted a laugh, but it came out as a rasping cough. "By the time they reach me, I shall be dead, and you must be long gone from here with my daughter and the book. Whatever happens, you must never let Alfredo get possession of either!"

Ivan stared at his friend, comprehension suddenly showing on his face. "You have cast the spell." It was not a question.

Tobias smiled faintly. "It was time."

"No!" Ivan cried desperately. "There must be another way, there has to be!"

Tobias smiled sadly. "There is no other way. I feel the drowsiness coming. It will not be long now. Go! Do as I have said, and at all costs, keep the book and my daughter safe!"

Ivan lingered for a moment longer, paralysed by indecision and grief. But even he could see it was too late. A look of intense peace drifted across Tobias's tired face, he gave a small sigh, then his eyes closed and he fell still.

Ivan stood motionless, allowing the tears to slide unchecked down his cheeks. He still held Tobias's hand fast in his own. Ivan could not imagine life without him. They had been best friends their entire lives. He could not remember a time when they had not been at each other's side.

A sudden snap made Ivan whip around. The book on the table had closed. A strange chink of greenish light shone momentarily from between its covers, then faded. Ivan moved as though he was sleepwalking and gingerly picked up the book. The leather covers were old and tattered at the edges. A pair of tarnished silver clasps held it shut. It felt strangely warm to his touch. Ivan tucked it under his tunic and walked into the adjoining room.

The baby's yells had long since subsided to a fretful whimpering, and her thumb was in her mouth. He looked down at her. Bright red hair stood out against creamy skin. Her eyes, only half-open now, were a startling blue. He thought of his own son, born only a few months before, and his throat constricted. How long before he too died, leaving his son without a father? Pushing the thought resolutely from his mind, he lifted the small, sleepy bundle, wrapped her in his cloak against the night time chill, and quietly slipped away.

Jeremiah answered at the first knock. He ushered Ivan in hurriedly, his eyes sweeping the narrow, deserted street. "You were not followed?"

Ivan shook his head. "Tobias sent me. He's... he is dead!" Ivan's voice broke on the last word.

Jeremiah looked down at the sleeping child cradled protectively in Ivan's arms. "So it has come to pass," he muttered half to himself. "Oh that I had never seen." He passed a hand across his eyes as though to block out an image only he could see. His eyes, as they rested on the baby, were sad and troubled. But the next moment he was himself again. Turning to a bewildered Ivan, he said quickly, "You must go. This child is in grave danger. She cannot stay here. You must hide her somewhere she can be safe."

Ivan frowned. "So, where can she go?"

"There is a world joined on to ours. A world that few people even know exists. There is a cross-over point, known to me alone. Now, I will share it with you."

"But I do not understand," Ivan protested.

"You must cross over to this other world, and leave the child there."

"But how can that be? How can there be other worlds joined on, and how can I cross? Are you sure no one else knows about it?"

"I will explain everything later," Jeremiah waved an inpatient hand. "You must leave now. Don't worry. You will be able to get back easily."

Ivan looked down at the small, warm bundle he held. "But can she ever return?"

Jeremiah sighed heavily. "One day she must. The survival of our people depends on her."

Ivan stared in horror from Jeremiah's face to the baby. Her thumb was still in her mouth. She looked so helpless and vulnerable. "You... you have seen this?" he stammered eventually.

Jeremiah nodded. "Her father knew of this too. When she comes of age, she will return here and fulfil the destiny marked out for her. But she must be allowed to grow up safely. Everything depends on her remaining alive and unharmed."

"And... and have you seen whether or not she will succeed?"

Jeremiah stroked the baby's silky cheek delicately with his forefinger. "That will depend on her. But you and I are the only ones who will know where she is. I may not be alive by the time she comes into her inheritance. It will fall to you, or one of your blood to travel to the other world and bring her back to her people."

Ivan thought of the book Tobias had entrusted to him, to guard for his child until she was ready to learn what it contained. "I will do whatever I can," he said solemnly, "I or those who come after me."

"Then come," said Jeremiah. "We do not have much time."

So that was how Ivan came to be in a world he had never known existed, in a park, at night, on the shore of a still, murky lake. He laid his burden gently on a park bench, where she was discovered the next morning. Ivan watched as she was taken away, then disappeared back into his own world. No one saw him come or go.

Nobody came forward to claim the abandoned baby girl, despite repeated appeals to the public. Eventually she was put up for adoption. She was snapped up almost at once, to begin a life in a world very different to that in which she had been born. Her past remained a mystery buried and never thought of. Sixteen years would pass before it would finally catch up with her.

# Part I

# The Book

# Chapter 1

## The Swimming Gala

James forced his way through the vast, milling crowd, searching for Fiona. It was a cold Friday afternoon in early January, but the swimming baths were already packed with people. It was the day of the swimming gala. This was an annual event, in which candidates from the county swimming team competed for a scholarship to the Fleetchester College of Athletics. The stifling air was heavy with the scent of chlorine. Shouts and laughter reverberated around the stone walls, mingling with the splashes of competitors diving in to swim warm-up laps.

James was tall for his age. Though not handsome in the usual sense, his face was pleasing. Bright brown eyes twinkled beneath an unruly mop of fair hair. His jaw was prominent, almost jutting, but his open, lopsided grin did much to soften his appearance.

He passed a hand across his sweaty forehead. Then pulled off his sweater and knotted it round his waist. His T-shirt was already clinging to him. He was going to have to spend at least two hours in this heat. At least the competitors would be cool. They'd either be in the water, or sitting drying off.

He spied Fiona coming out of the girls' changing room. She spotted him, and hurried over, grinning.

"You made it, great!"

"'Course I did, you didn't think I'd miss it?"

"But I thought you had football practice."

"I cried off. I told the coach I had too much homework."

"But the final's next Saturday."

"I know, but it couldn't be helped."

She punched him playfully on the arm. "I don't think your coach will see it that way. Still, thanks for coming. I need some support. Where's Carolyn? Isn't she coming?"

James looked slightly apologetic. "She had a late-running dance class, but she promised she'd get here as soon as she could."

Fiona laughed. "Evidently she has a better conscience than you. By the way, have you heard? Some of the girls were talking about it: someone vandalised the fence round the lake."

James frowned in puzzlement. "Why would they do that? It's suicide going anywhere near that lake."

Fiona shrugged unconcernedly. "Probably because it's forbidden. There are signs everywhere."

That's no reason, James thought grimly. Everyone knew the stories. Many people had been lost to those murky waters, and their bodies were never found. Even the divers who went looking for them never returned. He remembered the most famous disappearance. It had happened a couple of years before he was born, but the fence had been in place ever since. A girl, Alexandra or some such name, had gone swimming there, and never returned. She had been the daughter of the Mayor, and the story had been all over the papers and even on the news, so his mum had said. It turned out later that the relationship between the girl and her father had been difficult for some years. There had even been some speculation as to whether it had been a suicide attempt. The Mayor had stood down shortly afterwards, and retired from public life altogether.

Everyone warned their children to stay well clear of the lake, and James had needed little persuasion. He could never understand why anyone would want to swim in it. The waters looked cold and bleak, hardly inviting. But Fiona had always been curious, and had often tried to see how close she could get to the fence before a park attendant shooed her away. In fact, if he didn't know better, he would almost swear that Fiona was behind this, but she was no vandal. Still, she would welcome the chance for a swim in the lake. She was one of the strongest swimmers in the county, but James often felt she was over-confident. He wouldn't even trust someone of her abilities near that lake. She was watching him now, a thoughtful gleam in her eyes.

"Don't even think of it," he said firmly. "You've got more important things to worry about, like winning that scholarship."

She grinned mischievously up at him. "Always so sensible. Alright," she added hastily in response to his scowl. "I'll behave myself."

James glared suspiciously at her for a moment, then, thinking it better to change the subject, he nodded towards the other contestants leaving the changing rooms. "So, what do you make of the competition this year?"

Fiona made a dismissive gesture. "Nothing to worry about really. Adam Baxter's pretty good, I suppose, but I can beat him. I always do at practice sessions."

"I hear Louise Arden's a hot favourite."

Fiona let out a derisive snort. "The only reason she's a 'hot favourite' is because her swimming costume gets lower every week. I don't know why she doesn't just swim naked and be done with it."

"Is she any good?"

"She's not bad," Fiona admitted grudgingly. "But she's not really scholarship material. She wouldn't have made the team at all if her dad wasn't on the school's Board of Governors. Oh, look, here she comes now."

Louise Arden strolled out of the changing room as if she were a model striding along a catwalk. Several appreciative whistles greeted her appearance, all of them from watching boys. Louise gave them a coquettish wave and a smile. As Fiona had said, her costume left little to the imagination.

"I'd put your eyes back in if I were you," Fiona said innocently. "Carolyn's just arrived."

James started guiltily and looked around. A tall girl with shoulder-length blonde hair held off a slightly freckled face with a headband was making her way towards them. She hugged Fiona and kissed James.

"I thought I'd never get away," she said breathlessly. "Shouldn't you have started by now?"

"It won't be long now that Louise has made her entrance," said Fiona, cocking an eye at the crowd.

Carolyn, who was also looking at the pool, suddenly grabbed Fiona's arm.

"Hey, check out that lifeguard. Is he fit or what?"

Both Fiona and James looked where she pointed, and saw a boy of about their age. He was tall and athletic-looking. His wavy dark brown hair fell about his lean face. His skin was bronzed as though he'd been abroad, and a slightly sardonic smile played at the corners of his firm mouth. He was intent on his work, but every so often his eyes would flick to the people milling around or swimming in the pool, with almost appraising attention. There was something arresting about him. He looked the same as every other lifeguard, yet something about his appearance and the way he moved, caught and held the eye. He was checking the lane ropes, making sure they were secure.

"Well, what do you reckon?"

"I take your point," Fiona muttered, staring at the boy with obvious appreciation. He gave no indication that he was aware of the interest being shown him.

"How come you never mentioned him? I'd have got here earlier."

"I've never seen him before," Fiona said. "He's never been at any of our training sessions. I think I'd have remembered if he had."

"Am I missing something?" enquired James. "He doesn't seem anything special to me. He doesn't even look that friendly."

Fiona grinned wickedly. "Ah, Carolyn, I think your boyfriend might be jealous."

Carolyn immediately flung her arms round James. "Oh, don't worry, babe, he'll never be as cute as you."

James glowered at Fiona over Carolyn's head, but he couldn't keep it up for long.

Fiona was his best friend. They'd been inseparable ever since they'd first met at play group. When his mother had died of cancer, and his father had been too caught up in his own grief to attend to James, it had been Fiona who'd helped him come to terms with his loss.

Carolyn had only moved to their school the previous term, but she and Fiona had struck up an instant friendship. For weeks James had listened as Fiona elaborated Carolyn's numerous merits, which finally culminated in a "chance meeting". James suspected that Fiona had planned this from the start. Clearly she had nothing better to do than play matchmaker with two of her friends, but her plan had worked.

"I think I'll go and see if he needs a hand," said Fiona.

"Yeah, go for it!" said Carolyn. "Give yourself some Dutch courage for the scholarship."

James opened his mouth to object. The boy really did not look as if he would relish an interruption, but Fiona was already walking away. It wouldn't occur to her to be shy. Carolyn had presented her with a challenge. James watched her go.

She moved confidently, with the easy grace of an athlete. Many heads turned to follow her, some boys even managing to tear their eyes away from Louise's exposed flesh to spare her an appreciative glance, but she didn't even appear to notice.

Fiona was tall and slim. Her long legs still held the remains of last summer's tan. Her hair, which was at present concealed beneath her swimming cap, was a deep, coppery red. The eyes in her pale, heart-shaped face were a clear, brilliant blue, and when she smiled, she showed very white teeth. She could have had her pick of any boy here, James reflected, but she never seemed interested. There had been a few casual boyfriends, but none had lasted more than a couple of months. Fiona was too restless by nature, always wishing to move on to something new. The only things she really focused on were her swimming, and getting as much out of life as possible.

* * *

"Need any help?"

Christophe looked up. A tall girl was standing smiling at him, one hand outstretched.

"That depends."

Fiona took a step closer. "Depends on what?"

He straightened up to look at her. His eyes were very penetrating. They gave Fiona the impression that he was looking *through* her rather than at her. It made her feel a little uneasy. Then he suddenly smiled. "On the kind of help you're offering."

Fiona giggled and bent down to help him. His close proximity made her feel unaccountably giddy.

"I'm Christophe, by the way," the boy said casually. "And you are?"

"Fiona Armstrong. Have you just moved here? I don't think I've seen you around."

Christophe laughed. "Let's say I am just passing through. I never stay anywhere for long."

Fiona stared at him, puzzled, but Christophe went on before she could speak. His voice was slightly accented, though it was not strong enough for Fiona to make a guess at the origin. "I heard a lifeguard was needed, so I offered my services."

Fiona shrugged. "I suppose the others were busy."

Christophe turned to her suddenly, as though an idea had just struck him. "I will be here for a little while. I don't suppose you would care to show me around?"

Fiona could hardly believe her luck. "Yeah of course! When?"
"How about tomorrow? Perhaps early afternoon?"
"Whenever's good for you," said Fiona, blushing slightly.
Christophe reached into his pocket and withdrew a pencil and a scrap of paper. "Write your address on there."
She scribbled it, then handed it back. He glanced at it briefly, then smiling, tucked it back in his pocket. "I will see you tomorrow then. Now I have to go and change and you need to get ready. Good luck." He reached up to tuck a stray lock of hair beneath her cap, and was gone.

* * *

"Success!" cried Carolyn. "That's a turn-up, I must say."
James watched Fiona laugh at something the boy said, and then bend down. She seemed to be leaning rather close, yet the boy didn't appear to mind. If anything, he looked amused.
"She's smitten," said Carolyn. When James didn't respond, she turned to look at him. "What's up with you?"
James frowned over at the two bowed heads. "I don't know, there's just something about him that's not right. I've never seen her act like that over a boy."
"Well, it had to happen some time," Carolyn said cheerfully. "Even Fiona had to get bitten by the love bug sooner or later."
"She's only just seen him!" James protested.
Ignoring this, Carolyn tugged his arm. "Come on, let's get a seat, it's about to start."

* * *

Fiona stood in the pool, her hands resting lightly on the lane rope. Her whole body vibrated with excitement and energy. This was it. After years of training, she had reached the most important day of her life. For as long as she could remember, Fiona had loved to swim. She'd swum in many competitions, representing her school, her county, and even her country. She'd won more than her fair share of trophies and certificates. She was a trained athlete.
The Fleetchester College of Athletics was one of the top establishments of its kind in Britain. It took pupils from sixteen to eighteen. Only last year, one of its ex pupils, the twenty-one year old Melissa Bell, had won the gold medal for England in the Olympic Games. That was Fiona's dream. That was what she'd been building up to, and she was ready. She'd been ready for a year now. Pete, her trainer, had told her that she could have easily gone for the scholarship last year, if she hadn't been under age.
Fiona was in the middle lane. Adam Baxter and Louise Arden climbed down into the lanes on either side of her.
"I see you don't waste time, do you?" said Louise, staring pointedly at Christophe, who was just as pointedly ignoring her. Fiona couldn't hide a grin.

Louise scowled. She wasn't used to being ignored. "We'll see who's laughing after the gala."

Fiona's grin broadened. "Indeed we will."

"Good luck, Fiona," said Adam. He was a quiet, hard working boy, and, Fiona suspected, possibly her biggest threat, but she liked him nonetheless.

"And you."

James and Carolyn waved over at her, beaming encouragingly. Fiona gave them the thumbs-up in return.

"Let's do this," she muttered under her breath.

The first event was designed to test a candidate's ability to work under pressure, and deal with the unexpected. Someone was coming round now, giving everyone their instructions. They would be swimming one length, but not using the stroke of their choice.

"You'll be doing breaststroke," a man with a clipboard told Fiona. She groaned inwardly. That was her worst stroke. But she got into the starting position.

"On your marks," called the man with the clipboard. Christophe raised a whistle to his lips. For the briefest moment, Fiona was sure that his eyes had rested on her, but then he blew a sharp blast on the whistle, and she was away, streaking to the other side of the pool with the cheers and shouts of the onlookers resounding in her ears.

Adam was lucky. He was doing backstroke, which Fiona knew to be his best. They were swimming level, both their faces contorted in concentration. Then, at the last moment, Adam managed to pull away, slamming into the wall barely half a second ahead of Fiona, with Louise a more distant third.

Fiona leaned for a moment on the wall, breathing deeply. It hadn't been the start she could have wished. Adam had won the first event. True, she'd come a very close second, but a second all the same. The words of Pete, her trainer, filled her head. Don't get too cocky and lose your concentration. She knew he was right, but it was difficult. She could win this. She felt it in her bones.

She looked once more for her friends. There they were, waiting for the next event, with her whatever happened. She wished her parents could have made it as well, but neither of them had been able to get time off work.

Fiona's determination redoubled. She'd messed up once but it wouldn't happen again.

The next event measured personal best. A timed circuit of the pool. She was easily the fastest on the team. She gritted her teeth, her body tense. The swimmers would be called alphabetically.

"Take your marks," called the voice again, and the first up, Louise Arden, got into position. The whistle blew, and the crowd screamed its encouragement. She was pretty fast, but Fiona knew she could beat her.

"Twenty seconds," called the man with the stopwatch. Fiona nodded in satisfaction. She could beat that, no problem. The whistle rang out again, and she struck out in a powerful front crawl for the other side. It was a long pool, but she'd swum from end to end more times than she could count.

"Fourteen and a half seconds," said the man with the stopwatch. Fiona felt a surge of delight. She'd beaten her personal best. She stood, breathing quickly, her body tense, as Adam Baxter took his turn. He was fast, very fast. Fiona bit her lip and prayed silently.

"Fifteen seconds." Fiona breathed again. Only half a second difference. She'd clearly under-estimated Adam. She'd known of his potential, but hadn't bargained on his determination. They'd each won an event now. Would she be able to make it two?

The next event was diving. Each candidate had to make three dives, each from a different board, and ending with the highest. Once more they were called forward alphabetically. Louise dived first, but her dives were clumsy, and her position faulty. This might have been a cause for disqualification, but, no doubt because of her connections, Louise was allowed to remain. Fiona grimaced. She'd show the judges and Louise's father how it should be done.

Fiona climbed onto the lowest board, and assumed the right position; feet slightly apart, arms at medium height. The whistle blew, and she leapt. The plunge was not far, and nothing went wrong. Deafening cheers greeted her as she surfaced. She climbed to the medium board, and repeated the procedure. Then came the last board. She climbed onto it, and gazed at the sea of watching faces. This was her party piece. She stood poised, waiting. After what seemed like an eternity, the whistle blew, and she hurtled into space. Her body curved gracefully through the air, and hit the water, sinking at once, but she kicked hard, and almost immediately rose to the surface, and swam the short distance to the side. She felt a thrill of exaltation. She knew it had gone well, no awkward landings, and she'd kept her head.

Soon it was Adam's turn. His first two dives went well, and even Fiona had to admire his skill. But as he leapt into his third and final dive, his arms seemed to pin-wheel in the air, and he landed awkwardly, sinking immediately. Christophe prepared to jump in, but Adam rose up again and, gasping, swam to the side. As Christophe helped Adam to climb out, Fiona saw that he was clutching his side. It was plain to see he'd been winded badly. It was always important to hold your body at the correct angle when diving. Fiona supposed that Adam must've panicked. He was clearly in pain. There was a short discussion among the judges, but it was obvious to all that Adam could not continue. Fiona watched him limp away. After he'd been doing so well, it really was too cruel. Yet a small part of her could not help but feel relief. Adam was no longer in the running. She might really be in with a chance.

Next came the butterfly race. Fiona had never seen the point of swimming butterfly, but she'd practised hard all the same. The whistle blew, and the race began. Straight away Louise took the lead, showing surprising skill. To everyone's amazement, she won the race, with Fiona yet again a close second. Louise's fan club whooped and whistled, and Louise shot a triumphant grin at Fiona. It was unbelievable. Her performance in the other events had been well below the standard of the other competitors. Fiona's jaw clenched. There was one event left, and it looked as though it might be between her and Louise.

Adam would have made a much more worthy opponent. Well, her moment of glory was over. There was simply no way Fiona would allow Louise to beat her.

The final event was the relay. Whoever won this would receive the scholarship. Fiona positioned herself ready. She watched as Louise beamed at her adoring fans and her father waved at her, and her resolve tightened. She'd show him what happened when you put ambition over talent. She thought he might have glanced at her, but she stared resolutely ahead, waiting for the whistle.

"Go, Fiona!" yelled Carolyn into the silence.

"You can do it!" shouted James. Fiona almost waved, but caught herself. She had to concentrate.

The whistle blew, and Fiona flung herself forwards, infinitely relieved that this was free-style. There was a boy in front of her. She put on a spurt of speed and overtook him. She gained rapidly on Louise who, owing to her position, had got a slight head start. Louise was tiring, her strokes becoming slower. She saw Fiona coming up fast, and tried vainly to put on a spurt of speed and escape, but she was spent. Unlike Fiona, who had paced herself throughout the race, keeping some strength in reserve, Louise had expended herself too quickly. Fiona put on a spurt at the last moment and flashed ahead, leaving Louise and everyone else far behind. The final whistle was lost in the tumult of the crowd screaming its delight, as Fiona hoisted herself shakily out of the water. She'd done it. The scholarship was hers. She'd won.

James appeared from nowhere, and clasped her to him in a tight hug.

"I knew you could do it!" he cried ecstatically. She laughed with sheer delight.

"It was close, but I told you I'd do it."

Then Carolyn was there, jumping up and down. "You did it! You did it! That was fantastic!"

Fiona saw Louise storm off sobbing towards the changing rooms, while her father looked as though he'd just swallowed something extremely unpleasant. If anything could have set the seal on her victory, it was that.

Christophe suddenly appeared beside her. "That was well done," he murmured so only she could hear. He leaned forward quickly and kissed her. It was very brief, just a light brushing of his lips on hers, but Fiona's stomach did a back flip all the same. She turned to speak to him, but he was already lost in the crowd.

The head of the Board of Governors for the school stepped forward.

"Ladies and gentlemen, it is my great pleasure to award the scholarship to the Fleetchester College of Athletics, to Fiona Armstrong."

* * *

"I can't believe it!" Fiona, James and Carolyn were standing outside, getting a much needed breath of fresh air. A cool breeze blew Fiona's wet hair back from her face, which was flushed with triumph.

James seized her shoulders and swung her round. “You were fantastic!” he said grinning.

“I can’t believe it!” she said again. “After all this time, oh, I can’t wait to tell Mum and Dad.”

“Will they be home yet?” asked James.

“They should be. Come back home with me. I can’t celebrate without you.”

“Yeah, sure.”

“You too, Cas, the more the merrier.”

Carolyn shook her head regretfully. “I can’t, we’ve got family coming over tonight. I should’ve been back half an hour ago. I’m afraid you’ll have to have fun without me.” She gave Fiona another quick hug, and pecked James on the cheek. “See you tomorrow,” she called over her shoulder. “If I make it through tonight.”

“Come on,” said James. “Your mum and dad will be waiting.”

* * *

As she and James turned into her road, Fiona was pleased to see both her parents’ cars in the driveway. She broke into a run, whipping out her door key as she went. James followed at a more sedate pace. Fiona wrestled impatiently with the key, and flung open the front door, yelling at the top of her voice, “Mum! Dad! I’m home. I’ve got something to tell you.”

Mrs Armstrong came hurrying out of the kitchen, from which floated a delicious smell of cooking. Mr Armstrong stuck his head out of the living room. Seeing who it was, he ran down the hall. “Well?” he demanded. “Don’t keep us in suspense.”

“I won!” Fiona announced gleefully. Her mother seized her in a tight hug. “Oh, darling, that’s wonderful. I’m so proud of you. Oh, if only your dad and I could have made it. We must celebrate. James, I nearly didn’t see you. Come on in and have dinner with us.”

Mr Armstrong was now hugging Fiona. “Well done, darling. I knew you could do it.”

While Mrs Armstrong served up pasta and meatballs, Fiona talked them excitedly through the day’s events. “It was very close. This boy Adam, I was really afraid he’d beat me. He won the first race, but I managed to win the second. I actually beat my personal best, but it was a near thing. I think that the diving was my best event. Adam got injured and had to pull out. A pity, but it certainly lessened the competition. Louise Arden won the butterfly, if you’ll believe that. Her dad looked like the cat that got the cream. But you should’ve seen his face when I won the relay. It was brilliant!” Fiona drew breath, and used a piece of bread to mop up the sauce on her plate. Her mum beamed at her fondly.

“Congratulations, darling. Your dad and I are very proud of you.” Mrs Armstrong rose and began to dole out seconds.

“You’ll need new clothes,” Mrs Armstrong went on. “It would be nice to have a new wardrobe when you go away.”

Fiona rolled her eyes. "I'll be in my swimming costume most of the time, Mum."

"Not all the time you won't. You really could do with some new jeans, Fiona. Your others are literally coming apart at the seams. We'll have to go shopping. I'm sure your dad will give you an allowance."

Mr Armstrong nodded agreeably.

Fiona groaned. She loathed shopping of any description, but clothes shopping most of all.

James suppressed a grin with difficulty.

"Do you know when you're supposed to enrol and everything?" asked Mr Armstrong.

Fiona shook her head. "They're sending me the details in the post."

"Well, make sure you study hard. You need high GCSEs to get into that college. It would be a shame to do all that training and then have to turn it down."

"Yeah, yeah, I know," said Fiona dismissively.

"I mean it, Fiona. Now your training's over, you've got to get your grades up. There's no excuse—"

"I know, Dad!" Fiona interrupted. "I will work hard, I promise."

"More ice-cream, James?" asked Mrs Armstrong, who was firmly of the belief that James didn't get enough to eat at home and needed feeding up.

James pushed his bowl away regretfully and got to his feet. "No thanks, Mrs Armstrong. I really ought to get back."

"Alright, love. Come back soon, won't you?"

"Yeah, thanks for dinner."

Fiona went with James to the door.

"So, I'll see you tomorrow?"

Fiona shook her head. "Not tomorrow, I'm going out with Christophe."

James blinked. "Who's Christophe?"

"You know, the lifeguard I was chatting to earlier."

James raised his eyebrows. "That was quick work."

"What do you mean?"

"Well, you only talked to him for about a minute."

Fiona laughed. "I'm only showing him around. What's wrong with that?"

James shrugged. "Nothing, I suppose. There was just something about him that was… I don't know… not right," he finished lamely. "I mean, I've never seen him around before."

"That could be because he's just moved here," said Fiona, with exaggerated patience. "I'm just meeting him for an afternoon, and I promise I'll ask loads of questions and find out everything I can. I'll give you a report at school on Monday."

James punched her lightly on the shoulder. "I'll see you Monday then?"

"Yeah. If you're seeing Carolyn tomorrow, thank her again for coming."

"Yeah, I will."

## Chapter 2

### The Picnic

Christophe called for Fiona at half past twelve the following afternoon. Fiona had overslept after the previous day's excitement. When she finally awoke, it was gone eleven. She showered and dressed at top speed, terrified that Christophe would turn up any minute. Then she settled in the living room, rifling through a magazine. Every few minutes, she glanced out of the window, but the street was empty.

"Fiona, what is the matter with you?" Mrs Armstrong demanded, looking up from her book.

"I met this boy yesterday at the swimming gala. We're going out for a bit."

"You never mentioned him."

"Yeah, I forgot."

"So, what's he like?"

"He just moved here," said Fiona, not entirely answering the question. It was difficult to describe Christophe. He wasn't like any of the boys she knew. But he intrigued her. She was looking forward to discovering more.

"Well, make sure you're back in time for dinner. Everyone's coming over for a celebration."

"Oh, Mum!"

Mrs Armstrong frowned sternly. "They haven't been round in ages, Fiona. They just want to congratulate you."

Fiona sighed. She knew she should be flattered, but she had never liked family gatherings, and her relatives were not the kind to endear her to them. Her mother was watching her with a warning look in her eyes.

"Alright, I promise I'll be back in time."

The door bell rang. Fiona jumped up. "See you later, Mum."

"Have fun."

Fiona hurried down the hall. She could see Christophe's outline through the frosted glass pane in the door. She paused for a moment to compose herself. It would never do for Christophe to see her in such a flutter. She opened the door. "You're a little early."

Christophe pointed to the basket at his feet. "I thought we could have a picnic. It is quite mild today."

Fiona agreed readily. "Where do you want to go?"

"How about the park? I hear it is quite peaceful there."

"Yeah, sure."

They walked along companionably, Fiona pointing out the various shops, the cinema and the library as they passed them. "And that's St. Peters. I suppose you'll be starting there, won't you?"

"I might be."

Fiona looked at him, puzzled. "Where else would you go, the private school?"

Christophe shrugged.

"You'd better hope your mum and dad don't send you there, they're all snobs at that place. They think they're better than everyone else because their dads own expensive cars."

Christophe looked amused, though Fiona couldn't help noticing that the expression didn't reach his eyes. They remained cool, almost wary. She had the impression that even when he appeared to be relaxed, he was actually taking in everything around him. Watching, observing. She wondered what was bothering him, but decided she was probably imagining it. She had no wish to make a fool of herself.

"Have you always lived here?" he asked, as they walked across her school playing field.

"Yeah, all my life. Mum and Dad love this area. We've lived in our current house since I was five."

"And before that?"

"A bungalow on the other side of town. What about you, where did you use to live?"

He shrugged. "I don't know that I have ever lived anywhere."

Fiona frowned. "You mean your family move around a lot?"

Christophe nodded.

"Any brothers or sisters?"

He shook his head.

Fiona was even more intrigued. Christophe's life appeared to have been very different from her own. Though he seemed rather reluctant to discuss it, or indeed anything about himself. Perhaps he was shy, though he certainly didn't give that impression. She scrutinised his clothes. They were nothing special. The sort of clothes that blended in easily. He wasn't wearing any of the fashions that kids their age usually wore. Maybe he was a gypsy. Yes, that would explain his travelling existence, and his second-hand clothing. It would also explain his wariness towards her. After all, gypsies rarely socialised with anyone outside their own tight-knit communities. Maybe if she told him about her life, he'd realise he was safe with her and open up a bit.

They had entered the park now. It was deserted, unusually for a Saturday afternoon. Fiona pointed at a rough park bench. "I was found there."

He looked interested for the first time. "Really?"

"Yeah, I'm adopted. My real mum just left me there wrapped in a blanket."

"Do you remember your real parents?"

Fiona shook her head. "I was only a few weeks old."

"Do you know anything about them?"

"No."

"Would you not like to?"

Fiona's face hardened. "They didn't want to know me, so why should I bother with them?"

Christophe frowned. "Maybe they had to give you up. Maybe there was no other choice."

"So why didn't they leave a letter with me or something, explaining?" Fiona waved a dismissive hand. "I've got the best parents anyone could ask for. I don't need any others."

They walked in silence for a time.

"Shall we eat by the lake?"

Christophe smiled. "If you like."

They approached the broken fence. There was a sizable hole in the chain links, easily big enough for someone to fit through. Fiona slipped through first, then helped Christophe through with the basket. They stood still for a moment, staring into the murky depths of the lake.

"Loads of people have drowned here," said Fiona soberly. "That's why they put up the fence. Once those waters take you, that's it. No one's ever been found."

"So why would someone break the fence?"

Fiona shrugged. "Who knows; probably some kid did it on a dare. It's got a bit of a nasty reputation, understandably." She stared contemplatively into the water. Was it her imagination, or did the water seem to be moving sluggishly?

"I don't know why," she said musingly, "but I've always liked this place. I've always thought that the lake was, I don't know, hiding something, like a secret. I mean, all those people lost, even those who tried to rescue them. Why weren't they ever found? The lake's deep, but it can't be bottomless." She laughed. "Stupid, I know. My friend James thinks I'm crazy."

"There is nothing wrong with being curious," said Christophe. "How else will you learn anything? One day someone will discover the mystery of this lake. Why should it not be you?"

"Yeah, I suppose. But for now, I'll just concentrate on swimming pools. I don't fancy drowning just yet."

They settled themselves in the long grass, facing the lake. Christophe had brought a rug, which was just as well, for the grass was still damp from the many recent showers. While Fiona spread out the rug and began setting out rolls, fruit salad and crisps, Christophe busied himself pouring orange juice from a flask into two plastic cups.

"This looks really nice," said Fiona, settling on the blanket and accepting the cup Christophe offered her.

Fiona drained its contents in three gulps. As she selected a cheese roll and bit into it hungrily, Christophe wordlessly refilled her cup.

"You swam very well yesterday," he said. "I don't think I have ever seen anyone your age with such potential."

Fiona beamed with pleasure, but her smile turned almost at once into a yawn. "Oh, sorry."

"What happens now you have won the scholarship?" asked Christophe, moving closer to her in order to take something from the picnic basket.

Fiona felt a little light-headed.

"I go to this college for two years. If I'm good enough, I'll try out for the Olympics." She yawned again. "That's my dream you know. Someday I'll win a gold medal. I'll smash every record." She groaned, sinking her head into her hands.

"Are you alright?"

Fiona struggled to focus. Christophe's face was barely inches from her own, yet it seemed strangely blurred. Her head was swimming. "I don't know, suddenly I feel really strange." She lurched forward.

Christophe caught her in his arms. His grip was reassuringly strong. She sagged into his embrace, too dizzy to feel any embarrassment. With an enormous effort, she raised heavy eyes to his face. "What's happening?"

Christophe moved, dragging her with him. At first, she thought he was just shifting her to a more comfortable position. Then she realised to her horror, that he was dragging her towards the lake. "What are you doing?"

Everything was swirling before her eyes. The water was a foaming, roiling mass rushing towards her with frightening speed. The roaring in her ears was tremendous. She struggled, trying to break that terrifying hold, but her limbs felt oddly weak and heavy. She was as limp as a rag doll.

"Don't struggle," said Christophe. His voice was low, almost soothing. "Just close your eyes. It will all be over soon."

She felt so sleepy. But she mustn't give in. It would all be over in seconds. She gazed beseechingly into Christophe's grey eyes. They seemed as fathomless as the water, and just as cold.

"Please!" she said weakly. "Please don't do this!"

"Just close your eyes," his voice was even softer. "Sleep and you will have nothing to fear."

Her eyes fluttered closed. She could not prevent them. Her last conscious feeling was of being pushed forwards hard. She was falling into a cold, dark oblivion.

Christophe watched as Fiona was picked up by the heaving waters. He took two or three deep breaths, filling his lungs with air. The herbs he had slipped into Fiona's drink would insure that she would breathe, but he would not be so lucky. If he ran out of air on the way down it would be catastrophic for both of them. He plunged in. The whirlpool had him in an instant, sucking him into a well of blackness. Not even the strongest swimmer could hope to fight the whirlpool once it had them in its grip.

Christophe had learned long ago how to open his eyes under water. He stretched them to their fullest extent. If he didn't find her, who knew where she might come out? He spotted her almost straight away. He grabbed her spinning body, locking his arms tightly around her. The vile stench of the lake filled his nostrils and throat, despite the fact that his mouth was tightly shut. He fought not to gag. His chest ached and his head felt light from lack of oxygen, but he didn't panic. Lose his head and that would be it.

After what seemed an interminable length of time, the spinning stopped. The whirlpool had released him. Christophe gripped the waistband of Fiona's jeans tightly with one hand and began to fight his way upwards. At last his head broke the surface. He took several gasps of the clean, salty air, before drawing Fiona up too. He swam forwards, pulling Fiona behind him. She weighed almost nothing in the water. At last his feet touched bottom. He stood up and hoisted Fiona over his shoulder. Then he waded the short distance to the shore.

He was in a small cove. It was night. An entire sky of stars winked overhead, and a full moon shone. Tiny waves lapped gently against the sandy beach. Christophe stepped ashore, then collapsed in the sand. He lay there for a few minutes, utterly spent. He hoped fervently that he would never have to do that again. Still, at least he knew where he was. Not like the first time when he'd waded ashore and found himself in an unfamiliar world with a chain-link fence barring his way. He looked over at the girl he'd gone to fetch.

She lay in the sand next to him, on her side. Her eyes closed, hair clinging to her face and neck. She was pretty, he supposed. But he couldn't contain his uncertainty. When he'd first seen her, he'd even wondered if he'd got the right person, but she matched the description he'd been given perfectly. She'd confirmed that she was an orphan, and that she'd been found on the very park bench where Ivan had left her all those years ago. Then there was her love of the water. Watching her yesterday, it had been evident that she felt perfectly at home in it, as though she belonged there. From birth, he and all other children were taught to live by, and love the sea. They were as much at home on water as on land. He hadn't been lying when he'd told her she was the best he'd seen. Lastly, there was her affinity with the lake. No one from any other world would ever feel its pull. It had been calling Fiona home for sixteen years. The water had snatched her greedily, joyously. But she had been called back for a purpose, and Christophe doubted that she was ready for it.

He checked her pulse. It was strong and steady; her breathing slow and even. He scanned the beach, eyes and ears straining for the slightest movement or sound other than the lapping of waves or the calling of seabirds. The cove appeared to be deserted. Christophe frowned. Surely his absence could not have gone unnoticed this long. He had half expected to find a welcoming party waiting for him. Their absence made him uneasy. For a moment he considered leaving at once, but he was exhausted. He needed to rest, and Fiona would not wake before dawn. He would leave at first light as planned and, with any luck, he would be able to avoid pursuit and reach his destination safely.

With a sigh, Christophe got to his feet and hoisted Fiona over his shoulder once more. She was a heavy weight to carry, but he hadn't far to go. He picked his way carefully between several boulders, climbing a gentle slope. At last he reached a small wooden hut, concealed behind two stunted gorse bushes. The hut had no door, and its walls were crumbling. Christophe set Fiona down and felt around at the back of the hut. He quickly found what he was looking for; two thick blankets, just where he'd left them. He wrapped Fiona in the first blanket and settled her in a corner. She should sleep undisturbed through the night. He didn't dare light a fire, but the night was warm. He rolled himself in the second blanket and lay across the threshold with his head turned towards the sea. Despite his misgivings, a sigh of contentment escaped him. It was good to be home.

* * *

"So, at what time did your daughter leave the house?"

Mrs Armstrong stared at the policeman with wide, frightened eyes. James knew how she felt. The man sat there, calmly jotting in his notebook, while James wanted nothing more than to dash out of the house and scour every corner until he found Christophe, and wring his neck. The policeman cleared his throat delicately, waiting.

"It was about midday," Mrs Armstrong whispered.

James felt his anger mounting. They had been through this already. Why did the man insist on going over the same ground again and again? The man was still speaking, seemingly oblivious to James's steadily darkening brow, or the way Mrs Armstrong's clasped hands trembled in her lap.

"And your daughter did not tell you where she was going?"

Use her name! James thought furiously. She's not an object.

Mrs Armstrong shook her head. She looked on the verge of breaking down completely. James's heart ached for her.

"You're quite sure, Madam?" the policeman pressed. "The slightest detail might be important."

"She just said she was going out for a bit," Mrs Armstrong replied, her voice shaking.

The policeman finally seemed to notice her distress. "Alright, Madam," he said more gently. "And this boy she was with… what was his name?"

"Christophe," James said dully.

The policeman transferred his attention to him instead. "Christophe, yes, that's right. Had she known him long?"

"No," said James. "She only met him yesterday. He was a lifeguard down at the swimming pool. He told her he'd just moved to the area."

"I see." The policeman scribbled furiously.

"And she definitely went with this boy of her own free will? It's not possible that the boy could have abducted her?"

Mrs Armstrong let out a strangled cry, and hid her face in her hands.

James felt like hitting the man. "Fiona told me she was meeting Christophe," he said tightly.

The front door banged and Mr Armstrong came in, back from his own search. Spotting the policeman, he hurried forward eagerly. "Have you heard anything? Have you found her?"

"I've heard nothing yet, Sir, but my colleagues will soon return. They should be able to tell us more."

Mr Armstrong glared at him. "My daughter is missing, Officer. It's two in the morning. She's been missing for over twelve hours, and there's no trace of her. We've told you all we know, so why aren't you out there with the others, looking for her?"

The policeman gave Mr Armstrong what was clearly intended to be an understanding smile, but it looked patronizing to James.

"It is often necessary to go over things, Mr Armstrong, in order to make sure we have the facts absolutely right."

Mr Armstrong sat down on the sofa beside his wife and put an arm around her.

The policeman turned back to his notebook. "Now, I have a description of the boy. Perhaps you could just confirm it for me." He read out a few clipped sentences, then looked up expectantly.

"That's him," James said. The policeman looked towards Mr and Mrs Armstrong for their agreement.

"They've never met him," James said wearily.

"Ah, I see." The man shut his notebook with a snap and stowed the book and pen in his shirt pocket. "In that case, I think we'll leave it there. I expect we've got enough to be going—" a loud thumping on the front door drowned the rest of his words. Mr Armstrong leaped to his feet, and hurried to answer it.

He was back almost instantly, ushering in three policemen. One look at their faces told James they had some news. His stomach clenched and his throat constricted so that it was difficult to breathe.

Mrs Armstrong was on her feet too. "Have you found her? Is she safe? Where is she?"

There was a moment of awkward silence. Then one of the men stepped forward.

"I'm afraid not, Madam," he said kindly. "But we think we may have found a clue to your daughter's disappearance." He paused.

James realised he was holding his breath.

"We found an abandoned picnic basket down at the edge of the lake in the park. And also some signs of a struggle. I'm sure you know that the fence was vandalised a few days ago. We think it likely that the two incidents are connected. There was nothing else to hint at what might have happened to your daughter, but the area will be cordoned off tomorrow, and my men will conduct a thorough search."

Mrs Armstrong let out a wail of anguish. The policemen made noises of sympathy, punctuated by promises that they would do everything possible. Mr Armstrong was alternately bidding the policemen goodbye, and trying to comfort his wife, who had sunk onto the sofa, moaning softly.

"Oh, Fiona, my darling! My baby, no!"

The voices faded to meaningless noise in James's ears. Unseen by anyone, he quietly left the house.

Fiona was dead? It wasn't true, it couldn't be. The lake; if she'd disappeared there, they'd never find her. No one who entered those waters was ever seen again, alive or dead. He remembered Fiona's fascination with the lake. She'd had a thing about it as long as he could remember. He could vividly recall once trying to stop her from climbing the fence.

"Let me go," she had laughed. "You're such a scaredy cat."

"You'll drown!" he had protested, hanging on to her ankle for dear life. A park attendant had chased them away, whacking at their legs with his broom.

"I'll manage it one day," Fiona had vowed. "Someday, I'll climb over that fence, and swim in that lake too. And I'll come out again."

Fate had a cruel sense of humour. She had got her wish, but she wouldn't come back to tell him about it. Yet James couldn't believe Fiona would really be so stupid. Whatever she might say, she was no fool; impulsive, certainly. Her schemes had landed them both in more than one scrape over the years, but she wasn't foolish.

That left only one explanation. Christophe must have pushed her in. He was a lifeguard. He wouldn't go frolicking in those waters any more than Fiona would. And even if she'd insisted on going in, strong swimmer though she was, surely Christophe would have no trouble rescuing her if she got into difficulty. Then he could have seen her safely home. He had drowned her, James was sure of it, and then disappeared.

Well you won't hide from me, James thought grimly. Wherever you are, I'll find you, Christophe, and when I do… what would he do? He didn't know.

"But I will find him, Fiona," he said aloud. "I promise."

He stopped outside Carolyn's door and rang the bell. She was on her own this evening. Her parents were at a dinner party. It seemed impossible that only that day, he and Carolyn had spent an enjoyable afternoon, seeing a film, then going for a walk on the common. He had gone to bed that night overflowing with happiness, only to be woken at midnight by Mrs Armstrong's phone call. Fiona hadn't come home, had James seen her? James had rushed straight to the Armstrong's house. He'd phoned Carolyn to tell her what had happened, promising to come over as soon as he had news.

Carolyn was a minute in answering. She appeared in the doorway, her pyjamas crumpled and her eyes heavy with sleep. "I'm sorry! I fell asleep waiting up for you. Are you alright? What's happening?"

He took a step towards her, but his knees suddenly trembled alarmingly and he swayed where he stood.

Carolyn caught him, her face full of concern. "James! What is it? What's happened?"

He was ashamed to find that he was crying, weeping like a baby, his face buried in Carolyn's shoulder. She held him tightly, patting his back, making soothing noises.

"Fiona's dead!" he managed at last, his voice muffled in her shoulder. "She was drowned in the lake. Christophe killed her!"

"What? But James! How? How do you know?"

“She told me she was going out with him. The police found an abandoned picnic by the lake. They said there had been a struggle. The fence was vandalised a few days ago. You do the maths!”

“But James, are you saying he planned this?”

He looked up at her, his tear-streaked face livid, his eyes wild. “Of course I am!”

She took a step back from him, looking startled, but when she spoke, she endeavoured to keep her voice reasonable. “But James, you said he just moved here. You’re surely not suggesting that he came here just to kill Fiona?”

“How do we know that was true? He could’ve been playing a part; the stranger in town, to lure her off with him. He’s a psycho, Carolyn!”

“But James—”

He didn’t want to hear any more. Turning abruptly, he set off at a run. His eyes were dry now. He felt nothing. No grief, no anger, just a burning desire to prove his conviction. There would be time for feelings later.

The park was deserted. The police had plainly called it a night. James hurried towards the distant lake, his feet making scarcely any noise on the dew-soaked grass.

The sound of running feet made him spin around. Carolyn was racing towards him. She wore trainers on her bare feet and a jacket over her pyjamas.

“James! Wait up!” She skidded to a stop in front of him, panting. “What are you doing here?”

“I had to come,” he said quietly. He set off again, Carolyn falling in wordlessly alongside him. They stopped at the fence. James leaned on it and stared into the waters of the lake. They yawned below him like a dark, hungry mouth. He heard Carolyn give a small sob beside him.

“It’s horrible to think of her lost in there. She had her whole life ahead of her, and she waited so long to win that scholarship. But my dad always said no one could survive that lake.”

James wasn’t listening. He was staring at the bank. It was flooded. The ground was churned into a quagmire of mud. It seemed to have settled down somewhat, but it had clearly risen high. There was mud up to the fence. Twigs, leaves and other debris littered the ground.

“That’s weird,” murmured Carolyn. “It looks like it burst its banks, but there’s been no rain today.”

“Look at the water,” said James. They stared at it.

“What’s wrong with it?” Carolyn said uncertainly. The water was stirring sluggishly. It seemed to be settling down after a storm. Even as they watched, the ripples grew less.

James swung his legs over the fence, dropping in the mud with a squelch.

“James, what are you doing?” Carolyn called in alarm. He ignored her and began moving forward slowly. The ground was slippery and treacherous under foot.

“James!” He heard Carolyn land with a squelch behind him. He was at the water’s edge now. The water was still swirling lazily. There was something almost hypnotic about it.

“James, get away from there!” Carolyn’s voice was shrill with urgency. She seized the back of his jacket and attempted to tug him back.

“Carolyn, leave off!” He tried to shake free of her clutching hands. His foot slipped in the mud. For an instant, he seemed to teeter on the brink. Then he pitched forward. Instinctively he flung out his hands to break his fall. One hand slapped the water.

Instantly the water roared, shooting up in a terrific geezer. The greedy current seemed to snatch him. He was sliding forwards as huge waves swept up the bank and back again. James heard Carolyn’s panicked yell, and felt her clutch at his ankles in an effort to drag him back.

“No!” he shouted frantically over the roar of the waves. “It’ll pull you in too.” She ignored him, and made a grab for his ankles again. This time he felt her hands lock on to his legs. They were cold and shaking. Desperately he groped for something to hang on to. There was a weeping willow at the water’s edge. James stretched up and seized one of the low-hanging branches. He braced himself as another spout of water shot into the air and caught him slap in the face. Drenched and spluttering, he blinked the water out of his eyes and saw Carolyn lying face-down in the mud. She had somehow managed to keep hold of his legs and was attempting feebly to get to her knees.

“Let go!” he gasped. “I’ve got hold of this branch. I’ll try and haul myself into the tree, go and get help.”

She did so, then scrambled shakily to her feet. “Do you want a boost up?”

“No, don’t come any closer.” He locked his arms and heaved. His muscles felt like lead. For a moment he hung by his arms, his feet scrabbling frantically for a foothold in the slim trunk. Then, as though in slow motion, a great wall of water rose in the air and crashed down upon him. The last thing James heard as his hands were ripped from the branch, was Carolyn’s terrified scream, which was abruptly cut off as cold, dark water closed over him.

# Chapter 3

## Katie

She was on the deck of a ship which lay at anchor in a calm harbour beneath a blue sky. She held a fishing net in her hands. Her fingers worked busily, mending the broken strands. She was utterly absorbed. Beside her, the boy occasionally paused in his own work to give instructions or assistance when it was needed. She'd never seen him before, yet she worked alongside him without fear or unease. It was almost as though she belonged there. They were alone but for the continuous flocks of seabirds hunting for fish, and the dolphins at play in the waves. It was a glorious day. She smiled contentedly. They worked in companionable silence for several minutes, neither feeling the need to speak.

She was on an island she did not know. The boy was facing her, his expression a terrible mixture of rage and grief. She longed to run to him, to ask what was wrong, but she could not move a muscle.

Katie woke with a start, her breathing ragged, the thin, scratchy woollen blanket twisted round her limbs. She fought free of its clutches, but the effort made her head swim, and bile rose to her throat. She lay tense and motionless, waiting for the feeling to subside. As she knew it would, the nausea slowly receded and her body relaxed, though the feeling of fear and dread took longer to pass. Gradually she became aware of her surroundings, and lay for a while listening to the city sounds, as its citizens greeted the new day. When she felt able, she got out of bed and padded across to the open window and leaned out.

There was a slight breeze coming in from the sea. She could smell the salt in it. It felt soothing against her flushed cheeks. The remnants of the predawn mist were dissipating rapidly, leaving a completely cloudless blue sky. On a clear day such as this, it was possible to see as far as the beach, where a merchant ship was moored, its crew busily unloading their cargo. Her father's house stood like a sentinel atop a hill at the highest point of the city, impossible to miss. It was the largest landmark for miles.

Katie cupped her chin in her hands thoughtfully. The vision was still fresh in her mind. The images as sharp as though they had been pasted over her eyes. She gnawed at her lower lip, a frown creasing her brow. This vision had come three times now, never altering in detail. At first, she had been willing to dismiss it as a dream, but she couldn't use this argument any more. She could not fathom its meaning, but its portents was unmistakable. It concerned her in some way; her future perhaps. Did visions come unbidden to people? She had never heard of it happening before, but then she knew no one else who'd ever experienced visions, no one else like her.

Katie was no stranger to fragments of the future, or the past for that matter. Ask to see it, and it would be shown you while you slept, or while gazing into the heart of a fire, or into clear water. She knew about visions, she also knew that they did not appear to anyone, only a privileged few, no one else living that she knew of. That was why she was so important.

Katie chuckled mirthlessly. She was invaluable to Miguel. "His secret weapon" he named her to his associates. That was why he kept her around, and because her father paid him enough money to keep him living in the height of luxury while she had to earn her keep. She was living under his roof only through the kindness of his heart. No one else would take in someone else's child. Katie had once pointed out to Miguel that he wouldn't dare do anything else with her father being the most powerful man alive and ruler of an empire. She'd got her first beating then. It was shortly after that when she'd begun working for Miguel. He'd said it was with her father's approval, and it had never occurred to Katie to question the statement. You didn't question her father. He had never forbidden it with words, but his manner spoke clearer than any language. He never gave an order without a reason. If it wasn't for her father's sanction, Katie would have refused to work for Miguel. If it wasn't her father's wish that she remain under Miguel's roof, she would have left long ago.

Miguel was her guardian. She had been entrusted into the care of him and his wife from early infancy. Her mother was dead, and her father had told her, with one of his rare concessions, that as the daughter of an emperor, she must be kept safe. She was expected to be content with this. To some extent she was. She understood her father's reasoning, even if it frustrated her at times that she had so little freedom. In practical terms there was no better guardian than Miguel. He was the most accomplished spy in her father's network, a master at his craft. Though this could be attributed in some part to Katie and the use he made of her gift. Katie detested him. He had always treated her as an inconvenience that he'd been saddled with, and often complained that no money was worth keeping her, though he rubbed his hands in satisfaction when a new package arrived. Very little of it was spent on Katie's upkeep. She ate with the servants and wore their clothes. She did chores and slept in an attic bedroom. She had few possessions of her own.

When she was little, she had tried to ask Miguel questions about her parents and why her father would not let her live with him. But she only ever got a sharp retort or a blow for her trouble. If her father knew how she lived, he never commented on it, and Katie would've died rather than complain. The only person in the house Katie could really talk to was Miguel's wife Jessemine. She had nursed Katie when she was a baby. As she'd never had any children of her own, she had lavished all her love on Katie. Miguel treated her with a cool indifference, which Jessemine accepted with weary resignation, though it made Katie's blood boil. She was Katie's only friend. But even here there were barriers. Katie had asked Jessemine about her parents, but Jessemine either *could* not, or *would* not speak of them. Katie soon gave up asking. Jessemine was equally reticent about her husband. Katie had broached the subject more than once over the years. “Why did you marry him? I won’t believe you loved him, and how can you not mind the mistresses he parades through the house?” All she ever got was a weary sigh and a “We must all manage as best we can.” Consequently, Katie became withdrawn and secretive. The blank mask of her face hiding her inner thoughts, though she openly showed her contempt for Miguel at every opportunity.

Staring absent-mindedly at the harbour, Katie’s eye was caught by a handsome vessel gliding majestically towards the jetty. She did not need to see the pennant fluttering at the masthead (a sun-burned man on the deck of his ship holding aloft a glittering rod) to recognize her father’s ship. Katie’s breath caught. It had been nearly a year since she had last seen her father. He very rarely left the safety of his mansion. Something important must have occurred. Katie turned from the window and began to dress. On these visitations, he always asked to see her before departing. Katie both looked forward to, and dreaded these interviews, though they never lasted long. Her father always aroused a strange mixture of emotions within her. Excitement coupled with apprehension, and even a touch of awe. He was mysterious and unfathomable. He intrigued her. Katie longed for the day when she would be old enough to be considered worthy of being allowed to inhabit his world. He kept her at a distance, though she felt that, in his way, he loved her.

Katie hastened down to the kitchen, where she found the servants all in a bustle.

“Look lively, girl,” Blodwyn, the plump chief cook chided. “’urry up and eat your breakfast, you’re gettin’ under our feet. We’re to prepare a meal in your father’s honour, and he’ll most likely want to see you once ’e’s finished talkin’ with the master.”

“Why does he want to see Miguel?”

“Gawd blimey, ’ow should I know, and just you mind your P’s and Q’s an’ all, it ain’t any of your business. Now eat up, and go and sit quiet somewhere till your father sends for you.”

Katie obediently gulped down her honey bread and fruit, and exited the crowded, steamy kitchen. But she did not return to her room. Her father would have arrived by now, and was most likely closeted with Miguel in his study. Katie ascended the flight of stairs, and tiptoed along the hall. Thick rugs covered the wooden floor, which muffled her footsteps. She stole the length of the corridor, and descended three steps to a small landing. Here was nothing but a bay window set in a recess in the wall, and directly opposite, the study. The voices of her father and Miguel could be heard clearly. Her father’s low and even, Miguel’s unctuous and placating. Katie’s lip curled. Miguel could be very charming when he wished, particularly when he stood to gain something from it. He had long ago learned how to curry favour with those in power.

Katie knew she shouldn’t be here. Miguel would skin her alive if he caught her, and who knew what her father would do. Katie had never seen him angry, but she sensed intuitively that it would not be good to be on the receiving end of it. Yet her curiosity was aroused. Her father never visited unless it was of the utmost importance, and Miguel had spent a great deal of time away from home recently. He had told no one where he was going, nor demanded Katie's assistance, which was unusual. Perhaps now the mystery would be solved. Katie made herself comfortable on the large padded window seat, drew the musty velvet curtain around her, and settled down to listen.

* * *

Alfredo strode down the line of bowing servants, each of whom prostrated themselves as he reached them. He paused by a woman lying face-down in front of a small hall table on which sat a tray piled high with refreshments. Alfredo's eyes glittered with recognition.

"Rise!" his voice was low, not much above a whisper, yet it resonated with authority, and could be heard by everyone in the vicinity. Jessemine got to her feet. Though still quite young, her face was lined and care-worn, and her clothes had a worn-out look.

"Your husband knows I have arrived?"

"He has asked that you receive him in his study, master. He will be with you shortly."

Alfredo's lips twitched in a humourless smile. "Take me to his study, then go and inform your husband that if he ever keeps me waiting again, I will have him flogged before his entire household." He gestured at the men and women thronging the hall.

She bowed. "As you wish, master."

"And bring the tray."

"Yes, master."

He followed her in silence along a corridor and down three steps. The study door stood open. Alfredo marched in and settled himself in the chair behind the desk. Jessemine stayed only long enough to place the tray on a low table, before bowing once more, and withdrawing.

Alfredo got up and moved restlessly over to the window, staring down on his domain. It had taken him twenty years to come to this. Twenty years to build this city, this flourishing industry, his growing empire. Below, the people scurried about their daily business like a swarm of multicoloured ants. Those people were his. There wasn't one aspect of their lives that he didn't control. A percentage of everything the people earned was his. He was the richest person in the land. No one was allowed to possess more wealth than him. Every year new tribes and nations were trampled beneath his armies, to fall beneath the iron fist of his rule. Their young and healthy men conscripted into his army, while older men were put to work in the mines digging for precious metals, or else working the land. Women and children who could work joined them. Anyone who could not serve any purpose, such as the elderly or infants, were disposed of. Even those who earned their bread were little better than slaves. Alfredo's taxes saw to that. Fifty per cent of every person's profit was his by law. Every house, shop, or market stall was rented from him. He made sure to increase his prices regularly. Anyone who failed to keep up their payments was guaranteed a prison sentence. His spies hunted out those living on the streets who were then sold for slave labour. Those who resisted were removed, sometimes in secret, sometimes publicly, as a warning for anyone else planning to rebel. The ground about Traitor's Hill, where all public executions took place, was a mass of graves.

Yet, despite everything, Alfredo was far from content. He had power, he had domination, but it was not absolute. His spies could not rout out every rebel. Gangs still infested the back alleys. As fast as one was found and eradicated, another appeared to take its place. Then there were those who didn't even live on land. Traders, making their homes at sea, only coming ashore to buy and sell goods, or if they absolutely had to. They were at their weakest then, but once at sea, they were almost untouchable. When they docked, they were easy targets for his men, but for every ship he sank, another three escaped, living outside his rule, making profits unhindered. He knew that some of the larger nations had weapons for destroying ships, and ships designed specifically for battle, but they had refused to trade with him. Once he conquered them, they would learn to regret their foolishness, but until then, these floating travellers evaded his grasp. Even those who appeared outwardly respectful still had their private thoughts and emotions that he could not subdue. He couldn't completely trust the people in his employ. He knew they despised him. Only their fear of him keeping them loyal. He still did not have sufficient forces to conquer some of the larger neighbouring countries.

Frown lines creased Alfredo's already lined and furrowed brow. Though only in early middle age, he had the appearance of someone much older. He was abnormally pale, his face a studied, expressionless mask. He was thin as a wraith. The black suits he always wore were tailored to fit, topped by a black robe that swirled and billowed about him like a shroud, cloaking his body as he cloaked his life. His iron grey hair was close cropped. The eyes behind their thick spectacles glittered like gimlets, the spark in an otherwise lifeless face.

Alfredo drummed his fingers on the window sill. He had come close to achieving his goal. Sixteen years ago, the means for it had seemed assured, but he had been thwarted, the knowledge he craved taken beyond his reach and no amount of searching had yielded any results. But perhaps now, after all these years, it was in his grasp. At last he would fulfil his destiny. He would have absolute power. The people would be helpless to resist. Their every thought, every feeling would be under his control. He would quite literally rule the world. He was so close, but there were still obstacles in his path.

There came a tentative knock on the door.

"Enter," he called.

The door opened, and a man entered, bowing low, so that his nose almost touched the carpet.

"Sit down, Miguel," said Alfredo, pointing to the only chair. He himself remained standing, leaning casually against the mantlepiece.

If Miguel felt any anger at being ordered to sit down in his own study, he did not show it. He perched on the very edge of the chair, twisting his fingers together nervously.

Though a good deal shorter than Alfredo, Miguel was wiry and fit, with thick, powerful arms. His black hair, greying at the temples, was shaved closer than Alfredo's own, and his clothes were expensively cut. His sharp nose and narrow, close-set eyes always put Alfredo in mind of a fox or a weasel. Alfredo detested him, and secretly longed for the day when he could be disposed of, but Miguel was useful. He had a knack for noticing things others didn't, and was very skilled at gathering information. He could blend into a crowd, or slip off into shadows as quietly as a whisper.

"Your report is long overdue, Miguel," said Alfredo quietly. "I trust you now have something worthwhile to tell me."

"I crave your pardon, master," Miguel answered. His voice, though humble and tremulous, was as smooth and slick as oil. "But I think I am not being presumptuous in saying that your long wait has been worth it. Three men were apprehended by the looters. Two foolishly refused to speak, but the third Source was more forthcoming, though it did take a lot of persuasion."

Source was the name spies gave to those who passed on useful information to them, whether willingly or not. Miguel's men made a point of looting every ship not carefully guarded. When they could, they took people captive, and probed them for information about their leaders and any conspiracies they might be plotting. But it was rare that his men were ever able to force them to reveal anything important. Their loyalty was fierce, often prized above their own lives.

Alfredo felt a stirring of hope. "Did he tell you of the boy, Christophe?"

"Indeed, master. It seems that Christophe disappeared some days ago, and—"

"I am aware of that," interrupted Alfredo coolly. "Or I would not have sent you after him in the first place. What was the purpose of his journey?"

Miguel swallowed. Alfredo always made him nervous. It had probably been a mistake becoming involved with him. He always gave the appearance of a snake just about to strike, but his money was good.

"He has gone to the other world to find the child that went missing sixteen years ago. When he has located her, he intends to bring her back to this land. Further than that, I have not been able to learn."

Alfredo stroked his chin thoughtfully. "So!" he said, half to himself. "The boy means to bring the girl back. After all this time."

The boy had been gone several days, and Alfredo had set every spy he employed to hunt him as soon as he learned of it. It seemed his suspicions were correct. Alfredo's eyes took on a hungry gleam.

The story of the girl's disappearance was famous, with many varying versions. But they all agreed on one thing. One day, she would return. It was odd that it should be now. Why was this year different to any other? According to the stories, she would be given certain instructions that would enable her to lead a revolt and set her people free. Alfredo could guess what she would be told; he knew much of it himself but for one crucial point. The knowledge that had eluded him for so long. The secret that would be his glory or his downfall. Clearly Christophe had been assigned this weighty task. He supposed he should've known. Alfredo's pale hands clenched into fists. The boy had been a thorn in his side for many years now, and Alfredo had long suspected that he held the key to the information he craved. But he had so far evaded every attempt at capture, running rings round Alfredo's men on more than one occasion. Even Miguel, the best spy in his network, had never managed to lay hands on him. Alfredo dreamed of the day when Christophe's body would swing from a gallows on Traitor's Hill, with every man, woman and child in the city watching. Well, perhaps his dream would soon be a reality. It seemed Christophe had been designated this girl's protector. He would not find it so easy to hide with another in tow. With any luck, one would lead him to the other.

"Did your Source give you any clue as to when the boy would return?" he said now.

A faint sheen of sweat coated Miguel's forehead. "Er, no, master, he died before I could complete the questioning."

Alfredo fixed him with his burning gaze.

Miguel hastened to continue. "But he did tell me where Christophe now makes his home."

Alfredo masked his excitement with difficulty. Never before had anyone revealed the boy's hideout.

"Indeed?"

Miguel heard the note of interest in his master's voice, and inwardly breathed a sigh of relief. "He lives with the Travellers, master, on a ship called the *Dolphin*."

Alfredo kept his face expressionless, but inside he felt a surge of triumph. So that was how the boy had managed to remain so illusive. He had suspected for some time that Christophe was hiding onboard a ship, but as they were nearly impossible to pin down, he had never been able to put his theory to the test. This was a turnaround indeed. Soon he would have the girl, and the people's boy wonder would be out of his hair, one way or another.

Miguel watched him anxiously. He knew very well that Alfredo only tolerated him, and that when he had served his purpose, his body would have an appointment with the seabed, but Miguel had a plan. He had quite a substantial amount of money saved, and not all of it had been come by through his work for Alfredo. As soon as he got an inkling that his time was near, he would flee. He knew how to run and hide better than anyone. But his employer was cunning, and Miguel sometimes had a sneaking suspicion that Alfredo could see more than just outward appearances with those gleaming eyes. But for now he was fairly sure he was safe. Alfredo would want this girl found, and Miguel was the man to do it. And if he caught the boy as well, even Alfredo couldn't just throw him off a cliff.

Finally Alfredo spoke. "Very well, you will begin a search for the *Dolphin* immediately. I want that girl brought to me as soon as possible. Take the boy too if you can, if not, kill him! The girl is the priority."

Alfredo leaned towards Miguel, until their faces were barely a foot apart. "You will bring the girl to me alive and unharmed. Do you understand, Miguel?"

Miguel barely suppressed a gulp. He did not frighten easily, but Alfredo always succeeded in putting the wind up him with little apparent effort. Not for the first time he cursed the day he had first become involved with this man.

"Absolutely, master, the girl is as good as found."

Miguel rose to go, but just as his hand was on the door handle, Alfredo's quiet voice called him back. "Miguel!"

He spun around sharply. Alfredo was gazing steadily at him, his eyes seeming to penetrate his very soul. Miguel dropped his gaze.

"Yes, master?"

"This is the most important task you will ever undertake. I have been very lenient up to now, but you stretch my patience, and there are plenty of younger men who I'm sure would be more than capable of stepping into your shoes. Do not keep me waiting too long, and do not fail."

Miguel bowed repeatedly to hide his discomfort, and left the room.

* * *

Katie held her breath as the study door opened and Miguel bowed his way out, closing the door behind him. Her head was teaming with questions. She had heard of Christophe. He was a known outlaw. Miguel had never asked her to search for him. His pride had never allowed it, and Katie had never tried to search for him herself. She had believed him no more important than any other criminal. She had never been more mistaken, it seemed. He had gone to another world? How was that possible? And why was this girl important? What could her father possibly want with a girl from another world? Katie hugged her knees. She had never even suspected that other worlds existed. A strange excitement gripped her. Now, more than ever, she longed for her father's confidence, and felt a hot stab of jealousy that Miguel had been the one on the other side of that door. Miguel, who would have failed on more than one occasion to hunt down her father's enemies if not for her.

Katie uncurled her cramped limbs, preparing to return to her room and await her father's summons.

The velvet curtain was ripped aside, and Miguel's face was suddenly inches from Katie's own.

"I thought so!" he breathed. He seized her arm in an iron grip and dragged her off the sill. Katie landed hard, jarring her legs, and swayed a little before regaining her balance.

Miguel was twisting her arm in his powerful fingers, his nails digging into her bare flesh. "How dare you come here! How dare you listen! This is none of your business! I'll make you wish you'd never been born when your father has gone, you little—"

"Miguel?" Alfredo had opened the study door and was now leaning against the frame.

Miguel released Katie so suddenly it was as if he'd been burned. Katie resisted the urge to rub her arm and looked from Miguel to her father. Miguel's face was drained of colour, while Alfredo was quite expressionless.

"Katriana, I would speak with you. Miguel, I believe I gave you a job to do. Is there any reason you are still here?"

Miguel opened and shut his mouth like a fish out of water. "I... she... no, master."

"Then go!"

Miguel shot Katie a look which spoke of repercussions on his return. Then he turned on his heel, and strode off, vanishing quickly from view.

Alfredo beckoned to Katie. As she followed him into the study, Katie couldn't help but admire her father's nerve. Not every man would appropriate another man's domain, and dismiss him as though he were a servant.

Alfredo seated himself once more behind Miguel's desk, while Katie halted before him. He looked at her appraisingly, taking in every inch of her, including the full set of finger prints on her arm. Katie had to fight not to squirm. She felt sure her father knew what she had done, and that a reprimand was now coming. She forced herself to keep meeting his gaze, and waited silently for the blow to fall.

"How old are you now, Katriana?"

The question startled Katie, but she regained control again almost at once. "Sixteen last week, Father."

Alfredo nodded. "You are of marriageable age now. I shall have to consider that carefully. I can't have my daughter marrying just anyone."

Katie's heart sank. Marriage was the last thing she wanted, but all she said was, "Yes, Father."

"However," Alfredo continued, "I fear that is a distant event. I have a task for you, Katriana."

Katie could hardly believe her ears. He had never asked anything of her before. At last a chance to prove herself. To show him that she was worth his attention. "Of course, Father, what is it?"

"As I am sure you heard, a guest will shortly be lodging under this roof. I wish you to befriend her. Make her feel comfortable during her stay. Make her trust you and feel able to confide in you. I am counting on you, Katriana."

Katie felt her pulse quicken. The girl they'd spoken of from the other world, and he was trusting this task to her alone. She felt a rush of pride. Her new-found confidence emboldened her to ask a question. "Is there anything in particular you wish me to discover, Father?"

For a moment, she thought he was going to be angry, but then he said, "This girl is the bearer of a secret that is detrimental to myself and the empire. She does not yet know the full implications of her knowledge, so she is not yet a threat, but I must find out what she knows. All measures will be taken to gain her cooperation, but you are my last port of call. She should confide to you what she would be afraid to tell anyone else."

Katie nodded.

"You understand what I'm asking, Katriana. I wish you to take this girl under your wing. If, in the unlikely event she escapes or is rescued, I expect you to accompany her. Make yourself invaluable to her and her friends."

"I understand, Father. I will do as you ask. But how will I report back to you?"

"There are ways in which I can contact you. This is a dangerous game you are playing. If your true identity is discovered, you will most certainly be killed. I shall not be beside you. You will be completely alone. What do you say now?"

"Is Miguel in on this too?"

For the first time, a brief smile flitted across Alfredo's face. "He is unaware of your assignment, and will not be assisting you."

That settled it. If she was not working with Miguel, then she would be completely independent, answering to no one but herself. That would be one in the eye for Miguel. The fact that so much was being entrusted to her was a little daunting, but she was proud, and deeply touched that her father had placed so much faith in her. It was what she had always wanted ever since she was old enough to articulate the feeling.

"I will do everything I can, Father, I promise."

Alfredo's expression softened momentarily. "Very well. Now, I must be on my way, run along with you." He ruffled her hair briefly. It was the most affection he'd ever shown her. Katie's whole body tingled with pleasure as she left.

Once out of sight of the study, Katie broke into a run, heading for Jessemine's room. She had no intention of revealing her conversation with her father, but she needed an outlet for the feelings bubbling within her. She had never felt more alive or full of energy.

Jessemine was sitting sewing at her window. She looked up as Katie entered. "Well? Did you see your father?"

"Yes, but not for long. He had to leave again, and he was with Miguel for a while."

Jessemine threaded her needle with practised fingers. "I dare say they had something important to discuss. Miguel has been absent from home a great deal lately."

"Yes, hasn't it been peaceful? I wish father would send him away more often."

Jessemine smiled wanly. She always looks tired, Katie thought suddenly. She had never really noticed that before. She felt a pang of sadness as she gazed into that prematurely lined face, noting the telltale strain about the mouth and forehead, the pale, hollow cheeks, and the dark circles beneath her eyes. Katie longed more than ever to help her. To remove her from her unhappy existence. She'd been the closest thing to a parent Katie had ever known, and though she never admitted as much, Katie knew how miserable she was with Miguel. Maybe if she managed to carry out her father's wishes, she could ask as a reward that he do something about Jessemine's plight. She would never have dared imagine such a thing an hour ago, but now, anything seemed possible.

Jessemine's voice broke in on her thoughts. "Don't just sit there daydreaming, get out your needlework. You haven't practised for days."

Katie grimaced. She loathed sewing, and even after six years of Jessemine's tutelage, was no more than a passable needle woman. She dutifully took up her work, but it was slow and tedious. To relieve her boredom, she said, "My father thinks I am old enough to marry now."

Jessemine's face showed no expression. "I suppose you are. Sixteen is the customary age."

"But who would want to marry me?"

Jessemine raised an eyebrow. "You are an attractive young woman and the daughter of an emperor no less. Be careful!" Katie had jabbed her finger with a needle. Putting it in her mouth, she scowled at Jessemine.

She was not used to people. She rarely had dealings with anyone outside the household, and men were a completely unknown entity.

"He did say it wouldn't be for a while yet."

"Well then, why are you worrying?"

Katie gazed out of the window. Jessemine was right. She had much more important things to think about.

The glorious morning had been replaced by a dull, overcast afternoon, and a light drizzle had begun to fall. Looking towards the harbour, she was just in time to watch her father's ship hoist its sails, and begin gliding smoothly away from the jetty. She continued to watch it until it was lost from sight.

* * *

Miguel made his way swiftly through the narrow streets, his face concealed beneath his hood. His clothes were drenched, and the sky was as black as his mood. His career and his life were on the line. If something went wrong, Miguel wasn't sure how he would talk himself out of trouble. Also Katie's behaviour rankled. He could hardly believe she had had the audacity to spy on him. Just because she had assisted him a few times. She really was getting above herself. What she needed was a man to make her toe the line. Perhaps if this venture succeeded, he would suggest it to Alfredo. She would need humbling a bit first though, or no self-respecting man would have her. The thought caused a grim smile to twist his mouth.

He met no one. The shops had closed early. Most people were now safely in their homes. He hurried along a promenade lined with small, open-fronted shops and eating houses, until he came to a small inn overlooking the harbour. Miguel glanced down. Many ships and boats of all sizes were moored there. Miguel pulled his sodden coat around him in an effort to hold in some non-existent warmth. He hoped this infernal rain would let up soon. It would slow his search considerably. His only comfort was that Christophe would suffer too. This would certainly lessen his lead.

He pushed open the inn door. The air was so thick with smoke that it was difficult to see anyone clearly. Grime covered the cracked stone floor and walls like an extra coat of paint. Several men were congregated at the bar, smoking long pipes, the smoke billowing and eddying round them. Several tables and chairs lay overturned nearby, together with the smashed remnants of a bottle, whose contents meandered steadily over the floor.

Miguel made his way towards the two largest figures at the end of the counter. These two men were strikingly alike. Each man was enormous, with shaggy, matted hair falling to their shoulders. They were built like oxen, with barrel chests, and thick arms and legs. The only difference between them was that one wore heavy gold hoop earrings swinging from his ear lobes, and three studs in the top of each ear, while the other had tattoos all over his chest and arms. Not a single inch of skin had been spared. They were looking a bit the worse for wear. There had evidently been a fight. The man with the earrings had two black eyes, a cut lip, and was bleeding heavily from the nose. His brother wore his right arm in a sling, and his left cheek was swollen and bruised.

Miguel approached. "Good evening, gentlemen."

Both men turned sharply, looks of recognition dawning on their flabby faces. They had had dealings with Miguel in the past.

"What you doing out on a night like this?" one demanded.

"I wish to hire your services," Miguel answered smoothly.

The brother with the earrings, whose name was Claude, looked up from his mug of ale with a greedy expression in his small, close-set eyes. "A new job, eh? I 'ope it pays better than last time. Benjy rather thought you short-changed us. In fact," he looked at his brother, "didn't we tell 'im what we'd do to 'im if 'e showed 'is face 'ere again?"

"Per'aps we should refresh 'is memory," Benjy suggested, pinning Miguel against the wall.

Miguel tried to keep the contempt out of his face. He knew these men would never do him any harm, not so long as he was putting money into their greasy hands, but it really was galling to be expected to work with such people. They never missed an opportunity to scare or intimidate anyone. It was their main source of pleasure. But it would never do to let them know his real feelings. Dumb muscle was just what Miguel needed if he was ever to reach the girl. Christophe was sure to have her well protected, and these men knew how to fight. It was best to make them think they had the upper-hand.

Miguel's face assumed an apprehensive expression, and his voice shook as he replied. "You forget I am only a poor spy. I can never pay my assistants the money they deserve, but I am on an important mission for the master."

The brothers looked at each other. Alfredo! The big man. Any job he needed doing was always well rewarded if you did it right.

"What sort of mission?" asked Benjy slowly.

"There is a girl who the master very much wishes to find. She is currently under the protection of the boy Christophe."

At the mention of Christophe's name, both men made animal noises of fury. They hated that boy as much as anyone in the criminal underworld.

Miguel allowed himself a secret grin. They'd do whatever he asked them now.

“He is hiding with the girl somewhere in the city. Possibly on one of those filthy Travellers’ ships. I need to conduct a thorough search of the seaports. But we must hurry. The boy will no doubt learn that his precious charge is being hunted and will try to flee. That must not be allowed to happen. Alfredo wants the girl brought to him alive.”

A gleam appeared in both men’s eyes. They knew what that meant. The girl must be brought back alive, but not Christophe. It would be the brother’s absolute pleasure to put an end to him, and anyone else that got in the way.

The two brothers looked at each other. A chance to get rid of Christophe, and a big fat wad of cash at the end. They nodded. “We’ll do it,” they said together.

Miguel gave a huge sigh of relief. “You will? Oh, that is so very kind of you. Now we must begin the search as soon as possible. If only this confounded rain would cease. Otherwise, I fear it means waiting for morning.”

Claude frowned menacingly. “You givin’ us orders now, Miguel?”

“Yeah!” Benjy snarled, jabbing a thumb into Miguel’s ribs. “We’re in charge, remember?”

Miguel fought not to grind his teeth. One of these days these two imbeciles would get what was coming to them, and Miguel intended to be there to witness it.

“Of course you are,” he said soothingly. “I only meant that the master will be extremely angry if the girl is not delivered into his hands soon.”

The brothers nodded grudgingly. Even they could see the sense in that. They shambled out of the inn, Miguel trailing behind them.

# Chapter 4

## The Appointed

Fiona lay on the hard, sandy floor and listened to the gulls screaming outside. It was that which had woken her, but she felt drowsy enough to drop back off again. She had never felt so tired. Her limbs felt like lead, and her head was so fuzzy that it was difficult to think straight. She tried cracking open an eye, but that was more than she felt equal to just yet. It was really much easier to lie where she was. She registered dimly that she was lying on something solid, nothing at all like her bed. Had she perhaps rolled out onto the floor? Also, the blanket over her felt thin and scratchy. Like some sort of rough wool. She groaned and twisted, trying to get comfortable. How had she ever managed to sleep at all?

Memories came to her, jumbled and fragmented. Dreams of being chased through a wood. Of being stalked through her house by a presence she couldn't see. Of coming home to find her parents and James dead and her house burnt to the ground. She trembled and tried to burrow further beneath the blanket. They were bad dreams, that was all, just nightmares. Like the one of that boy throwing her into a lake. That had been the most vivid of all. And there had been something familiar about the boy. She knew him from somewhere. Odd, who did she know who would want to kill her? It hadn't been James, she was sure of it. He'd looked a bit like that boy she'd met at the swimming gala. She'd gone on a picnic with him. By a lake… memory came rushing back. Christophe had lured her away from her home. He had tried to drown her. Yet she was still alive. How was that possible?

"Good morning," said a voice.

Fiona's eyes flew open. She shot upright, the sudden movement making her head spin. She placed one hand on the floor to steady herself. With the other she clutched the blanket around her as though it were a shield. She appeared to be in some kind of shack. Christophe sat across from her, watching her calmly. She could hear the sound of breaking waves. Warm, bright sunlight made her blink, and a cool breeze brushed soothing tendrils across her face. She stared at Christophe, a knot of panic constricting her chest.

"Where… where am I?"

"We call it Fledgling Cove, on account of all the birds that come to breed here. It is also known as The Crossing Point, the boundary between worlds." He smiled slightly at her blank look, though it did not touch his eyes.

She backed away from that smile, shuffling until her back was up against the wall. "How did I get here? The last thing I remember…" She broke off, seeing again that black, swirling mass rushing to meet her. "You tried to kill me!" she whispered.

"Well, clearly I didn't, as you are still alive. I drugged you, that is all."

That was all? How could he dismiss it so lightly? But none of this made sense. He'd drugged her, then tossed her in a lake. What had he expected her to do, swim laps? Of course she would have drowned. But she hadn't. Why? There was only one explanation. Christophe must have saved her, but why, when he'd thrown her in the lake in the first place? And how had they got here? This was like no beach she knew.

"Where am I?" she said more forcibly. "Why did you drug me? What's going on?"

He sighed with exaggerated patience, the sardonic smile still in place. "So many questions. I had to kidnap you. You would not have come with me otherwise. It was necessary."

"Come with you where? If you wanted to go to the seaside, you wouldn't have needed to drug me, and why am I still alive after you..." she broke off, swallowing the bile that rose to her throat.

"We are no longer on Earth. This is the land where you were born. Where you would have lived and grown up if your parents had survived. You were sent to Earth for your own protection, from those hunting you and your family."

Fiona stared at him incredulously. Her mouth opened, but no words came out. The boy was absolutely mad. Other worlds? Sent to Earth for protection? What was he on about?

"You're mad!" she spluttered finally, fury replacing fear. "You can take me home now. In fact, for your sake, you'd have been better off letting me drown, because as soon as I get out of here, I'll have you chucked in a mental home for the rest of your life."

Christophe seemed utterly unperturbed by her tirade. If anything, that made Fiona even angrier.

"This is your home," he said firmly. "This is where you belong from now on. Earth was never meant to be your home. You must let go of your old life."

Fiona stared at him, eyes blazing. She wanted to slap him. No, that was too lenient, after what he'd put her through. She could feel the hysteria rising. "And what about the lake?" she spat. "Thought I could have a farewell dip before I left, did you?"

The smile was gone from Christophe's face. His eyes were as hard as flint. "The entrance to this world is through that lake."

Fiona had had enough. Springing to her feet, she backhanded Christophe as hard as she could across the face. "Stop it!" she screamed at him. "This is all stupid! Ridiculous! You've had your joke, now take me home!"

Christophe was on his feet too. In the confined space, there was no escape. "If I were you," he said softly, "I would not try that again."

But Fiona was past caring. She never stopped to consider any consequences, The dam of barely controlled terror was about ready to burst. She lashed out the only way she could. She swung her arm again, but Christophe's fingers closed on her wrist in an iron grip. She met his unflinching gaze. There was no hope of breaking free. She was quite sure that, should Christophe choose, he could break her wrist easily. He was immensely strong for a boy his age. They stared at each other in silence for a moment, then Christophe released her. Fiona resisted the urge to rub her wrist. She refused to show any weakness in front of this boy. She could feel tears bubbling behind her lids. Angrily she forced them back.

"We must go," said Christophe. "With any luck, there should be a boat somewhere nearby."

Fiona followed him silently along a gravel path that descended steeply to the sandy beach below. As soon as they were on level ground, Christophe ducked beneath an overhang of rock jutting out from the sheer cliff wall. He gave a satisfied grunt. "Yes, it's here."

Fiona didn't wait. As Christophe started to drag the small rowing boat down to the water, she bolted in the opposite direction. She still felt weak from whatever drug Christophe had given her, and her knees threatened to fold any second, but she struggled on. If she could just reach a town, there might be a phone box where she could call for help. The sand was deep and hard to run through.

An arm wrapped around her from behind, pulling her to a stop.

"Let me go!" she screamed, trying desperately to break Christophe's grip, but she did not have the strength. Christophe simply picked her up, and carried her to the waiting boat. He deposited her in the stern, pushed the boat out into the waves, then leapt lightly in himself, taking up the oars.

Fiona remained where she was, utterly defeated, watching as the shore receded. The oars dipped and rose with rhythmic, powerful strokes.

Fiona shivered. The sun had gone in, and there was a definite chill in the air. Glancing skywards, she saw black clouds massing overhead, bringing an unwelcome promise of rain. She surveyed the water anxiously. The waves looked large to her, and the sea had gone from clear blue, to iron grey. She opened her mouth to demand where Christophe was taking her, when a flash of movement caught her eye. At first she thought it was a dolphin, then, to her horror, a head rose above the water. It was a person. A person struggling to keep afloat, but Fiona could tell that they were at the end of their strength. Even as she watched, the head sank beneath the waves.

"There's someone in the water! They're drowning!"

Christophe looked up immediately. "Where?"

Fiona pointed to where the head had disappeared. Only a stream of bubbles remained.

Christophe cursed and began rowing hard in the direction she'd indicated. "There's a rope under the seat," he snapped. "Get it out and tie it on to something, quickly!"

Fiona hastened to obey. Her hands were shaking violently. Her own narrow escape was too fresh in her mind.

Christophe seized the end of the rope, and knotted it around his waist. Then without a word, he dived over the side, the rope playing out behind him. The boat bobbed up and down, as Fiona held her breath and waited. She gripped the rope, ready to haul Christophe up.

After what seemed like an age, she felt the rope tighten. The water erupted, and Christophe appeared, a limp form in his arms. Fiona reached out to help haul the body into the boat. Then she looked down at the still form lying at her feet. Her scream sent flocks of seagulls soaring from their perches with indignant squawks.

"James! Oh my god, it's James!"

"Be quiet, girl!" Christophe snarled. "Take the oars, get us back to shore."

Fiona silently obeyed. She'd been on a sailing holiday with her parents the year before, and had taken to it well.

Christophe got down beside James, which was difficult in the confined space. He laid a hand on James's chest. "Not breathing," he muttered.

Fiona let out a sob, but continued rowing as fast as she could for the cove. It wasn't far, but the tide was going out, and the water was becoming increasingly choppy. Fiona wasn't sure if that was rain or spray hitting her face. The sun had vanished completely now, and she was shivering, though from cold or shock it was impossible to say.

How had James got here? She supposed he must have tried to come after her.

Christophe lowered his face to James's and began to breathe into his mouth. Deep slow breaths, with a few seconds' pause after each. He worked James's chest with his hands. But nothing happened. Tears mingled with the spray and rain pouring down Fiona's face. She could hardly see where she was going. He was dead, and it was because of her. He'd died trying to save her. The oars felt so clumsy and heavy in her grasp. Again and again Christophe breathed life into James's body. It seemed as though he would never stop.

Then, James's chest suddenly convulsed beneath Christophe's hands. Christophe immediately turned him on his side. Fiona dropped the oars as she bent forward. Christophe wordlessly pushed her aside, and resumed rowing. James's eyes fluttered open, then he vomited over the side of the boat. At last, he fell back, gasping. There wasn't room for him to lie full out. Fiona cradled his head in her lap, staring down into his white face.

"Fiona?" he croaked.

"James! Oh thank god, James!"

"You're alive?"

"Just rest for a minute, we'll be on land soon." He lay back obediently. She smoothed his wet hair back from his face with one hand, while wiping away tears of relief with the other, and trying to contain the sobs that still welled up in her. He was alive!

"Where are we?" he said, his voice stronger now.

"That's a good question," said Fiona, with a furious glance at Christophe, who'd remained silent all the while. Now that her terror for James was over, anger rose to take its place. If not for him, she would never have gone missing, and James's life would never have been in danger.

James followed her gaze, and tried to sit up. His movement was so sudden that it caused the boat to rock alarmingly.

Fiona gripped him tightly. "Easy, James, you'll have us over!"

"Him! He tried to kill you! I'll—"

"James, no, later!"

In another minute they were at the beach once more. Lying James in the bottom of the boat, Fiona helped Christophe to haul it up onto the sand. Then she helped James to climb out.

"Get him to the hut," Christophe said curtly, then he walked off.

Fiona frowned after him. Where was he going? James sagged against her before righting himself, and she pushed Christophe from her mind.

"Can you walk? It's not far." Supporting him with one arm, she guided him to the hut, which was out of the wind, and offered some shelter from the driving rain. Forcing him to sit, she found the blanket she'd slept under, and wrapped it around him. He was shivering. She sat pressed up against him, trying to lend him some of her warmth, though she didn't have much to give, one arm around him.

"You idiot," she said softly. "What in the world did you think you were doing? You know you're not a strong swimmer."

"It was… a sort of accident. I was down at the lake with Carolyn, and I sort of fell in."

"What do you mean?"

"Well, the bank was flooded, like there'd been a storm. I slipped in the mud, and one of my hands touched the water. Then it all foamed up like a whirlpool and dragged me in."

"And Carolyn? She didn't fall in too, did she?"

"No, I sent her for help, she's safe." He looked around bleakly. "Which is more than can be said for us. Where on earth are we?"

"I don't know, I woke up here. The last thing I remember is Christophe pushing me in the lake. It all foamed up like you said, and then I was here." She frowned worriedly. "He says I belong here, that I was sent to Earth only for my own protection."

"He's mad!" James said sharply. "He tried to kill you, for god's sake!"

"But I'm still alive. He didn't let me drown. He said he drugged me to bring me here. He said it was necessary."

"I don't care what he thought was necessary. Because of him, we both nearly died! If you hadn't happened along when you did, I'd be dead by now. Where was he taking you anyway?"

Fiona shook her head. "No idea."

"Well, this is stopping right now. He's taking us home whether he likes it or not."

Fiona said nothing. She doubted it would be that simple.

"Where is he anyway?" James demanded.

As though in answer, Christophe appeared, an arm-load of firewood clutched to his chest. "We shall have to stay here while this rain lasts," he announced.

“There’s no point setting out until then.” He set the damp logs down on a ring of stones near the hut entrance, and began rummaging in his pocket.

“Let’s get one thing straight, Christophe,” said James. “The only place we’re going, is back where we belong. You can take us there yourself, or just give us directions, but this is stopping right now, are we clear?”

Christophe ignored him. He produced a box of matches that Fiona didn’t remember seeing on him before, and struck one. It took several attempts, and several spent matches before the damp wood finally caught, and a few more to get the fire going properly. All three of them huddled gratefully around the meagre blaze, Fiona wrapping the remaining blanket around herself.

James immediately resumed the attack. “So, are you going to tell us how to get out of here?”

“You cannot leave here by yourselves.”

“Excuse me?”

“I will send you back if you wish, but I imagine you would rather stay with your friend.”

“And why won’t you let her go?”

“I need her,” Christophe said simply. “The entire land needs her.”

Both Fiona and James stared at Christophe, open-mouthed.

“What for?” Fiona spluttered. “And what makes you think I’d do anything for you after everything you’ve put me through?”

Christophe raised an eyebrow. “What exactly have I done?”

“What have you done?” echoed James incredulously. “Not much. Only taken Fiona away from her family to this godforsaken place, only nearly killed her in the process, and if that wasn’t enough, you nearly killed me too. Her parents are frantic! They have no idea where she is. They think she’s dead. Apart from that, you’re innocent.”

Fiona had gone white. “They think I’m dead?” she whispered. It was James’s turn to put a comforting arm around her, while glaring at Christophe.

Christophe looked completely unfazed. “I don’t know why you both keep insisting that I tried to kill anyone.” He pointed at Fiona. “I could have let you drown. It would have been so easy. But instead I risked my neck to keep you alive. And…” he nodded at James, “if memory serves correctly, I just saved your life.”

James shifted uncomfortably, and Fiona looked down. There was no denying Christophe’s words. He had undoubtedly saved James’s life.

Fiona recovered first. “You put his life in danger in the first place. He wouldn’t be here if you hadn’t kidnapped me.”

“Yes,” said Christophe musingly. “A brave deed, if incredibly foolish. That lake swallows anyone it touches. How, pray, were you intending to survive?”

“I fell in by accident,” James snarled.

A slight sneer tugged at the corners of Christophe’s mouth. “So, it was not even an act of bravery. In that case, you have no one to blame for your predicament but yourself. You could have remained safe in your own world.”

James tried to get to his feet, uttering an inarticulate sound of fury, but Fiona restrained him with a hand on his arm. Her mind was racing. Despite the circumstances of her capture, she was curious to know what had made this boy risk so much for her. She was also curious to see what arguments he could possibly use that would convince her to help him. He would never tell them how to return home, but if they appeared to cooperate, his mood might soften. If the worst came to the worst, she could simply refuse to help him, and he would have no choice but to send them home.

Affecting a sigh of resignation, she said, "Alright, Christophe, you win. It's obvious we're at your mercy. Just tell me what you want."

Christophe stared at her long and hard for several moments. Fiona had to fight hard not to squirm. His expression was unreadable.

Finally he said, "This land is ruled by a tyrant. His name is Alfredo. He has been ruler of this country, and all the bordering lands for twenty years. He has a small empire at his disposal. The people are poor. They are overworked and underpaid. They scratch out a living as best they can, trying to feed their families from the pittance left after Alfredo's taxes. His spies hunt out resistance and crush it ruthlessly. Alfredo needs one thing only to make his power complete, and seal the doom of those he has enslaved."

Christophe paused to gaze at his audience. Both James and Fiona were listening raptly, all animosity momentarily forgotten.

Christophe took a breath and continued. "A man named Tobias opposed Alfredo. He was the chief of a network of spies who made it their business to find out Alfredo's plans and destroy them if they could. Alfredo was always looking for new ways to increase his power. It soon became apparent that he was after something in particular. What this was, Tobias also became determined to learn. It soon became clear that it involved the merpeople, for Alfredo began persecuting them shortly after. The merpeople hold great wisdom and power, so whatever he hoped to force them to reveal would have been awesome indeed. But they fled, and Alfredo was left to nurse his hatred and frustration. The merpeople were never seen again."

Fiona let out a derisive laugh. "Oh, come on, Christophe, you can do better than that. Merpeople? Please! They're just a kid's fairytale."

James nodded his agreement.

Christophe regarded them coldly. "In your world, perhaps they are. But I think I am correct in saying that if two people went back and tried to tell their friends that they had been kidnapped and taken to another world by means of an enchanted lake, their story too would be dismissed as just a fairytale. Yet here you are."

Neither James nor Fiona were able to dispute this. Christophe was right, of course he was. They lapsed into silence.

Christophe took advantage of this to go on with his story. "Tobias and his allies also continued searching for the merpeople, for they were a grievous loss. They still hoped to learn what it was Alfredo coveted so much, so that it could be destroyed.

"Tobias eventually returned after many months' absence. He met with his closest friend, a man named Ivan, and instructed him to gather all who were loyal to an urgent meeting. However, Tobias was captured. Alfredo's men knew he had gone to search for the merpeople, to try to learn the secret of the power Alfredo sought. He was imprisoned for many months. When he was finally rescued, he was weak from lack of food, and his body severely damaged from continuous torture. His health was failing, despite everything the healers tried. He lived out the remainder of his life in hiding with his wife. He only confided in Ivan, and all he said was that he knew what Alfredo desired, and what the merpeople had tried to deny him. He would not name it, except to say that it would lead to disaster, and he was the only one who could stop it. Yet he was in no condition to act.

"Shortly after this, two disasters occurred in quick succession. First, Tobias's wife died giving birth to their first child, a girl, leaving her to the care of an ailing father. Secondly, Alfredo's men discovered Tobias's hiding place. He feared they might harm his daughter to force him to reveal what he knew, and he feared he would not have the strength to withhold it from them. He called Ivan to him, and then drank some poison he had hidden away. When Ivan arrived, he found his friend dying. In his final moments, Tobias charged Ivan to send his daughter to Earth, in order to protect her. He also entrusted to his care, a book with tarnished silver clasps, with instructions to guard it until his daughter came of age. His daughter was then to return to this world, and receive the book. Ivan concluded that the book held the knowledge that Tobias had guarded so well, and through such hardship. He did as Tobias asked, and took his daughter out of this world, by a way known to few. He tried to read the book, but it would not open. No one could open it. It was for one person only. That person is you!"

Christophe concentrated his full gaze on Fiona. "You are Tobias's daughter. You are the baby that was sent to Earth sixteen years ago. Now you are a woman, and you must take up your birthright. You, and no other can discover the secret your father hid for so long. You, and no other can act on what you find. You are the land's last hope. You are The Appointed!"

Fiona started. She had been so caught up in Christophe's tale that it took a moment to realise that he was addressing her directly. As his last words sank in, she went from surprise, to astonishment, to outright disbelief. That pronouncement, uttered in that tone, aroused a powerful emotion that she could not at first put a name to. It took her a moment to realise that the shiver running the length of her body was fear.

"I am the what?" she said shakily.

"You are The Appointed," Christophe repeated. "You are the one chosen by your father's dying wish to continue his work."

"This is ridiculous!" James snapped. "I've never heard such a load of rubbish in my life. It sounds like something out of a book. I mean, for god's sake, how can you expect us to believe you?"

For the first time, a hint of anger blazed in Christophe's grey eyes, and his voice was cold as winter. "Are you so ignorant that you will not believe what is before your eyes? Here you are, in another world. A world to which you were transported under impossible circumstances. Do you think anyone else would have survived being tossed into a foaming lake? Did you never stop to wonder where all those who entered the lake disappeared to? Your name is whispered by mothers as they soothe their frightened children, as an antidote to their fears. Slaves driven almost past endurance, struggle on in the hope that The Appointed will one day come to set them free. Men and women live with conditions that you could not possibly imagine. Their children are born and die in squalor and filth. They are forced to watch quietly as the money that might have kept them from starvation is taken from them coin by coin. These people endure all this and more, yet the thought of The Appointed sustains them. They suffer their pain only because they believe that some day it will end if they can only be patient and hold on. People are willing to give up their lives in the name of The Appointed. They have done, and will go on doing so, even when it seems there is no point. There is always a purpose while The Appointed lives. And you would dismiss their hopes as just a story?

"There is a price of 5000 gold sovereigns on my head, dead or alive. Do you have any concept of what that could do for a family? And yet they sit tight and say nothing, while Alfredo's men raid their houses searching for me. There is a threat of death to anyone sheltering me, but they keep quiet. And why? Because I am bringing The Appointed to set them free." He spat contemptuously.

Fiona realised that she was trembling. She gripped James's hand tightly, unable to meet Christophe's eyes. Fear still roiled in her, but mixed in with it was a sense of shame. She didn't like the feeling. It meant admitting that what Christophe said was true. That he was right. She didn't think she had ever met anyone so calm, yet so passionate.

She suddenly raised her head, glaring at him. "Prove it!" she snapped.

He blinked. "What?"

"So, what you say is true, fine! You explained why you kidnapped me, but how do you know I'm the one, The Appointed?" The words seemed to stick in her throat.

Christophe met her challenging stare levelly. "You told me yourself that you were abandoned on a park bench. You said that you knew nothing of your parents, that they gave no explanation for abandoning you. When you were brought to this world, you were left on a park bench, the very same one on which you told me you had been found. Ivan told me that he hid and watched until you were picked up. Your mother, Alexandra, disappeared a year or two before you were born. It was thought she had drowned, a tragic accident. I saw her picture in your newspapers. She matches the description Ivan gave me exactly. Finally, you said that you had always felt a certain affinity towards that lake. No one else shared your feelings. They thought it dangerous. That was why a fence surrounded the water's edge. Only someone from this world would feel such a pull. I felt it tugging at me the entire time I was in your world."

"The mayor's daughter who disappeared!" Fiona breathed. "Her name was Alexandra. And it was you who vandalised the fence!"

Christophe was unremorseful. “Of course! How else was I supposed to get you away?”

“But what if someone else had fallen in by mistake?”

Christophe shrugged unconcernedly. “They would have been stuck here for ever. It happens from time to time. Strange people arrive from strange places, and all have the same explanation for how it happened. They never return. Usually they are glad to leave their old lives behind them.”

Fiona stared at him, momentarily lost for words, but James had another question. “Why did Ivan confide in you so much? What’s so special about you?”

Christophe waited a while before answering. He busied himself throwing more logs on the fire, not looking at them. Fiona thought he was choosing to ignore the question. But then he turned and looked full at them. “He was my father.”

# Chapter 5

## A Simple Plan

The rest of that day was not a comfortable one for Fiona. After Christophe's extraordinary pronouncement, she just sat there, not knowing what to say.

James was equally speechless. What sort of a response could you give to that?

Christophe did not wait for them to recover. "We will have to stay here for the night. This rain looks as though it's set in for the day. I will go and see if I can find us something to eat." He strode out of the hut, and the driving rain soon obscured him from view.

Fiona looked helplessly at James. "What do we do now?"

James shook his head.

Fiona hugged her knees and stared into the heart of the fire. She felt as though everything she knew to be real and possible was slipping away. She had been sucked through a portal into another world, and if she accepted that that was true, then she had to believe the rest of Christophe's story too. She was here to accomplish something important, and there were a lot of expectations riding on her shoulders; a whole nation's, in fact. Resentment boiled hot and strong in her chest. Why couldn't they solve their own problems? They were not her concern. Except, they were, weren't they? They were her people.

A thought suddenly struck her. "We can go back."

"What?" James frowned at her.

Fiona felt excitement momentarily rise to blot out her resentment. "The lake is obviously a portal between the two worlds."

"So?"

"So, it's not just a one way ticket. You can travel between them. Those people could've gone home if they'd wanted to. Christophe can travel back and forth whenever he likes."

"How do you reckon we get back?"

Fiona frowned. "The lake brought us to this cove, so the portal is somewhere round here."

James shook his head. "Christophe brought you here. This was where you found yourself when you woke. You don't know how far he brought you."

Fiona bit her lip. "We found you in the ocean. The lake spat you out into the sea, not that far from land…" She stopped, realising what she'd just said. Christophe would've swum to shore with her, and it would have taken much longer swimming than by boat. And who knew how far James had been swept by the current. Somewhere in that vast, heaving ocean, the way back to Earth was located.

"It may as well not exist at all," she muttered dully. But Christophe had known exactly where he was coming out. He could leave and return whenever he pleased. Fiona sank her head in her hands. Christophe was not going to tell them. That was certain. It was the only hold he had over them. She could almost feel the jaws of the trap closing in. She was caught as surely as a fish in a net.

James seemed to have read her thoughts. He put an arm around her shoulder and squeezed gently. "Look, Christophe can't be the only person who knows about this. Someone must have told his dad. We'll find someone who'll show us the way back."

"How?" Fiona's voice was expressionless, muffled between her hands.

"We'll wait till nightfall. The rain might've let up by then. We'll wait till Christophe's asleep, then we'll steal the boat and make a break for the mainland. I shouldn't think it's too far. That's probably where Christophe was taking you."

Fiona raised her head, a spark of hope in her eyes. "Do you really reckon it could work?"

"We can give it a try. We'll be cooperative all day. Make him think he's won. If he thinks we'll give him no more trouble, he'll drop his guard. Then we'll run for it."

"Yeah, OK." She grinned. "It'll be a shock for him when he finds his boat's gone." Neither of them felt any compunction about leaving Christophe on this godforsaken spit of land. It seemed a just revenge.

So, for the rest of the day, they were suitably docile. Christophe returned a few hours later, carrying a brace of dead rabbits. Fiona tried hard not to watch as he skinned and cleaned the animals. Her thoughts kept straying to the pet rabbit she'd had when she was little, that had lived in a hutch at the bottom of the garden. To take her mind off it, she asked Christophe where he'd found the various objects he'd brought with him. A knife, a cooking pot, and more matches.

"You would be surprised what you can store under the seat of a boat," he replied dryly. "I left it ready for my return." He sent Fiona off with the cooking pot and directions to the nearest stream. And after very careful descriptions, sent James off in quest of some strange-looking roots and leaves that neither James nor Fiona had ever seen before. He did not seem to think for one moment that they would try to escape. Fiona marvelled at his foolishness, but it was all to the good.

Christophe added the roots and leaves to the rabbit meat in the pot. They took turns eating the stew from the pot with a ladle. It was very tasty, but the memory of Flopsy hopping over the lawn kept Fiona from enjoying hers.

Christophe cooked all the meat, though he did not add all of it to the stew. He wrapped some of it up in broad flat leaves. "It will do for breakfast tomorrow," he said. "Rabbit is just as nice cold."

During the meal, Fiona asked where they were going.

"We will be making for one of the shipping ports," said Christophe. "I hope to catch up with the *Dolphin*. She has been my home these last six years, and she will be a good place to lay low for a time while we make our plans. They are good people on that ship, and they will have been on the lookout for us these past two weeks."

When the meal was over, Christophe sent Fiona to rinse the pot and ladle in the stream. The rain had stopped now, leaving the air smelling fresh and clean. It was a warm night, and the sea was calm once more, with barely a ripple stirring the pond-like surface. Even better, there was a full moon overhead. The conditions for their night-time journey would be perfect, and Fiona was reasonably confident of her sailing.

When she returned, Christophe was rolling himself into one of the blankets.

"Better get some sleep," he said gruffly. "We must leave early tomorrow."

Fiona and James nodded dutifully. They shared the second blanket, huddling close together. Fiona lay wide awake with her eyes closed, pressed against James, listening to the sounds of the night. This was the tricky bit. They had to be sure Christophe was asleep.

After what seemed like an age, the hut was filled with regular, quiet breathing. Fiona felt James stir cautiously, and knew he was checking to make sure. Fiona held her breath. Then she felt James's breath on her cheek and heard his whisper.

"Coast is clear, let's go."

Fiona opened her eyes and sat up slowly. Turning her head, she saw that Christophe was lying on his side, his face buried in the crook of one arm. James was rolling up their blanket. He picked up the food parcels and slipped them into the makeshift sack. The leaves crackled a little. It sounded very loud, and they both froze, staring at Christophe, but he never so much as twitched. Fiona hesitated over the cooking pot, but then decided against it. It would be cumbersome to carry, and they were already burdened by the blanket. They'd just have to have a good long drink at the stream first.

They slipped out of the hut, and began to pick their way down the steep, rocky path to the beach. The full moon lit their way perfectly. Overhead, the sky was a deep, blood red. It would be a glorious day tomorrow. Fiona reached level ground with relief. She had been half afraid she would stumble and send a rock flying, but they'd been lucky. Fiona set off at a run for the little cove. James, who was carrying the rolled-up blanket, followed at a slower pace. So it was, that Fiona, running flat out, reached the little beach first, and drew up short with a cry of dismay.

"What is it?" James called, quickening his pace. He came panting up beside her, and saw for himself. The boat was gone. The stretch of sand running to the water's edge was completely smooth, except where a channel had been made by something heavy being dragged away.

Hot rage coursed through James. "He must have hidden it!" he hissed through clenched teeth. Such a simple idea, yet it stymied their plan completely.

"We'll split up," Fiona said. There was a hint of desperation in her voice. "He can't have dragged it far." They combed the entire inlet. They peered behind boulders and into patches of scrub, but the boat was nowhere to be seen. In the end, they had to concede defeat. James retrieved the blanket and the food, and they trudged wearily back to the hut.

Christophe was still sleeping peacefully, exactly as they had left him. James felt like kicking his head, but he would not give Christophe the satisfaction of knowing his plan had worked. No wonder he'd given them so much freedom. They never had any chance of escaping. The thought was bitter.

Fiona was sitting on the floor, looking utterly defeated. James had never seen her looking so lost and vulnerable. She looked like a little girl, rocking backwards and forwards, her eyes huge and frightened. James put his arms around her. She hid her face in his shoulder, tears sliding down her cheeks. Fiona never cried. James didn't know what to do.

"It's no use," she mumbled into his jacket. "The only way we're getting out of here, is if he tells us how." She shot a venomous glance at Christophe. "And the only way he'll tell us how to leave, is if I do what he wants."

"Hey, come on," James said awkwardly. He'd never seen her fall apart like this. "Don't give up, we'll get out of here somehow."

"I might never see Mum and Dad again."

"Yes you will," James said firmly. "We will get home again, and if that means following Christophe's harebrained scheme first, then we'll do it together. I won't leave you."

She raised her tear-stained face from his shoulder and hugged him back. "Thanks, James," she whispered. She was silent a moment. Then, so softly that he barely heard her, "I'm glad you're here with me."

"Me too. Now let's try to get some sleep."

They snuggled beneath the blanket once more, huddling close together for comfort. Fiona fell asleep at once, but James turned his head to look at the corner where Christophe lay sleeping. There would come a day, he swore silently, when Christophe would pay for what he'd done to Fiona. A wave of tiredness swept over him, and before he could decide exactly how Christophe would pay, he was asleep.

* * *

Christophe waited until he heard his companion's slow breathing, before rolling onto his other side. His arm was numb from having lain on it for so long. He had watched as Fiona and James collected their meagre possessions and sneaked out of the hut exactly as he'd expected. It was just as well that he'd hidden the boat earlier while he'd been out hunting. He had known they would try to escape. They were both determined and stubborn. They would never help him unless they had no other choice. He had watched them return, the girl defeated and tired, but he had underestimated the boy's feelings for her. He was clearly devoted to the girl, and listening to their conversation, hearing the fear in the girl's voice at the thought of never seeing her parents, and the boy's avowal that he would stick by her, he felt a twinge of remorse. He'd secured Fiona's help, but it was a hollow victory. If they survived this, and The Appointed managed to do what was required of her, then he would take her home again. He would keep this promise to himself of course, but she would live to see her parents again. He would make sure of that. It didn't matter that this was her home. She had been in that other world too long. She would never truly belong in this one. Christophe sighed, wrapped the blanket more closely around him, and allowed his thoughts to carry him off to sleep.

# Chapter 6

## The Festival of Mer

Fiona was woken by the deafening chorus of birds greeting the new day. She lay perfectly still, her eyes squeezed tightly shut. If she kept them closed and remained where she was, then she could pretend that all this was a dream. That what she was hearing was not the mournful call of gulls, but the cheerful song of sparrows and blackbirds. This wasn't hard floor beneath her, but her own bed at home. Everything would be just a memory, a nightmare. The image was so real, that she nearly opened her eyes, but the illusion was shattered as she felt a hand on her shoulder. She gave a small cry of fear and bolted upright, her eyes flying open.

It was morning. The hut was full of warm sunlight. Christophe was portioning out the leftover meat from last night's meal. There was no sign of James.

"Where's James?" she demanded, staring about for him. She did not want to be left alone with Christophe.

"I sent him to get some water. There will be none between here and the shipping port, and it is hot out under the sun." He paused, looking at her. She couldn't make out his expression.

"There is no need to be afraid of me, you know. I mean you no harm."

She snorted. "Suddenly my confidence is completely restored. What will you do when I've saved the world? I won't be much use to you then."

He let out a sigh of exasperation. "What do I have to do to convince you that I am not some kind of monster?"

"Let me go home."

"You know I will not do that. Unlike you, I have more than just myself to think of."

Fiona opened her mouth furiously, but the retort died as James appeared, carefully carrying the full cooking pot. He grinned at Fiona. "You're awake then?"

She glared at him. "You could've woken me."

"I thought I'd let you sleep a bit longer. You never were a morning person." He set the pot down and, pointedly ignoring Christophe, sat down and began his breakfast. Fiona and Christophe followed suit.

No one made any mention of the disastrous escape attempt of the night before, but James and Fiona chatted animatedly throughout the meal, while Christophe was deliberately excluded. Fiona sneaked a sidelong glance at Christophe to see how he felt about this treatment, but he just continued eating his breakfast, apparently indifferent.

They took turns drinking (Fiona and James making sure Christophe was last in line) then Christophe began gathering up their belongings, after first using earth and leaves to hide the remnants of the fire and the rabbit bones. Fiona and James stood side by side, watching as Christophe heaved the blankets onto his shoulders and bent to pick up the pot and ladle and shoved the remaining matches into his pockets. When he straightened up, he looked like a loaded down pack mule. He peered at them over his load. “Would I be correct in thinking that you are both just going to stand there?”

“You would,” said James flatly. “We may be your hostages, but we’re not your slaves.”

Christophe made no response beyond a slight tightening of his lips, and strode off. Fiona and James fell into step behind him.

Despite herself, Fiona couldn’t help but admire his self-control. She would have been foaming at the mouth by now.

When they reached the little inlet, both James and Fiona watched Christophe keenly. They had searched this entire beach for the boat without finding it. Surely Christophe had some really clever hiding place. To their utter fury, Christophe simply set down his burden, walked over to a patch of scrub and small rocks identical to all the others and pushed it all aside to reveal the boat. Fiona and James couldn’t quite mask their looks of incredulity. Surely they’d looked there.

“If you want to hide something well,” Christophe said quietly, “hide it in plain sight.” Then, as Fiona and James glared at him, he began stowing his gear back beneath a small hatch that lifted out of the base of the boat’s seat and dropped neatly back into place once more. Then, without waiting for them to get in, he began pushing the boat into the waves, causing Fiona and James to flounder hurriedly after him.

“Wait up!” Fiona called after him, but Christophe did not even slow down. He pushed the boat out further and further, so that Fiona and James were actually wading in water up to their knees. Christophe leaped into the boat and took up the oars. For one awful moment, Fiona thought he was going to row away and leave them marooned, but he merely sat watching as they came splashing up to him. The water was by now nearly up to their waists, though it was blessedly warm. Fiona managed to scramble aboard fairly easily, but James nearly slipped twice and had to be helped in by Fiona.

He collapsed beside Fiona and glared at Christophe as the boat began to pull away from the shore. “What was the idea?” he demanded furiously.

Christophe raised his eyebrows. “You said yourself, you are not slaves. I cannot make you come with me. Since you find my company so unbearable, I thought you were staying behind.” He glanced at their wet clothes. “It seems I was mistaken after all. Still, don’t worry. Once we are out on the open sea, the sun will soon dry you off.”

Neither James nor Fiona could think of a response to this. Fiona sat in silence, feeling the boat rise and fall gently beneath her, enjoying the feel of the sun on her back and the breeze that lifted her hair. She trailed a hand in the warm water. She did like being at sea. She'd loved every minute of that sailing holiday. The water was so much cleaner here too. The blue sky reflected in it perfectly. She could see right down into the depths where brightly coloured fish swirled lazily by.

Then, in a shock of spray, two dolphins surfaced no more than ten feet away. Fiona gave a cry of delight, and even James, who was not used to sailing and had been looking rather pale, stared in wonder. Another dolphin rose to join the first two. Then another and another. Soon six dolphins were cavorting in the water, leaping impossibly high and falling back again with huge splashes, calling to each other with squeaks and clicks. Fiona gazed at them, so happy and carefree, and longed to join them. It was one of her life's dreams to swim with dolphins. She wanted to dive over the side of the boat and swim in among them, to leap and play. But then she saw Christophe's face, and momentarily forgot everything else.

Gone was that hard penetrating gaze and that expressionless mask that hid so much. His eyes shone, and a smile of pure joy lit up his face. It made him look a completely different person. It showed him for the boy he was. Fiona stared in amazement, but then the spell was broken. The dolphins disappeared below the surface and did not return. Fiona remembered once more where she was and what she was facing; Christophe's smile was gone, replaced by a look of determined concentration as he carried her onward to whatever fate awaited her. She fell back to wondering what was going to happen to her. How she would be received by the people of this land. The prodigal daughter returned to fulfil her destiny. Would she be able to do what they wanted? Could she live up to their expectations? Did she even want to? Images of her parents and the home she had left behind rose up in her mind. They seemed so far away. She wished more than anything that she was back with them safe once more. She had to fight down her rising panic. She looked at James. He was staring fixedly ahead, his face faintly green. She reached for his hand and gave it a reassuring squeeze, and felt comfort in the pressure of his response. Whatever happened, James would be beside her. Nothing would ever change that.

It felt like no time at all before they reached their destination, though Fiona was sure it must have been an hour or more. One moment it seemed, Fiona was watching, entranced as the dolphins played in the open sea, and then she was watching the land rise up like a mountain from the water. It was a dock thronged with people. They swarmed about the decks of their ships, making sure the moorings were secure, or else unloading cargo. She was deafened as people competed with each other to be heard, orders were shouted, and hawkers tried vainly to sell their wares, struggling to make their cries heard. Children ran everywhere, fetching and carrying, or simply playing. Chasing each other along the pier, or paddling in the warm sea, splashing water at each other. Seabirds added their clamour to the racket, as though determined not to be outdone. The air was heavy with the smells of fish and sea salt. They had slowed to a crawl. They were in a queue inching slowly towards the jetty. Boats and ships of all sizes were behind and ahead of them, waiting to tie up, their owners calling and gesticulating impatiently to those in their way.

Fiona was able to get a good look at the people around her. The women wore brightly patterned pinafore dresses with full, flared skirts that fell to just below the calf. They were of every shade imaginable, and so vivid that they dazzled the eye. Sky blue, lime green, dusky pink, there were reds, purples and oranges in every conceivable hue, and every pattern imaginable. Spots, stripes, prints, squares, polka dots and swirls. The exposed skin of their arms and legs was bronzed golden by the sun.

The men wore wide-legged baggy trousers that flared extravagantly at the bottom, and loose-fitting tunics, also in the same vivid colours and patterns. Everyone wore brightly-coloured sashes at their waists, and many tied back their hair with bright headscarves. Many of the men had hair as long as the women's, and as a variation to the scarves of the women, they wore their hair tied back with braided leather cords. Many people wore flat open-toed sandals in plain neutral colours, contrasting with their gay apparel, though a large number went barefoot, and all the children did so.

The women were festooned with beads. They hung from their necks and adorned their wrists. They were all gaudy colours and Fiona was reminded of the kind of thing seen on the stall at a school fête. They seemed to clip together magnetically, and could be made as long or as short as the women wished. Finger rings covered their hands and hoops and drops swung from their ears, and from many of the men's. They also had a cheep, tacky look to them.

They were nearing the jetty now, and Fiona saw that Christophe was making a beeline for one of the larger ships. She had been so busy watching the people, that she'd hardly spared a glance for the harbour. There were ships and boats of all sizes, all of which appeared to be made of brightly painted wooden timbers. Many of the larger vessels had a sleek, majestic look to them, with their prows and mastheads carved in intricate designs of sea creatures or birds. Fiona marvelled at the detail that had gone into those carvings, but it was to one ship in particular that her eyes were drawn.

It was to the forefront of all the larger vessels, and reminded Fiona strongly of the pirate galleons she'd seen depicted in school history books. It lay at rest, like a quiescent denizen of the deep. Its prow and masthead were carved in the likeness of dolphins leaping out of the waves. The detail was so lifelike, that Fiona even fancied she could see droplets of moisture glistening on the dolphins' backs. Every curve and contour of their fins and tails was revealed in stunning clarity, and the eyes of the dolphins seemed to flash in the morning sun, as though with life. The ship was turned so that the carvings faced out to sea, as though longing to ride in the embrace of its waves once again. This was a ship that was born for the ocean. And the skills of those who had made it and the love they had poured into their work made Fiona's breath catch in her throat. She was unsurprised to see that it had also been named for its figurehead.

Christophe lowered his oars, and half raised himself upright. He waved towards the deck of the *Dolphin*. Several people on the neighbouring ships looked round in surprise at the small boat, but their looks of puzzlement changed quickly to smiles of recognition. In his clothes that he'd taken from Fiona's world, Christophe stood out immediately from the crowd. People began shouting his name, pointing excitedly at the boat. Christophe had taken up his oars again, and was guiding the boat in alongside the *Dolphin*. Someone rushed to the ship's side and threw a rope.

Christophe turned to Fiona. "When we get near enough, grab the rope and tie her off." Fiona nodded dumbly.

The people seemed transported. They were leaping up and down on the decks, pointing, waving and cheering. On the shore, people were becoming aware of what was happening. They ceased what they were doing and pressed forward. Parents lifted children up on their shoulders so they were above the heads of the crowd. The people on the *Dolphin* alone stood motionless, crowded on the deck.

Fiona felt a mounting sense of panic. Surely, all these people hadn't gathered to see her? It wasn't possible. It wasn't real. Yet the boat had drawn alongside the *Dolphin*. She was reaching out with the rope as though in a trance. She was barely aware of it leaving her grip, and a man moving forward to tighten it securely. Then hands were grasping her, hauling her aboard, and she was standing on the deck, with James beside her, looking equally bemused. Only then did she become aware that the shouting and cheering had stopped, and complete silence had descended over the throng. Even the birds had ceased their racket. All that could be heard now was the gentle lapping of waves. All eyes were turned towards the *Dolphin*; towards her. She turned frantically to find Christophe.

"What are they doing? What's going on?"

For answer, Christophe took her hand and pulled her forward. Everyone else cleared a space for her.

James tried to follow, but he was hemmed in, and Christophe shot him a warning look.

She stood alone now with Christophe. He released her, and addressed the crowd in a strong clear voice. "People of the sea. Travellers and outcasts from your rightful home, The Appointed has returned! The one whose coming has been foretold among us. The one who will give back to us the land and the freedom that have been denied us so long. Acknowledge her!"

To Fiona's horror, every man, woman and child assembled there bowed low to her. Many sank to their knees, and some pressed their faces to the ground. Fiona felt a sudden, hysterical urge to laugh. All these people kneeling to her? It was ridiculous. Surely they couldn't believe that… she broke off that train of thought abruptly and looked instead toward Christophe for help.

He alone had not bowed or knelt, but as she watched, he inclined his head slightly in her direction and placed one hand across his heart. As though this were a signal, several men and women stepped forward, the crowd parting to let them through.

They could not have made more of a contrast to the people around them. They all wore loose-fitting leggings and tunics in hues of green and brown. Colours that seemed drab in comparison with the bright colours of the rest. They wore no jewellery, and every one of them, the men and women alike, wore their hair braided with brown cords of twine.

They all carried weapons. Many had braces of knives at their waists, and nearly all carried bows or quarterstaffs. As one, they halted in a line directly before Fiona. Like Christophe, they inclined their heads, and placed their right hands over their hearts. Then one of them intoned, "We are the Guardians. We dedicate our lives to the protection of this land and its people from the abomination of Alfredo's rule. We join with our comrade, Christophe, in the people's cause, and our lives are pledged to you whenever you have need of them."

Fiona gaped at him. Their lives were pledged to her? Surely this man wasn't really saying he would die for her? That was ridiculous. Some of the Guardians were her own age. They had their whole lives ahead of them. It dawned on Fiona that the Guardians were all watching her, waiting. Waiting for what? Was she supposed to respond somehow? What should she say? She didn't want anyone to die for her, and she certainly wasn't planning on dying herself, but the silence was becoming more pronounced.

Fiona's throat felt dry as sand. She cleared it in a futile attempt to work up some saliva so she could speak, but her voice came out as a rasping croak. "Er, thanks, that's very… nice of you." She swallowed again. "But there's been a mistake. I'm not…" She stopped speaking abruptly. She'd been going to say that she wasn't The Appointed, that Christophe had made a mistake, but she caught his eye, and the look he gave her was so fierce that it froze her tongue in her mouth.

"…I'm not sure we should discuss it yet. I need to…" She needed to what? To run; to get as far away from this madness as she could.

"Please," she muttered. "Just… just carry on with whatever you were doing. And stand up, for god's sake! I'm not… my name is Fiona. You don't need to bow and scrape like I'm the queen or something. It's…" embarrassing "…really not necessary." She felt her cheeks grow hot and bowed her head.

Then she became aware that someone had moved forward to stand beside her. Looking down, she found the eyes of a little girl, hardly more than six or so, in a red dress with two long dark beaded braids hanging below her shoulders. She held in her outstretched hands a garland of pink and purple flowers that Fiona did not recognize, though their fragrance was delightful.

"Appointed," she said in a clear, bold voice. "I want to give you this. Mama said I could wear it tonight at the festival, but you should have it." So saying, she reached up, and placed the garland on Fiona's head like a crown and stepped back.

Fiona didn't know what to say. Finally she managed, "Thank you."

The little girl dropped a curtsy and turned away.

"Wait!" Fiona called. The little girl turned back to look at her.

"What's your name?"

"Lena."

Fiona reached up to touch the flowers. She wanted to say something, to thank the child. She was deeply touched by the gift, but instead she said awkwardly, "But I wouldn't want you to not have anything to wear in your hair at the festival."

"Esther will make me another one," Lena said cheerfully, indicating a girl of about Fiona's own age standing a little off to one side. "Or Christophe will."

Fiona blinked. She found that idea hard to imagine.

Lena smiled happily at her. "It looks prettier on you anyway." With that, she scampered back to Esther, as the whole throng broke into cheers once more.

"The Appointed has returned! The Appointed has returned!" Then they began to break up and in twos and threes, began returning to their tasks and occupations once more.

Fiona stood in a kind of bemused stupor. Her eyes saw what was happening, but her brain still fought to accept it. Funny how cheering could sound so different, she thought hazily. When they'd cheered after she'd won the swimming gala, she'd felt exultant. Now, as the crowd shouted her name, or, more accurately, the name they had given her, she felt a rising sense of panic. It was creeping up on her by degrees; threatening to consume her completely. These people clearly thought their prayers were about to be answered, and she had no idea how to set them straight. She felt herself sway where she stood, fighting down a rush of fear and anger. It was easier now that everyone was no longer gaping at her.

"Appointed?" said a timid voice at her elbow. Fiona jumped as though she'd been stung and whirled around. The girl whom Lena had indicated was beside her. She started in turn at Fiona's abrupt reaction.

"Forgive me!" she stammered, one hand going to her mouth. "I did not mean to startle you."

Fiona forced herself under control with an effort and managed a weak smile. "It's OK, sorry! I was miles away."

"I thought you might like to sit out of the sun for a while," the girl said shyly. "You look a little faint."

Fiona had to fight down a laugh. Shade wouldn't even begin to solve her problems. "Er, yeah, that'd be great."

Esther led Fiona over to a makeshift awning set up to one side of the deck. Fiona had hardly noticed the sun's heat during her welcome, but as soon as she was seated on a rug, and the glare was no longer on her, she felt instantly relieved. Sweat ran down her back and under her arms. She really would have to borrow some of those bright clothes. They looked blessedly cool. It seemed hard to believe that back on Earth it was still winter.

Esther dropped to the blanket beside her. She was roughly the same height as Fiona. Her arms and legs tanned golden from the sun. She wore a blue pinafore dress and a matching scarf tied up her thick, dark hair. She had a kind, open face which, though not exactly pretty, was nevertheless pleasing. Perhaps her one beauty was her eyes. They were a soft, warm hazel, like liquid pools, gentle and reassuring. Despite her fears, Fiona felt herself relaxing in Esther's company.

It suddenly struck her then that James had disappeared. She was about to ask Esther if she had seen him (he'd be sure to stand out in his jeans) when he appeared, his jacket knotted at his waist, and accompanied by a boy who could only be Esther's brother.

He was taller than Esther by about a head, and he was dressed in the clothes of a Guardian. Yet his resemblance to his sister was striking. Fiona was willing to bet that they were twins. His dark brown hair was braided with a brown cord. His eyes, the mirror image of his sisters', were frank and intelligent, and he had the same pleasant, open smile. Yet there was something about him that Esther lacked. A toughness, an alertness that reminded Fiona forcibly of Christophe. He did not have his sister's innocence.

James's grin was a little forced. "Well, that was quite a welcome. At least you know now there's no pressure."

Fiona scowled at him as he flopped down at her feet. But she was deeply relieved to see him.

The boy bowed to her. "Appointed, my name is Gideon. I am brother to Esther and Lena. My mother and father will join us presently, as soon as they have found some refreshments. You must be hungry after your journey."

Fiona groaned. "Oh, please, call me Fiona. This Appointed stuff is just too weird. I'm just like you, really."

"I will try to remember, App… Fiona."

"And you don't need to bow either."

Gideon grinned, his natural good humour breaking through his formality. "As you wish." He sat down on Fiona's other side.

"Where's Christophe?" Fiona asked, looking around.

Gideon shook his head. "I believe he may be consulting some of those who've been in port since he left, catching up on the news."

"He seems well respected," James said dryly.

Gideon missed his tone. "He is a leader among us younger men, and even our true leaders sometimes ask him for his opinion. When he is older and has more experience, he will make a fine leader for the Guardians." His grin flashed at Fiona once more. "He is almost as honoured as you."

Fiona stared at James. Until now, Christophe had just seemed like an ordinary teenager. Seeing him in this new light, so utterly removed from any of the people she'd grown up with, from all her ideas of a normal sixteen-year-old boy, made Fiona feel distinctly uncomfortable. It made Christophe seem even more alien.

James wore a stubborn expression. It didn't matter how much Christophe was respected by his own people. To James, he was still the boy who had snatched Fiona away from her home and family, thereby landing them both in this mess.

"He doesn't tell you much though, does he?" James said coolly.

"He can be hard to approach sometimes," said Esther. "He always acts in his own time and for his own reasons, but he has appointed himself your protector,

Fiona, and I can assure you, you will not find a better. Your lives are safer in his hands than anyone else's."

Something about the look in Esther's eyes, and the softened tone of her voice, set off a warning bell in Fiona's brain. She'd gossiped with too many girls in the past not to recognize the signs. Carolyn looked exactly like that whenever James's name was mentioned. She wondered if Christophe returned Esther's feelings. It would be interesting to watch them. At least it would provide a temporary diversion from her own dilemma.

"Does he have any family?" James asked.

"No one knows very much about him," said Esther. "He refuses to speak of his family to anyone. We know little of his past."

Gideon nodded. "He was ten years old when we found him, or you might say he found us! He was just there one day, while we were in port to drop off some cargo. He was in rags and clearly starving. He had obviously been in a fight. His face was bloody and swollen, and he walked with difficulty. Mama took one look at him and demanded he let her feed him and dress his wounds. He has lived with us ever since."

"He never spoke a word for three days," Esther smiled reminiscently. "Gideon and I were only children ourselves then. We tried to get him to tell us where he came from, and where his parents were, but he refused to answer. After a while though, he opened up a little. He said he had lived among the street gangs, but that was all. It soon became clear that his fighting skills were quite advanced for a child his age, and he had a knack for being in the right place for picking up useful information. Mama and Papa more or less adopted him after that."

"Talk of the devil," James muttered.

Fiona looked up. Christophe was walking towards them. He had changed out of the clothes he'd stolen from Earth. He was now dressed in the brown leggings and tunic of the Guardians, with a cord tying back his hair. An impressive array of knives now hung at his waist, and he wore knee-length laced boots of worn brown leather. Somewhat to Fiona's surprise, Lena was clinging to his hand, pulling him eagerly along. In her other hand, she carried a fresh bunch of flowers. She made straight for Esther, tugging Christophe with her.

"There," she said brightly, dropping the flowers in Esther's lap. "Make me another garland quickly, Esther, the festival will be starting."

Esther obediently took up the flowers and set to work, while Gideon rose to introduce the three people who Fiona now saw had followed Christophe and Lena.

"Appointed, please allow me to present my parents. My father, Antonio, leader of the Guardians, and my mother, Josephine. Also my grandfather, Jeremiah. He is my mother's father."

Fiona got to her feet, wincing inwardly at Gideon's abrupt return to formality. James rose with her.

She shook hands all round. Antonio and Josephine had the same sun-browned appearance and open countenance as their children, but their faces were marred by lines of strain about the corners of their mouths and eyes, and they had a tired, careworn look that Esther and Gideon lacked. Though still fairly young, both had flecks of grey in their hair.

Jeremiah looked extremely old and frail. His hand seemed to be all bones and veins, and the skin felt as dry as paper. Yet his grip on Fiona's fingers was surprisingly strong, and his eyes on her were as keen as Christophe's.

"It's, er, nice to meet you, but please call me Fiona." They all smiled and nodded, shaking hands with James too.

"This is James," Fiona said awkwardly. "He's my friend, from my… from the world I came from."

"You are both very welcome," said Josephine. "And we are honoured that you have chosen the *Dolphin* as your home while you stay with us. Please feel free to come and go as you wish. My husband and I, and my children, are always available if you need us."

She sat down and set a covered plate on the blanket in front of her. "The festival of Mer begins shortly, but the meal is not yet prepared. Perhaps an appetizer while we wait. It is very refreshing after a hot day." She twitched aside the wrapping and Fiona saw that the plate was piled high with melon wedges.

Everyone sat down and Fiona took a piece of the succulent fruit. The juice soothed her parched throat, reminding her of holidays abroad with her parents, sitting by the pool munching melon while the sun warmed her back. She had a sudden desire to swim in the sea. She felt sure the water would be delightful.

Lena had settled herself next to Christophe, and was leaning against him contentedly. Once more, Fiona expected him to push the little girl away, but he looked more at ease than she'd ever seen him, leaning back, an arm around her slender shoulders.

James was also looking better. The fruit appeared to be helping with his seasickness. Fiona's mother had always suggested eating something as a cure for travel sickness.

"You must've had a difficult journey," Josephine said solicitously. "When did you arrive back here?"

"Yesterday," answered Christophe. "I would have set out at once, but the storm was too great." He frowned. "I only hope our delay won't have given anyone a chance to pick up our trail."

"You think you were followed?" Antonio said sharply.

Christophe shook his head. "I don't think so. That storm would have caused as much inconvenience to a pursuer as it did to us, but it appears Miguel learned of my absence somehow."

Gideon made a noise between his teeth, and Esther's fingers stilled momentarily.

"How do you know?" Josephine breathed.

"I spoke to someone from the *Great White*. Their ship was attacked by looters two weeks ago, and three of their crew were captured. They sent scouts out to try to learn what had become of them. They found their corpses, on a gibbet on Traitor's Hill. They hastened here as soon as they could."

"We only arrived half an hour before you," Antonio said grimly. "We have not had the chance yet to enquire for news. And they are certain it was Miguel's men?"

Christophe nodded.

"Who is Miguel?" James demanded. "Why would he be looking for you?"

"For us!" Christophe corrected. "Miguel is Alfredo's most skilled and trusted spy. He will have learned of my absence, and now he may have learned the reason."

"So Fiona's in danger?" James snapped.

Christophe regarded James almost pityingly. "She has been in danger from the moment she set foot in this world. She is the one person who can put a stop to Alfredo once and for all. Naturally he will be looking for her."

"So what are you going to do about it?" James shouted. "While you sit there at your ease, some psycho even crazier than you is looking to cut Fiona's throat."

"That will not happen!" Antonio said firmly. "Fiona is the Appointed. We will do everything we can to ensure that she and you remain safe."

"I will go to the city tomorrow to try and find out Miguel's movements," said Christophe. He looked directly at Fiona. "While I am gone, I want you and James to remain below deck. Keep out of sight."

Josephine laid a reassuring hand on Fiona's arm. "The *Dolphin* can be ready to depart at a moment's notice. We will be away long before Miguel knows we are here."

Fiona tried to smile, but her jaw seemed locked in place. Her barely controlled panic was threatening to rear its head once more.

"I believe the feast is ready," said Esther.

Josephine rose at once and beckoned to Fiona and James. "Come, the Festival of Mer is about to begin."

It was a meagre feast. Fiona sat with James and Christophe, together with Esther and her family and at least two hundred other people around fires burning at intervals along the beach. The meal consisted of smoked fish that reminded Fiona of salmon, potatoes and beans and slices of bread. Fiona ate her portion, but she had no appetite. The words of Christophe and James kept revolving through her mind. She is the one person who can stop Alfredo; naturally he will be looking for her. Some psycho wants to cut her throat. She felt sick, and despite the warm night, she shivered. To try and divert her thoughts, she asked Esther, "What is The Festival of Mer?"

"The merpeople are our kin. Once they lived among us, protecting the creatures of the sea, and enriching the lives of all the people of the land. We have not been whole since their disappearance. Every year we commemorate their memory, and celebrate the coming of age of our children to adulthood."

Fiona stared at her. "What do you mean they're your kin? I mean, you're human, I don't see any fish's tales."

Christophe rolled his eyes, but Esther laughed. "Yet it is true. The merpeople are our descendants. We are born of the sea, and to the sea, we surrender the phases of our lives. Children surrender their childhood to the sea when it is time to enter adulthood. Married couples surrender their single status and emerge as one, and in death our bodies are given up to the sea to begin our final journey. Our bodies are food for the creatures that dwell in the deep, and so the balance of nature is maintained."

"How do you surrender your childhood and become adults?" asked James curiously.

Esther smiled. "Watch and you will see."

The meal did not last long. When it was over, all the children gathered up their family's bowls and spoons and took them away to rinse them in huge water buckets before returning to their places in their family circles. A hush fell over the crowd as about two dozen boys and girls, all about Fiona and James's age, rose from their places and stood facing the crowd.

Jeremiah got laboriously to his feet. He looked as though a blast of wind might blow him over, but when he spoke, his voice rang through the assembly. "People of the sea, the rite for the coming of age is upon your sons and daughters. In the presence of all these witnesses, they will renounce their former lives, and embrace their new lives as adults and equals among their people."

He sat down. For a moment, nothing happened. Then, one by one, the small group of teenagers began to undress. Fiona stared in disbelief as one by one, their clothes slid to the sand. Naked, they formed a line, and began to walk towards the sea.

"What are they doing?" Fiona breathed.

"Hush!" Christophe whispered.

Fiona watched as the line entered the waves, and began to wade forward.

"It's sort of like a baptism," James whispered.

Fiona nodded. "Except that in our world, they don't take all their clothes off."

"Silence!" Christophe snapped. "No one may speak during the Coming of Age."

Fiona scowled, but subsided. She and James watched together as the line of boys and girls continued to wade further and further from the shore. Fiona was surprised. She had expected them just to wade up to their knees and duck their heads, but the water was nearly to their waists. Her surprise changed to alarm as the water rose towards their shoulders. They couldn't possibly keep their feet much longer. The water would soon be up to their chins, and the waves would surely throw them off balance. Then, just as she was about to call out, they stopped, and as one, let themselves sink beneath the waves.

James let out an audible gasp.

Fiona expected them to bob up again at once, but they didn't. The seconds passed, and still no one rose.

"What are they doing?" Fiona gasped, barely managing to keep her voice to a whisper.

"They are counting the years they are returning to the sea," Esther whispered. "One second for each year."

Fiona looked back in time to see a boy's head break the surface, water rolling like tears down his cheeks. Then one by one the others rose too, and they began the wade back to shore. Family members rushed forward. Parents pulling their children into tight embraces as soon as they came within reach. They were dragged over to the warmth of the fires and wrapped in blankets. Then Fiona felt Christophe's hand on her arm.

"Now it is your turn."

She gaped at him. "What?"

"You must also perform the rite. You are of age."

"Are you mad? You want me to strip off in front of all these people? I don't think so! You may be happy showing your bits off to everyone, but I'm not."

"No one will be looking at you!" he snapped impatiently.

"What sort of boys did you grow up with?"

"You can't make her do this!" James said heatedly.

Christophe's face seemed to close. "Very well. Stand up and tell them that you aren't The Appointed; that you can't help them after all. Go on, what are you waiting for?"

Fiona bounded to her feet, eyes blazing. Now was her chance to end this madness. If she told everyone the truth, Christophe would have to let her go home. But the moment she stood up, everyone fell silent once more. They were all looking at her, expectation written across every face, and she knew it was hopeless. Her denial would make no difference. Telling them she couldn't help them was no use. They believed in her. She wasn't just a human; she was the symbol of their hopes and dreams. They would give her all the time in the world to find herself, to discover what she had to do. They would never take her defeatism seriously. They could not afford to. The fury drained off her like water, and a wave of helplessness took its place. Wordlessly, she walked out to the cleared space, and began to undress.

She longed to turn her back to all those watching eyes. She waited in mortified anticipation for the whistles and catcalls, the heat rising to her face in expectation, but they never came. The crowd watched in utter silence as she waded into the sea.

The water was warm, and she could feel it tugging at her legs. A soft breeze lifted her hair and caressed her bare skin. She fought to keep her hands to her sides, fighting the instinct to cover herself, and walked in deeper. When she could go no further, she allowed herself to slip beneath the waves.

It was oddly peaceful under water, away from all those watching eyes. A strange feeling of contentment stole over her. It was as if she had come home. But that wouldn't last long, until the moment she ran out of breath. What was it she had to do? One second for every year she was returning to the sea. She began to count slowly to sixteen.

A torrent of sound greeted her as she surfaced. Everyone was on their feet, cheering and hugging each other. Many were weeping. Ironic, she thought as she waded back to shore.

Josephine was waiting for her. She flung a blanket around Fiona and clasped her tightly to her chest. “Antonio and I will be your parents in place of your own if you would have us,” she whispered.

Fiona could only nod. Sudden tears filled her eyes as she wondered what her own parents would have made of it. Josephine pushed wet hair off her face and led her to sit in front of the nearest fire.

Jeremiah had risen once more. “Now The Appointed has truly been returned to us, and we shall—”

“Wait!”

Fiona jumped in astonishment. James was on his feet. He looked flushed and more than a little nervous, but his voice was steady. “Let me do this too, this… this coming of age.”

There was a moment’s stunned silence.

“You are not of this world,” Christophe said coolly. “Our rights are not yours, they do not concern you.”

“You were not born of the sea,” Gideon added worriedly. “The god of the sea may refuse to accept you.”

“Fiona is my best friend,” James said stolidly. “I swore to stand by her always, no matter what. What happens to her, happens to me.”

Fiona could only hug the blanket to her. Her throat was too constricted for speech.

“Very well,” said Jeremiah after a brief hesitation.

James walked out to the clear space of sand. He looked more nervous than ever. No doubt his escape of the day before was still fresh in his mind. Fiona wanted to call out, to stop him, but he was already wading out to sea.

When he slipped beneath the waves, Fiona held her breath. He only had to count to sixteen, what was taking so long? She was about to hurl the blanket aside and rush to his aid, when he rose, spluttering, and began to make his way unsteadily back to shore.

Gideon and Esther both jumped up to help him, Esther keeping her eyes averted. Gideon wrapped a blanket around James and led him to sit with Fiona.

“Welcome, James of the two worlds,” said Jeremiah solemnly. “The Appointed has indeed found a worthy friend in you.”

Everyone broke into cheers once more as James sat down shakily, clutching the blanket firmly around him. No parent had come forward to embrace him.

Fiona leaned forward carefully to keep her own blanket in place, and kissed his cheek. “Thank you,” she whispered.

He reddened. “That’s OK, just don’t expect me to do anything like that again. There is a limit, you know.”

She laughed, even as tears blurred her vision. “I won’t.”

Everyone was settling down once more, and a hush fell as Esther rose and made her way out to the clear stretch of sand.

“What’s happening now?” Fiona asked Christophe.

“Esther will tell the story of the merpeople,” he replied.

Gideon went to join his sister, producing from his pocket a wooden flute. Another boy joined them holding a dulcimer, and a third sat down and placed a drum between his knees. Lena crawled into Christophe's lap and curled up there, her small face turned towards the musicians. He put an arm over her as the first cord was struck and the crowd fell silent. Then, to the slow, steady beat of the drum, the dulcimer began to strum out the cords and Esther began to sing, Gideon's flute playing in harmony with her.

The song spoke of times gone. Of the god of the sea who created the land and the humans who populated it. Of the merpeople who were his children, and the sacrifice of those who took human form and went to live among people to teach them wisdom and how to care for the land. How the merpeople and humans mingled freely and how the merpeople rose from the depths of the ocean on nights when the moon was full, and filled the night with their singing. And all who heard their songs were enriched and blessed, and their crops flourished and their children grew healthy and strong.

But then the story took a different turn, as Alfredo, filled with fear and rage against these precious beings, persecuted them and drove them away until they were never seen again, so their songs would never more enrich the land and the lives of its people.

The final cord rang out, and Esther's voice ceased, breaking the spell. Fiona blinked and roused herself. She had listened as enthralled as the rest, and as Esther sang of the merpeople's disappearance, she had felt a powerful sense of loss, like an ache within her. But it felt as though she was waking from a dream. The song still hung in the air, but already the enchantment was fading. Fiona's situation seemed to return more clearly than ever after her brief respite. She longed for Esther to sing again, to lose herself once more in the story her words and voice unfolded.

James sat motionless, a look of wonder on his face. Around them, people were starting to drift away back to their ships. She nudged him and nodded to their clothes, which lay where they had discarded them. They dressed with their backs to each other. Out of the corner of her eye, Fiona saw Christophe.

He had not left with the others. He was still exactly where he had been sitting. His gaze directed out to sea, his face sad and pale beneath its tan. It struck her suddenly how vulnerable he looked. Lost, as if he did not know where to turn. He seemed completely oblivious to everyone around him. Lena was asleep on his lap, and his hand absently stroked her hair.

"Come," said Esther. "It grows late."

Her voice, so close at hand, seemed to rouse Christophe out of his reverie. He stirred and looked down at Lena. "Sleeping," he said softly.

"I will take her, Christophe," said Gideon.

Christophe shook his head. "Let her be."

He stood, and Fiona and James rose to follow him. Lena stirred a little in the cradle of his arms, but she merely snuggled her face into his shoulder and went back to sleep. Christophe led the way back to the *Dolphin*.

The sleeping quarters were sparsely furnished. When Fiona and James entered the tiny cabin, they saw only two rickety bunks, with a cot squeezed between them, and a small, battered chest against one wall.

"You shall have the bunks," said Gideon.

"But where will you sleep?" asked Fiona, looking around the cabin. There wasn't room for one more bed, let alone two.

"We shall be quite comfortable on the floor," said Gideon with a laugh. "At least as comfortable as you will be."

Christophe laid Lena gently on the cot, and turned to Fiona and James. "I shall be gone when you wake. Please do as I said, and stay out of sight as much as you can. I shall try to return quickly. Goodnight." With that, he turned and left.

James frowned after Christophe. "Friendly, isn't he?"

Esther, who was tucking Lena in to bed, laughed.

"He was ever that way. You will get used to him in time."

Neither Fiona nor James answered. Fiona felt that Christophe's ways would take an awful lot of getting used to, and she would probably never learn them all. He constantly surprised her.

Despite the ceremony on the beach, or perhaps because of it, neither Fiona nor James felt like undressing in front of anyone, and they had nothing to change into. They kicked off their shoes and scrambled into bed fully clothed. Gideon, who had left briefly, returned carrying blankets and he and Esther curled up on the floor.

Fiona felt sure she would never sleep. The mattress was lumpy, and the pillow scratchy, and she felt uncomfortably warm. She wriggled about, trying to find a comfortable position, but the bunk creaked loudly every time she moved and it wobbled dangerously. Fiona lay curled in a tight ball, her eyes closed, listening to the breathing of the others, and the gentle lapping of waves against the ship's prow. The story of the merpeople came back to her. The sad words with their haunting melody. It was the remembered sound of Esther's voice that eventually lulled her to sleep.

# Chapter 7

## Trapped

James's light touch on her shoulder woke her. Fiona stretched and yawned. Her neck was very stiff. She gave her pillow a reproachful look. "I don't know how they manage to sleep in these beds, or how I managed to for that matter."

"And a good morning to you too," James laughed. "It looks like Esther and Gideon have been up a while already." He nodded to the blankets, which had been rolled up neatly and laid on Lena's empty cot. "And someone's left some clothes out for us. Look!"

Fiona saw a neatly folded pile lying on the end of her bed. There was an identical pile on James's. She picked it up. There was a pair of brown leggings and a green tunic identical to those the Guardians wore, and even a brown leather cord for her hair. Nearly out of sight under the bed was a pair of boots. On closer inspection, they were revealed to be made of brown leather, worn and travel-stained, but with no holes that she could see. The tunic and leggings appeared to be made of a rough wool.

James had unearthed similar garments, though no cord had been provided for him. His hair was too short. James looked from the boots in his hand to Fiona. "I suppose we should put them on?" he said doubtfully.

Fiona shrugged. "I guess. At least we won't stick out as much."

They each sat facing the wall while the other dressed. As Fiona discarded her jeans and pulled on the leggings, she felt an odd sense of loss. It felt as though she was shedding the final trappings of her old identity, and assuming her new one. One she still didn't want. They both kept their undergarments, as no fresh ones had been provided. Fiona had no comb, so she teased the tangles from her hair as best she could with her fingers and tied it back in the fashion of the Guardians. She wished she had a mirror to see how she looked, but the clothes seemed to fit well, and were comfortable. The boots fitted surprisingly well, considering whoever had provided them had only been able to guess at her size. She and James sat on their beds across from each other. There was so little space between them that their knees bumped.

"You look great," Fiona said with a forced grin.

James laughed self-consciously. "So do you. It feels strange though, doesn't it?"

Fiona nodded, though she wasn't sure whether James meant their clothes or the entire situation. As if reading her thoughts, James said, "What do you make of all this, everything that's happened, I mean?"

Fiona gave a brittle laugh. "What, me being The Appointed? To be honest, James, I don't know whether to laugh in their faces or hide under the bed. I can't help them. I can't deliver them from this Alfredo, but I have no idea how to tell them. The worst thing is, I like them. I can't bear the thought of letting them down, but I will sooner or later, even if we continue this charade. I just want to go home."

"We could still try to find someone who'll show us the way back," James suggested half-heartedly.

Fiona snorted. "Oh yeah? Even if we managed to get past everyone without being seen, we don't even know where to start looking."

She was on her feet. James hated to see her like this, biting her nails and pacing backwards and forwards restlessly in the tiny space. She reminded him vividly of a caged animal at a zoo. She had always been so free and full of life. Now she just looked tired and defeated. Desperate to comfort her, he blurted out, "We could ask someone here. There's bound to be someone other than Christophe who can help us."

Fiona stopped in mid stride, a spark of hope suddenly rekindling in her eyes. "I never thought of that." But then her face clouded once more. "But where would we start? We'd look a bit suspicious if we started asking questions all over the shop."

"Gideon and Esther," James suggested. "We could just drop it casually into conversation. We don't have to make it look like we're really interested."

"But why should they know above anyone else?"

"They're Christophe's friends aren't they? He might have told them."

Fiona's expression cleared. "Yeah, you're right. Come on, let's go and find them. I'm starving anyway."

Another glorious day greeted them as they emerged on deck. Fiona squinted a little in the bright sun. The sea was blue and as flat as a pond, and a gentle breeze relieved the heat somewhat. I'd have loved this under any other circumstances, Fiona reflected sadly.

Gideon hailed them. "Good morning. I was just coming to wake you. Did you sleep well?"

"Great, thanks," Fiona lied.

Gideon seemed to know her thoughts. He laughed. "You are very tactful, but those beds are dreadfully hard for someone who is unused to them."

"I am still not used to them," said Lena, who was sitting nearby with Esther.

"Nonsense," said Esther. "You would sleep anywhere if given the chance." She turned to Fiona and James.

"You must be hungry; I will fetch you some breakfast. Make yourselves comfortable."

Fiona and James sat down on the rug with Lena, and Gideon joined them.

It struck Fiona suddenly that it was a good deal quieter than yesterday. "Where is everyone?" she said, looking at the harbour. All the bigger ships still seemed to be there, but many of the smaller fishing boats were missing.

"The salmon harvest has begun," Gideon replied. "At this time of year, the salmon return to these shores to breed. Each year for us begins the day after the festival, the first of the harvest. This is the only time of year when we gather in such numbers for any length of time. Normally we just drop off and collect cargo. We never stay long in one place. It is not safe. All the Travellers will have made for their nearest port to partake of the harvest and honour the festival."

Esther returned then, carrying a plate piled high with what looked like flat bread or cakes. Honey oozed out of them, and Fiona thought she could see dried fruits buried in them. In her other hand, Esther carried two glasses of a cloudy juice that gave off a delightful fragrance.

"A meagre meal I fear," she said apologetically, setting down her burden and dropping to sit with them on the rug. "Poor fare indeed for The Appointed, but times are hard."

"Don't worry about it," Fiona muttered awkwardly.

"This looks fine to me," said James. He picked up a honey cake and bit into it hungrily.

Lena shot a covetous look at the plate as Fiona took a cake.

"You have had your breakfast already," Esther chided. Lena ignored this and took one anyway.

"Did you like the festival?" she asked Fiona.

"Erm," Fiona stalled. She didn't know how to describe her experience of the night before, and didn't want to say anything offensive. "It was—"

"Different," James supplied. "There's nothing like that in our world."

"There probably is," Fiona amended. "Just not where we come from."

"But how do you celebrate your passage into adulthood?" Esther asked.

Fiona and James looked at each other.

"Well," said Fiona. "Where we come from, we're not adults until we're eighteen. Then people usually have a big party with their family or friends."

"A party?" said Gideon, puzzled. "I have not heard this word before."

"You know, to have fun. Loads of people getting together and dancing and drinking and stuff," Fiona finished lamely. Esther and Gideon were looking a bit shocked.

"Are the parents not there to exercise some restraint?" asked Gideon.

Fiona smiled. "Sometimes, but more often than not they join in as well."

Esther and Gideon stared, but Lena looked untroubled.

"So when you reach your eighteenth year," she said to James, "you will have a party…" she stumbled a little over the unfamiliar word, "as well?"

"I doubt it," said James dryly.

"But why not?"

"I don't really have any family. My mum died when I was quite little, and my dad and I don't really get on."

They looked stricken.

"We are sorry for your loss," said Esther softly. "To grow up without parents is a grievous thing."

James looked uncomfortable. Fiona searched for a way to move the conversation away from this topic, but it was Lena who came to James's rescue.

"Do they have ships where you come from?"

"Not like these," said Fiona. "There were some once, a long time ago, but not any more."

"What happened to them?"

Fiona shrugged. "They're all at the bottom of the sea most likely."

"There are some in museums," said James. "Places where people can go and look at things from years ago," he added in response to Esther and Gideon's puzzled looks.

"We do have a navy, you know, war ships, but most of our ships take people on cruises."

"Cruises?" asked Esther.

"It's when people pay a load of money to be taken around the world," Fiona explained. "They visit famous cities and landmarks."

"The people do not live on ships?" asked Gideon.

"While they're on the cruises they do, but we mostly live on land."

"Our people lived on land once," Esther said wistfully. "We tended it and cared for it until Alfredo drove us away. It was part of the long ago pact that our first ancestors made with the god of the sea. That we guard and nurture the land he had created. We have failed him."

"No!" said Fiona. "It wasn't your fault Alfredo came to power."

"You are right," said Gideon. "But it is a bitter comfort. We have no home to call our own, unless it is the ships that carry us, and life is hard at sea. Every waking moment is a fight for survival, be it against disease, starvation, storms or capture."

"But all that will change now," said Lena. "Now The Appointed has come, and Alfredo will be sent away for ever, and we can go home again."

Fiona bowed her head, unable to bear the confidence in the small girl's eyes.

"Has no one ever been to our world?" James asked quickly. "I mean, people from Earth have found their way here."

"There must be a way to travel between your world and ours," said Gideon. "After all, Christophe has proved that, but as far as I know, he is the only one to have done so."

"But he must have learned the way from someone?" James prompted.

"He did not confide in us," said Esther. "He just announced one day that he would be leaving. He did not say how long he would be gone, but when he returned, he would bring The Appointed with him."

"Many people do not even believe that there is a portal between your world and ours," said Gideon. "They regard it as a legend. Few of our people are concerned with anything beyond their everyday lives." A slight bitterness had crept into his voice.

"But you're not?" James asked.

Gideon looked half ashamed. "It is just that I grow weary. This life is not enough for me. I feel trapped here. There are no opportunities to discover and learn new things."

"Then you are a fool," said Esther sternly. "When you have lived as long as Mama or Papa or Grandpapa, then you will have learned much, and when there is nothing left to teach you, your life will end, as every life does. Be content with your lot."

"But I cannot be content," Gideon said stubbornly. "There was a time when this land was full of learned men. They learned the language of letters and studied many wondrous things. You are a woman; you will have a husband and children to fill your life."

A pained look crossed Esther's face. "I will have neither, brother, as you well know."

Gideon looked instantly remorseful. "I spoke in haste, sister, forgive me!"

She smiled sadly. "You often do, brother, and now the time draws near for your training."

As though on queue, a loud bell rang out from the direction of the harbour. Gideon leaped up and turned to James. "Now the Guardians begin their morning training. Would you care to watch?"

"Er, yeah, alright," said James. He looked down at Fiona. She had remained silent for some time.

"Go!" she said. "I'll be along in a while."

Gideon and James left, and Lena ran off to join the other children playing on the beach. Fiona and Esther were left alone together.

Esther picked up a broken net and set about mending it, her fingers moving deftly.

"That looks difficult," said Fiona, wishing to break the silence.

Esther smiled. "It is easy once you know how. I have had many years' practice."

Fiona, wishing for something to distract her thoughts, said, "Can you show me?"

Esther hesitated.

Fiona sighed. "Yes, mending nets is fit work for The Appointed. You've got to stop treating me as if I was somebody special."

"To us you are," said Esther. "We have long awaited your coming."

"Well, I promise you, there is nothing special about me, and the sooner you all realise it, the better. I'm only one person and I don't know anything about your world. Why not look to Christophe to save you?"

She broke off. She had not meant to say any of that, but the words had just come pouring out of her, everything she'd held bottled up inside her since her reception the day before. Esther and Gideon's admission that they knew no way back to Earth, and that few people knew, let alone believed that another world even existed, had been the final nail in her coffin. She looked at Esther, expecting to see her looking crushed and disappointed, but in her eyes, there was only understanding and sympathy.

"A terrible burden has been laid upon you," she said gently. "The expectation of an entire people rests on your shoulders." She seemed to think for a moment. "But it would seem to me that a person who faces her peril with fear and doubt, but does what she can in spite of it, is very special indeed. It is important to be aware of your weaknesses, for how else will you overcome them? Christophe will not allow himself to show weakness. He sees it as failure, and he does not believe in failure. Consequently, he is hard on those who show weakness."

Fiona stared at Esther in silent gratitude. Words failed her utterly. She wanted to thank Esther for her kindness and understanding, but instead she said, "I'm sure Gideon didn't mean what he said earlier. You'll marry Christophe one day."

Esther laughed. "Gideon has a warm heart, and I love him dearly, but he is often hasty, saying what he feels before he thinks. But he is restless. He thrives on excitement and longs for adventure. He joined the Guardians the day after his coming of age. Lena is very like him."

"And you?"

For answer, Esther tossed Fiona another broken net. "Come, these nets will not mend themselves, and Mama will expect them all to be finished on her return. This is how it is done."

* * *

James followed Gideon along the beach. In the distance he could hear shouts and the loud clash of weapons.

"Do you learn to fight in your world?" asked Gideon.

"Sometimes, but we mainly learn because we want to, not because we have to."

"What weapons do you fight with? The knife? The bow? The quarterstaff?"

James smiled. "Not exactly, our army tends to use guns and bombs."

Gideon frowned. "I have not heard of these weapons."

"Think yourself lucky," said James grimly. "Bombs are great explosions that can wipe out an entire city at a single blast. They can kill loads of people just like that!" he snapped his fingers.

Gideon looked horrified. "What terrible magic made a weapon that can destroy so many?"

"Science."

"But how can your rulers allow it?" Gideon seemed unable to comprehend how such atrocities could be committed by one human against another. Even Alfredo, in all his malice and cruelty and lust for power, had never devised such a weapon as far as Gideon knew.

James sought to reassure him. "Most people hate them and would never use them, but it's a way for some people to show their power over others."

Gideon looked thoughtful. "It seems that your world is not unlike ours after all."

James nodded. "I suppose so."

"I am thankful that Alfredo does not know the way to your world," said Gideon. "It would be disastrous for us if he were to gain such knowledge."

"Yeah, I guess it would."

They had reached the training ground. It was a wide clear space of sand, on which men and women were engaged in various methods of combat, supervised by a number of older men. James watched as two men squared up to each other, each clutching a wooden stick.

"A quarterstaff," Gideon murmured.

Both men stood motionless, eyes locked on each other. James had the impression that they were sizing each other up, trying to predict their opponent's first move. They looked evenly matched, neither having any obvious advantage over the other that James could see. They were perfectly balanced, legs a little apart, poised to strike, yet still neither moved. Then, suddenly, one man's arm shot out, the staff aiming for his opponent's head. James was taken aback. There had been no warning; surely the other man would not deflect it in time. But quick as lightning, the other man's arm shot out to block the blow, and both staffs met with a clash of wood on wood. The first man danced lightly away from the impact, moving on his toes, staff whirling, but again the other man blocked the blow. Then, with an underhand flick of his wrist, he drove one end of his staff into the other man's side as he turned. The man grunted and stumbled but regained his balance almost at once and dodged a blow aimed at his legs. Back and forth they danced, first one gaining the upper hand, then the other, but neither keeping it for long. Then, quite suddenly, one of the fighters struck his opponent a crack across the forehead. The man stumbled, and before he could regain his equilibrium, the other man's staff was tangled in his legs. He fell and lay still, a trickle of blood running down his forehead. One of the trainers came over and began instructing the men as the winner helped the loser to his feet.

"But he was doing so well," said James. "How did that happen?"

"He let down his guard," Gideon said simply. "Fighting with the quarterstaff takes immense concentration. You have to keep moving all the time. You must always plan ahead. Plan your next move as you make your first, anticipate his next as you defend his last. It is all about keeping ahead of your opponent. Misjudge once, and it can be fatal. You must allow nothing to disrupt your concentration even for a second. That's all it takes. Come now, and watch Carlotta. She is one of the best shots we have."

James followed Gideon to where a girl stood alone before a target. She held a strung bow in her hand and was on the point of nocking an arrow. She paid not the slightest attention to her audience. Taking ten paces back, she raised the bow to her shoulder and loosed in one fluid movement. There was a twang and a thunk, and the arrow stuck quivering in the exact centre of the target.

Carlotta repeated the same procedure from twenty paces away, then thirty. Finally, at seventy paces away, she shot her final arrow. She had positioned the target carefully, and judged her shot. Once more her aim was true. She hadn't missed a single shot.

She did the same thing with a set of knives which she produced from various places beneath her clothing and even from her boot. James felt rather sick as with unerring accuracy, she hit every target, even when one fellow Guardian wobbled the target to and fro in an effort to throw her off stride. But every time she hit her mark. James tried very hard not to think about those daggers embedding themselves in human flesh. Had he been less preoccupied, he might have noticed that Gideon also watched Carlotta with a glint of more than just passing admiration in his eyes. To distract himself, he said, "So you allow men and women to fight in the Guardians?"

"Women only fight as long as they are maidens. When they marry, they give up everything in order to care for their husbands and children."

"Why?"

"When a woman marries, her life is dedicated to her husband and her children. That becomes her sole duty."

"But isn't the husband's life dedicated to his wife?"

"Indeed, but his duty is not only as provider and protector for his family, but also of his land, to cultivate and defend it in time of need. He accepts that pact when he reaches adulthood, and again when he marries. The woman's pact is to succour the land and its people."

"So all women give up their jobs when they marry?"

"Some become healers and care for the sick and the wounded, or help to bring children into the world."

"Fiona wouldn't like that," said James with a grin.

"Are things done differently in your world?"

James laughed. "I should say so. Where I come from, men and women work all their lives, often alongside each other. Women don't even stop when they have children. They quite often get other people to look after them while they work, and in some cases, the man stays home."

Gideon looked astonished. "The women work even when they are married?"

"Yep," said James, amused by Gideon's incredulity. "Some women never marry. They just live with men."

Gideon's expression changed from astonishment to horror. "They share a bed out of wedlock? But that would make their children bastards!"

"Well, yeah, but no one minds that."

Gideon frowned. "You come from a very strange world, my friend. This must seem so alien to you."

"Well it does a bit, but I think Fiona is finding it harder than me. This is so different from everything she's ever known, and finding she's The Appointed and everything…"

"Yes," said Gideon seriously. "I can see how that would be difficult for her, when so much depends on her. But come, I have loitered long enough, my practice awaits."

"Are you doing the staff or the bow and arrow?"

Gideon shook his head. "I will do that later, but we have also another method of fighting, and perfected only by us. Our founder devised it. We use no weapons but hands and feet only. I am reckoned to be quite skilled at it. Come and you shall see."

James followed after him. As he left, he was in time to see Carlotta whirling a slingshot around her head. Her arm was moving so fast it was blurred. At the height of her arc, the stone shot forth, to land squarely on the temple of a wooden manikin held out by one of the trainers. Making a mental note to give Carlotta a wide birth in future, James hurried after Gideon.

* * *

The women of the camp returned a few hours later. Esther explained that they had gone to market to buy provisions for their next voyage, and to sell what little goods they had brought with them. The men returned at about the same time, their boats laden with the first salmon catch of the season. Some of the fish would be eaten that day, and a small portion would be taken to the market to be sold, but the majority of the catch would be cooked and salted and added to the food stores aboard the ships. Fiona and James had spent an enjoyable morning. Once the nets were repaired, Esther and Fiona had strolled over to the training ground in time to watch Gideon defeat a man twice his size in the Guardian's Combat, as many named the fights that involved hands and feet only.

Josephine served up a meal of new baked bread and cheese fresh from the market, and for a while Fiona was able to forget her troubles and enjoy the company of those around her. She was growing to like them more and more. Their lives were hard and frugal, and a far cry from the way she lived at home, but they were a warm and caring people, and there was a real sense of community among them. Everyone looked out for everyone else, not just the members of their own families, and it was clear that they regarded each individual as precious, from the youngest child to the oldest grandparent. Fiona had to admit that the people of her town were not as solicitous of each other's needs and comforts. She doubted she could name one person living in the next street from hers, and was barely on speaking terms with her immediate neighbours. But the simple way these people lived made her realise exactly how much she had taken for granted back on Earth, when here, even hot water was a luxury. It made her miss her home all the more. Still, now that Esther and Gideon had stopped bowing and scraping to her, and treated her normally, she had begun to let down her guard and relax a little, and she sat with the others, eating her meagre lunch, feeling happier than she had done since she'd arrived.

But the sight of Christophe making his way through the diners towards her brought her back to reality with an unpleasant bump. Several people smiled and waved at him, and Lena jumped up and ran to him, holding out a wedge of bread and cheese. Christophe smiled as he took it from her, and ruffled her hair before coming over to join them.

Fiona glared at his approach, but he appeared not to notice.

"Well, Miguel does not appear to be in the city," he said, dropping down beside Lena. "No one has seen him."

"Isn't that good?" said James. "Surely that means he hasn't caught up with us yet."

"I fear it means the exact opposite," said Christophe, accepting a water skin from Esther and draining it. "You are forgetting the man from the *Great White*. I fear Miguel may have learned a lot from him. Everyone I spoke to said his men were looking for me, and I saw at least four placards offering a thousand gold crowns for my head." At these words, Esther gasped, and Lena moved closer to Christophe.

"They won't get you," she said fiercely. "I won't let them."

"Hush, Lena!" said Esther, who was very pale. Christophe put an arm around Lena.

"So you think he could be in hiding?" said Antonio.

Christophe nodded. "I am sure he is not in the city. As you ordered, I set friends to monitor as many of Alfredo's men as they can. They are trustworthy, and will not lose him once he is seen, but I think he could be watching the fishing ports. He knows we return at this time of year, and he may have learned which ship is sheltering me."

"You do not know that for sure," Gideon objected. "Our men would die rather than betray us, and Miguel kills those who reveal any information as well as those who do not."

"When it comes to the safety of The Appointed, I will not take any chances," said Christophe flatly. "We will be hard pressed to find Miguel if he does not wish it, but I will resume my search of the ports this afternoon."

"But it is not safe for you!" cried Esther. "They will all be on the lookout for you. You cannot search for Miguel alone!"

"She is right," said Antonio. "You should take some of the Guardians with you, if only to watch your back."

Christophe hesitated. He was used to working alone, and often preferred it. But Antonio was his leader, and he was bound to obey. His own skills were formidable, but what Antonio suggested was sensible and he knew it. He must remain alive and free at all costs if The Appointed were to be kept safe. Christophe was confident that there was no better protector for her than himself.

"Very well. I could take a small group, perhaps about half a dozen. I shall leave in ten minutes. I must first speak with The Appointed."

Gideon dashed away at once to select those who would accompany them. He himself would make one of the number. Everyone else wandered off too, Esther looking extremely troubled.

Christophe beckoned to Fiona. With a sigh, she got to her feet. James rose with her.

"I must speak to The Appointed alone!" Christophe said pointedly.

"You can't have anything to tell me that James shouldn't hear," said Fiona.

"Very well," said Christophe with a slight sneer. "If you need him to hold your hand." He walked away.

James made to start after him with a cry of rage, but Fiona grabbed his arm. "Leave it! I don't want him to think I'm weak, that'll give him even more advantage."

"Alright, but one more crack like that and I'll punch his face for him, Guardian or not."

Christophe's cabin was tiny, barely larger than a fair sized cupboard. It contained nothing but a bunk fastened to the wall, and three drawers underneath, in which, Fiona supposed, Christophe kept his clothes and any other possessions. It was a dingy place, and did not put Fiona any more at ease.

She did not follow Christophe inside, but stood in the doorway. Two people would have been a squash in any case in such a confined space.

Christophe stood regarding her.

"You seem to have settled in quickly."

"What do you want?" Fiona said shortly.

Christophe smiled humourlessly. "So friendly. As a matter of fact, I have something for you. Something that belonged to your father."

Fiona was instantly wary. "What?"

For answer, Christophe reached beneath his mattress, and extracted, of all things, a book. It was very old. The leather was worn and cracked, and the silver clasps that held the book closed were tarnished. Christophe held it out to Fiona, but she made no move to take it.

"What is it?"

Christophe rolled his eyes. "A book, what does it look like?"

"I gathered that," Fiona snapped. "I mean, is it a diary?"

"No one knows what the book contains. It was given into my father's care by your father just before he died. He charged my father to protect you and the book with his life, and when you came of age, the book was to be returned to you."

"But surely you know what it says."

Christophe's face hardened. "I would not presume to read something that was not meant for my eyes. In any case, the book is impossible to read. The clasps will not yield to any touch."

"Oh, come on," Fiona scoffed. "It's just stiff, that's all. It's pretty old."

"Do not take me for a fool," Christophe said quietly. "This book has been sealed magically. Your father wished only you to know its contents, and he specifically said that the book was yours. Undoubtedly, it contains the secret that he was tortured and imprisoned for. The knowledge that he gave his life to protect. The thing Alfredo craves for, and possibly how to stop him. This book may be the answer to Alfredo's downfall. He meant you to read it, and carry on the work that he started." He once more thrust the book at Fiona, who recoiled as if it were diseased.

"No!" she cried desperately. "I am not The Appointed. My name is Fiona Armstrong. I don't come from this world. I can't save your people. I haven't the foggiest idea how to begin."

"This book will guide you. That is why your father left it for you. It is your inheritance."

Fiona snatched the book from him and hurled it across the tiny cabin. It hit the wall and dropped to the bunk with a sad thump. Fiona was breathing rapidly. Tears glistened on her lashes.

"I can't do this," she whispered. "Please don't ask this of me. Just let me go home."

"You will not be alone," Christophe said quietly. "I will protect you with my dying breath."

“But I don’t want your protection!” she screamed. “I don’t want anyone to die for me. I just want to go home. You’ll never be able to keep me safe for ever. What happens when someone slits your throat? Who’s between me and Alfredo then? Once he has my head on a spike, that’ll be the end of your precious Appointed.” The tears were pouring freely down her face now, and she made no effort to check them. She no longer cared who saw her despair.

“Your father had great power at his command,” said Christophe. “It was what helped him to be such an efficient spy. It has made the book useless, even if it should fall into enemy hands. He would not have left it for you if there was no hope. Don’t you care about your own people? Is yourself all that matters to you?”

“Of course I care about them,” Fiona said tightly. “That’s my point. I can’t bear the thought of letting them down. I hate seeing the hope in their eyes. I hate knowing there are people willing to die for me, and for what. Even if I somehow managed to read this book, I haven’t any magic powers, I can’t save anyone. I’m begging you, Christophe, please, please, let me go home!”

They stared at each other in silence. Fiona gazed into Christophe’s eyes with her red, swollen ones. They were as unreadable as ever. She couldn’t tell if he had heard what she had said, or if he was utterly indifferent. He had never before shown any consideration for her feelings. She was just a tool to him, a means to an end. Nothing mattered but that she fulfilled her duty as he saw it.

At last he broke the silence, and though his voice was still calm, the sardonic note was gone. “Read the book, then make up your mind.”

“But I can’t read it. You said yourself that no one knows how to open it.”

“The book is yours. I have a feeling it will open for you. You must find the way.”

“So I even have to do that on my own,” Fiona said bitterly.

“I cannot help you.” He brushed past her, leaving her alone in the tiny cabin.

Fiona threw herself face-down on the hard, narrow bunk, knocking the book to the floor. How long she lay there, she didn’t know. She barely moved, and she wasn’t aware of thinking anything. She felt numb. Her last hope was gone. There was no way out. No one came to disturb her. Not even James. Perhaps Christophe had told him to stay away, but she didn’t think that would have stopped him. At last she sat up and peered out of the little porthole. The sun had set and night was falling. Christophe would be returning soon. She couldn’t bear another encounter with him. She made her way back to her own cabin and climbed into bed.

James came in shortly afterwards. “Fiona?” he said tentatively.

She made no answer, but lay still, pretending to be asleep. James couldn’t share this with her. The responsibility was not his. Christophe would send him home if he wished. But not her, not even when she begged. She knew in her heart that she would never see her family again. Esther and Gideon came to bed, and she buried her head beneath the scratchy blanket, ignoring their whispers.

Little by little, a longing grew in her to escape her prison, if only for a little while. She would be found of course, either by Christophe or Alfredo, but neither thought was enough to dissuade her. She lay awake and listened to the quiet breathing of the others. Then very stealthily, she rose and took a long hooded cloak that Gideon had hung over the door. Then she sat on the edge of the bed and waited for morning.

The hours seemed to crawl by at a snail's pace, but finally the first rays of the new risen sun could be seen through the portholes. Fiona tiptoed from the cabin. She had to move now. The inhabitants of the *Dolphin* were early risers. She had no clear destination in mind. She knew nothing beyond the harbour. She just felt the overwhelming urge to run. To get as far away from this place as possible. She drew the cloak around her, and pulled the hood up to obscure her face.

"Who goes there?" the sentry on duty demanded as soon as she appeared on deck.

"Esther," said Fiona's voice, muffled by her hood. "I've got an urgent message to deliver for Christophe."

"You should not go alone," said the sentry.

"This is urgent," said Fiona brusquely.

The sentry deliberated a moment, then lowered the gangplank.

"Very well, go carefully."

Fiona hurried down the gangplank and set off at a brisk walk. No doubt the sentry was puzzled by the abrupt manner of the usually gentle Esther, but that didn't matter. She was off the ship. She was free.

She forced herself to keep up a measured, purposeful stride, so that it would indeed appear to anyone watching that she had a job to do and no time to waste. But it was difficult. With every step she took, she fought the urge to run, to put as much distance between herself and the *Dolphin* as possible.

She tried hard not to think about James and what he would do when he found her gone. Hopefully, he would return home. Christophe had no use for him. As for her, if she couldn't go home, she would not be Christophe's tool.

The beach was out of sight now, and the road before her rose in a gentle slope.

Despite the earliness of the hour, there were a number of people about. None of them looked twice at Fiona, but hurried on their way, intent on their business. They all seemed to be heading in the same general direction, and Fiona followed them, watching them curiously.

An old man was on the path just ahead of her, driving a laden donkey. He was breathing heavily as he ascended the slope, leaning on the donkey and a stick for support. The donkey plodded patiently along. Its coat looked shabby, and Fiona could see every bone clearly.

A woman was striding along, head held erect, a basket of mangoes balanced there. It was impossible to tell her age. Her step was sure enough, but her face was deeply lined, and her eyes looked as though they had seen things beyond her years.

A sudden rumbling of wheels sounded behind her, followed by the sharp crack of a whip. Fiona spun around, and only just got out of the way in time. A wagon was bearing down on her; the horses going at a reckless pace. The large bearded man on the wagon seat cracked his whip and urged them to still greater exertion, while the wagon lurched from side to side. The man and woman also tried to get out of the wagon's way, but less successfully. The old man's stick got tangled around his ankles and he fell with a cry, trying to grab at the donkey. The donkey danced back a little, so that the man was dragged along a good way before he could halt the animal. The woman leapt aside and her basket slipped. She lunged for it, but it hit the ground, fruit rolling everywhere, which was promptly trampled beneath the hooves of the horses and the wagon's wheels. The driver never so much as glanced back at the consternation he had caused. A sheet of dust was flung up in his wake, and he was gone.

Fiona stepped across to the old man, offering her hand.

"Here, I'll help you up."

With her aid, the man was able to regain his feet. Still holding his arm with one hand, Fiona bent to retrieve his stick. It was miraculously unharmed. He was breathing heavily, and looked severely shaken, but he managed to give Fiona a wan smile.

"Thank you kindly."

Next, Fiona turned her attention to the woman, who was scrabbling around in the road for the mangoes. Fiona bent to help, but it was a sorry collection. Many of the mangoes had been squashed to pulp. Others were so coated with dust and grit that they were inedible. It was a sad and forlorn pile that was eventually stowed in the basket once more.

The woman looked furious. She shook her fist in the direction of the departed wagon. "Vicious brute! Could have run us down!" She looked dispiritedly into her basket. "Another profit lost."

"Who was he?" asked Fiona.

"One of them farmers most likely. From the country. They drive up here most weeks to sell their turnips or whatever up at the market. Have no consideration for the rest of us. Think cos we come from the city, we got it easy." She spat contemptuously and strode away without so much as a thank you or farewell.

Fiona walked on. The farmer had certainly been better dressed than the man and woman. They looked half-starved. It was a sobering thought that a person's income for the week could depend solely on a basket of fruit. It was a far cry from her own life on Earth. She had never gone hungry in her life. What would happen to the woman if she couldn't sell her fruit, which was very likely now? Where would she find her next meal? Did she have a family? Was selling mangoes her only means of feeding them? Had that farmer in his arrogance, just condemned children to a week without food?

She soon reached the city. The quiet of the road was instantly replaced by noisy activity. It was impossible to move for carts and donkeys. Many people wove their way expertly through them, balancing baskets on their heads. Ragged barefoot children ran everywhere, and, to Fiona's disgust, almost as many rats. Shaggy, flee-bitten dogs snarled over bones on the ground. The streets twisted and turned, alleys appearing everywhere. The road was little more than hard-packed dirt, rutted and potholed.

Sound assailed Fiona on every side. She had expected the market to be set up in a square, but people had put up their stalls everywhere along the main thoroughfare, where people would have to negotiate their way past them, and so be easily waylaid. Many people just walked through the crowds, crying their wares at the tops of their voices.

There were stalls selling cheeses and bread. Other stalls selling sweetmeats and honey cakes. There were wagons full of turnips, potatoes, leeks and other root vegetables. There were mango sellers, melon hawkers, and many other varieties of fruit. And everywhere, there were fish stalls. Some of it fresh, some of it salted. The air was thick with the smell of the fish, but it did not entirely mask other scents. Now and then Fiona caught a whiff of stagnant water or rotting rubbish. The ground was covered in litter. Fiona saw a little boy duck down behind a stall and snatch a half-rotten apple from the dirt. Without even bothering to clean it, he shoved the fruit whole into his mouth.

The people all had a starved, ravaged look. The children were hollow-cheeked, some of them with sores on their arms and legs. The women's faces wore deep lines of care carved into them, as though to map out their suffering. The men were so emaciated that they resembled walking skeletons. Many wore desperate looks, like hunted animals. Fiona hurried past two of them, fighting over the last piece of bread on a stall. It was so stale that it looked more like a brown brick than food.

Everyone wore drab, dull colours that contrasted strongly with the brighter shades of the Travellers. Fiona hurried on, keen to put as much distance between herself and the squalor as she could.

The sun was properly up now, but the breeze of the past few days was missing.

Fiona was sweating profusely beneath the cape. Despite the smell, she let her hood fall back to get some air to her hot face.

The road continued to slope upwards. The whole city seemed to have been built on an incline, rising at its peak to a large and forbidding house that seemed to frown down on the people below. Fiona shuddered. She knew without being told that this was Alfredo's house. It was the highest landmark for miles, impossible to miss. Fiona tried hard not to think about what it would be like to be trapped in there. Almost on a level with it was a large squat tower surrounded by high walls. Fiona could just make out the moving silhouettes of men patrolling there. She supposed it was the city jail and averted her gaze.

She had left the crowds behind, and was now walking past houses, which were really little more than hovels. They appeared to be made of wood with thatched roofs. Fiona gave the straw a doubtful look. Surely it would be like kindling in this heat if a fire were to break out. The houses were so close together, that they would be consumed in no time. Outside one house, a man was working in his garden, or what passed for a garden. It was really little more than a brown patch of earth in which a few sorry-looking vegetables were struggling to grow. The man was pulling up weeds from his potato bed, and throwing them over his shoulder. Stoop, pull, and throw. Stoop, pull and throw. The man did not even look up as Fiona passed, but carried on relentlessly, performing the chore that Fiona suspected he had been doing for perhaps all of his adult life. She was surprised the monotony hadn't driven him crazy, or perhaps it had. Perhaps that was all his life consisted of now. The same thing day in and day out as he struggled to make his living.

A little further on, Fiona saw some thin, ragged blankets that had been draped over a stunted bush to dry in the sun. A little boy, no older than two or three came hurtling out of the house, clearly making a bid for freedom. His mother, who was heavily pregnant, came hurrying out after him, but her stomach was so huge that she could only manage an ungainly waddle.

"Elijah!" she shrieked. "You come back here this minute!" The little boy ignored her. As he darted past her, Fiona made a lunge and grabbed the small brown hand. The little boy let out an indignant squeal as Fiona led him back to his mother. She seized him from Fiona and clutched him to her swollen stomach as though she thought Fiona might run off with him. Her scolding carried on the air long after Fiona had walked away.

Soon her surroundings changed again. She was entering streets that were less dirty. Several buildings were still gutted ruins, but they had an air of lost grandeur about them. Among these were what appeared to be newly built houses, some with small, tidy gardens. The people were more smartly dressed too, and looked better fed. They also seemed to be making for a single point. Fiona followed them.

Soon their destination was revealed to be a huge arena, raised in three tiers. The first two tiers were comprised of stone benches, while the topmost level was a stone dais.

Fiona felt oddly exposed here. She tried to turn back the way she had come, but people jostled her on every side, and she was swept along. She was shunted into the first row. Unable to think of anything else to do, she perched on the very end of the bench, her head bowed, praying that no one would notice her. She had a clear view of the arena below her. Everyone was seated now, and their faces were turned towards the arena with an air of expectation. A silence had fallen. Fiona's sense of foreboding increased, but it was impossible to slip out now. She'd draw attention to herself at once. She had no choice but to watch with the rest.

The sound of marching feet drew near, accompanied by an ominous clanking, and what sounded like the crack of a whip. Fiona let out a stifled gasp of horror, as into the arena marched a column of people. They were dressed in little more than rags, and ranged from men as old as Jeremiah, to children younger than Lena. They were bound together by long chains connected to manacles around their ankles. There were two men with the column, one at the head, and one at the rear. They each carried a long and lethal-looking whip.

The line of people was halted in the exact centre of the arena. They were jerked up so sharply that many fell to their knees. They all looked exhausted, and many of the elderly and the little children had been stumbling and limping. The stronger and fitter sought to comfort their companions. Many of them clutching loved ones. There was terror on all the children's faces. On the adults, resignation. Some people were crying, though softly, as though they feared to draw attention to themselves, while others tried, equally quietly, to soothe them. One of the men left his position and marched up onto the dais, and Fiona realised with a sick certainty what was about to happen. She longed to run, but could not look away.

The remaining slave trader stepped forward and detached a woman from the line, dragging her roughly forward, the manacle still around her ankle. The man on the dais launched into his spiel.

"Well, ladies and gentlemen, here we have a fine specimen for you. A wench in her prime. Strong, healthy. Ideal on the farm or in the kitchen or for anything else you might have in mind." Several men laughed at this.

The woman, Fiona noticed, had not taken her eyes off a frail-looking woman near the end of the line. There was a blazing look in them, as though she dared any of those men to try and touch her.

"I'll start the bidding at ten silver crowns, who'll give me... twenty! Very well, twenty, how about fifty? Fifty silver crowns for this fine young wench. An asset to anyone's household."

"Five gold crowns," said a man in the row behind Fiona, making her jump.

The slave trader looked delighted. "Five gold crowns! Any more offers? Going once, going twice, and sold for five gold crowns to the gentleman in the second row, and may you enjoy your purchase, Sir."

The man looked as though he had every intention of doing just that. He was smiling as he beckoned a servant forward who led the woman away.

The frail-looking woman let out a piteous cry and tried to follow her daughter, but the other slave trader struck her a vicious blow across the face with his whip that knocked her to the ground. Fiona's answering cry was drowned by the woman's high, thin wail. Fiona clapped her hands over her ears, but no one took any notice of the woman. The terrible auction was still continuing.

A boy no older than the toddler Fiona had rescued earlier was wrenched away from his father. The man went berserk, straining against his chains, desperate to reach his son. The slave trader laid about the man's head with his whip until the man was forced to his knees. From there, he was forced to watch, blood running down his face, as his son was sold for two silver crowns and led away.

I can't watch this! Fiona thought desperately. I can't stand it! She turned, meaning to leap over the bench, occupants and all, to run as far from this terrible place as possible and back to the safety of the *Dolphin*, when she felt a hand close on her shoulder.

She whipped around. The man sitting directly beside her on the bench was looking full at her. One hand still on her shoulder. He was smiling.

* * *

It seemed to Christophe that he had no sooner closed his eyes than he was jerked suddenly awake by the pounding on his cabin door. He'd had a tiring day. The search for Miguel had once more proved fruitless, and his last conversation with The Appointed was still on his mind. He had hoped that she would have come round to her destiny and accepted her duty to her people, but she still refused to believe him. She still clung fervently to her old life, and he feared she would do something desperate. Feeling that she needed some time alone, he had talked Gideon into persuading James to accompany them. He had returned to find his cabin deserted, and the book lying on the floor.

Deciding that the best course of action would be to leave on the *Dolphin* when she sailed the following day, Christophe returned the book to its hiding place, determining to make a second attempt to persuade The Appointed once they were at sea. He could make no further plans until she had read the book and learned what it was that her father expected of her, and at least she would be safe from Miguel's clutches. It bothered him that no one had seen hide nor hair of Miguel, but it couldn't be helped. They would be away at first light.

A great weariness stole over him. It felt as though he'd hardly stopped to draw breath since snatching The Appointed. He wouldn't think any more tonight. Christophe sighed deeply and lay down without bothering to get undressed.

The next thing he knew, someone was pounding on his door as if they meant to smash it from its hinges, and yelling his name at the top of their voice.

Christophe slid the bar across and the door flew open.

James stood there, a wild look in his eyes, his face chalk white.

"What—?" Christophe began, but James cut across him.

"She's gone!"

Christophe stared at him. "What are you talking about?"

"Fiona!" James bellowed. "She's run away, and it's all your fault! You drove her to this. She was perfectly happy until you turned up and decided to—"

"Are you sure?" Christophe snapped.

"Of course I'm sure!" James yelled. "She was gone when we woke up, and so was Gideon's cape. When we went up to ask the sentry if he'd seen her, he said he'd let Esther go because she said she was on an errand for you."

"And Esther?"

"She was here all the time!"

Christophe sat down heavily on the edge of his bunk. It had happened, as he had feared it would. The stupid girl! He felt like strangling her.

"Come on!" he said harshly. "Get Gideon to round up as many Guardians as he can. We need to search the city. Let us hope we find her before Miguel does."

"And what am I to do?"

Christophe hesitated fractionally, but there was no point telling James to remain behind. The mood he was in, he'd be sure to do something reckless. Best to have him where he could keep an eye on him.

"You're with me, now go!"

James turned, but halfway out of the door, he looked over his shoulder. His eyes bored unblinkingly into Christophe's. "If anything happens to her, I swear I'll kill you!" Then he was gone.

* * *

As he walked at Christophe's side, James fought the sick dread that had taken possession of him ever since he'd discovered Fiona was missing. It wasn't so much her running away that baffled him, but the fact that she'd gone without him. He'd sworn to her, and to himself, that he would protect her. What could have happened that was so desperate that she'd fled without even saying goodbye?

James thought back. What had happened yesterday? They'd watched Gideon fight, they'd had lunch, Christophe had returned and asked to speak to Fiona alone.

James rounded on Christophe. "What did you say to her?"

"What?" Christophe snapped. He was leading the two dozen men that had been quickly gathered to the city, and had remained preoccupied and silent ever since they had set out.

James was undaunted. "Yesterday, you and Fiona talked together alone. She was fine before that, so what did you say to her?"

"I gave her a book."

James stared at him. "What?"

"It was her father's. He gave it to my father just before he died. It was supposed to tell The Appointed how to put an end to Alfredo."

"So she must have read something in there that freaked her out?"

"I doubt it. The book was lying on the floor when I returned. I do not believe she even looked at it." He did not tell James how frantic she had been. About her tears, and how she'd pleaded with him to release her. He didn't think he'd forget that in a hurry. He paused before the open city gates.

"Divide into groups and comb every inch of the city. If you meet any gangs who are friendly to us, get them to help. Someone should try all the inns. It's possible she may be hiding in one of them. If you have not found her by sunset, return to the *Dolphin* and send out the next search party."

He would not return. He did not intend to rest until The Appointed was safe under his eye once more. A tight knot of fear formed in his chest every time the unbidden image of The Appointed in Alfredo's clutches swam into his mind. He dreaded to think what Alfredo would do to her, regardless of the fact that she was not yet a threat. He beckoned to Gideon and James, and without a word, he strode off, Gideon and James hurrying to keep up.

"Where do we start?" James asked.

"We will begin with the market," said Christophe. "Stay close. It is easy to get lost in these crowds."

James obediently stuck close to Christophe's side as they wended their way along the twisting narrow streets. People jostled them on all sides, and more than once they were accosted by a fruit seller or cheese seller, anxious to make a profit. Christophe shouldered them aside, and they moved smartly out of his way when they saw the quarterstaff in his hand and the long dagger at his belt. Every now and then, an alley would open up and Christophe or Gideon would dart down it while James remained where he was, scanning the passers-by for any sign of Fiona. At any other time, the squalor and poverty of the city would have appalled him, but he barely noticed, praying all the time for a glimpse of Fiona's distinctive coppery head bobbing through the crowd.

Their progress was slow, as Christophe and Gideon stopped to question anyone they recognized. James could feel his impatience mounting.

Then they reached a point where two streets forked. James was at the rear, and just as he reached the fork, a hand shot out and grabbed him.

"Buy a cheese, Sir? Just come off the ship it has, fresh and salty."

"Er, no thanks," said James, trying to free himself from the man's grip.

"Come on, Sir," the man coaxed, tightening his hold. "You won't find better cheese in all the city. I sell nothing but the best."

"No!" James snapped, wrenching himself free. "I'm in a hurry!"

"But it's only half a silver crown," the man wheedled.

"Look, I haven't any money, so just get lost, will you?"

The man walked off scowling.

James looked around everywhere, but Gideon and Christophe were nowhere in sight. He swore loudly. Which way should he take? But as he stood there, undecided, Gideon came hurrying towards him from the right-hand street.

"James! I thought I had lost you!"

"Some stupid cheese seller grabbed me. Where's Christophe?"

"I did not see," said Gideon. "We were separated. I thought he had gone that way," he indicated the street he'd just emerged from, "But there is no sign of him."

"He must have taken the left way," said James. "Come on!"

* * *

The man was slim and wiry, Fiona saw, with a narrow, fox-like face, and his smile did not extend to his sharp, cold eyes, which were fixed intently on her. She twisted to free her shoulder, but he tightened his grip, still smiling.

"Not so fast, my dear. I wish to speak with you."

"What do you want?" Fiona tried to keep the fear from her voice.

"I have not seen you before. Are you new to this city?"

"What makes you ask that?" Fiona snapped.

The man's smile broadened. "You will forgive me for saying so, my dear, but you do rather stand out. Your unusual colouring and your hair!" He reached out to touch it, and Fiona flinched away from him.

"Just leave me alone, will you? I'm staying with friends if it's any of your business."

"These friends of yours," the man said softly. "Would one of them perhaps go by the name of Christophe?"

Fiona ran. Wrenching herself free in one desperate movement, she vaulted over the bench and leaped down the steps, sprinting across the arena to the street beyond. The crowd stared and the slave auctioneer halted in mid flow.

Miguel let out a shrill whistle, and at once men appeared from among the spectators. "After her!"

Fiona cast a terrified look over her shoulder. Two huge men were bearing down on her, arms outstretched. More men were vaulting over the benches. With a gasping cry, Fiona darted away down the first street she came to. Her breath came in panicked gasps. She could hear shouting and pounding boots getting closer. Her foot caught in a rut and she stumbled. An arm swung out of nowhere and seized her cape, but she tore free with a scream and ran on. Down one street, then another, twisting and turning. If she could just confuse them, she could get away. A narrow alley opened up invitingly on her left. She dived down it, running as hard as she could go.

She hit the wall headlong. She hadn't even seen it in her blind panic, looking desperately for another turning. She reeled backwards, blood streaming down her face. Her skull felt as though it had split in two. The ground seemed to lurch horribly. She put out a hand to steady herself, wiping blood from her eyes with the other. It was a dead end. There was a solid brick wall in front of her, and behind her… six huge men were blocking the alley. Miguel was foremost. She stared around her like a hunted animal, blood still pouring from a deep gash in her forehead while her nose throbbed in time with her rapidly beating heart. She was trapped.

"The chase is up, Appointed," said Miguel softly. "You cannot run from us."

Fiona gazed into his eyes. She had thought Christophe was hard, but there was no mercy in this man's gaze.

"Bind her!" Miguel rapped. Two men seized her and forced her to the ground. She was too dizzy to put up a struggle. One man tied her ankles together while another forced her hands behind her back and bound them. A wad of some foul-smelling material was forced into her mouth.

Suddenly, the man guarding the street toppled forward with a muffled grunt. The men holding Fiona let her fall as they turned to examine their comrade. Twisting her head, Fiona saw that he was lying face-down with a knife buried in his back up to the hilt.

Christophe stepped over the man's body, and bent to retrieve his knife. In his other hand he held a quarterstaff.

"Well," said Miguel. "Nice of you to drop by, Christophe."

"Let her go," said Christophe quietly.

Miguel appeared to deliberate a moment. "No, I don't think I will. You see, you may have felled one of my men, but there are four others here. Of the two of us, I think I am in the position to make demands. Leave now, and I will spare your life, although there is a thousand gold crown price on your head which would fill my pocket nicely. But I am a merciful man. I have what I came for."

Christophe looked down at Fiona. Her terrified eyes met his for only a second before his gaze snapped back to Miguel.

"And if I refuse?"

Miguel let out a sigh that almost managed to sound regretful. He raised a hand, and as one, the men attacked.

Fiona's cry was stifled by the material blocking her mouth. She tried feebly to get to her knees, to crawl over to Christophe, but as she raised her head, a wave of pain and nausea swept over her. Bile rose to her throat, which she was forced to swallow, and her head fell back weakly. She could do nothing but watch. All the time she was aware of Miguel standing over her, like a hunter with his prize.

* * *

When Christophe realised that Gideon and James were no longer following him, he cursed. He debated going back for them, but decided against it. They would realise their mistake and catch up soon enough, and Gideon would look after James. He was alone.

His short cut brought him out near the arena. There was a lot of shouting and running feet. Two men darted out of the arena and down a side street. Christophe recognized their uniforms immediately. They were Miguel's men. He followed. With any luck, they would lead him straight to The Appointed. He wished he had his own men with him. He would need them if it came to a fight, as it undoubtedly would. But there was no time to go back for them. He halted a short distance away, and peered around the corner. The men had disappeared into an alley. Only one watched the street. Christophe drew his knife and took aim. At that range, it was an easy target.

His worst fears were confirmed when he saw The Appointed lying on the ground, bound and gagged. Her face was swollen and bruised and blood trickled down her forehead. He saw the look of terrified entreaty in her eyes when he met them briefly, and as Miguel's men rushed at him, he was ready.

He spun on one foot, staff whipping round to smack his first attacker across the forehead, while his other foot sent the dagger spinning from the man's hand. Ducking low, he rammed the staff between the legs of another attacker who was charging at him. The man screamed and slashed at him. As he fended him off, a man came up from behind. Christophe felt the man's knife bite deeply into his side. Warm blood ran down his thigh, but only a part of his brain registered the pain. The other half was too busy calculating his next move. But his body knew what had happened. He stumbled, and as he was thrown off balance, the third attacker brought his own quarterstaff smashing down with terrific force on Christophe's hand. There was a crack, and pain exploded through Christophe's arm and shoulder. The knife fell from his limp fingers. He tried to draw another from one of the many hidden in his clothing, but he could not move his arm. He now had only one fighting hand, and the loss of blood from his side was weakening him. He recognized at least two of his assailants. Claude and Benjy; two of Miguel's best thugs. What they lacked in skill, they made up for with sheer strength. He was reduced to ducking their blows, searching for an opening, but his dodges grew less and less nimble, and the combined pain of his arm and side threatened to make him black out. He would have been more than a match for any of these men in single combat, but they were four on one, and so far he had inflicted little damage.

He saw the eyes of The Appointed, huge in her terror-stricken face as she lay helpless at Miguel's feet while he stood impassively watching. Anger filled him, momentarily drowning out the pain. He would finish Miguel off if he did nothing else. He lunged towards him, hammering his staff into one attacker's face. The man lurched away, his face a bloody mess. Christophe's foot drove into the belly of another, who doubled up, momentarily winded, but Claude and Benjy were not so easily despatched.

Claude leapt on Christophe's back, forcing him to his knees, while Benjy stamped down viciously on the hand that still clutched the quarterstaff. It snapped cleanly in two. The brothers did not give Christophe time to rise. They drove punishing punches into his chest and ribs, relentlessly forcing him to the ground. Christophe fought to gain some leverage to use his feet, but their weight was too great. They pinned him to the ground, and he could do nothing except try to protect his face, while they rained down blow after blow on his back and head. Everything was swirling around him. Everything was pain. He saw Fiona's face swimming before him, oddly close. I'm sorry! He thought weakly as the current swept him away.

# Chapter 8

## Captivity

Fiona lay like a sack over a broad shoulder. Her head hung down, and she could still feel blood trickling into her eyes. Someone had pulled her hood over her face, shutting out sunlight completely, but they could not block out the images that filled her mind. The silent movie revolved continuously. She watched Christophe's prostrate form fall in the dirt beside her, his clothes sodden with his own blood which pooled around him. He lay on his side, utterly motionless. But she'd barely had time to absorb what she was seeing before she was lifted up and carried away, bumping up and down through the city's endless streets and alleyways. Gradually, her shock receded, only to be replaced by a growing fear. It crawled icy fingers over her skin and clutched her heart in a vice. She was helpless, utterly alone, and a prisoner of enemies who held her very life in their hands.

How long she was carried, she could not have said. Time seemed to have melded into an endless pattern of movement, pain and fear. Then she found herself being roughly set on her feet and the hood thrown off. She blinked in the bright sunlight and staggered. Her ankles were still bound, and she was dizzy and nauseous from the blow to her head.

She was standing in the courtyard of what appeared to be one of the more recently built houses. She was certainly in a grander part of the city than she had yet visited. The sweeping lawns to her left and right were neatly kept and their flower beds carefully tended. The gravel approach to the front steps was swept clean.

The house itself was a squat, ugly building. The thatched roof replaced instead by shingle. There were few lights in any of the windows. The entire aspect was far from welcoming.

Two men seized her arms and held her upright between them. They were so huge that she felt like a doll in the hands of two giants. Another man stepped towards her, drawing a knife. She flinched away from him, eyes dilating in panic, but he merely bent down and, with one quick slash, cut the cords binding her ankles. He did the same to the ropes securing her wrists and ripped the gag away from her mouth. She took several deep breaths, fighting the urge to spit out the foul taste the gag had left behind.

Miguel regarded her dispassionately. "You are in our hands now, Appointed. Your protector lies dying in the filth of a back alley. No one knows where he is, and when your friends from the *Dolphin* begin their search, they will find no trace of you. After all, dead men tell no tales. You would do well to cooperate with us."

Fiona said nothing. She did her best to stand up straight, to keep looking into those merciless eyes. But it was difficult. Once again she was in the hands of someone who had designs for her and, once again, she was helpless to save herself.

"Take her to her quarters," Miguel instructed the two men holding her. He started to walk away as the men began dragging Fiona towards the house. But then he paused and called over his shoulder. "We will have another little chat tomorrow, Appointed!" The last word was uttered in a mocking tone that made the other men laugh.

She was taken along many corridors and up numerous staircases before finally halting before a plain door with peeling paint. One man drew out a key and inserted it into the rusty lock. With a violent shove, the other man sent Fiona flying backwards through the door to sprawl on the floor. The door slammed, the key turned, and the men's footsteps gradually faded to silence. Fiona was alone.

For some time, Fiona lay where she was, too numb with fear and despair to move. Her head throbbed and she still felt sick. She could feel the congealed blood on her face, and her wrists and ankles were cramping painfully. Slowly she sat up and began rubbing her limbs to restore the circulation. Her head swam and, as feeling returned, agonising pins and needles shot through her hands and feet. However, after a couple of minutes, she was able to get unsteadily to her feet, and begin exploring her prison.

It didn't take long. She appeared to be in an attic. A lumpy bed had been fastened to the wall, but there were no other items of furniture in the room. Outside, the sun was setting, casting flickering shadows on the walls. There was a tiny window set high in the sloping roof. Fiona climbed unsteadily onto the bed. Even then her head was not quite level with the window. Only by craning her neck and standing on tiptoe, holding tight to the sill, could she see anything. She could dimly make out the roofs of other houses. They were terraced. She appeared to be in the middle of a row of five. She was too high up to risk climbing out. She'd break her neck. And there was also the small problem of the thick iron bars set in the skylight opening with virtually no gap between them.

Stepping down from the bed, head spinning, Fiona stumbled across to the door and bent down to examine it. It was plain and unremarkable. There was a tiny gap at the bottom, perhaps big enough for her to insert her little finger.

Though she knew it was hopeless, Fiona began tapping her way around the walls. She looked into every corner, even bending to peer under the bed, but it was useless. Finally she gave up and curled up on the hard, rickety bed. It was a relief to rest her aching head. Her stomach rumbled loudly, reminding her that she'd had no food that day. She felt exhausted, worn out by shock and fear. She closed her eyes, but all she saw was Christophe lying next to her in a pool of blood. She snapped them open again, a small sob catching in her throat.

Christophe had tried to protect her. He had probably died doing so. Despite the fact that he had abducted her, and tried to force her to do his bidding, Fiona had to admit that he had not physically tried to harm her. He had kept her safe, introduced her to his people. Why had she left his protection? Much as she hated to admit it, he was her one ticket out of this world. If she'd held out just a bit longer, he would have been forced to let her go. Whatever happened, her life would not have been in danger. Christophe would have kept her alive, if only for the sake of his people. She had no idea what he'd intended to do with her if she'd been successful and rid his people of Alfredo, but at least she'd been safe from him for a time, and she'd had some hold over him, some power. What did she have now?

Christophe had said that the book probably contained the secret or whatever it was that would lead to Alfredo's downfall. Goodness knows what that could be. It could be anything. A means to give him more power? But he had that already. The people were under his control. What more could he possibly want? More likely, it was a way of defeating him, but how? There would have to be a war of some kind. Fiona let out a bitter laugh. If everyone expected her to lead the people in some mighty battle to re-conquer the land and free the people, they were sorely mistaken. She knew nothing at all about battle strategy. The book would have told her of course, but she hadn't read it. She hadn't even tried to open it. But Miguel was not to know this. He would try to pry the information from her, and not accept her pleas that she knew nothing and was no threat to his master or to anyone. She felt sick as her brain presented the various methods Miguel might adopt to wrest the truth from her, and when he finally realised that she had no information to give, why, she would be of no further use. There was no reason to keep her alive.

"Damn you, Christophe!" she said aloud, her voice muffled in the pillow. "Damn you for getting me into this!" She had been safe on earth. Safe and happy. And now she would probably never see her home again. Then a truly dreadful thought struck her. She wouldn't see Earth again, but soon that wouldn't matter. She would probably be dead. But she had condemned James to this cruel, violent place for the rest of his life. Christophe's death ended the only hope James had ever had of returning home. She had abandoned him, and he would never know what had become of her. She closed her eyes in despair, feeling the tears squeeze through her closed lids to trickle down her cheeks.

Her tears stopped abruptly as the key grated in the lock. Fiona tried to sit up, but her head protested sharply. She gave up with a groan and rolled onto her back, eyes trained on the door. It opened and a flood of dancing light made Fiona blink. The sun had long since set, casting the little attic into shadow.

A girl entered, bearing a loaded tray. On it was a plate of bread and some strips of dried meat, a pitcher of water, and two candles. These were the source of the light. The girl bent to set the tray down carefully on the floor. Picking up the candles, she set them in two wall brackets. They filled the room with their warm, comforting glow, and by their light, the two girls examined each other.

Fiona saw a girl of her own age, dressed in the uniform of a servant: a patched smock over a drab pinafore dress. She was small and slight. Midnight black hair framed a thin, pale face, and was bound up with a scarf. Her eyes were like two beads of jet, bright with intelligence. They were fixed on Fiona's face. But then the girl suddenly seemed to realise what she was doing. Hurriedly she bent to pick up the tray, and proffered it to Fiona.

"Something to eat, Miss? You must be thirsty too." She had a low, quiet voice, but it was quite well spoken. It took Fiona by surprise. She'd expected a servant's accent. She chided herself silently. Who could tell where this girl had come from. She was most probably a slave. An image of the slave market returned and she repressed a shudder with difficulty. Still, this girl did not look too badly off. Though thin, she appeared well fed, and her clothes, though patched and darned in many places, were nevertheless better than the rags she'd seen on many of the people on the streets.

She sat up slowly, shuffling back until she could lean back against the wall. She put her pillow behind her, and the girl stepped forward to lay the tray across her knees.

"Thank you," she mumbled.

The girl made no reply. Her gaze had come to rest on Fiona's head. Fiona knew she must look quite a sight.

"That is a nasty cut you have there."

Fiona nodded and took a bite of bread. It was stale, but by this time she no longer cared. The girl stood watching her eat. Fiona noticed that, though her manner was meek and servile, there was a bold directness to her gaze that she could not quite hide. Fiona didn't mind. It put her more at ease. A cringing servant, terrified of everyone would not have been willing to speak, but this girl's evident curiosity might mean that she was prepared to answer questions. She took another mouthful of bread and a sip of water. It tasted hard and stale, but it soothed her parched throat.

"Where am I?"

"This is the home of Miguel Fernandez."

Fiona's heart sank. Alfredo's right-hand man. She could barely get out her next question. "Does… does Alfredo live here too?"

"Oh no, Alfredo's house is way up at the top of the city. All his most important prisoners are brought to Miguel's house first for questioning."

Fiona felt sick. She laid down the strip of meat she had just lifted to her mouth.

The girl noticed her reaction. "Would you like me to fetch a healer? That cut really should be seen to."

Fiona stared at her in surprise. "There's a healer living here?"

For the first time, the girl smiled. "There are all sorts of people living here."

"But won't Miguel notice if too many people start coming here?"

At this, the girl actually laughed. It was a harsh sound, completely devoid of humour. "Miguel is absent from home this evening. No doubt he is celebrating with his comrades over his latest capture." A spasm of contempt crossed her face.

Fiona found herself liking the girl. Servitude certainly did not appear to have affected her spirit.

Then a thought struck her. "Could he not have gone to report to Alfredo that he's got me?"

The girl's face softened. She laid a hand lightly on Fiona's shoulder. "Try not to worry. I promise you are safe, at least for tonight. I cannot say what tomorrow will bring, but not all of us here are monsters like Miguel."

Fiona nodded again. She felt a little comforted.

"Why don't I fetch that healer while you finish your meal? Who knows when your next one will be."

She started for the door.

"Wait!" Fiona called suddenly. The girl paused in the doorway and looked enquiringly back at her.

"I don't know your name," Fiona said awkwardly.

The girl smiled. "My name is Katie."

"I'm Fiona."

Katie gave her another friendly smile and departed. Fiona noticed that she locked the door behind her. She felt a moment of dismay, until she considered that it was probably for the best. Miguel's men could easily be on the watch, especially if what Katie had said was true, and there were some servants not loyal to Miguel. They would be on the lookout for any attempt at escape. She finished her meal and drained the pitcher.

True to her word, Katie returned, bringing a woman with her.

"This is Jessemine," she said. "She was once a healer before she came to live here."

Though still quite young, the woman's face was lined and weary and utterly expressionless. She said not a word as she produced several strips of cloth and a small glass bottle from her pocket. When she removed the cork, a strong antiseptic aroma filled the room. Still in silence, she wet one of the strips of cloth with a little of the bottle's contents. The woman's hand was gentle as she cleaned the cut and wiped away the congealed blood, but it stung horribly and Fiona drew in a sharp breath through her teeth.

Katie moved to Fiona's side, and supplied the commentary. "This is an antiseptic lotion made from boiling leaves. It helps prevent wounds from becoming infected and begins the healing process. You are lucky you did not need stitches. This…" as the woman began spreading a salve with cool fingers over her bruised and swollen nose and forehead. It felt wonderful against her skin. "…is a salve for reducing swellings."

When the woman was finished, Katie held out a goblet to Fiona. It was brim full of a completely clear liquid that gave off the strong smell of spirits. Fiona eyed it doubtfully. "What is it?"

Katie laughed. "It is a liquor made from crushed berries. It will help to relieve the pain and will help you sleep."

Fiona accepted the glass and took a cautious sip. The liquid stung her throat, making her splutter. Her eyes watered. "Yuck!"

"Drink it all," Katie said firmly. "It will make you feel better."

Fiona grimaced, but obeyed. Sip by careful sip, she emptied the goblet. The liquor warmed her stomach, and gradually she felt the nausea and dizziness fade. The dull, throbbing pain in her head eased, and a warm, pleasant drowsiness stole over her. She was hardly aware of the woman leaving quietly, taking the empty food tray with her. Katie helped Fiona to lie back down and made her as comfortable as she could.

"Why didn't that woman speak?" she murmured sleepily.

"It is always wise to guard your tongue," Katie replied darkly. "In this house, even the walls have ears."

Fiona sighed. The candles bathed her in their hazy glow. "Goodnight, Katie," she murmured. Then her eyes closed and she was asleep.

"Sleep well, Appointed," Katie whispered, before tiptoeing from the room.

For the last few mornings, it had been the call of seabirds that had roused Fiona to consciousness. This morning, a far more ominous sound disturbed her uneasy dreams. Some instinct opened her eyes and alerted her to the footsteps approaching. There was more than one person. She could hear their voices murmuring low to each other. The clouds of sleep faded and she was on her feet, her eyes on the door, a thrill of apprehension stealing over her.

The key turned and the door was flung open theatrically. Fiona saw the two huge silhouettes of the men who'd dragged her up here, as they stepped into the shaft of sunlight filtering through the bars on her window.

"Well, fancy that, Claude," one observed. "It seems she's expectin' us."

"Sleep well, my pretty one?" Claude asked with mock solicitude.

Fiona made no answer. Claude's companion stepped forward and jabbed her hard in the ribs, making her gasp.

"It's not polite to ignore your elders. Miguel wants a word with you, and if yer smart, you'll tell 'im what 'e wants to know. If not…" he paused dramatically, grinning at his companion. It struck Fiona suddenly how alike they were. They could have been brothers.

Claude grinned back, displaying a set of broken brown teeth. "Now, Benjy, no need to frighten the little girl." Chuckling, they each seized an arm, and frogmarched Fiona between them down through the house.

Fiona remained silent, refusing to look at her captors. She hoped to catch a glimpse of Katie, but though she saw plenty of servants, they were all strangers. They hurried about their business with their eyes averted. Fiona noticed that several of the women cast Claude and Benjy fearful glances as they passed.

They came at last to a solid door of polished oak on which Benjy knocked. A voice ordered them to enter. Fiona recognized it at once. She thought that it would be ingrained on her memory for ever.

The room was furnished as a study. Miguel sat behind a large writing desk littered with papers. He looked up and smiled as they entered. "Well, my dear, I trust you passed an agreeable night?"

Fiona said nothing.

Miguel gestured Claude and Benjy to deposit Fiona in a high-backed wooden chair. She was pushed down onto it roughly, and Claude and Benjy immediately set about binding her arms and legs to the chair. Miguel began calmly stacking his papers and piling them neatly into a drawer. Once Claude and Benjy had made sure that Fiona was tied so tightly that she could hardly move, they took up positions behind her chair, one on either side.

Fiona could not take her eyes from Miguel, who had sat back in his chair, and was now regarding her impassively. A leaden ball of fear had lodged in Fiona's chest. She was utterly defenceless, subject to Miguel's every whim, but she did her best to meet his gaze without flinching, all the while aware of the two hulking figures at her back.

"Now then," Miguel began in a pleasant voice. "I would like you to tell us your name."

Fiona supposed there was no harm in answering this question. It was hardly a treasured secret.

"My name is Fiona," she said expressionlessly.

"And how do you come to be in our world?"

Fiona started a little. Miguel did not know about the hidden entrance.

"I was brought here."

It was best to give a little of the truth where possible. Perhaps they would believe she was cooperating with them and go easy on her.

"How were you brought here?"

Fiona said nothing. Without warning, Claude struck her hard across the face. Her head snapped back against the chair's wooden back. Instinctively she tried to raise her hands to defend herself, but she could not move her arms.

"I will ask you again," Miguel said quietly. "How were you able to return to this world from the alternative place to which you were sent as a child?"

"I don't know," Fiona mumbled. That was technically true. She had been unconscious when Christophe had transported her. It was only through James that she had learned how the lake worked. Still, she knew her answer was not a satisfactory one, and she braced herself for another slap. Her head still rang from the first blow.

Miguel sighed. When he spoke, he used the tone of someone explaining something to a dim-witted child. "Do not play games with me. I am fully aware that you were spirited away to an alternative world when you were a baby. Your father wished to protect you so that one day you could return and fulfil the destiny marked out for you. The people have built up a legend around you. They call you The Appointed. They believe that you will save all their miserable lives and once more give them freedom to pursue their idle and pointless existences."

There was a pregnant silence.

"Where is the sceptre?" Miguel wrapped suddenly.

Fiona was taken by surprise. The sceptre? What was he talking about? She stared speechlessly at Miguel.

This time it was Benjy who struck. His full-armed slap made her head jerk and took her breath away. She felt blood trickle from the corner of her mouth. It felt as though her jaw might be broken.

"My patience grows thin!" Miguel said.

Claude seized Fiona's wrist. It felt very frail in his spade-like hand. Fiona winced.

"Where is the sceptre hidden?"

"I don't know." Claude twisted sharply. Fiona gritted her teeth.

"What safeguards are in place to protect it?"

"I don't know!" Claude twisted harder.

"Do the merpeople have it?"

"I don't know!"

"Where are they hiding?"

"I don't know!"

"How were you intending to destroy it?"

"I don't know!" Her arm was surely going to break. She couldn't stand this much longer.

"Look, I don't know what you're talking about!" she shouted. "I've never heard of this sceptre, I don't know where it is, and I've no idea who has it or how to destroy it. I'm not The Appointed!"

She broke off with a strangled gasp as Benjy punched her savagely in the stomach. She doubled over, all the breath driven from her body. She did not realise straight away that Claude had let go of her wrist.

When she was finally able to raise her head, she saw that Miguel had got to his feet. He gestured to Claude, who, with his brother's help, rolled the desk away from the wall. A trap door was revealed, set into the floor. Benjy threw this back, to reveal a deep, yawning shaft. Fiona saw that a winch and pulley system appeared to have been rigged up to enable a descent. At a nod from Miguel, Claude and Benjy hauled on this, and with a loud clanking, drew up a metal cage. They pushed Fiona's chair into this contraption, and Miguel, after lighting a candle stepped in beside her. Then they were carefully lowered into the darkness.

In no time, it seemed to Fiona, they were at the bottom. She blinked, her eyes adjusting to the gloom. Soon she saw that she was in a large underground chamber or cavern. It stretched away beyond the range of her vision. Miguel held up the candle and, by its light, Fiona saw wicked-looking knives arranged in racks along the wall. Below them hung an array of lethal-tongued whips. Miguel let his light extend a little further, and Fiona glimpsed other implements of torture too hideous to contemplate. Miguel allowed her a good long look before snuffing out the candle and giving three sharp tugs to the winch. With a rattling and a clanking, the cage ascended once more to the sunlit study.

Miguel did not say a word until the desk was replaced and all was as it had been before. Then he bent over Fiona's chair, staring unblinkingly into her large, frightened eyes. "Those instruments have broken the resilience of far stronger people than you," he said softly. "Think about that, and maybe tomorrow, you will be in a better frame of mind to answer my questions."

He straightened and turned to Benjy and Claude. "Return The Appointed to her quarters."

It was well that Fiona had the support of Benjy and Claude. She could hardly stand upright, her stomach hurt so badly. They half dragged, half carried her all the way to her cell door in silence. Benjy unlocked it while Claude watched Fiona lean heavily against the wall for support. He eyed her bruised and swollen face maliciously.

"Not so high and mighty now eh, Appointed?" They shoved her bodily through the door, and Fiona heard their laughter receding into the distance.

She crawled to the bed and curled up there. She felt sick. Gingerly she examined her face with her good arm. Her lip was cut and swollen and one eye was closed. Her jaw felt tender, but she could move it, and there appeared to be no teeth missing. She lay motionless, feeling her various aches and pains, wondering what the morrow would bring. Every time she thought of those knives and whips and other terrible apparatus, she wished she were dead. She could give Miguel no information. But what state would she be in when he finally conceded defeat? He would not give up easily.

The afternoon wore away slowly, and Fiona remained where she was. The pain in her stomach gradually subsided, though it still felt tender. Her jaw felt stiff and awkward. Her arm throbbed. A little experimenting revealed that it was not broken. She could move her fingers. It was obviously just badly bruised. The ache spread all the way up her arm into her shoulder and even to her neck. Darkness fell outside, but Fiona never noticed.

What finally roused her was the sound of the key turning once more. She struggled painfully into a sitting position.

"Who's there?"

Her swollen lip made her speech a little indistinct.

Katie entered, carrying a loaded tray as before. It contained a pitcher of water, and another of broth, and some fresh candles, but there were other things on there too. Fiona recognized the jar that had held the salve the woman had used on her the night before. Katie removed the old candles and placed the new ones in the brackets. Then without a word she crossed the room to examine Fiona. Fiona saw anger and disgust in her eyes.

"Here," she said softly. Sitting next to Fiona on the bed, she applied the salve with infinite gentleness to Fiona's face. Her touch was so light that Fiona barely winced at all.

"Are you hurt anywhere else?" she said after a while.

Fiona extended her arm. It was a mass of purple bruises. Claude's finger marks stood out on her skin like a brand. Katie rubbed the salve into the skin, then handed Fiona the broth.

"Drink this before it gets cold."

"Thank you."

"What happened to you?" Katie asked.

"Miguel questioned me, but he didn't much like my answers."

Katie nodded sympathetically. "Miguel always seems to know when a person is lying to him. It is unwise to try."

"But that's just it!" Fiona said desperately. "I wasn't lying. I hadn't a clue what he was talking about."

"What did he ask you?"

"He was going on about something called a sceptre. He wanted to know where it was and how it could be destroyed. He also kept asking if the merpeople had it and where they were hiding."

"Why should you know these things?"

Fiona sighed. "Because I'm The Appointed, or at least that's what everyone believes. They think I'm going to defeat Alfredo and save the world."

"And you're not The Appointed?"

"I don't know. I'm not sure of anything anymore. I come from another world. I was brought here." She told Katie everything. How Christophe had gone to Earth and kidnapped her. How James had also been accidentally drawn into this world too. How Christophe's people had welcomed her as the answer to all their prayers. Christophe's insistence that it was her destiny. That it was her duty to save her people, and his refusal to take her home.

"Then he gave me this book. He said it was given to his father by mine, and that it would tell me everything I needed to know to stop Alfredo."

"And did it?"

"I never read it. I ran away, but Miguel caught me. Christophe came after me, he tried to save me, but…" she broke off. Once again the image of Christophe as she had last beheld him filled her mind.

Katie put a comforting hand on her shoulder. "Did Miguel kill him?" she asked gently.

Fiona gulped. "He thinks so. He said he was as good as dead. There was blood everywhere."

She began to tremble. Katie put her arms around her and Fiona relaxed into her embrace.

"What of your friend – James?"

"I don't know where he is. He wasn't with Christophe. He's probably still on the *Dolphin*. That's the worst of it. With Christophe dead, James can never go home!"

"Christophe may still be alive," Katie pointed out.

Fiona raised her head from Katie's shoulder. "Really? But it was five against one. He was stabbed at least once!"

Katie made no answer to this.

"Don't worry, Fiona, I'll try to think of a way to get you out of here. It won't be easy. This place is heavily guarded."

"I don't think I've got long. It won't take Miguel long to see I'm of no use to him. He won't keep me around after that."

"So we need to change his mind."

"How?"

Katie bit her lip, thinking. "You must lie to him," she said eventually. "Tell him a story, but put in as much truth as you can. Make him think you are weakening. That should buy us the time we need."

Fiona stared at Katie in horror. It would be extremely risky. Katie herself had said that Miguel was difficult to deceive. If he discovered she was lying to him, the consequences did not bear thinking about.

"He showed me his torture chamber," she whispered.

"He would not dare subject you to that!" Katie said sharply.

"Why?" said Fiona, taken aback.

Katie's eyes had flashed fiercely, but then she seemed to recollect herself. "Miguel is only a spy, a collector of information for his master. He could not afford to hurt you. What if Alfredo needs you to retrieve the sceptre? He is expendable. You are not."

Fiona did not feel greatly reassured. Sooner or later Miguel would learn the truth. But it was the only plan they had. She would just have to pray she could keep up the deception long enough to give Katie time to come up with a plan of escape.

"Alright," she said reluctantly. "There's no other choice."

Katie squeezed her shoulder. "I will think of something, I promise. You will see James and your home again." She picked up the tray and departed.

* * *

Once alone in her room, Katie seated herself at the window and gazed unseeingly out at the city below. It was a clear, starry night, and her view was unbroken to the calm waters of the sea. But Katie barely noticed.

Miguel, the fool, had got it wrong. He had allowed his men to leave the boy Christophe for dead, instead of capturing him and forcing him, under threat of Fiona's safety, to reveal what he knew. He had gone to fetch Fiona from her world. He was obviously the key. Her father had mentioned something that was dangerous to his rule. That must be the sceptre. Had Christophe been going to tell Fiona how to use it against her father? Why was Fiona needed to wield it? Why couldn't Christophe make use of it himself?

Katie bit her lip. Her father had told her to befriend Fiona, to become her confidante. But she genuinely liked the girl. She clearly was no threat at all. She was nothing more than a pawn in this boy Christophe's game. She did not deserve to be left in Miguel's hands, to die a slow, painful death, as befell all traitors to her father's rule. At the very least she deserved to be allowed to return to where she came from. It was where she belonged and clearly wanted to be. Then any possible threat from her would be over. That just left Christophe. If only he was alive, then she could return Fiona to him somehow and perhaps learn what he intended. She was sure he would reveal his plans to no one else. He clearly had something specific in mind, or he wouldn't have abducted Fiona, much less given up his life for her. And there was that book he had tried to give Fiona. It was vital to find out what it contained. No, she would have to return Fiona to Christophe.

Miguel had said he was as good as dead. Well "as good as" did not mean certain. It would be just like Miguel in his arrogance not to check.

Katie snuffed the candles and got into bed. She lay there beneath the thin blanket and listened to the night noises that floated into her through the open window. When she felt herself becoming drowsy, she formed the question in her mind, as she had done so often before, and kept repeating it over and over inside her head.

"Is Christophe alive, and where can I find him? Is Christophe alive, and where can I find him? Is… Christophe…?"

She was in the back room of a small, two-roomed hovel. A dirty sheet had been drawn across the one small window. The only source of illumination came from a fire burning in the grate. The room was uncomfortably warm. A woman with wispy white hair was bending over a figure lying on a bed. He was on his back, his mouth open, his face a nasty grey colour. The harsh rasp of his breathing filled the silent room.

The boy's tunic had been removed and one side of his leggings had been cut away. His blood-stained tunic lay in a heap on the floor. There was a terrible gash in the boy's side. The blanket on which he lay was already stained with red. The woman gestured.

A young girl who had been stirring a pot over the blazing fire, from which issued the aroma of healing herbs, came hurrying over with some wads of cloth. The woman began mopping up the boy's wound, wiping away fresh and clotting blood. The boy half-opened his eyes and groaned. The girl lifted a flask to his lips and trickled some liquid down his throat.

Over by the fire, a small girl stirred the pot of boiling herbs and banked up the fire, silent tears pouring down her face all the while.

The older girl held the boy's hand and murmured soothingly to him. Her pale face was strained and anxious in the firelight.

Two boys stood on either side of the door as though on guard. Both of them wore grim expressions. One was dark, like the two girls, and kept fingering the knife at his belt. The other was fair-haired and pale.

Katie awoke sweating and breathing rapidly as she always did after a vision. She could still see the hovel, as well as the street it was in. It was as though a map had been imprinted on her brain.

Well, at least Christophe was alive. Now all she had to do was pay him a visit.

Katie rolled over, and returned instantly to dreamless sleep.

* * *

When Claude and Benjy came for her the following morning, Fiona was ready. She'd spent a largely sleepless night trying to figure out a convincing lie, piecing together fragments from what Christophe had told her and from what Miguel had let slip during the previous days' questioning.

It seemed that Alfredo had discovered a weapon which he was very anxious to obtain. For what reason, Fiona could not guess. This was obviously no ordinary weapon like a sword or bow and arrow. Miguel had called it a sceptre. From stories she'd read as a child, Fiona knew that sceptres were often imbued with magical properties, and were used by their wielders in battle against their foes. Why Alfredo wanted such a thing was a mystery to Fiona. He controlled every aspect of his subject's lives. Surely no enemy posed a severe enough threat that he needed magic to suppress them.

Then there was the matter of her father, or the man Christophe claimed was her father; she still could not accept this. He must have discovered the whereabouts of this weapon, and that was the information Alfredo and his followers had tried to force from him. This presumably was the information contained in that book Christophe had tried to give her. Perhaps it was a journal. What he expected her to do about it, Fiona didn't know and didn't want to think about. The important thing now was to keep herself alive long enough for Katie to engineer her rescue. To do this, she must deceive Miguel. This was no easy task. Miguel was a spy, a master of trickery and deceit. Surely he would see through her as transparently as if she were made of glass. But she had to try, and hope that Katie acted soon. She knew she was placing a lot of faith in the servant girl, but she had no choice. Katie was the only ally she had.

When the door was flung wide and Claude's bulky form was framed in the narrow opening, it was to find Fiona slumped on the floor against the wall, head in hands, the very picture of defeat. Claude grinned with satisfaction. "Well, well!" he gloated as he hauled Fiona roughly to her feet. "Look at this, Benjy, not quite so 'igh and mighty any more, is she?"

Benjy leered at Fiona over his brother's shoulder. Fiona stood with her head bowed and her eyes on the floor.

"I'll tell Miguel whatever he likes. I can't stand this any more!"

Benjy cackled gleefully and grasped one of Fiona's arms while Claude took the other.

"Works every time," Benjy sneered. "Usually just a glimpse of that chamber 'as 'em spillin' the beans. Some last for a couple o' days, but they all end up squealin' like pigs in the end. Even you, my pretty one." Grunting with amusement, they marched off down the endless stairs and corridors with Fiona, unresisting, between them.

When Miguel bade them enter, they strode into his study with Fiona suspended aloft between them as though she were a trophy. They dropped her into the waiting chair facing Miguel, and she immediately slumped forwards.

Her face was tired and drawn, her yellowing bruises standing out against her pale skin. When she spoke, her voice was a frightened whisper, and she could not lift her eyes to Miguel's impassive face.

"I'll tell you everything, everything I know, I promise! Just please don't..." she broke off and pointed a shaking finger down at the floor, beneath which Miguel's torture chamber was waiting. She raised pleading eyes to his face, in time to see a fleeting look of satisfaction flit across it, to be replaced almost instantly by his customary impassivity.

He turned to Claude and Benjy, hovering eagerly just inside the door. "You will wait outside and escort the young lady back to her room."

The brothers looked furious, but they had little choice but to obey. They backed out sullenly, slamming the door behind them.

Miguel barely noticed. His attention returned instantly to the girl cowering in the chair opposite him. He sought to put her at her ease. "Come now, my dear, you have made a wise decision by agreeing to help me. Be truthful with me, and no harm will come to you. Lie to me," his voice hardened. "And you will wish you were dead." The girl gave an audible gulp. Good, people would do anything out of fear, especially if they saw a ray of hope. Of course she would be killed the instant her usefulness wore out, but she would not suspect. It never ceased to amaze Miguel how deluded people could be. How could they possibly believe that they would be safe if they cooperated? But they did. They were desperate to believe it, and the looks of shocked incredulity on their faces as the knife slid home never varied. Still, it would be a shame to kill this one. She was a pretty thing. Perhaps the master would allow him to keep her as a reward. He couldn't suppress a thin-lipped smile. Reaching forward, he lifted the girl's chin and held it so that she was forced to look him directly in the eyes. Eye contact was vital during interrogations such as these. You never knew if the victim was lying or holding back. It had happened before, though no one had lived to try it a second time. He spoke softly, soothingly.

"Now then, my dear, where is the lost sceptre?"

The girl's voice shook as she replied. Her eyes were wide and fearful. "My father was a spy for many years. He and his friends believed that somehow, they would find a way to oppose Alfredo's rule. When my father learned that this sceptre existed, he tried to learn everything he could about it. He knew that Alfredo wanted it, and that made him scared. He wanted to find it for himself and use it against Alfredo."

"And did he discover where it was hidden?"

"No, but he learned who had it."

Miguel's grip on Fiona's head tensed. She had to fight not to flinch, but his touch made her skin crawl.

"And who has it?"

"A secret organization. They have a castle far away from here, and they took it there to try and discover how to destroy it."

Miguel's face lost some of its colour. "It's gone? They destroyed it?"

Fiona took a deep breath. Now for the tricky bit. She was basing her fabrication on the many fantasy movies she'd watched over the years. She only hoped her imagination wouldn't prove her undoing.

"They couldn't destroy it. It was a thing of magic, and only someone with magic in their blood would be able to use or destroy it."

"Ah!" Miguel breathed. So that was what Alfredo planned to do. He would use his own magic to command the power of the sceptre. No wonder none of the fools had tried to take it for themselves. They would have known it was no use to them. This was presumably why Tobias, having located the sceptre, had not brought it back in triumph to his people. But that didn't explain why he needed the girl, unless… Miguel drew in a sharp breath.

"Your father couldn't destroy the sceptre because he didn't have magical blood, but you?"

Fiona bowed her head as if crushed. She wished she could force tears into her eyes. "It is in our family, but it skipped my father's generation. When I was born, a mer person told my father that the magic was alive once again in me, and I would destroy the sceptre and free the people."

Miguel had let go of her. He was gazing at her bent head. "Look at me!" he wrapped suddenly.

Fiona started and sat up. Miguel was gazing at her intently. She felt herself beginning to tremble.

"How do you know all this?" he almost whispered.

"Christophe told me," Fiona croaked. "My father sent me to another world to keep me safe, but he told Christophe's father how to find me. Christophe said I wouldn't come into my power until I came of age. That's why he waited so long before coming to find me. He drugged me and brought me here. I don't remember how I got here. Christophe was going to take me to a man from this secret society who lives at a neighbouring sea port. He's a merchant. He was going to take me to someone who could show me how to awaken and use my magic. And then we would go to find and destroy the sceptre. But Christophe's dead. I can't do this without him. We're all lost! I've failed them all."

To her surprise, Fiona felt a tear slide down her cheek. She was really getting into this.

"How were you to recognize this merchant?" Miguel said.

Fiona thought rapidly. "We would know him by the mermaid carved into his dagger. It's the symbol of the organization. They all carry knives with a mermaid carved into them." She leaned towards Miguel, pleading.

"So you see I can't hurt you. Christophe is dead, and without him, I've no chance of finding the man who will awaken my powers. Let me return to the world I came from."

Miguel smiled. "I think not, my dear, though your story appears to be genuine. If I had been Christophe, I would not have pinned the hopes of my people's freedom on a snivelling wretch like you, but I must verify your story."

Fiona's heart plummeted. "What are you going to do?" she managed finally.

Miguel's smile widened. "Why, I think I'll pay this merchant a visit. He seems a veritable mine of information. It would be a shame to waste it. Meanwhile, you can stay here safe and sound until my return. If what you have said is true, perhaps we can return you to the planet you came from. After all, without this merchant's help, you are no use to us, or your people, you are no use to anyone, and I think it's best we leave it that way."

Fiona put her head in her hands as if devastated, but she had difficulty concealing her relief. The plan had worked. He'd bought it. What he would do when he discovered the truth, she dreaded to think. She had no illusions. He would never let her go, even if her story had turned out to be true. She was dead regardless. But at least she had time. If Katie acted soon, she could be away before Miguel returned.

Fiona made no complaint as she was returned to her cell. She sat on her bed, waiting for Katie. She had fulfilled her part of the plan. Now, it was up to Katie.

# Chapter 9

## Grim Tidings

Alfredo sat on his balcony, reading the letter that the messenger crow had delivered. The bird was perched on the balcony railing, waiting patiently for a return message, or else a much longed for crumb. But Alfredo had no attention to spare for the crow's wants. His eyes devoured Miguel's latest report hungrily. It was better than he could have hoped. The boy Christophe was dead. The most persistent threat to his rule was snuffed out, eliminated, and with his death the people had lost a popular hero. Even better, The Appointed was now in Miguel's custody, doubtless being interrogated for information. Alfredo doubted how far Miguel would get. Miguel was not a patient man, and Alfredo could not afford for him to break the girl just yet, not when her usefulness was still in question.

His thoughts turned to his daughter. He had commanded her to befriend the girl and learn what she could. She was resourceful. Alfredo had no doubt that she would succeed better than Miguel. He felt a faint surge of pride. She was growing up fast. She was rapidly reaching marriageable age, but Alfredo had no wish to waste her considerable talents. Perhaps it was time for her to live with him permanently. He was the one who could best put her gift to use, and then he could replace Miguel at last. He had long suspected the spy of having an agenda of his own. But Miguel would be no threat to him once he had the sceptre. Alfredo felt a tightening in his chest. At last, the time was approaching when the plan of the warlocks would come to fruition. The people's lives would be altered irrevocably, and Alfredo and his kind would have supreme control. He had waited for it for so long.

When he had been selected for the great task of finding and obtaining the sceptre, when he had realised that he was the one on whom all the warlock's hopes depended, he had been full of optimism. He had been ambitious even then, and had welcomed the challenge. Subjugating and dominating the people was easy, particularly once the merpeople had been driven into exile. There were still people being born with magical abilities, but with the merpeople gone, there were no tutors to train them in the use of their powers. Those who had mastered their abilities were eliminated one by one. Alfredo had felt a grim satisfaction in snuffing out each new threat as it presented itself. But this was also tempered with frustration, as the sceptre continued to elude him.

And then there was The Appointed, and all the prophecy surrounding her. He had searched high and low for her, but he had never been able to discover the location of this mysterious portal to another world. No one he had questioned even knew of its existence. It seemed it was not a matter of public knowledge.

As the years had passed, Alfredo had come steadily closer to despair. He had watched the people carefully for signs of magic. Everyone with power gave off traces which were easy enough to detect. They didn't even need to use it, though the pulses were much stronger when active. Magic wielders left traces in the air and in the ground on which their feet trod. Alfredo monitored these carefully. It was only a matter of time before the cleverest gained a rough mastery over their powers and were able to mount a defence. But raw magical ability had been on the decline in recent years. Alfredo was at a loss to understand why, though it gave him a temporary respite.

He redoubled his search for the sceptre and The Appointed. This was about the time that Christophe and his Travellers had become active, presenting a small but united front against his rule.

Alfredo felt sure that Christophe had the information he sought, but he had proved as elusive as The Appointed. Until now.

Alfredo had reasoned that the boy would one day reveal The Appointed. He would bring her out of hiding and use her to set his people free. So Alfredo had waited, reasoning that Christophe would eventually bring The Appointed to him. And his gamble had paid off. He would actually be looking forward to his messages from now on.

* * *

Miguel banged up and down the cabin of what felt like the umpteenth merchant ship. They had been here three days now and so far their search had proved fruitless. He and his men had searched every merchant ship and tavern on the quay at least a dozen times. He had demanded ships to turn out their cargo, and he had cornered men in bars and forced them to hand over their weapons. He had raided merchants' houses and tried to force them to reveal the whereabouts of this organization, but they had known nothing. The more guarded simply assumed expressionless masks and those less subtle looked puzzled. Not even threats to their families had elicited any results, even when he'd made an example of one family to teach the people a lesson.

Miguel had been a spy over half his life. He knew what to do to make people talk. He knew how to reduce them to such a state of terror that they sang like birds. Very few held out for long. Either they gave in, or they drove out those they were sheltering, or they tried to flee. But they were ferreted out in the end. Miguel might have given more time to the business if he'd been alone. But time was something Miguel simply didn't have. Also, there was the fact that he had sent a report to his master the moment the girl had left his study. He had been flushed with his success. Now the master would be expecting results and speedily, and he was well aware of what would happen to him if he didn't produce the goods. His men were raiding the villages for miles around and still others had been sent to contact spies in other sea ports.

He returned to the inn where he was staying. As he entered the common room, he saw a man beckoning to him from a nearby table. The man was dressed from head to foot in black. His face concealed beneath a cowl. Miguel recognized him. He was in charge of enforcing the street curfews that Alfredo had set in place after nightfall. His men had too often been attacked under cover of darkness, and it was this man's job to patrol the streets and taverns to ensure that no one was behaving in a suspicious manner. He had a considerable number of men at his disposal. If anyone could help Miguel, it was this man.

Miguel approached the table guardedly. "Well?"

"Miguel! Haven't seen you for a while, let me buy you a drink."

Miguel made no move to sit. "I asked you to meet me here to answer a question. I haven't got time for chatter."

The man shrugged. "Well, just as you like. Those boys of yours..." he indicated Claude and Benjy who were at a nearby table, their faces buried in their fourth tankard of ale. "They said you were after a merchant who belonged to a secret society, whose emblem is a dagger with a mermaid carving on it."

"Well?" Miguel snapped.

The smile the man gave him was distinctly mocking. Miguel forced down his annoyance with difficulty.

"You're slipping, Miguel. There was a time when I would have been asking you that question."

"Alfredo," said Miguel in a dangerously low voice, "is extremely anxious for this information, and his patience is wearing thin. Neither he nor I have time for your games. Now, once and for all, are there no undercover operations in this city as far as you know?"

"I know for certain there are none. If there were, I'd have sniffed them out. Whoever told you this must have taken you for a ride. I wonder how they did it." He chuckled softly. "I would not have thought it possible."

Miguel retired to his room in silent fury. He had been duped. How was it possible? He was the most accomplished spy in Alfredo's network. He knew every trick in the book, and he'd been sent on a wild goose chase by a mere slip of a girl. It was galling. How had he been taken in? He supposed she'd told him what he wanted to hear, and he'd allowed himself to believe her. He had not previously considered her as a serious threat. How could he have misjudged so badly?

But what was her plan? She must have a good idea what would happen to her on his return. Unless... the realisation struck him like a physical blow. She'd got him out of the way so she could escape. It was obvious. Clearly she knew someone who was living under his roof. A servant perhaps, and they were waiting until he was safely out of the way before smuggling her to safety.

A blind rage filled Miguel so that he could hardly think straight. He stormed back to the common room and bellowed at his men, "Make ready the boats! We return immediately!"

His acquaintance gave him a cheery smile and a wave as he left, but he hardly noticed. He would find her. He would find her if it was the last thing he did. He would drag the truth from her, piece by agonizing piece, and only her screams for mercy would be just repayment for the fool she'd made of him.

* * *

Alfredo read the letter with rising fury. The fool! How could he have let this happen? Sent on a wild goose chase by a child? He spat contemptuously. The crow let out a hopeful caw, but Alfredo threw his chair at it and it flew off, shrieking indignantly. Perhaps all was not lost. Perhaps Miguel would get there in time. The girl would not find it easy to escape from such a heavily guarded building. Utter catastrophe could still be avoided.

Alfredo ground his teeth. All he needed now was for Christophe to still be alive.

* * *

Katie had disappeared. Fiona paced anxiously up and down the tiny attic. She cast frequent glances out of the tiny window as though hoping to see Katie strolling up the drive.

She had last seen her three days ago. She had sat waiting for Katie to come to her after her last interview with Miguel. Sure enough, with the sun's setting, Katie had appeared, bringing food and candles as usual. Fiona had explained what she had done and they giggled over it for an hour. Katie had left, telling Fiona that everything would be alright and to leave the rest to her.

But she hadn't come the next night. It was the silent woman who had dressed Fiona's various cuts and bruises that brought her food. Fiona could get little out of her. She learned that Miguel had left, but the woman would tell her nothing of Katie. She seemed anxious and uneasy. Two more nights followed and Katie still did not appear. Fiona really began to be afraid. If Katie didn't come soon, Miguel would return and that would be that.

She woke abruptly a few hours later as the door flew open and crashed back violently against the wall. Before she could gather her fogged wits, Miguel had crossed the length of the room and seized her by her hair. He hoisted her half off the bed. Fiona screamed in pain and tried to wrench her head free, but Miguel was shaking her so hard that the room became a blur.

"Thought you could trick me, did you? You foolish child! I gave you the chance to tell me freely. Now I shall drag your torment out until you will think death is the only release left to you. Then when you've poured out every scrap of knowledge in your pathetic little brain, maybe then I will end your suffering."

He threw her from him. She fell in a crumpled heap, but even before she could scramble to her feet, he was looming over her, face contorted with rage. Seizing her hair once more, he yanked her to her feet and began to drag her behind him down the corridors and staircases, deeper and deeper into the bowels of the house. The air grew colder, and a damp, musty smell filled Fiona's nostrils.

Fiona's face was twisted in pain. Tears streamed down her cheeks. It felt as though Miguel was going to rip her hair out by the roots. He paused. Still gripping her tightly with one hand, he took a set of keys from his belt with the other. He unlocked the door directly facing them and flung it wide. Fiona found herself staring into a well of blackness from which an icy draft rushed, and squeakings and scufflings could be heard.

"The rats are lonely!" Miguel said viciously. "It is a long time since they entertained a guest. I think I will leave you to their tender care for the night, and if there's anything left of you by morning, then we'll pay a little visit to my chamber. I do hope they leave you your tongue."

He sent her flying through the door, and slammed it behind her.

* * *

The tapping woke Alfredo from a fitful doze. He flung back the rumpled blankets and strode quickly to the window. Flinging it open, he saw a crow perched on the sill, tapping its beak against the window pane. There was a letter attached to its leg.

Alfredo unrolled it hastily. He had not expected Miguel to write so soon. Surely nothing else could have gone wrong in so short a time.

To his surprise, the letter was not from Miguel. The writing was unfamiliar.

*Miguel is gone. Things are well in hand. The girl is no serious threat. I go to seek the Travellers. The key lies with them.*

Alfredo read this twice, his brow furrowed thoughtfully. His daughter had left the house. And she had seemingly waited until Miguel was out of the way. Had she perhaps sent him away deliberately? What was she planning? It was risky for her to venture into the city alone and by night. He had instructed her to stay close to the girl.

Alfredo clenched his fists in frustration. Katriana would never betray him. She had been only too eager to give her help, and she would never involve Miguel in anything she planned. That must be why she had waited until he was safely removed. He would just have to trust her and await developments.

He debated sending a reply, but decided against it. He had no idea where his daughter was. He snapped a sharp word to the crow, which took to the air at once.

Alfredo watched the crow out of sight and returned to his bed. All he could do now was wait.

# Chapter 10

## Rescue

Pain; it invaded every particle of his awareness. It was hard to tell where the pain ended and he began. With every beat of his heart his body throbbed. It was difficult to draw breath.

Christophe groaned and half opened his eyes. He had a dim picture of a fire-lit room, but it was really so much easier to let his lids droop once more. He felt a hand raise his head and heard a gentle voice.

"Hush, Christophe, drink this." He felt liquid trickle between his parched lips. He swallowed once, twice, then his eyes opened fully. Esther was bending over him. He could see her pale, frightened face illuminated by the fire's glow. He was in a little one-roomed hovel. A healer's hut. She was rummaging in a box and ignoring him. Gideon and James were standing on either side of the door, and, to his surprise, Lena was tending the fire, stirring a bubbling pot. When they saw that he was conscious, Lena burst into tears and James and Gideon hurried forward.

"Christophe! You have returned to us! What happened? James and I got there as soon as we could, but by the time we found you…"

James said nothing. He looked ill.

Christophe struggled to speak, though the pain was growing worse, particularly in his side, a deep life-sapping ache.

"The Appointed!" he rasped. "Captured… Miguel…"

"Hush!" Esther said sharply. "You must not talk." She glared at her brother. What little colour there was in James's face left it.

"Fiona? Captured?" he breathed.

Before Christophe could muster the strength to answer, the healer came bustling forward with needle and thread.

"That wound in your side will need stitching. I've put your arm in a splint. That should heal in about a month. The rest are just bruises, but you've lost a lot of blood. You, girl!" she wrapped at Esther. "Make a dressing and soak it in that pot on the fire. It will help prevent infection and reduce the risk of fever." Esther hastened to obey. The healer bent and forced a wad of material between Christophe's teeth. He made no effort to resist. He had seen this done before. He would need it.

Gideon and James moved back and Lena came to kneel on Christophe's other side and took his hand.

Those next five or ten minutes were the longest and most arduous of Christophe's life. He had felt pain before but nothing like this. The healer's fingers were deft, but that made little difference. If it had not been for the rag in his mouth, he would have screamed in agony. Distantly, he heard James going outside to be sick.

But at last it was over. Christophe fell back. He was breathing rapidly and a faint sheen of sweat covered his forehead. He was ashamed to realise that he had been crushing Lena's fingers between his own. He let go, and she stepped back without wincing. Esther came forward with the soaked bandage and the woman bound it tightly over the wound in his side. This was painful too, but it was nothing to what he'd just undergone.

Then the healer took down a glass phial. "Drink this. It will help to relieve the pain and make you sleep."

Esther raised his head once more and the healer poured the concoction down his throat. Christophe slipped gratefully back into oblivion.

When he next came to himself, he was lying in his cabin aboard the *Dolphin.* He had no memory of having been brought there.

He felt exhausted, utterly drained of strength. His ribs still hurt when he breathed, and he could not easily move his right arm. He tried to sit up, but the movement caused a spasm of pain to shoot through his side.

The door opened and Esther was there, pushing him back onto the bunk.

"Don't try to sit up yet. You must take things slowly. I will bring you some food in a little while if you are hungry. Now you must rest."

"I have no time for rest," he said, weakly trying to push her hands away so he could sit up once more. It took little effort for her to restrain him. With one hand she held him still while feeling his forehead with the other.

"Your fever has broken at last. We have been dreadfully anxious. But your side is healing and there is no sign of infection."

"How long have I been here?"

"Three days."

Three days. It had been three days since The Appointed was captured. Who knew what Miguel had done to her? She might even be in Alfredo's hands by now, or dead.

Christophe turned his head away. His helplessness infuriated him, but what was threatening to overpower him was his sense of failure. He had allowed The Appointed to fall into enemy hands, after swearing to protect her. He had failed her, his father, and his people. How had this happened? How had he allowed it to happen? If The Appointed was dead, then all their hopes were dead with her, and it was his fault.

He could not suppress a low moan.

Esther was bending over him at once, her face full of concern. "Christophe, what is it? Are you in pain?"

"Leave me!" he muttered.

She straightened, but then, in that way she sometimes had, as though she could read his mind, she whispered, "It was not your fault, Christophe." But this, far from comforting him, only made him angry, and that gave him strength. He sat up.

"No? Then whose fault was it? The Appointed was under my protection and I failed her! I swore to myself that I would fulfil my father's duty and I failed. The Appointed is lost, and by the time I have recovered my strength, it will be too late."

Esther rounded on him. He had never seen her look angry before, but her eyes flashed and a bright spot of colour had appeared in each cheek.

"No!" she said passionately. "You have not failed! You returned The Appointed to us. If not for you, we would have no hope at all. We will get her back. We will never give up, and we need you. Do not give up now. Whatever task The Appointed must undertake, there is no better person to help her than you."

Christophe did not reply. He lay back wearily and closed his eyes. Esther looked down at him in silence for several moments. Then she said quietly, "I will bring some food in a little while," and left.

Over the next few days, Christophe slowly regained his strength. His appetite returned and his bruised ribs eased. His side still troubled him, though it was healing well. Any exertion brought on shortness of breath and he tired easily. He sent for the healer who had tended him, and she assured him that his tiredness would pass in time, and was due to his fever and the amount of blood he had lost. She said his side would heal too, though she thought it would be some time before he recovered his full strength. The wound had been deep. She advised him to rest but he could not. His frustration at his own weakness left him restless and irritable. He was even more reserved than usual and was moody with almost everyone. He could not bear the poky solitude of his cabin, and ventured on deck only a day after regaining consciousness, ignoring the protests of Esther and her mother, though the effort left him exhausted.

Antonio sent men to scout around Miguel's house, searching for a weak spot in Miguel's defences. The scouts reported back that the house was heavily guarded at every entrance with archers and hunting dogs and constantly changing patrols around the drive and garden.

A raiding party of twenty men was also sent under cover of night, hoping to overwhelm the guards by sheer numbers. Only three returned and all of them were wounded. The only positive thing was that Miguel's extra security meant that The Appointed was almost certainly being held there. Christophe was able to take some small comfort from this. At least they knew where she was, and one scout was able to learn from one of Miguel's servants that The Appointed was definitely alive. The question was how to get to her.

What they really needed was a way of breaking into the house without approaching it from the outside, so that Miguel and his men could be taken completely by surprise. His men were trying to approach Miguel's servants to learn what they could tell them, but it wasn't easy.

And then one evening, nearly a week after Fiona's capture, when Christophe was in his cabin resting, there came a tentative knock on his door.

"Yes?" he snapped.

Gideon poked his head in cautiously. "There is a girl to see you, Christophe; she will speak to no one else. She is a servant in Miguel's house."

Christophe felt a faint twinge of curiosity. One of Miguel's servants! How she had managed to escape from the house, let alone find her way here was a mystery, but that could wait.

"Bring her to my cabin," he told Gideon. "I will speak to her."

* * *

Katie had been surprised at how easy it had been to find the *Dolphin*. She had no knowledge of the city but the directions in her vision had steered her true.

Her tension grew as she neared the ship. She had no idea how she would be received, or if Christophe would see her. He might not be enough recovered. Would she be able to gain his trust? Her father's plan depended on it.

She also felt a powerful sense of curiosity. She had heard so much about Christophe. He was much loved in the city and his exploits were whispered among the servants. He lived with the sea folk that wandered from port to port, and it was rumoured that he was a prominent member of the elite and highly skilled band of warriors known as the Guardians. She knew that reward posters had been put up in the city, offering large amounts of money for any information that would lead to his capture. What must it be like to live like that? With a sentence of death hanging over you. Not knowing if each day was your last. And he had managed to kidnap The Appointed single-handed, and nearly lost his life defending her. Despite the fact that he was a traitor, Katie couldn't help admiring his courage and loyalty.

She had barely reached the ship, lying placidly at anchor, when she was hailed by a sentry.

"Halt! State your business."

Katie took a deep breath. She must appear composed and confident. Never mind the fact that she could be killed on sight. She mustn't let her feelings show. She must appear as if she was in complete control of the situation, whether it was true or not. She called back, her voice strong and clear, "My name is Katie. I am a servant in Miguel's house. I wish to speak to Christophe. I have news for him about The Appointed."

"What do you know of The Appointed? What concern is she of yours?"

"I will give my information to Christophe and no one else, refuse, and it may cost The Appointed her life."

The man turned away and called to someone else. Katie saw a boy about her own age approach and confer in whispers with the man. They were so alike that Katie suspected that they were probably father and son.

The boy vanished below deck and the man turned back to his watch, ignoring Katie completely. She waited with mounting trepidation. What if he wouldn't see her? What if she was simply killed? She claimed to have information about The Appointed. Surely they would keep her alive, at least for a while. She wondered if Fiona was alright. If she wasn't rescued soon it would be too late. She would be lucky if Miguel didn't kill her outright after the trick she'd played on him. Miguel did not suffer fools gladly, still less being made to look a fool himself. His pride would not allow it.

The boy returned and said something to his father. The man pulled on a rope and a gangplank thudded to the path.

"Cross," he called to Katie. "Christophe will see you."

Katie walked up the gangplank, head erect, eyes scanning everywhere for danger, though her posture was relaxed and confident. She smiled at the man and his son and offered her hand, but neither made any move to take it. Their faces were identical expressionless masks, betraying nothing of their true feelings.

"Give me any weapons you have," the boy demanded.

"I am unarmed." He didn't seem prepared to take her word for it. His hands performed a lightning search over her body. It was so quick that Katie only became aware of what he was doing once he had stopped. He did not give her time to react.

"Follow me." Katie followed him across the deck and down through a hatch to the sleeping quarters. There was very little activity going on. It seemed that most of the ship's occupants were in bed.

The boy halted before a door and knocked. A voice called to him to enter. The boy opened the door and gave Katie a push. The moment she was through, he closed it behind her, but he did not move away. Katie suspected he had taken up a position outside, ready to rush in at the slightest sign of trouble. She almost smiled.

It was a tiny cabin, sparsely furnished, with nothing but a rude bunk with two drawers beneath it. But the presence of the boy overwhelmed it completely. It was like those rare meetings with her father. He too had always dominated whichever room he was in.

The boy was watching her, his gaze alert and intense. There were dark circles beneath his hard grey eyes and pain had carved premature lines into his face. His skin was pale beneath his tan, and at present marred by deep bruising. Katie felt a little disconcerted. It felt as though the boy was reading her soul with his gaze, just like her father. It was amazing how alike they were. But she mastered herself almost immediately.

"Christophe, my name is Katie. I am a servant in Miguel's house."

"Indeed? And what is your business with me?"

"The Appointed is in terrible danger and I wish to help her. All our hopes depend on her after all."

"How do you come to be a servant for Miguel?"

Katie bowed her head. "Because of what I can do. My father gave me to Miguel as a gift. But he is vicious and cruel. I hate him! And what he's doing to The Appointed…" she broke off, letting his own imagination supply the picture.

"Sit!" Christophe said.

Katie dropped down to the hard, narrow bunk. Christophe remained standing, though it was clear that this gave him pain.

"Will you not sit also?" Katie said. "You are ill, and I will not harm you. I have no weapon."

For the first time, Christophe smiled slightly. "You would not have been allowed to see me if you had. You would not have left this ship alive." He hesitated, then sat beside Katie. They tried to keep their distance from one another, but the confined space meant that they were pressed close together.

Katie felt a strange sensation at Christophe's proximity. It was half unease, half excitement. With difficulty she mastered her thoughts and said, "I bring The Appointed her meals. We have become friends. We, Miguel's servants, have often spoken of The Appointed, out of our master's hearing of course. Very few of us work for him willingly."

"And what is it that you can do?"

"I can see things," said Katie quietly. "I can learn things about the past or the future. I just ask a question before I sleep and hold it in my mind and the answer comes to me as a dream. That is how I knew you were alive and where to find you. Fiona told me about you. About how you fetched her from another world and how you were wounded and left for dead when Miguel and his men took her prisoner. She has told me everything and I want to help her."

Christophe's expression was unreadable.

"A useful gift indeed. I am surprised Miguel ever let you out of his sight. You must have learned a lot of useful information for him. You do realise that by placing yourself in our hands, you effectively sealed your own death. We cannot possibly allow you to go free."

"I would never betray you!" Katie said fiercely. "Do you think I would help Miguel after the way he has treated me? I could have told him that you were alive and his men would have sunk your ship where it lies. But I said nothing. I came here at my own risk. I wish to rescue The Appointed and I am your only hope. Kill me, and you will have lost her for ever."

Christophe was looking at her intently, and there was something almost like respect in his eyes. Perhaps no one has ever stood up to him before, Katie reflected.

"What is your price?" he said simply.

Katie took a deep breath. This was it. All or nothing. The big gamble. She tried not to think that the cost might be her life.

"I know a way into Miguel's house. Many of these old merchant's houses have underground passages that lead from caves on the beach to their cellars. They used to use them for smuggling and probably still do. Miguel has been a smuggler for years. How do you think he obtained his wealth? But he believes the whereabouts of the passage is a secret known only to him. He certainly doesn't know that I know of it. I can lead your men to this passage and I have first-hand knowledge of the interior of the house. If we succeed in rescuing The Appointed, I ask that you take me with you. My gift could be useful."

"And what makes you think I would trust a single word you say? Given what you have told me."

Katie felt herself growing angry. "What difference does your trust make to me? I am dead either way. If I have deceived you, then you will kill me. If not you, then Miguel will. I have betrayed him. I cannot win. But I will not return to

Miguel, I refuse to spy for him. Send me away or kill me now. The power lies with you."

Christophe smiled. "So it seems. I will speak with Antonio. You will have the decision in the morning. You will spend tonight on the ship under guard, but you will be treated courteously. Gideon!"

The door opened and the boy who had escorted Katie stuck his head in.

"This girl is to spend the night on the ship as my guest. See that she is given food and a bed and place a guard to watch over her."

Gideon nodded and beckoned to Katie. She followed him out of the little cabin, her eyes on Christophe all the while.

As soon as she was gone, Christophe settled back on his bunk, deep in thought. His weariness had momentarily lessened its hold of him. His thoughts were all of Katie. He wondered why he had never heard of her before. A girl with a gift such as that would have been a gold mine for any spy. She was clearly a descendant of one of the original mer families, and she had learned to use her gift unaided. Miguel clearly valued her highly, and he had hidden her successfully.

Christophe tried to think of any reason why she would betray him. There was the possibility of course that she had been sent by Miguel to lure them into a trap, so destroying all Alfredo's enemies with one blow. But there was also the problem that Katie could have been entirely truthful. After all, the majority of servants of rich families were slaves caught and sold at auctions. They had no loyalty to their masters. Katie had risked a lot to leave Miguel and come to find him. If he ignored her, he could be sentencing The Appointed to death. If he followed Katie, he could be dooming not only The Appointed, but a number of good men as well. Men the Guardians could ill afford to lose.

Christophe wrestled with his indecision. What made it more difficult was the affect Katie's presence had had on him. It had been wholly unexpected. He remembered how agreeable it had been to feel her slight body pressed so close to his own. He remembered the quick, bright intelligence of her gaze and the scent of her hair… Christophe forced himself to break off this train of thought, but he was disturbed. He had never felt anything more than a passing regard for any girl before. But for Katie, he felt a powerful sense of curiosity, mingled with admiration of her courage.

He sighed. He must go before Antonio, but what should he say? He could not bear to fail a second time. The consequences would be far worse than a wound in his side. Apart from the lives that would be forfeited, there was also the matter of his self-respect. He had precious little of that at present.

There came another knock at his door.

"Who is it?" he said wearily. His tiredness was creeping up on him once more, and he felt the pain of his side more acutely than he had all day.

"It's James," came the reply.

Christophe was mildly surprised. He hadn't seen much of James since his return to consciousness. He'd had the feeling that James was avoiding him. He supposed he couldn't blame him.

"Come in," he called.

James backed into the little cabin as Christophe once more pulled himself into a sitting position.

"That girl," James began immediately. "The one who came to see you. She had some news about Fiona?"

Christophe nodded.

"Is she alive?"

Close to, James looked as ill as Christophe. His face had a tight, strained look. His eyes were red from lack of sleep, and worry lines criss-crossed his forehead. Christophe felt an unexpected stab of pity for the other boy.

"She is alive. The girl comes offering her help and a plan of rescue. She is one of Miguel's slaves."

James's eyebrows rose. "But how did she find us?"

His alarm was understandable. Christophe wished he could offer some reassurance, but he himself was already half expecting an attack force to strike at any moment.

"She has a powerful magic that enables her to learn anything she wishes to know. She asks a question, and is shown the answer in a dream. She has befriended The Appointed and wishes to help her. She used her talent to locate us."

"That was really brave!" James said, unable to keep the admiration from his voice. "Miguel will kill her if he finds out."

"Very possible."

There was a look of hope and excitement in James's eyes now.

"And she says she knows how we can rescue Fiona? How?"

"She claims that there is a secret passage that leads from somewhere on the beach, directly into Miguel's cellar."

"Why would there be a passage into Miguel's house?"

"Lots of smugglers use passages for transferring goods to their houses. Alfredo has banned smuggling, so this enables people like Miguel to carry on in secret. It's also useful for a spy to have a secret way in or out of his house. It means he can come and go unmolested."

"But this is perfect!" James exclaimed, his face alive with excitement. "We've tried to get in from the outside and it's impossible. This way, we can sneak up, and by the time they realise we're there, it'll be too late. Miguel won't know what hit him."

Christophe said nothing, but frowned pensively at his knees. His lack of enthusiasm was not lost on James.

"I take it you're not overly keen on this idea?"

Christophe nodded.

"But why not? We haven't any better plan, and time's running out on us. It won't be long before Miguel realises that Fiona's no threat to his master, and then..." he couldn't bear to finish that particular sentence. He took several deep breaths. "What exactly is your problem?"

"Has it not occurred to you that Miguel could have planned this whole thing? He sends his most trusted servant to lure us into his trap with The Appointed as the bait. We come out into that cellar to find twenty knives pointed at our throats. Miguel's men promptly dispatch us and Miguel kills The Appointed when he or his master chooses. All threats dealt with in one swoop. Quite neat, wouldn't you agree?"

James was breathing rapidly, gnawing at his lower lip, his hands clenched fists at his sides. "But she could be telling the truth. If there's even the smallest chance of rescuing Fiona, then we've got to try! Or isn't she important enough to risk your neck for?"

There was an awful pause. Christophe got to his feet. Ignoring the pain, he stood facing James, his eyes blazing. "I would remind you that just under a week ago, I was attacked and left for dead 'risking my neck' as you put it, for The Appointed. I entered your violent and polluted world to find her and bring her back to my people. When my parents' house was burning, I escaped with the book that had been given to my father, instead of staying to help my parents!" His voice broke. He collapsed once more on the bunk, his face turned away from James. His side throbbed worse than ever and his heart was racing. What on earth had made him say that? He had never spoken about his past to anyone.

He felt a tentative hand on his shoulder and looked up. James was crouched beside him, his face stricken.

"I'm really sorry, Christophe, I shouldn't have said that. It wasn't fair."

Christophe was surprised and touched. James had shown nothing but hostility towards him until now. Perhaps for the first time, he really saw James for what he was. Until that moment he had viewed him as a nuisance who had interfered in matters that were not his concern. Now, he saw a boy not unlike himself. They had more in common than he had previously thought. They were both, in their different ways, devoted to The Appointed, and her safety and well-being was their primary concern. They should be allies, not enemies.

"It is of no matter," Christophe said gruffly. "Though I would prefer it if you kept what I have told you to yourself. Not even The Appointed needs to know."

"Sure!" James said hastily. And in that moment, a current of understanding passed between them. It needed no words, and James left immediately after. But they both knew what Christophe's decision would be, and both slept better that night than any since Fiona's capture.

* * *

Katie found it difficult to sleep. Her body ached with exhaustion, but her brain was active and would not allow her eyes to close. Her ears strained for any sound. She half expected men to come storming in any minute. After all, if it was decided that she was a threat, she would not escape.

Her thoughts turned to Christophe. She wasn't exactly sure what she had been expecting. She had imagined a thug, a ruffian, brutish and insolent, after everything she'd heard. But these descriptions did not even begin to match the boy who had sat so close to her. He had been a curious mixture of courtesy and danger. He had remained outwardly cool, displaying nothing of his emotions. He reminded her forcibly of her father, and she felt disturbed and intrigued by him. He was quite good looking too in a battered kind of way. She saw again his intense grey eyes. The lines of pain carved into his lean face, the wayward lock of dark hair that fell across his forehead. She wanted to know more of him. Perhaps she would before this mission was done.

She supposed she must have fallen asleep at last, because the next thing she was aware of was someone knocking at her door. She shot bolt upright. Shafts of sunlight were filtering through the tiny porthole. She threw an arm across her eyes.

"Yes?" she called groggily.

The boy who had taken her to Christophe entered.

"You must come with me."

"Where?" Katie demanded, fully awake now and alert. What was happening? Had Christophe decided to let her be killed after all?

"There is a meeting. Your presence is required. Come!" Without another word, he strode out of the cabin.

Katie hurried after him, hastily attempting to smooth her rumpled hair and clothing. Well, it didn't look as if they were going to kill her yet. Or, her pessimistic side wondered, perhaps this was a trial, and her sentence of execution would be decided. She briefly allowed her imagination to indulge in a picture of a jeering crowd voting among themselves the manner of her death, before resolutely pushing the thought away. Whatever happened, she would not show fear. If she was to die, she would not give Christophe or anyone else that satisfaction.

The crowd was even more vast than she had imagined. Young and old, men and women, children and adults, they thronged the quayside. As she was led ashore, they all followed her with their eyes. Some wore expressions of mild curiosity, others, pronounced mistrust. Katie's eyes sought out Christophe. She spotted him almost immediately, standing to the forefront of the crowd, a fair-haired boy at his side. Katie's eyes widened slightly in recognition. He had been one of the boys with Christophe in that hovel. And now she came to think of it, the boy escorting her had been there too. She came to a halt, facing Christophe and the crowd, with her escort on her right, and a girl who could only be his sister on her left.

The girl ignored her completely, but the fair-haired boy next to Christophe was staring fixedly at her. She wondered if this was the friend Fiona had mentioned. He looked pale and strained, and the look in his eyes was clear, a mixture of eagerness and anticipation. He had pinned his hopes on her whatever the others said.

Christophe stepped forward then and all talk ceased instantly. Katie was reminded once again of the way people behaved in her father's presence. Christophe too instantly demanded respect, though he was so young. His face was tired, but his eyes were as alert as ever. A gentle breeze lifted his dark hair.

He stood unaided, proud and upright, and if he felt any pain or discomfort, he gave no sign. Katie felt her admiration increase.

"People," Christophe began. "As you know, The Appointed still remains captive. So far, every plan of rescue we have attempted has failed, and time is rapidly running out, for us, as well as for her. Alfredo grows stronger with every passing moon. He needs one thing only to make him unstoppable. Our one hope for salvation lies in The Appointed. She must be rescued if we are to have any hope of ending Alfredo's rule for ever."

He beckoned to Katie, who stared at him, surprised, then walked over to stand beside him.

Without looking at her again, Christophe continued. "This girl came to visit me last night. She is a servant in Miguel's house, and has watched over The Appointed during her captivity. She comes with a proposal for rescuing The Appointed, and to offer her aid. I now invite her to speak."

Katie's jaw dropped. What was Christophe doing? She had not expected this at all. She had thought to win Christophe over, not an entire crowd of strangers, many of whom were looking at her with thinly veiled hostility. She knew a moment of panic. Christophe had stepped back from her, one of the crowd. She was alone.

"Thank you, Christophe," she said awkwardly, inclining her head in his direction. She swallowed again and continued, her words coming more fluently as she spoke. "My name is Katie. I have looked after The Appointed during her captivity and heard her story. My master, Miguel, has been ordered to extract from The Appointed whatever she can tell him of the treasure Alfredo seeks, and then to destroy her. I am Miguel's servant, but I have no loyalty to him. I, like many of his slaves, and like you also, have long cherished the hope that The Appointed would one day come to free us. I for one, wish to help her in any way I can, and her need is dire. I come with a plan to break into Miguel's house and remove The Appointed as speedily as we can."

"And how do you suggest we do that?" someone demanded loudly. "We have tried every possible method of breaking into that house. It is like a fortress. Alfredo himself could not be more closely guarded. There are sentries at every entrance. Regular patrols prowl like jackals. There is no way to approach the house unseen."

"What you say is true," Katie said. "It is impossible to surprise Miguel from the outside. The house is impregnable. Therefore, we must approach The Appointed from within."

There was a moment of stunned silence.

"Is this a trick, girl?" a thick-set man demanded, stepping forward menacingly, a hand to his dagger. A man whom Katie presumed to be the leader of the Guardians raised a warning hand and the man froze in his tracks.

"We will hear her out," he said quietly. The man returned to his place in the crowd.

Katie felt shaken, and it was with an effort that she collected her thoughts. "There is a passage leading from one of the old smuggler's caves directly into

Miguel's cellar. Miguel believes the passage to be a secret and has placed no guard there, or in the cellar at the other end. It was by this route that I was able to come to you. You will have the element of surprise on your side. While your fighters distract Miguel's men, I will lead you to The Appointed and guide you all safely out again."

There was a moment's absolute silence. Katie longed to slip away. She was not used to being the centre of attention. She felt utterly exposed and vulnerable. Why had Christophe placed her in this position? Was it a test? If the crowd turned on her, would he lift a finger to stop them? He still had not said what his own feelings were. She felt a dribble of sweat slide down her spine. The sun burned the back of her neck.

"You are asking us to trust you?" the thick-set man demanded. "You expect us to believe you? One of Miguel's servants?" He made a derisive noise, then addressed his people.

"This girl is a spy! Follow her, and you will be led into a trap. Miguel has sent this girl to lure us out of hiding. I say we do not give her the chance. I would die before I would accept help from the likes of her!" He spat contemptuously.

Katie felt a rush of anger. This had gone on long enough. Some people were muttering in agreement, while others still remained doubtful. Christophe's face gave nothing away. Katie decided all at once to end this game. She would not be toyed with. It was with a considerable effort that she kept her voice calm as she looked her accuser squarely in the eye.

"Kill me then, but remember that when you do, The Appointed dies with me, along with all hope of freedom. End my life and bear that on your conscience. You will have very little time to wonder if you did the right thing."

The man lunged forward with a cry, drawing his dagger, but Christophe took a step forward, one hand coming up. Only Katie saw him wince.

"Enough!" the single word cut the air like a whip crack. Christophe's eyes flashed and the man froze once more where he stood. "Remember your oaths, Brock. No one kills unless in defence of their life or in battle and never the unarmed or helpless. Even a traitor is not killed unless a unanimous verdict of treachery is reached. You would do well to remember that, unless you wish to lose your guardianship."

Brock flushed and shuffled his feet, but looked no less defiant.

"What then would you have us do?"

"I would have us use our common sense," Christophe replied. "We must rescue The Appointed. This is the only way. I see no other. We will let this girl's conduct vouch for her. If she is true, and The Appointed is returned to us, then she will be given a place of honour among us. If she plays us false," Christophe hesitated fractionally, then continued, "then the sentence is death, as befits all traitors."

All eyes now turned to the leader of the Guardians, who nodded. "I believe that what Christophe says is true. Let us put it to the vote. All in favour?"

Instantly, James's hand shot into the air. Christophe's was only fractionally slower. Hands went up all over the quay, until only Brock was left standing with his hands balled into fists at his sides. Everyone stared at him. Then, with a shrug, as though the whole affair was of no further interest, he raised his hand, and retreated to his place, sheathing his dagger.

Katie felt slightly dizzy with relief. She had done it. She had some time. Christophe had given her that. But if he had saved her with one hand, he had doomed her with the other. If something went wrong or her intent was discovered, then she would die by a unanimous vote. Still, she had been given a chance.

The crowd was breaking up now. Katie turned, wanting to say something to Christophe, though she hardly knew what. But he was already moving away, supported between the brother and sister who had stood with her. He did not so much as glance in her direction. Katie was puzzled. He had saved her life, but he seemed to want nothing more to do with her. She felt oddly hurt by this, and this in turn made her angry. What did she care? Christophe was a criminal. She needed neither his notice nor his pity, but she was hurt all the same by his abrupt dismissal of her. She debated going after him, but at that moment, the fair-haired boy accosted her.

"You said you'd been looking after Fiona." It wasn't a question. Katie nodded, wondering what was coming now.

"Is she alright? Are they hurting her?"

Close to, Katie could see the dark circles under his eyes. He looked so pale and anxious that her anger faded. She tried to smile reassuringly.

"I have been taking care of her. She has not been badly hurt. She has told Miguel a fabricated story that has sent him away from home and bought us some time. At the moment, she is as safe as she can be." That was, unless Miguel returned before she did.

James nodded. "What are our chances of getting her out of there? Realistically."

Katie sighed. "Realistically, they are not high. Our one advantage will be that Miguel has not guarded the passage. We should be able to take him by surprise. But Miguel's men are hardened fighters. They will not simply allow us to walk away unmolested. It is more than their lives are worth. These Guardians had better be able to live up to their name."

James nodded once more. "But why are you helping Fiona? You don't need to. I expect Miguel will kill you if he catches you."

Katie's laugh was short and harsh. "And these people will kill me if Miguel catches you. There is little hope for me either way."

James remained silent, still waiting for an answer to his question.

Katie sighed. "I like Fiona," she said truthfully. "She has told me how she came to be here. She is the innocent one in all this. I would not see her harmed."

James's voice was thick. "Neither would I." He started to turn away, then paused. "I trust you," he said simply, then he was gone.

Katie bowed her head. She felt James's trust like a weight around her neck. More final than any death sentence.

* * *

Christophe was once more alone in his cabin. The decision was made. They would rescue The Appointed tonight. His side twinged painfully. He was in no condition to be attempting dangerous rescue missions. He ignored it. Of course he would be there. He had sworn to protect The Appointed.

His thoughts turned once more to Katie. She had handled herself well. He had sought to test her and she had risen to the challenge with courage and skill. She had convinced almost the entire population of the Travellers, no easy task. He could not help but admire her. He would like to have told her so, but he could not be seen to be showing any favour towards her when her credibility was still in doubt.

There came a knock on his door.

"Enter!"

James, Gideon and Esther squeezed into the tiny cabin, purposeful looks on their faces.

Christophe shot them a quizzical look. "Well?"

"We've been thinking," James began awkwardly.

"Oh? What about?"

"About you," James pressed on. "We don't think you should come with us to rescue Fiona. We think you should stay behind."

Christophe's face darkened. "Of course I am coming," he said shortly. "The Appointed is my responsibility."

"But you are hurt!" Esther said earnestly. "You cannot fight Miguel's men. You will be killed."

"I have as much chance of surviving as anyone else," Christophe said sharply.

"Don't be thick," James said. "That might have been true a couple of weeks ago, but you've had your side slashed open since then, and you've only got full use of one arm. You're no good to anyone dead, least of all Fiona."

Christophe was silent. There was truth in that. He had to admit it, though it was a serious blow to his pride. His sense of frustration was acute. He was not used to being helpless.

"I would protect her in your place," Gideon said quietly. "I would lay down my life for her."

"Please, Christophe," there were tears in Esther's eyes. "You can go with The Appointed when she leaves us, just as you planned, but stay here and get well."

They were right. He knew it, though it infuriated him. He was in no condition to hold off Miguel's ruffians. He had made it his duty to protect The Appointed, to keep her safe until her task was done. He had failed her once. He could not let that happen again. He needed to recover his strength. He nodded. The relief on all their faces was evident. He turned away.

"Leave me!" They exited in silence.

* * *

Night fell over the city, covering it in a blanket of darkness and expectation. There was a storm coming. All could feel it. The tension in the air was almost palpable, and it had a heavy, muggy feel. All over the city, there was a sense of foreboding. Shops and stalls had shut up early. People had barricaded themselves inside their houses, fearing for their crops, remembering how the last storm had destroyed them utterly, and wondering where they would get the money for their next meal. An unnatural hush had descended. Even the seabirds had ceased their incessant calling, and huddled in their nests to wait out the coming storm.

In his house, Alfredo sat brooding over Miguel's failure, and hoping that it was not too late for his daughter to fix the situation.

Miguel had paid no attention to the weather as he hurried home, too incensed to care, and now, it only matched his mood.

In the cellars, Fiona was not aware of anything but the huge, grey shapes that scuttled ever closer, growing braver with every passing minute, and her own sense of fear and despair.

Christophe paced uneasily up and down the watch deck, pain and fatigue forgotten, shunning all attempts at conversation. His thoughts following the little fleet of row boats as it pulled away from the *Dolphin*, the sound of oars very loud in the unnatural silence.

James kept his head bent, feeling the rise and fall of the boat beneath him, the stillness only increasing his trepidation. He was in the lead boat with Katie, and also Gideon, Brock, and Carlotta, the girl he had watched use the bow and slingshot to such great effect. They made up three of the twenty Guardians who had been assigned to The Appointed. Her personal protection. Some of the most hardened and experienced fighters hand-picked by Antonio. Katie and himself brought the number to twenty-two altogether. He hoped that would be enough. He had never done any fighting except with his fists, and he could count the number of occasions on one hand. He was not a violent person, and it had only ever been out of the necessity to defend himself. He wondered how much experience Katie had. Not much, he guessed. She was not there to fight. She was there to guide them to Fiona, and safely away once more.

There were lanterns in the boats to guide the way, turned low, so that they illuminated only what was immediately ahead. Shapes loomed suddenly out of the night, only to disappear again just as suddenly.

James realised he was sitting rigidly in his seat and forced himself to relax. Though the night was warm, he could not suppress the chill that crept over his skin. His eyes scanned the darkness continuously, searching for he hardly knew what. Then, as a sudden patch of rocky headland rose up ahead of them, he heard Katie's low murmur.

"This is the place."

Brock and Gideon did not pause the rhythm of their oars, but Carlotta nodded once to show she had heard, and signalled to the boat immediately behind. Antonio made a sign in response, and signalled the boat following him.

Gideon and the Guardians had developed a system of signs and symbols, a language with which they could communicate in difficult situations. There were at least four or five ways of saying the same thing, so that it was impossible for anyone studying the communication to decipher a code or pattern. It also meant that the Guardians could make plans and pass on information in perfect silence.

Carlotta turned up the lantern a little to light their way more clearly. It was a nasty stretch of water. The rocks rose sheer and cruel, with jagged edges reminiscent of human jaws waiting to swallow unwary ships. It took all of the Guardians' considerable skill to guide the little boats safely through to the small pebble beach. James stepped down into the shallows and helped to drag the little craft ashore. He could hear others doing the same. They concealed the boats as best they could in some sparse patches of scrub. It was a perfect drop-off point for smugglers. No one would willingly attempt to navigate those treacherous rocks who didn't know them well. James wondered how many ships had been wrecked off this coast, and how many men had been sent to their doom.

When the boats were safely hidden, Antonio called them all around him and they gathered in a close huddle, barely able to see one another in the blackness.

"Now for it, friends," he whispered. He beckoned Katie forward and gave her one of the lanterns. "You will lead us to the caves and this passage. When we arrive, you will take a couple of us to The Appointed and—"

"I'm going with her," James said firmly. "Fiona's my friend. She hardly knows any of you." His jaw was set stubbornly. Antonio opened his mouth to object, then seemed to think better of it.

"Very well. Gideon and Carlotta will go with you as your personal protection. When you have The Appointed, come straight back here as soon as you can. Do not wait for us. Your task is to get The Appointed away as quickly and as safely as possible. The rest of us will seek to distract Miguel's men and buy you time. Do you understand?" Everyone nodded.

Antonio nodded at Katie. "Lead on."

Without a word, Katie began leading the way up the beach, picking her way with care, the lantern held up before her. James followed immediately after her slight figure.

He and Katie, like the rest of the Guardians, were dressed in black, so that they blended seamlessly into the night around them. Their faces were hooded, and James could only see their ghostly silhouettes flitting through the night like wraiths. The crunch of gravel under his feet sounded excessively loud and he winced. The Guardians hardly seemed to make any noise at all. They were like night hunters intent on their prey. James tried to tread carefully, but it made no difference. The ground was rocky and uneven and ascended steeply. Every now and then he stumbled, sending a rock skittering from under his feet away down the slope. He was breathing heavily by the time the ground levelled out.

Katie stepped behind a massive boulder and stopped. She held up the lantern and cast its light in a wide arc. Before her, a well of even deeper darkness yawned like a cavernous hungry mouth.

"These are the caves," she said. "The old smuggler's caves. They lead right up into the city and branch off into the sewers. There are catacombs beneath every street."

"And you can get us to Miguel's house, can you? Without getting lost?" It was Brock. His voice was harsh and sceptical. He turned to Antonio. "I say we tie her up and put a dagger to her throat. That should get rid of any temptation to go running off and leave us lost in the maze."

Katie stiffened, but Antonio spoke up firmly.

"That will not be necessary, Brock. We are all comrades here, or should be. However, I think we should all be roped together for safety's sake. That way there is no risk of any of us getting separated."

Brock nodded grudgingly. "But who is going to be tied to her. It ought to be someone armed in case she tries anything."

"Enough, Brock!" Antonio snapped.

"I'll go next," James said quickly, hoping that by putting himself in the way it would keep Katie safe from anyone like-minded as Brock. They needed Katie alive and well at all costs, or Fiona was lost.

Antonio nodded and unwound a thick coil of tough fishing line from his waist, playing it out to its full length. He handed one end to James who stepped forward. He looked questioningly at Katie who nodded and allowed him to tie the rope about her waist. James then attached himself with Antonio a step behind him. When they were all linked up, Katie stepped forward into the blackness.

It felt to James as though he was stepping into Hell. Katie led them through one cave after another; a seemingly endless maze. The floor was slippery and rutted and their muffled footsteps echoed eerily.

Katie paused at last in a cave that seemed no different to any of the others they'd passed through, and swept the ground all around her feet with the lantern. It fell on a metal ring sunk deep into the floor. Katie set the lantern down and bent to the ring, heaving at it. James bent to lend a hand. They heaved and, with a grating sound, a piece of the rock floor swung up and over revealing a deep shaft below. A powerful draught rushed up into James's face and he shivered. Katie held the lantern to show what lay before them. A flight of shallow steps, hewn from the rock, leading down into the bowels of the earth. Without a word, Katie led the way forward, James close on her heels.

The steps seemed to go on for ever, but at last they ended. James stepped down into a low tunnel that wound away from him into the distance. Katie did not even check her pace. The passage sloped steeply downwards, carrying them even deeper underground. There were forks and side turnings. It was a veritable maze of passages, all descending. Katie walked on confidently, never hesitating. James marvelled at how she could find her way with such apparent ease. He could not know that the visions Katie had been sent guided her as surely as a map imprinted on her brain. Her memory never forgot a thing once it was shown her.

The air was thick with the smell of the sea, and underneath it, a damp musty smell that grew stronger as they descended. It was unmistakably the sewers. The air was damp and freezing. James was shivering as he walked. Every now and then a large drop of water would drip from the walls to land with a loud plink. James began to wonder if they'd ever get out, or if they'd be wandering these loathsome tunnels for ever. Perhaps Brock was right and Katie was simply intending to lead them so far underground that they would have no hope of finding their way out again, and then abandon them. But almost as soon as the thought formed, he realised that the passage had begun to rise. Soon it was climbing steeply. James could feel sweat on his face and running down his back, while his feet still remained numb with cold. Then a flight of stone steps rose before them. They ascended these swiftly, until they ended abruptly in a solid stone wall. Katie held up the lantern once more, and James saw an iron ring set into the wall, identical to the one that gained them entrance to the passages. He stepped forward, and he and Katie tugged the ring up. A slab of stone swung out of the wall, and they all stepped through into an underground room, filled with boxes and cases of every size and shape imaginable. They filled almost every available space, and some piles reached halfway up the wall. James let out his breath. Mïguel certainly didn't do anything by halves. But he didn't have time to dwell on this, for the others were already untying themselves, and Antonio was whispering rapid orders.

"James, you and Katie will go with Gideon and Carlotta and rescue The Appointed. Give us a chance to get clear of you. A minute will do. When you have recovered her, return to the boats. The rest of us will make our way back by whatever path we can. If you don't find any of us waiting for you, return to the *Dolphin* as quickly as you can. We must aim to return before the storm strikes."

James felt the rope slip free.

"Good luck, everyone," said Antonio. "May courage and fortune be yours." It was the usual farewell. The Guardians laid their hands briefly over one another's, including James and Katie's, then they separated.

James gave them a few moments to get clear, forcing himself to wait until the last footsteps had receded, and then counting to sixty in his head.

"Where now?" he whispered.

"The Appointed is locked in one of the attics at the top of the house." Katie whispered back. "Come!" She led the way, James immediately behind her. Gideon and Carlotta brought up the rear, weapons drawn. James was thankful for their presence.

As they emerged from the cellars, distant shouts reached their ears.

"It has begun," Gideon said grimly, his hand tightening on his knife. Carlotta nocked an arrow to her bow, her face an expressionless mask.

Katie did not hesitate. She flitted along passages as silently as a ghost. The shouting grew louder, mixed with the definite sounds of battle.

They hurried up a staircase and came out on a landing where a lone Guardian was battling against two huge men built like tanks. There was yet another staircase leading upwards, and one glance at Katie's face told James that was exactly where they needed to go, but how? Gideon and Carlotta didn't hesitate. They leaped to their comrade's aid.

"Go on!" Gideon shouted. "We will catch up to you."

Katie darted for the stairs, James following, but with a roar of fury, one of the men rose to block their way, both massive fists swinging. One sent Katie flying, the other knocked James head over heels. The man lunged again, but froze with a grunt. James lifted his head in time to see the man pitch forward onto his face, a feathered arrow protruding from his back. James felt ill. His head swam. He could not take his eyes from the lifeless form, but then Katie seized his arm and hauled him to his feet.

"Move!" she screamed.

They ran up the next staircase and started along a new landing. There was a sense of urgency in James now, a barely controlled feeling of panic. How on earth was he to get Fiona out of this?

Then just as they were passing a door set back into a small alcove, it opened and a woman's face looked out, her eyes fixing on Katie. She looked pale, but if she was afraid, her face showed no sign. And her voice when she spoke was urgent but perfectly steady.

"Miguel has moved her. He took her to the cellars about an hour ago."

Katie paused.

"Jessemine!" she began, but the woman shut the door in her face with a snap.

"Come on!" she called frantically to James. "She is in the cellars. We must get to her before Miguel does! Now he knows we have come to rescue Fiona, he will kill her!"

James made no argument. His heart was beating rapidly as cold fear and dread stabbed through him. In the cellars! If only they'd known! They could have sneaked her away and Miguel would have been none the wiser. And now it could be too late. Miguel would kill Fiona rather than give her the chance to escape. If his master couldn't have what he wanted, then no one would. James dashed after Katie, yelling frantically to Gideon and Carlotta as they passed.

"She's in the cellars! Quick, before Miguel gets to her!"

Gideon and Carlotta, along with the other Guardian were fighting the other huge man. He seemed to have worked himself into a frenzy, and it was taking the combined efforts of all three Guardians to subdue him. As James and Katie appeared, they finally succeeded in bringing the man to the ground. At James's words, Gideon and Carlotta broke off the attack and ran after him. James saw their comrade leap on the fallen man, his knife glinting, but he wrenched his eyes away and kept running.

They had reached the ground floor now, they were almost there. Then James skidded. His feet slid in separate directions and he fell. Looking down, he saw to his horror that he was kneeling in a pool of blood.

Brock lay nearby, bleeding from knife wounds to his chest, stomach and head, his blood forming an ever widening pool around him.

The others turned back to find him and saw Brock.

"Father!" the word was wrenched from Carlotta as she flung herself down at Brock's side. James realised that this was the first word he had heard her speak.

At the sound of her voice, Brock's eyes flickered open. Incredibly, the man was still alive, though not for long, even James could see that.

"Father!" Carlotta whispered. She was trembling. The dying man reached for her hand and grasped it.

"Daughter, you must leave here. Do what you came here to do."

"We cannot leave you!" Gideon said firmly. "We will take you with us."

"No!" Brock snapped. "I would slow you down. The Appointed is your first concern. Save her." A spasm of pain wracked him. "Look after your mother!" he gasped to Carlotta. "And your brothers and sisters. Protect them in my stead. I am counting on you."

Tight-lipped, Carlotta nodded. Brock sighed once, then fell still.

For a moment, they all froze where they were, numbed by horror and grief. Then rapidly nearing yells brought them back to their senses.

"They have found us," breathed Gideon. He turned to James and Katie. "Save The Appointed. Carlotta and I will hold them off."

James nodded. He and Katie turned and began to run once more. The men burst into the passage behind them, and they heard Carlotta's scream of fury as she threw herself at her attackers. Neither looked back.

The cellars were quiet. There were at least ten identical doors lining the corridors. James felt his heart sink. Which one was Fiona in? And how would they get her out? They had no key. James turned to Katie, a question forming on his lips, when a voice spoke behind them.

"Looking for these?" James and Katie whirled. Miguel was smiling at them, a bunch of keys cupped loosely in his hand. His eyes, as they bored into them, were murderous. This is it, James thought dully. He must have been with those men. He's set them on Gideon and Carlotta so he could come after us.

Miguel's eyes fixed on Katie. "So here is my little runaway. You used the passage I suppose. I had no idea you even knew it existed, but then, I suppose your other worldly senses told you. And you," his gaze shifted to James. "A friend of The Appointed, come to rescue her, perhaps? How very foolish of you. How exceedingly—"

Katie sprang. It was so sudden that it took both Miguel and James utterly by surprise. She fastened onto him like a leech. Nails tearing at his face. Heels driving into his ribs. Miguel snarled in pain and tried to throw her off, but her grip was tenacious. She was like some wild cat, her face a rictus of fury. Miguel tried to reach for his belt. James saw a glint of steel. With a cry, he leaped forward. He seized Miguel's wrist and twisted, at the same time driving his knee into the man's stomach. Miguel was winded but not beaten. Abandoning the attempt to reach his knife, he swung up his free hand and landed James a dizzying blow on the side of the head. Lights exploded behind James's eyes.

Katie was trying to pry Miguel's fingers from the bunch of keys, but Miguel's free hand had found her throat. Katie choked for air, but did not let go. Blinking the dizziness from his head, James flung himself into Miguel, and bore him to the ground in an awkward tackle, but Katie fell beneath him. Miguel was on top of her, hands still tight around her throat.

Then Carlotta and Gideon were there. They were on him in a flash and he was forced to release Katie. She rolled clear and James helped her to her feet. Her lip was bleeding and one eye was already beginning to close. She gasped for breath, leaning heavily against the wall. Gideon struck Miguel a well practised blow to his temple and the man lost consciousness instantly. He slumped to the floor, the keys sliding from his slack fingers. At once, Carlotta's knife was at his throat.

"No, don't kill him!"

Gideon and Carlotta turned to stare at James. Both were wounded. One sleeve of Carlotta's tunic was soaked with blood, and Gideon was using the wall as he supported himself. But their faces were grim, and Carlotta's eyes were as cold as winter.

"He has murdered many of our people," she said quietly. "And my father lies dead at his order. I will not spare such a man as that. He does not deserve it!" She spat the last words.

James felt sorry for her, but he stood his ground. "Don't kill him," he repeated firmly. "He's helpless. I didn't think the Guardians killed those who couldn't fight back, whoever they were. They'd be no better than their enemies then." They stared at him in astonishment, but he didn't wait for their objections.

"Carlotta, watch the passage. Gideon, look after Katie." Without waiting for arguments, he retrieved the fallen keys and moved back down the passage to the doors. He tried door after door, which took some time as he had to find which key fitted each door.

"Fiona, are you there? If you can hear me, answer me!" Another door, still no luck. Then a voice, faint and scared.

"James? Is that you? Is it really you?" He froze.

"Fiona? Where are you?"

"Here! I'm in here!"

James listened. The voice seemed to come from behind the last door; two doors along from where he was now. He hurried over, frantically shoving a key into the lock. It didn't fit. He tried another with the same result. The third key did it. The door swung open with a squeak of protest and Fiona tumbled out into his waiting arms.

"James! I never thought I'd see you again!" She clung to him, sobbing and trembling. He held her for a few moments, letting her cry, stroking her hair over and over. His relief at having found her again was so powerful that he felt tears blur his own vision. He held her tightly, and waited for both their emotions to subside. At last, he pushed her gently from him and examined her face. She was pale and drawn and her face was bruised and battered. There was a half-healed scab on her forehead, and she was very thin.

"Are you alright? Are you hurt?"

"I'm fine now, but how did you find me?"

"There's no time to explain. We've got to get out of here. It was Katie, she brought us to you."

Fiona stared at him in disbelief. "Katie?"

James put an arm around her and led her back to the others.

Carlotta was still scanning the empty passage. Katie was upright once more, standing away from the wall, and Gideon had torn his cloak into strips, which he was using to bind and gag a still prostrate Miguel.

Katie grinned when she saw Fiona. "I said I would find a way to rescue you. And now, I really think we should be going."

Fiona stared at her speechlessly for a moment, then, breaking free of James, she rushed over to the other girl and hugged her tightly. "Thank you so much, Katie, I don't know how I'll ever repay you for this."

Katie blushed and returned the embrace somewhat awkwardly. She was not used to physical demonstrations of affection and did not know how to respond.

"We should leave," said Carlotta. "I think I hear men coming."

They left Miguel locked in the cellar that had been Fiona's prison, and Katie led them once more through the trapdoor and back through the endless maze of passages and tunnels to the beach beyond. It seemed to take half the time it had taken to reach the cellars, but an unpleasant surprise awaited them when they eventually reached fresh air once more. A wind had got up and a few heavy spots of rain were already beginning to fall. In the distance, a low rumble of thunder sounded ominously.

Gideon wasted no time. Limping as quickly as a clearly injured ankle would allow, he made for the nearest boat. "Come, there isn't a moment to lose."

They dragged the boat down to the waves and piled in. Gideon and Carlotta took up the oars once again, while Katie, James and Fiona huddled together in the stern.

If the journey out of the caves had seemed half as long, then the return journey to the *Dolphin* took twice the time. No sooner were they out on the open sea, than the waves rose up alarmingly, threatening to swamp their little craft entirely. The boat pitched and rolled in the ever increasing swells and freezing spray was tipped over them in bucket loads. All the rowers could do was struggle through the turbulent waters, fighting with rapidly decreasing strength to keep the boat on course. The boat's passengers could only bow their heads and cling on for dear life as the wind tossed the boat like a plaything and freezing water soaked and chilled them to the marrow.

Then, just as Gideon and Carlotta were nearing the limit of their endurance, and James had about given them all up for dead, lights hove into view. Ships' lanterns signalling them home. Ropes were thrown and they were being hauled on board, to land in wet, shivering heaps on the deck. Then, with a flash of lightning that tore the sky in half, and a deafening clap of thunder, the storm broke over them. Driving rain fell in torrents, and there was a mad rush to get below. James wondered, as he was swept along with the others, if the rest of the rescue party would make it. He didn't hold out much hope for any of them.

# Chapter 11

## Tobias' Story

"Are you planning to sleep the day away by any chance?"

At the sound of James's voice, Fiona stirred reluctantly into wakefulness. The sun was well up, indicating how long she must have slept. All traces of the storm of the night before were gone as if it had never been.

She sat up and stretched, blinking against the sun. "This is the first decent night's sleep I've had in over a week."

James grinned and sat down on the bunk across from her. "You must have been exhausted to have slept through that storm. The rest of us have hardly closed our eyes all night."

"Was it really that bad?"

James's face grew serious. "I've never seen anything like it. The waves were enormous! I've never seen waves that high. One whole section of the jetty just disappeared; swept into the sea as if it had never existed. The Travellers certainly aren't stupid. It's lucky we're moored where we are."

Fiona nodded her agreement.

Her memories of the night before were patchy. She remembered her rescue and flight from Miguel's house clearly. And then there had been their struggle through the storm to reach the *Dolphin*, fearing that any moment they would capsize. She had a confused impression of faces and then someone leading her below, and after that, nothing. The terror she had lived through and her relief at being alive and safe once more, had given way to an exhaustion so profound that not even the storm's fury could trouble her.

"Did everyone get back OK?"

James shook his head. "We lost five men. They were killed fighting Miguel's thugs, but the others managed to bring their bodies back. One boat never turned up. Men were sent out to look for it as soon as the storm cleared. Only half the men that went with Katie and I to rescue you made it back. Gideon and his dad are OK though."

Fiona bowed her head. All those men dead because of her. The very thing she had never wanted to happen. She felt the guilt of their deaths like a physical weight in her chest. Their poor families! How they must hate her. She would in their place. Nothing she did would make up for their loss.

James gripped her shoulder firmly. "It wasn't your fault. They weren't forced to come. They were volunteers. They all wanted to see you safe."

"But it's my fault they're dead. It's because of me."

James could think of no reply to that. He hugged her tightly. Though he was sad for the men and their families, Fiona was safe once more, and that outweighed every other emotion. His joy and relief at finding her again had been so powerful that it had taken even him by surprise. He had not realised until she was taken from him, how empty his life was when she was not with him. The revelation had shocked and confused him. He didn't know what it meant. They had known each other since they were little. There had never been a time when Fiona was not an integral part of his life. She was his best friend, but that no longer seemed quite enough.

Fiona drew away from him finally.

"I missed you, James. I didn't think I'd see you again. I thought I was a goner. If not for you and Katie…" she broke off suddenly. Christophe had not been there last night. James had made no mention of him. Had anyone found him?

"Christophe," she said uncertainly. "Is he alive?"

"Yeah, amazingly. He was nearly dead when Gideon and I found him. He was unconscious and he had a really deep gash in his side. He was a real mess. But we took him to a healer Gideon knew of and she sorted him out. He's a lot better now, but his strength isn't fully back. With an injury like that, I reckon he'll never be what he was. It was with difficulty that we managed to persuade him to stay behind. He was all for coming with us, but he's not up to heroics yet, whatever he might think."

"Can I see him? I ought to, you know, thank him. I mean, he did try to save me."

"Sure! They're having the funerals for the men now, but I reckon you can speak to him after that."

Fiona sat up and fumbled for her boots.

"I want to go to the funeral. I owe those men that much."

"OK."

As she got to her feet, James put an arm round her to support her. She was still weak from lack of food.

"Are you alright?" he asked anxiously as they left the cabin. "Esther said you were covered in bruises."

The evidence was not entirely gone from her face.

Fiona did not reply, but a shadow of remembered pain and fear crossed her face briefly.

"Did they hurt you?" James said gently.

"A bit," Fiona muttered, "but I'm OK. It was Benjy and Claude. They're Miguel's chief thugs."

"They're dead," James said quietly.

Fiona stopped abruptly, turning to look up into his face.

"You're sure?"

James nodded. He didn't think he'd forget in a hurry the sight of that lifeless form with an arrow protruding from its back as the blood formed a pool around it.

He felt Fiona begin to tremble.

"Miguel just let them do their stuff while he sat and watched. He never batted an eyelid. I never thought anyone could be so…" she broke off, blinking furiously.

"Look, you don't have to meet the others yet. You've earned a rest. Wait till you're ready. They'll understand."

"No!" Fiona rubbed her sleeve fiercely across her eyes. "I need to do this. Please!"

James hesitated a moment, then, giving her arm a reassuring squeeze, he led her up on deck.

It seemed as though everyone had turned out for the ceremony. Not only those from the *Dolphin*, but also people from the other ships currently moored in the harbour.

The beach thronged with them, as it had on the day Fiona had first arrived. But unlike then, nobody made a sound. The bright clothes were gone, to be replaced by black or brown. There was no laughter or chatter. People stood in clusters, their faces sombre, apart from when they drifted over to offer condolences to the bereaved.

They were not hard to pick out. Dressed head to foot in black, with black bands on their arms and holding back their hair. The women had them sewn around the hems of their skirts as well.

As on the night of the festival of Mer, a clear space had been made. But there was no line of eager boys and girls there now.

Fiona's chest tightened as she saw the driftwood pyres, and the mounds completely covered by blankets that rested peacefully on each, as though they were merely sleeping. Fiona's eyes prickled, but no tears came, as much as she longed for their release. She had never known these men who had given their lives for her. She could never tell them how grateful she was, or how sorry. She felt she should speak to their families, but her heart quailed at the very thought. She could barely bring herself to look at them.

She was grateful when James led her over to stand with Esther and her family. Christophe was with them, with Katie standing close by. Katie smiled at Fiona, who ran and hugged her.

"I don't know what to say," she whispered into the other girl's hair. "You saved my life. If there's anything…" Katie laughed and gently pushed her away.

Then Fiona's eyes found Christophe. He was watching her, his gaze as intense and unreadable as ever. Fiona swallowed. With one arm in a sling and his battered face, he looked a mess. She had no idea what to say to him.

"How are you?" she finally managed. She wanted the words back as soon as they'd left her lips. What a stupid question. He was changed. His face was older and marked by premature lines around his mouth and eyes. Though he stood straight and upright, the pain was still visible in his face, and his eyes were dark with weariness. Fiona felt a stab of pity, an emotion she would never have expected to feel for this boy, and her guilt returned tenfold. She tried to cover it with a weak laugh.

"I thought you were dead."

A slight smile tugged at the corners of Christophe's lips. "Not quite."

Fiona blushed. Then impulsively, she held out her hand. "Thank you for what you did. I… I'm really glad you're OK. All the time I was shut up in Miguel's house, I thought you were…"

A spasm of emotion flitted across Christophe's face. It was hard to read. Fiona thought it might have been disgust, though not at her, she thought.

"I deserved to be. This wound will always remind me of the fate that should have been mine. If you will thank someone, thank Katie. She is the one you owe your life to, not I."

His voice was so hard and bitter that Fiona drew back startled. She wanted to deny his words, but did not know how. A pregnant pause followed, and it was Christophe who broke it.

"Are you well? Did they harm you?"

Fiona nodded distractedly. Then the words tumbled from her before she could change her mind. "If you still have that book, I'll read it. I'm not making any promises, mind, but I'll see what it has to say."

Christophe looked surprised. "Are you sure?"

Fiona sighed heavily. Her next words would seal her fate irrevocably, but it was the least she could do. "Yeah, I'm sure."

Christophe smiled genuinely for the first time. He clasped her fingers briefly.

"No promises, remember," Fiona said warningly. "I'm just reading it, OK?"

Christophe nodded.

"By the way," she added. "I didn't tell Miguel anything."

Christophe actually laughed. "What could you have told him, even if you had wanted to?"

Fiona made no answer. She had the feeling that she would have told Miguel everything he wanted to know, whether she knew anything or not. She turned to watch the funeral rites with the others.

A silence fell over the crowd. Fiona heard the sound of a few women weeping, the sound very audible in the sudden stillness. Even the birds had stilled their usual racket, as though in deference to the mourners. In contrast to the night before, the sea was completely smooth, the waves making hardly any noise as they broke over the sand.

Four men stepped forward bearing buckets of oil, which they proceeded to pour over the garments of the dead. Everyone broke into a low, murmuring chant, the soft cadence of their voices interspersed with sounds of sorrow.

It was a terrible sound. Fiona longed to cover her ears, to hide her eyes, to run, but she forced herself to stand and watch, her hands resolutely at her sides. Only she, Katie and James watched in silence, not being familiar with the words of the ceremony. But Fiona's lips moved along with everyone else's, as though her heart knew the words they were saying.

Then, at the last words, a sudden silence fell once more. The same four men stepped forward, all weeping freely, bearing burning brands of sticks and dried grass, also coated with oil. These they set to the pyres of driftwood which caught instantly. Then some women and children came forward, also with burning torches. Fiona realised with a jolt that these must be the dead men's families. They too added their fuel to the flames, saying as they did so, "It was the sea that gave you to us, and to the sea you now return. May you always have a place at the sea god's table."

By now the pyres were ablaze, the flames beginning to crackle fiercely. Fiona wondered if they would have to stay and watch the bodies be consumed, but people were already moving away.

As though she had read Fiona's thoughts, Esther said quietly, "No one may witness the god of the sea as he welcomes his children home. No one will return to the spot until every last trace of the ashes has been washed out with the tide. Only then will we know that our brothers are truly home where they belong."

Fiona made no answer. She could think of nothing to say. No words of hers could alter what had happened. She had to relieve her guilt or go mad, and she saw only one way.

"I'll see you later," she said to James. "I've got to find Christophe."

"Are you sure you want to do this? You don't have to, you know, no one can make you."

Fiona smiled wearily. "*I'm* making me. I have to do something. You understand, don't you?"

James squeezed her shoulder. "Yeah, of course I do. See you later then."

Christophe was in his cabin, exactly where she knew he would be. He was sitting on the narrow bunk, but rose as she entered, the book in one hand. Fighting a sudden feeling of foreboding, Fiona took it from him. It lay in her hands, nondescript, old and tattered. There was no inscription on the cover.

"I will leave you in peace," Christophe said.

"I don't want to turn you out of your cabin, you must need to rest."

Christophe grimaced. "If I spend any more time in this cabin, I shall go mad. I have seen more than enough of it these last few days."

Fiona gave a brittle laugh.

"I will be with James and Katie," said Christophe. "Come and find us when you have read what it has to say."

Fiona nodded and sat down heavily on the hard bunk.

Christophe left, closing the door quietly behind him.

Fiona sat motionless for several long moments after he had gone, staring at the closed door. The feeling of foreboding was back worse than before. She longed to hurl open that door and run as far and as fast as she could. But there was nowhere for her to go. She thought again of those men who had died for her. They had given up everything. Home, loved ones, all for her. It was a debt she could never repay, but she had to try, and if this was the only way then so be it. Sighing, she drew her legs up and settled with her back against the wall, Christophe's pillow behind her. Might as well be comfortable, she thought grimly.

She looked down once more at the book in her hands. The silver clasps holding the book shut were old and tarnished, but they looked sturdy. Christophe had said that no one had been able to open it. Perhaps she wouldn't either. A seed of hope blossomed in her chest. If she couldn't open it, then she would have done all she could. Her conscience would be clear. She could go home and forget this place for good. With this thought to spur her on, she tried to prise the clasps apart.

Her hopes fell away the next moment as the clasps sprang apart with no resistance at all, and the book fell open in her hands.

A chill breeze swept through the cabin, the cold so intense that it pierced Fiona to the marrow and made every breath hurt in her chest. A paralysis gripped her limbs with iron bands and as her eyes widened in shock, the pages began to snap and crackle in the wind. Finally, the book twitched itself completely out of her hands, to land on the floor with an audible thump. Fiona tried to scream, but the sound seemed trapped somewhere in the back of her throat.

The pages of the book were fluttering wildly now, though the chilling wind had not intensified. Finally it came to rest, lying open about halfway through. As Fiona watched in horrified fascination, a greenish mist began to rise from the heart of the book, swirling an eddying in the combined space. At first the mist simply drifted randomly about, but then it began to gather in on itself until it was hovering directly above the open book. Tendrils of fog started to coalesce into a shape and, as they did so, Fiona felt the iron bands gripping her limbs and crushing her chest begin to loosen. She gasped great lungfuls of air as the death numbing chill slowly receded from her bones.

Then Fiona saw the man. He was seated cross-legged on the floor, resting, in fact, in the very heart of the book. For a moment, Fiona's bemused brain grappled with this phenomenon. How could a fully grown man be sitting in a book as though it were a cosy armchair?

Even sitting down, Fiona could see that he was a big man. He wore a tunic and leggings similar to those the Guardians wore, though his feet were bare. He was very thin. His hair and beard were snow-white and the hands which were clasped on his knees were knotted and skeletal looking. His face was hollow and sunken as though he had been ill a long time, but the eyes, which were a deep clear blue, were bright and alert, and they were fixed on Fiona.

"Back at last." His voice made Fiona start. It filled the cabin, but at the same time seemed to come from far away. It echoed, as though it were calling to Fiona from the other end of a huge chamber. It was then that Fiona realised that the man himself was not completely there either. He seemed perfectly solid, but her perception of him was hazy, as though she were viewing him through misted glass. More a reflection than real living flesh and blood.

"Who are you?" she whispered. "What are you?"

"My name is Tobias," came the distant reply. "For sixteen years I have remained trapped between the world of flesh and spirit awaiting the time when my daughter would release me from my captivity and summon me back to fulfil my final task." He smiled at her then, the lined face softening so that he looked much younger.

"You have become a very attractive young woman. When last I saw you, you were a helpless infant. I had no idea what would become of you when I left you to be raised by strangers so far from the home where you were born. For years I have been tormented by the fear that I would never see you again. That you would never open the book and Alfredo would triumph over humankind for ever, yet here you are."

"Wait a minute!" Fiona cried desperately. "I was given this book. I know nothing about you. Why should I be your daughter? I just opened a book. I'm losing it," she muttered distractedly. "That time in Miguel's house has tipped me over the edge. This is a dream, a hallucination."

Tobias gazed at her, and there was understanding and sympathy in his eyes.

"You are my daughter," he said gently. "Only one of my blood could unlock the book and release me. It was a precaution I had to take in case the book ever fell into the wrong hands."

Fiona shook her head vehemently. "No! you're wrong! My name is Fiona Armstrong. I live at twelve Portland Close. I was born and adopted on Earth. I was just brought here by a mad boy. For all I know, this is just some horrid nightmare and I'll wake up soon." These last words were spoken rather half-heartedly. Fiona had long since given up hope of waking to find herself safe and sound in her own bed, with all that had happened nothing more than a dim, frightful memory.

To her surprise, Tobias laughed.

"You are just like your mother. It took her a long time to accept this world and her existence here as real. You have her hair and face," he added speculatively. "And her pale skin too. But you have my eyes. It is nice to know I managed to pass something on."

Fiona stared at him incredulously. "My mother was from Earth?"

Tobias sighed wistfully. "Her name was Alexandra. She came here quite by accident, through an enchanted lake which is a portal between this world and the one you call Earth. She was very unhappy in her own world. Her father was a very important man in society and she saw little of him. Her mother died when she was very young, and her father buried his grief in his work, leaving his daughter to the care of several minders. He had very high expectations of her, and as she grew older he placed more and more restrictions on her. His reputation was everything to him, and his daughter was forbidden to do anything that might tarnish it.

"She rebelled. She associated with people her father disapproved of and neglected her studies. She roamed the streets and got on the wrong side of the law. Finally, a chance meeting with a boy left her carrying his child and her father cast her out. Alone and friendless, and with no way of supporting herself or her child, Alexandra decided to end her life and her suffering once and for all.

"Imagine her surprise when, instead of the oblivion she had sought, she awoke to find herself in a completely different world." He paused, his eyes far away, lost in his memories.

"I was out fishing just off the coast where she surfaced. I saw her struggling to keep afloat. She looked frightened and confused and her sodden clothing was dragging her down. I helped her into my boat and took her back to my village."

"And the baby?" Fiona breathed.

"The child did not survive. The waters are always very cold at that time of year, and your mother was weak from lack of food and from the toxins she had put into her system. She lost the child that very night.

"But in time she recovered and settled into her new life. She felt more at home here than she had ever done in her old world. We were married a year after her arrival. She was the best friend I ever had, and a strong and fearless fighter in our cause. I miss her terribly, and thanks to my self-imposed exile, I was not reunited with her when my mortal life ended."

Fiona gazed into her father's sad eyes. Her father! She couldn't believe it. In any scenes she'd ever imagined where her real parents suddenly appeared, there had been nothing like this. She had certainly not been sitting holding a conversation with a ghost whose soul was unable to rest. She had definitely passed beyond all notions of sanity now. Yet she could not doubt his story. He knew about Alexandra. Her disappearance had happened exactly as he had described it. And it also explained how he had found out about the lake and knew to send her there.

Her mother had come from Earth. She was a product of two worlds, two civilizations. It was a sobering thought. Things might have been very different had her parents lived. She would never have known James or her adopted parents. She and Christophe would have grown up together. Their fathers had been friends. They might have been friends too. No, she couldn't imagine that. Christophe had no friends. But then, would he have been a different person too, if his parents had lived?

Her father's voice broke urgently in on her reflections.

"My time runs short. My spirit will not remain long on this world now that you have released it. I must explain your destiny."

"OK," Fiona said reluctantly.

Tobias sighed heavily. "What do you know already? What has Ivan told you?"

Fiona was mystified. "Ivan? Oh, you mean Christophe's dad? I think he's dead. It was his son Christophe who brought me here."

A spasm of pain flitted across her father's ghostly face.

Fiona could have bitten out her tongue. Of course. They had been friends. Best friends. Christophe had said so.

"I'm sorry," she said contritely.

Tobias passed his hand wearily across his eyes. "I should have known they would not have let him live long after he helped get you to safety. What about his wife Natasha. Did she survive?"

"I don't think so. At least, Christophe never mentions her. He's been living with the Travellers for the last six years. No one knows what happened to him before that."

"It is quite remarkable that he survived at all. He was just a baby a few months older than you when I saw him last. And he brought you back from the other world and gave you the book?"

Fiona nodded. "He said his father had given it to him, and it would tell me how to defeat Alfredo. He said nothing about what form the information would take," she added a little reproachfully.

Tobias laughed at her expression. "I am sorry I startled you. But Christophe could not have known what the book contained. Even his father did not fully understand. The boy was as ignorant as you."

"So what do you want me to do?"

"There is a weapon which, if it were to fall into Alfredo's hands, would make him the most powerful man in the world. He would be invincible."

There was a chilling silence. Fiona shuddered involuntarily.

"But what is it?" she whispered. "No weapon is unstoppable."

Tobias leaned towards her, his face very serious. Once again, Fiona felt the icy chill on her skin.

"This is not a weapon crafted by human hands. This is something that was created using magic. And not any ordinary magic, but dark, forbidden powers that no decent human being would ever tamper with. To even have a chance of challenging it, there would have to be another weapon to stand against it, and it would take an exceptionally strong person to wield it. One who was free from the taint of corruption and the lust for power. One whose motives were entirely unselfish. There are not many people like that in the world. I doubt that there is any. The capacity for wrong doing resides in all of us, though in some it is more pronounced than others."

"But I don't understand," Fiona said desperately. "How was such a thing created? What does it do?"

Tobias sat back on his heels and clasped his hands on his knees. His eyes never once left Fiona's face.

"Long ago, when our world was first created and some of the merpeople were given human form so they could populate the land, it was discovered that many of the earlier generations of humans exhibited signs of the magic that their mer ancestors once possessed. This magic could take many forms, and as the humans populated and their mer-blood dwindled, these signs grew less. Often skipping several generations unless it was a family where the mer-blood was particularly strong. Whenever a child showed signs of magical ability, the merpeople would teach them how to control it and use it for the benefit of their people.

"But the merpeople underestimated the flaws of human nature. Inevitably there were some who wished to use their magic, not to aid their people, but to dominate and control them. They considered themselves superior to ordinary men and women.

"When the merpeople discovered this, they refused to tutor them, but the damage was done. They simply carried on alone. They took to living apart from their fellow human beings in remote, lonely areas. They conducted experiments and searched the land for people who they could guide and influence. They were known as warlocks."

"And Alfredo is one of them?" Fiona breathed.

"He is indeed, but let's not get ahead of ourselves."

"The warlocks' greatest ambition, as I have already said was the domination of their fellow men and the merpeople too if they could manage it. But as long as the merpeople remained powerful and strong and as long as there were still those who practised good magic, they were thwarted. Despite their gradual increase in numbers, they were still not enough to take on the might of the merpeople alone. They needed a weapon.

"They fashioned a weapon using the darkest arts that the merpeople never taught. The forbidden magic. They poured into this weapon all their malice and cruelty and lust for power and their iron determination. In other words, they gave it their souls. There now was a weapon whose source of power was the souls of the most evil men and women living at that time. They were encased within it as my spirit was within this book."

Fiona was trembling. "But… but how did it work?"

"It worked," Tobias said grimly, "by feeding off the emotions of the one who held it. The sceptre, as it was known, converts the emotions and desires of its holder into energy which unleashes the power of the trapped souls within. The stronger the character, the greater the release of power. With the sceptre, a wielder only has to think a thing and it is done. Wish somebody dead, and a burst of magic would strike them instantly dead where they stood. You could induce pain or fear or submission, whatever you liked. In short, you could effectively rule the world. Your only limit would be the scope of your imagination. The sceptre feeds on the holder's emotions, the holder wields the power, the power crushes the victim's resistance and strength of will, rendering them utterly powerless. Their strength in turn is absorbed by the greedy captive souls to fuel their power. It was a perfect plan. Men were mortal. The warlocks' domination would last only so long as they lived. With the aid of the sceptre, their domination would be complete and never-ending. It would just be passed to a new holder when the old one died."

Fiona's face was drained of all colour. She stared at her father, her eyes wide and terrified. She thought of all the wicked people of her own world. With all that power at their command; they are able to achieve any desire. If someone like Hitler had possessed the sceptre, he could have killed the British forces as they went into battle. He could have had the British people on their knees before him, his helpless subjects.

"And Alfredo wants this sceptre? That's what he's looking for?"

Tobias nodded. "He has been searching for it these last twenty years."

"But what happened to it? Why didn't the warlocks use it as soon as they had the chance? No one would have been able to stand against them."

Tobias gave her a wry smile. "An excellent question. The reason the warlocks were never able to use the sceptre, was because it was stolen by the merpeople."

Fiona was incredulous. "How?"

"The sceptre was created at a fortress on a remote island. Flushed with their success, the creators set off for the mainland, anxious to show the sceptre to their brothers and sisters and begin the war they had been so long preparing for.

"But the merpeople recognized their ship and created a storm. The ship was sent to the bottom of the sea, its precious cargo and passengers with it, and no doubt the merpeople breathed a sigh of relief.

"But then Alfredo came on the scene. He was born during a generation when, for some reason, the magical blood was particularly strong. Alfredo and I were of an age with each other and grew up as neighbours living in the city.

"His father was a rich merchant who had little time for his son's extraordinary talents. Alfredo's mother died when he was still a small child, and he was left to be raised by a man who had nothing in common with him. All Alfredo's father was concerned with was maintaining a profitable business, and he saw no way in which magic could help with this. But Alfredo was desperate to explore his wondrous skills, and they were indeed formidable. He was easily the most powerful of his generation. When it became clear that he had no interest in his father's business, his father turned him out into the world to make his own fortune. He had long since ceased studying with the merpeople, frustrated by the restrictions they placed on the use of his magic and the direction they wished him to take with it. With no one to guide him, it is not surprising that he fell under the influence of the warlocks. He disappeared for years, and nothing was seen or heard of him.

"I completed my own magical studies and moved to a small fishing village."

"What can you do?" Fiona asked curiously.

"I came from a magical background. Both my parents had the blood, though it was only my father's gift that was passed on to me. My father had the ability to separate his spirit from his body while he still lived. Once free, he could go anywhere in spirit form. Nowhere was barred to him. He always said that it was a shame I did not inherit my mother's gift. She was able to immobilize any attacker by freezing their limbs. She could manipulate the body like a puppet. She could make an attacker drop their weapons, thereby rendering them helpless. At least her gift was of some use. My father had never found a use for his, and I did not think I would either. So I became a simple fisherman instead."

"I can't do those things," said Fiona, disappointed. She couldn't help thinking how convenient it would have been to just freeze Miguel and his thugs where they stood before they could reach her.

Tobias laughed. "I did say that it skipped generations, and only one of your parents possessed magical blood."

"Yeah, I know," Fiona muttered. "Go on."

"Well, after about ten years, Alfredo reappeared. I am sure I do not need to tell you about his rise to power. You must have heard it from Christophe. Many men flocked to him. Some out of fear, some eager to use their untrained magic, others because they knew how to attach themselves to those in power.

"It was not long before Alfredo had made himself emperor, and his domination over his people was almost absolute. He needed only one thing to make his victory complete."

"The sceptre," Fiona muttered.

"Correct, and what is more, he nearly found out where it was hidden."

"What?" Fiona was aghast. "But it was lost in a shipwreck!"

"So we believed. But the merpeople retrieved it and hid it away. All their efforts to destroy it had failed. They hid it deep beneath the sea away from any human hands. I learned this from a merman I knew from my tutoring days."

"But how did Alfredo learn of it?"

Tobias sighed heavily. "There was a young mermaid who fell in love with Alfredo."

"In love with him? But why?"

"It is possible that it was not of her own free will. Alfredo knew that the sceptre had been lost in a shipwreck. He surmised that if anyone had found it, it would have been the merpeople. He may well have charmed or seduced the mermaid somehow or befuddled her with magic. We will never know. But it was she who told him that the merpeople had the sceptre, but before she could reveal its whereabouts to Alfredo, she was discovered."

"What happened to her?"

Tobias shrugged. "Who can say? I daresay she was punished for betraying her people. But Alfredo's schemes were effectively halted in their tracks.

"He began persecuting the merpeople after that. He was getting desperate. He was under great pressure from his brothers and sisters who were still in hiding, and he knew that the sceptre was the only thing that would make him completely safe. There was always the chance that someone powerful might one day arise to challenge him, and he wanted to be ready."

A sad, haunted look came into Tobias's eyes. "He shot them with harpoon guns and left them wounded and bleeding on the beach unable to return to the water. He poisoned the water so they would sicken and die. Eventually the merpeople fled and none of us ever saw them again."

His face hardened. "That was the last straw for me. I and many others had been actively resisting Alfredo for some time. He had taken everything from us. Our way of life, our freedom. We could not even sleep safely in our own beds. And now he had taken the merpeople. So I formed a plan. It was time at last to put my hitherto dormant abilities to use.

"I determined to visit the merpeople's caves at the bottom of the sea in spirit form to learn what I could about the sceptre. Maybe, together, we could find a way to destroy it. I travelled to a lonely beach where my body was unlikely to be disturbed. I hid myself among the rocks and departed.

"I do not know how long it took me to find the caves, they are fathoms beneath the seabed, but when I reached their ancient home, I found it completely deserted. I searched everywhere but I found no trace of the merpeople or the sceptre. I searched through every underwater cave, but it was like searching through a tomb. Finally, just when I had almost given up hope, I found it, or at least, I found where it had been hidden."

"It was gone? But why? Who took it?"

"I am afraid I never found that out, but I had found what I had sought, or at least, I had found something which might help us.

“In a cavern full of statues and carvings, I found a pedestal with a likeness of a sceptre carved above it. But instead of the sceptre, there was only a scroll, yellow with age, and a dull rusty key.

“I did not waste time trying to decipher it down there. I needed daylight, and the body begins to die if the spirit is absent for too long. I had already been in the caves for hours, much longer than was wise. I returned to my village safely with the key and the scroll, but it was not until I was back under the sun once more that I fully realised what it was I had found. In the cavern, the key had appeared bent and rusty, but in the sun, it shone a pure silver, completely untarnished. At first I thought it was just the poor light in the cave that had made it look so dull, but when I showed it to your mother, and to Ivan, they saw nothing of its beauty. I spoke to an acquaintance who had the power to create illusions, and he confirmed that the key was indeed under an illusion, and for some reason, it would only reveal itself to me, even though I had no power to break through its disguise.

“As for the scroll, it turned out to be a short message, a list of instructions in the form of a poem. I was at a loss to understand it, so I called an emergency meeting of our followers, but before I could reveal what I had found, I was betrayed. Someone tipped Alfredo off, and his men came for me.

“They were led by Miguel, one of Alfredo’s most trusted spies. He had learned of my trip to the mer caves. I should have been prepared for him. Nothing escapes his eyes for long.”

Fiona said nothing. She knew the truth of those words only too well.

“They came for me one night,” Tobias said softly. “They held a knife to your mother’s throat. They gave me a simple choice, come with them willingly, or they would kill her in front of me. What else could I do? I followed them. Your mother tried to come to my aid. She screamed my name over and over again, but they just knocked her unconscious and led me away.”

He was silent for a few minutes as his memories swept over him once more. Fiona sat quietly, waiting for him to continue.

“Three months I was in Alfredo’s house. His men tried everything to make me reveal what I had learned.”

He did not look at Fiona as he said these words, and Fiona shuddered.

“But at last they were forced to let me go. I was barely alive, and it was clear that they would learn nothing. They put me on a hand cart, drove me into the heart of the city and left me there. I would have died if a kind farmer had not seen me and taken me to his home. His good wife nursed me, and eventually, I was able to return home. But the damage was done. I had suffered too much to ever fully recover, and my extended absence from my body had exacted a heavier price than even I had anticipated. I was dying.”

He stared at Fiona, and there was a pleading look in his eyes.

“There was nothing else I could do. I knew I could never find the sceptre, and yet by now, I was convinced that the task was meant for me. I had had plenty of time to think. Why was it that the key would reveal itself to me and no other? And then there was the fact that the merpeople obviously intended someone to find their instructions, yet only I had the power to visit their caves. I pored obsessively over that scroll, and though its meaning is still unclear, I believe I know what the writer intended."

He paused suddenly, and an anxious look came into his eyes. "My time grows short," he muttered. "I have not got long, and there is so much still to say."

"What do you mean?" said Fiona, alarmed, but her father ignored her.

"I took what steps I could. If I could not fulfil the merpeople's quest, I had to ensure that someone of my blood could finish what I had begun. I memorised the words of the scroll and burned it. I asked a seer called Jeremiah where the best place would be to hide you, and he told me of the world your mother had come from and how to reach it. I hid the key with a friend, the man who created illusions. He is a merchant, and he often disguised the goods in his shop from unwelcome customers. I knew the key would be safe with him. Finally I sent for Ivan and took some poison. I knew by then that Miguel had discovered that I was still alive, and I could not risk dying without leaving my message behind. I encased my spirit within the pages of a book. The entrapment was such that only one could release me; the rightful owner of the key and bearer of the task that had been placed on us. In other words, one of my own blood – you! With my last breath, I told Ivan to take you to Jeremiah, who would tell him how to take you into the other world, where I could be sure you would be safe, and I charged him to guard the book until you came of age, when he was to come for you."

"What did the scroll say?" Fiona asked hesitantly, not sure that she really wanted to know.

Tobias recited:

*"First find the key that unlocks all doors,*
*Except for those within.*
*Unlock the secret of the mountain's heart,*
*Without which you cannot win.*
*Cross to the island you cannot see,*
*and if you would reach your goal,*
*Follow the path of truth and find what is hidden within your soul."*

Fiona stared at her father incredulously. "But what the hell does that mean? A load of cryptic rhymes? What am I supposed to do with that? You expect me to pull off some kind of miracle? I cannot believe you waited sixteen years for that!"

Her father's form was losing solidarity, becoming hazier. Fiona could see it happening. Panic built within her, threatening to swallow her whole.

"The merpeople knew Alfredo was hunting for the sceptre, so they removed it. They could not destroy it themselves, but obviously they believed someone else could."

"But how? No human could do it. You said yourself the merpeople are much more powerful than they are."

"Yet the merpeople believed differently. Otherwise, why did they move the sceptre? It was perfectly safe where it was. Alfredo could not get to it. Why else did they leave a message explaining how to find it? Why would they want a human to find it if not to destroy it? It would not be safe, just guarded. There was always the risk that it would be found and its keeper destroyed."

"But I don't know what that message means," Fiona shouted, tears of frustration and fear in her eyes. "I'll have no better luck than anyone else who tries to follow those stupid directions. Why should I be the one to do this?"

"It is appointed for you," Tobias said softly.

"But you don't know that. You're only guessing."

"I do," he said earnestly.

Fiona wished she could shake him. He was making no sense.

"How? How do you know for sure that I'm meant to do this?"

"The seer, Jeremiah," Tobias said sadly. "He saw you. He saw you return. He saw you set out to search for the sceptre."

"I don't suppose he saw if I returned?" Fiona enquired sarcastically, but her father's face remained grave.

"No, he did not."

Fiona snorted. "Why am I not surprised?" She hid her face in her hands.

"I know this is hard for you," her father began quietly.

Fiona's head snapped up. "No, you don't know the half of it! I was happy on Earth. It was my home. I had parents, friends, a life. I was normal. Then Christophe just turns up out of the blue and carries me off and why? Because of a guess? A theory? People bow and scrape because they think I'm their saviour. They die because of me. Or else they believe I'm some kind of monster who should be done away with the first chance they get. I don't have any magical powers. I'm no one special. I never asked for any of this!"

"There is the key, the first part of the message. Follow the clues and all will be revealed. They would not have left a message if there was no hope of succeeding. They were often able to read the future. They also must have seen what Jeremiah saw."

"That's really reassuring," Fiona muttered.

"You must try!" her father pleaded. There was desperation in his eyes. "Do you think I like this any better than you do? Sending my child into peril? Knowing I can do nothing to help her? How I wish with all my heart that I was the one meant to find the sceptre. If I had to send anyone, why did it have to be my only daughter?" His voice broke. It was the only solid thing left of him. His form was shrouded in mist. It was sucking him in. He was becoming part of it.

"Will you do it?" he called desperately. "Will you destroy the sceptre and free our people?"

Fiona thought of those people in the market place, being sold as if they were horses or cattle. She thought of the men who had given their lives for her. And Christophe who had nearly died trying to protect her. Surely there must be some hope. The merpeople wouldn't have left the message and the key if there was no hope. They would tell her what to do if only she could manage to find them. And she would not be alone. Christophe would protect her, and James would never leave her. James – if for no other reason, she had to do this for him, so he could go home, back to Carolyn. She owed him that. Even if she never got back, James deserved to. He was only here because of her.

"Alright," she said, and as she spoke, it felt as though she were sealing her own death sentence. "I'll try."

The mist seemed to swim, and for a moment, her father's face was clearly visible once more. There were tears in his eyes, but he was smiling.

"That is all anyone has a right to ask of you."

Fiona nodded. She felt unable to speak. Now that she had actually spoken the words, her mind felt nothing. She just stared into her father's eyes and saw the love mirrored there.

"Your mother would have been proud of you," he said gently. "And so am I."

Then the mist roiled into a freezing, billowing cloud. There was a gentle sigh, then, nothing. Her father was gone. The mist had vanished. The cabin was warm again. Once more, she could hear the sound of seabirds, voices calling to each other, and the sound of waves breaking over rocks. Normal everyday sounds that Fiona only dimly realised had been absent throughout her father's appearance.

Looking down, she saw on the floor a pile of dust the colour of grey parchment. And glinting dully in the midst of the dust, two tarnished silver clasps. All that remained of Tobias's story.

# Part II

# The Sceptre

# Chapter 12

## Retribution

They looked peaceful, Fiona thought as she emerged on deck.

It was a relief to be free from the close confines of Christophe's cabin. A gentle breeze wafted soothingly over her hot forehead, but it did nothing to cool the fever of her thoughts. It was only just now beginning to sink in that she had agreed to go on this foolhardy quest. She had promised to destroy a weapon that threatened an entire civilization, and she didn't have a clue how she was going to do it, nor even if it could be done. She could have laughed, or wept.

They all stopped what they were doing at once. Esther and her mother, who were mending nets with some help from Lena, froze in their work and looked up at her questioningly.

Gideon laid aside the arrows he had been fletching and Antonio and Jeremiah knocked out their pipes.

Christophe and Katie, who Fiona noted with some surprise, were sitting together and speaking quietly, broke off their conversation and watched her in silence. Christophe's face was unreadable as usual, but Katie's gaze was curious, almost eager.

They were the only ones on deck apart from James. He stood at the ship's rail, gazing unseeingly out to sea, completely unaware of those around him. But at the sudden silence, he turned sharply around.

Fiona stopped uncertainly. All those eyes on her made her nervous, particularly in light of what she had come to tell them.

James hurried to her side immediately.

"Are you OK?" He looked keenly into her face. "You're pale!" Without another word he took her arm and steered her over to the rail where he had been standing. He stationed himself at her side and waited.

Fiona's knees were threatening to fold, but she forced herself to remain standing and to meet their enquiring looks eye to eye. It was an effort.

"The book that Christophe gave me," she began hesitantly, "contained the spirit of my dead father." She paused. The memory was still so fresh, yet the words sounded ridiculous. Even she still had trouble believing it. She forced herself to go on.

"My father was able to separate his spirit from his body and that was how he managed to spy on Alfredo. When he knew he was dying, he encased his spirit within the book until the time when I would be old enough to hear what he had learned. He's gone now, and the book has crumbled into dust."

She stopped again. Her throat was dry and she felt more alone than she ever had in her entire life, even with everyone there watching her, hanging on her every word.

It was Katie who came to her rescue. She alone seemed unfazed by Fiona's revelation.

"What did he tell you, Fiona?" she asked gently.

Fiona took another deep breath. Not looking at James, she said, "There's a weapon, a sceptre, that the warlocks made long ago to conquer this world and enslave the people. The merpeople found out about it and stole it, but one of them told Alfredo about it."

"That cannot be true!" Gideon broke in hotly. "The merpeople would never betray one of their own!"

"That's what my father said," Fiona replied. "He said she fell in love with him. My father reckons Alfredo might have seduced her somehow. Why would he say it if it wasn't true?"

Gideon made no comment and Fiona continued. "The merpeople found out about her betrayal and sent her away before she could tell Alfredo where it was hidden. So Alfredo started persecuting them until they were forced to go into hiding.

"My father used his gift to leave his body and go down under the sea to search for them. He never found any of them, but he did find a message and a key. He believes the message is the clue to finding and destroying the sceptre. And he thinks that the merpeople must have learned of a prophecy that meant he or his descendants were the chosen ones, as he was the only one who would be able to find them. Also, the key was protected by an illusion and only he could see its true shape. He managed to hide the key with a friend, but he was captured. By the time he was rescued, he was too ill and weak to go after the sceptre himself. When I was born, he took me to a seer called Jeremiah who—" Fiona suddenly broke off with a gasp, realising what she had just said. It hit her like a thunder clap.

A seer called Jeremiah! Jeremiah, the old man who had presided at the festival of Mer. Esther and Gideon's grandfather. He must be who her father had meant. She shot Gideon a swift glance. He was regarding her intently, and as their eyes met, an invisible current of understanding seemed to pass between them.

Christophe was also watching her keenly, and she saw by his expression that he had worked out the truth. But how had he known? Then it hit her. Of course! Christophe must have gone to Jeremiah to find out the way to cross to Earth and bring her back. He was Ivan's son. Jeremiah would have known he possessed the book. Jeremiah had probably told him of his vision of Fiona on the hunt for the sceptre. Christophe had probably known all along. How foolish her denials must have sounded. He could have at least told her. She shot him an angry look, but then recovered and went on.

"Jeremiah told him how to find Earth. My father knew it existed because my mum came from there." At this, Christophe's eyebrows lifted, and Fiona felt a stab of satisfaction. "Jeremiah also told my father that he'd had a vision of me looking for the sceptre years later. So my father took some poison and trapped his spirit in the book which he gave to Christophe's dad. And he made Christophe's dad take me to Jeremiah so that I could be sent away to Earth and protected until I reached sixteen."

"But what does this weapon do?" said Antonio. "You said it was made by the warlocks, so how can Alfredo use it?"

Fiona was startled. "But Alfredo *is* a warlock. He was from a family with strong magical blood and he was very powerful. He hated the restrictions the merpeople put on him and their expectations of how he should use his magic, so he studied with the warlocks instead."

They stared at her, varying degrees of shock and consternation on their faces. Fiona couldn't believe that this was news to any of them. But apparently it was. Katie in particular looked utterly incredulous. She said nothing, but the colour had drained from her face.

Fiona sat down cross-legged on the deck with her back to the railing. She didn't think her legs would support her much longer. James dropped down beside her, and his closeness gave her comfort.

"The warlocks made the sceptre by trapping some of their souls within it. It's powered by the wielder's emotions, the bad ones obviously, and that releases all the trapped magic and performs the holder's will. It can kill people or control them so that they'll do whatever they're told. It sort of boosts the power the holder already has."

There was a terrible silence. Fiona saw fear on every face, and she felt helpless to reassure them. What hope did she have against a warlock? Even without the sceptre, Alfredo was powerful. Why shouldn't he just swat her aside like a troublesome fly and walk off with the sceptre. She wouldn't be able to stop him. But there had to be some way. She must remember that. The merpeople wouldn't have left the message and the key if it was impossible. She had to believe that or collapse right here and now in a gibbering heap while the people suffered and died around her. For Alfredo would find the sceptre. She knew that. Even without her help he would have stumbled on it eventually. Her appearance would only spur him to greater exertion, and he must not have it. She must prevent that from happening at all costs. If she couldn't destroy it, then she at least had to keep it from falling into Alfredo's hands. Especially now that she knew what it could do. She sank her head into her hands and felt James's gentle hand on her shoulder. She wished she could turn to him and let him fix everything. She'd relied on his strength so often before. But not even James could help her this time. It was up to her.

"He would be unstoppable," Christophe said quietly.

Josephine reached for her children, hugging her daughters close.

"What did the message say?" said Katie.

Fiona recited in a dull monotone.

*"First find the key that unlocks all doors*
*Except for those within.*

*Unlock the secret of the mountain's heart*
*Without which you cannot win.*
*Cross to the island you cannot see,*
*And if you would reach your goal,*
*Follow the path of truth and find what is hidden within your soul."*

"What the heck does that mean?" said James.

Fiona shrugged helplessly.

"You said your father found the key," said Katie. "Where is it?"

"A friend of his has a shop. He's a master of illusion and he often bewitches his goods. He has the key."

"We must go there first then," said Christophe.

"But where from there?" demanded James. "Assuming the key reveals itself to Fiona."

"It will," said Jeremiah quietly. "Make no mistake about that. It has been foretold."

"The rhyme said something about the mountain's heart," murmured Esther.

"The nearest mountains are on the other side of the desert which begins on the outskirts of this city," said Christophe. "I have heard it is vast. It would take us many days to cross, but at least the mountains will not be hard to miss."

"You will need plenty of supplies," Josephine said matter-of-factly. "It will be almost certain death crossing that desert, for there is nothing there worth hunting, and I have heard there is no water to be had for miles."

"Who'll be coming?" asked Fiona.

"You and I, obviously," replied Christophe. "And James. He will not be separated from you."

"Of course I'm coming," James said hastily, squeezing Fiona's shoulder.

"I will go with you," said Katie. "I will be some help to you I think."

Fiona was startled. She didn't know what help Katie could possibly be, but she was too glad to have the other girl's company to argue. Christophe also made no objection, which surprised Fiona.

"You will need Guardians," Gideon said eagerly. "There is sure to be fighting required and The Appointed must be kept safe at all costs. With respect, Christophe, you cannot defend three people alone. I will gladly volunteer."

Fiona was horrified. Not more men risking their lives for her. And not Gideon. She couldn't bear it. She was about to protest, but Christophe spoke first.

"I shall consider carefully who among the Guardians will travel with us. We need speed and a large number will slow us down. Also the Travellers will be on their way soon and they too need protection. The ships sail in three days. By that time, we will have food and supplies, and I will have made my choice. We depart in three days."

* * *

Katie sat alone and ignored in a corner of the deck as everyone else went about their business. She leaned against the ship's rail, hands clasped over her drawn up knees, her mind reeling from all she had heard.

Her father a warlock? It couldn't be true. Why hadn't he told her? Why hadn't Jessemine or anyone else told her? It couldn't be true, and yet it did explain some things. Now she knew where her strange abilities had come from. She had never found a satisfactory reason to account for what she could do, and Jessemine's vague response that some children were just born lucky had never been a good enough explanation.

Who had her mother been then? Had she been a warlock too? Why had it been necessary to keep so much from her? Who could she have told? Until she had met Christophe and Fiona, she had never had dealings with anyone outside Miguel's household. Why had her father not wanted her with him, if they both had magical abilities? She knew that her father had wanted to keep her safe for her own protection, but why couldn't he have left her with people like her, instead of Miguel? Hurt and resentment stirred within her. Was she only worth noticing when her father wanted something? Until he had asked her to befriend Fiona and find out what it was she had been brought here to do, he hadn't really paid her much attention. He hadn't told her much then either, and she had been so delighted that he had finally entrusted her with something worthwhile, and for a chance to get one over on Miguel, that she had not enquired too closely.

By all accounts, this sceptre sounded like an awesome weapon, but she couldn't see what use her father would have for it. He was already emperor. His empire was vast and growing. Every person for uncounted leagues was subject to his laws, his rule. He had supreme power already. Why on earth would he want more?

When he had first broached the subject in his study, he had mentioned a threat to his rule. Katie had assumed at the time that he meant Fiona, but what if she was wrong? What if her father had actually meant the sceptre? Perhaps Fiona's father had been mistaken. Perhaps her father did want to destroy it. After all, something that powerful would be a serious threat if it fell into the wrong hands, and surely only someone who possessed magic could destroy it. What chance did Fiona have really? In that case, surely it was her duty to take it to her father. Why should Fiona die needlessly?

She liked the girl, and that only added to her confusion.

As for Christophe, Katie simply didn't know what to think. She had never felt such a powerful, intense emotion for anyone, and she wasn't even sure what that emotion was. All she knew was that her being seemed to come alive when she was with him; as though she was on fire. When she was with him, her mind was focused on nothing else. When she was away from him, he filled her thoughts. He intrigued and fascinated her. The voice that whispered that he was a criminal and opposed to her father was growing weaker by the day. She found herself making excuses to be near him, and not even her fear of her father's wrath if he found out was enough to deter her. She wished she had someone to talk to. Jessemine would have been able to help her. She wouldn't have pronounced judgement. She would have listened in her quiet way and offered advice. But Jessemine was still under Miguel's thumb. There was no one who could help her through her doubt and confusion. She was alone.

As though he had heard her thoughts, Christophe suddenly appeared beside her. He stood looking down at her.

"Why are you up here by yourself?"

Katie looked around. Sure enough, everyone else had gone. "I... I was just thinking," she said lamely, feeling the usual quickening of her pulse that always came when she was close to him.

"Do you mind if I join you? I need to ask you something."

Katie took a firm grip on her agitation. "No, of course not."

Christophe lowered himself to the deck beside her. She saw him wince slightly as he did so.

"Is your side still giving you pain?"

Christophe grimaced. "Sometimes, but it gets better every day."

"Are you sure you will be fit to travel in three days' time?"

"I've got to be. I promised I would protect The Appointed in my father's stead and I intend to keep that promise." His voice took on a bitter note. "I have failed so far."

"That was not your fault!" Katie said hotly, remembering how she had first seen Christophe, lying as though dead with the blood flowing from his side. "You did your best. What else could you have done?"

Christophe smiled sadly. "You are kind."

Katie felt a flush of guilt stain her cheeks. If only he knew. She was nothing of the sort. But Christophe was speaking again.

"You said you could be of some help to The Appointed. Did you mean your gift?"

Katie nodded. "I told you I am a seer. It could come in useful if there is anything we urgently need to find out."

"Do you think you would be able to find out where the sceptre is, and how to destroy it?"

"I could try, but I doubt it will be that easy. Still, I will do all I can."

Christophe smiled at her. It was rare for an expression of genuine pleasure to cross his face, and Katie felt her heart skip a beat.

Just then, Lena appeared on deck from the direction of the harbour. Her eyes were swollen and red with crying and the tears still ran down her cheeks.

Christophe was on his feet at once. "Lena, what is this?" She ran to him, throwing her small, thin arms around his waist. Without a word, Christophe sat down again, taking the little girl on his lap. She buried her face against his chest.

"Now, tell me what all this is about?"

Lena's voice was muffled. "I do not want you to go away!"

"Why? I've been away many times before and you have never minded."

"But this is different. What if Alfredo gets you? What if you die?"

Christophe was touched. "That will not happen," he said gently. "Alfredo has been trying to kill me for years and he has never succeeded. The Appointed and I will be quite safe."

"Is your side better now?" she asked anxiously, laying a hand gently over the wound.

"Yes, I am quite recovered."

She raised her face from his tunic front, looking up at him through swimming eyes. Christophe pushed the hair back from her wet cheeks, then gripped a brown, hot little hand in his.

"We all must be brave, Lena. It is likely that your father and brother will be travelling with us, so I want you to watch over your mother and sister while they are gone. Will you do that?"

She hesitated a moment, then nodded gravely. "I promise, Christophe."

"Good girl, off you go now."

She gave his hand a squeeze, then scrambled off his lap, rubbing a dirty sleeve across her eyes.

Half turned to go, she suddenly said over her shoulder, "Esther really likes you. I think she wants to marry you." With that, she was gone.

Katie had watched the entire scene in silence. The little girl with the scratched knees and the tearstained face, and the boy with the eyes that had seen too much. She was deeply moved, and her mind felt suddenly a good deal clearer. Criminal he may be, but Katie knew as surely as she had ever known anything that here was a good person sitting beside her. She would get the sceptre to her father if that was what he wanted, but she would also do everything in her power to ensure that Christophe and Fiona remained safe.

* * *

"Say something!" Fiona implored. "You've been quiet for ages!" She and James were in a quiet, secluded corner of the beach. Fiona had felt the need to be away from people, but she dreaded being alone with her thoughts. She peered into James's face. "You think I've lost it, don't you? You think this place has finally tipped me over the edge. That I'm hearing voices sending me divine messages. He was there, James! I know it sounds crazy but it's the truth!" She suddenly realised she was shouting and shut her mouth abruptly.

James was looking at her, his face intense.

"I believe you, though you have to admit, it's a bit weird! But you surely don't actually mean to go ahead with this?"

Fiona laughed bitterly. "The time when I had a choice in things was over ages ago. Christophe would drag me kicking and screaming if I didn't go of my own free will."

"This isn't funny, Fiona," James said earnestly. "We might never get back. We have no magic powers. We're more than likely walking to our deaths."

Fiona noted the word "we".

"You're still coming along? You could go home, back to Carolyn. I wouldn't mind, honestly."

"And worry myself stupid over what might be happening to you? No thanks! I said I'd stick by you and I will. I just hope you know what you're getting yourself into."

Fiona squeezed his hand. "I haven't a clue, but it won't be so bad if you're there." She laughed. "It's like those movies isn't it? Where a group of friends go off on some harebrained quest."

James's smile was grim. "Except that they usually have happy endings. I'm not sure ours will."

"But we'll be together though?"

"'Course we will. Don't think I'm letting you out of my sight for one minute."

Fiona grinned. Getting to her feet, she brushed sand from her clothes.

"I'll see you later. I want a word with Jeremiah."

"Sure."

Jeremiah was in his cabin. He was usually to be found there of an afternoon, when he often retired to rest. But when Fiona knocked and was told briskly to enter, she found Jeremiah sitting at a scrubbed wooden table, poring intently over some old and yellowing bits of parchment. A rough wooden bench and a hard narrow bunk were the only other items of furniture in the room.

"Well?" he said briskly. "What is it?"

Fiona was undaunted by his abrupt manner. She didn't care if he was busy or not. There were things she had to know.

"What did you see about me?" she demanded without preamble. "Tell me everything!"

Jeremiah gave her a stern look from beneath his rather bushy eyebrows.

"Were you never taught to respect your elders?"

"I'm about to risk my neck for you!" Fiona said indignantly. "Believe it or not, manners aren't that important to me right now."

Jeremiah laughed, showing surprisingly white teeth. "Well spoken. Why don't you sit down?"

Fiona perched herself on the bunk and waited expectantly.

Jeremiah steepled his fingers and regarded her thoughtfully over them.

"The truth is, I cannot tell you much. Your father brought you to me shortly after your birth. He was dying and he did not know what to do for the best regarding the sceptre. I saw two visions. One showed a man with a red-haired baby girl slipping through a portal to another world.

"The other was of this same child but grown, hunting for something of the utmost importance. That child was you. I recognized you the moment I saw you that first day on the *Dolphin*. It was on this information that your father made his decision. The man I saw carrying you to safety was Ivan."

"That was it? You didn't see anything else?"

"Only what I have told you."

"So you don't know if I'll succeed? If I'll even live to tell the tale?"

"I am afraid not."

There was a hint of desperation in Fiona's voice. "Couldn't you look again now that I'm here?"

Jeremiah sighed. "I have tried many times since you arrived, but there is nothing. Your future is doubtful. I think it will be up to you to decide it."

"I doubt it," Fiona said bitterly. "I haven't exactly had much say in things so far."

"On the contrary," said Jeremiah. "People always have a choice. You could have refused your father."

"But then I couldn't have fulfilled the second vision."

Jeremiah smiled. "That is correct."

"So it wasn't my choice. It was fate, or something."

"It was the path you chose."

Fiona put a hand to her temple. "I feel a headache coming on."

Jeremiah chuckled.

He extracted a role of parchment from among those littering the table. It was torn and yellow with age, but he unrolled it for Fiona's inspection.

"This is a map of the desert and the mountains and the surrounding countryside. As I am sure you have learned how to read, you may find this useful."

Fiona studied it. The writing was small and faded, but the landscape was clearly sketched; the desert and mountains skilfully drawn.

"Thanks," she said, rolling it up carefully.

"It is one of a very old collection," said Jeremiah. "I doubt there are many copies still intact. Be sure to return it safe and sound."

"I'll try."

* * *

The next three days passed all too quickly for Fiona's liking. Everything was all bustle and activity in the harbour as the Travellers made ready to depart. Last minute cargo was taken on board, and there were daily trips to the market to stock up on food supplies.

Fiona realised that she would miss the *Dolphin* and her crew. Almost against her will, she had grown to regard the ship as a sort of home, somewhere she felt safe. Esther and Gideon and their extended family had made her welcome and she was grateful to them. She couldn't help feeling that a few weeks at sea was infinitely preferable to toiling across a desert.

Preparations for her own journey were also under way. Christophe disappeared often into the city and the Guardians he had picked to accompany them were drilling constantly. Among these, to Fiona's alarm, was Gideon, and the reserved fighter Carlotta. Fiona appealed desperately to Esther.

"Why did Christophe pick Gideon? I couldn't stand it if he dies. I couldn't look any of you in the face again!"

Esther smiled sadly. "Gideon has the making of a fine Guardian. He may even have what it takes to be leader some day, but he is anxious to prove himself. He has been waiting for just such a chance ever since he joined. Besides, Christophe and he are friends. It was inevitable really."

"I don't suppose there's any way to talk him out of it?" Fiona asked without much hope.

Esther sighed and shook her head. "None at all."

Looking at her, Fiona suddenly realised how difficult this must be for Esther. Not only was her brother going into danger, but the boy she loved too. Fiona shuddered as she imagined what it must be like to live with that dread hanging over you, waiting to descend. Yet Esther was doing an admirable job of hiding her feelings. She bustled about as busily as anyone. On impulse, Fiona suddenly hugged her friend.

"I'll try and bring them back safely," she said huskily.

Esther hugged her back. "I shall miss you, Fiona," she murmured softly.

"Me too!"

There was to be a farewell feast on the last night to wish The Appointed well on her journey. All the Travellers currently on land would attend, and the women busied themselves over cooking fires for most of that day.

The feast began at sunset. There was roasted fowl and goat, as well as a deeply fragrant vegetable and herb broth, bread and various cheeses and honey cakes. It was plain, simple food, but full of good flavour, and Fiona loaded her plate with a will.

She and James joined the *Dolphin* party as usual, together with Christophe and Katie. Spirits were high. Everyone was full of hope and expectation, hopeful that the tyranny of Alfredo's rule was at last nearing its end. Despite her own fears and anxieties, Fiona found the mood infectious. Even Christophe seemed caught up by it, and was more talkative than usual.

"I heard some good news in the city today," he said, accepting a honey cake from a passing platter. "Good news for us, at any rate."

"What was that?" enquired James around a mouthful of bread and cheese.

"Alfredo has issued a warrant for Miguel's arrest. He is to be imprisoned and publicly executed a few days from now by Alfredo's order."

"They will be lucky to catch him," Antonio said grimly. "That man can hide better than a fox down its hole when he chooses."

"Why would Alfredo want Miguel arrested?" asked Lena. "He was his best spy."

"I think Alfredo would disagree," said Christophe with evident satisfaction. "He allowed The Appointed to escape, and," he touched a hand briefly to his side, "Christophe the criminal survived as well." There was appreciative laughter all round.

"But what will become of his servants and the rest of his household?" asked Esther.

"They are to be given to the slave traders," said Christophe. Beside him, he felt Katie tense. He waited until everyone else was lost in conversation, then leaned close to her. She looked pale, and was twirling a piece of bread absently between her fingers.

“Are you alright?” he murmured quietly. She looked up at him, and he was startled to see the hint of tears in her eyes. The sight distressed him. He felt a powerful urge to comfort her, though he had no idea how.

“They were good people,” she said hoarsely. “They were never in league with him. They do not deserve this!”

“They were your friends?”

“Some of them. One in particular, his wife Jessemine. She raised me. She always hated Miguel. She never said so, but I knew.” Before he could think better of it, Christophe reached for Katie’s hand and held it. When she didn’t pull away, he said gently, “If you wish to go and try to save your friends, I would understand. I would willingly help you, but my place is with The Appointed.” She was tempted. He could see it in her eyes. A sudden irrational fear clutched at his heart. She would leave. He would never see her again. Appalled with himself he crushed the feeling. They were the nearest thing she had to a family. She had every right to go to them. But when she spoke, she surprised him.

“I would do no good to them. I could not rescue them alone.” She laughed bitterly. “Besides, I was a member of Miguel’s house. That makes me a slave now too. I would not be much use to anyone caught.”

Christophe couldn’t help but feel relieved, no matter how he tried to quell the emotion.

“When this is over, I promise I and the Guardians will help set them free.” He felt the slight pressure of her fingers against his, then she let him go.

“But why would Alfredo order punishment against innocent people?”

Christophe was startled that this information should come as a shock.

“That is how he likes to work. An example made of the innocent is a lesson quickly learned and not easily forgotten.”

She stared at him incredulously for a moment, then her face became expressionless and she lapsed into silence.

Christophe was glad when the feast eventually broke up. Katie’s pensive mood had ruined his enjoyment of the evening. He wanted nothing more than to find his bed and sleep.

People drifted to their beds. Everyone would be up early for departure tomorrow. One by one the lanterns on the mastheads of the ships were extinguished, and soon everyone was sleeping save the sentries, watchful and alert as ever.

* * *

They came like ghosts in the night. No one heard or saw them. Under cover of the music and merriment, they made themselves comfortable among the sand dunes or behind boulders and waited.

At last the beach was deserted. Everyone had retired to their beds, happy and hopeful. There were only the sentries left. At a whispered command from their leader, the intruders nocked arrows, sighted and drew. Every arrow found its mark. The unsuspecting sentries had no time to react. They were looking for danger elsewhere, not in their very midst. Many fell without a sound, killed instantly. Those that lay wounded were quickly silenced. This done, the intruders set about their night's work.

Climbing aboard the unprotected ships, they proceeded to soar through the ropes supporting the ladders that led below deck. They were skilful, never cutting quite through. To someone in a hurry, the ropes would appear untouched. Lighting brands of twigs and brush, they tossed them into the sails and riggings. The cloth kindled at once. Hurrying now, anxious to leave before the fires spread, they hastily knocked holes in every lifeboat or dingy they could see before jumping over board once more and slipping away as quietly as they had come.

Miguel looked back at the rising plumes of smoke with satisfaction. He did not have much time left before his execution. Alfredo would find him soon. There was no point trying to hide from him. Perhaps he would even give himself up. Play the penitent servant. But he had won. All of his master's hopes would go up in smoke tonight, along with the girl who could supposedly lead him to his treasure, the wandering peasants who had made such a fool of him, and the girl who had been the bane of his life for so long and had effectively sealed the deaths of him and his companions. Like him, they all had much to lose, since Alfredo's brat of a child had alerted her father to the undercurrent smuggling trade in the city, and were thirsty for vengeance. Miguel's smile widened as he and his men rode away. Behind them, the first panicked cries rent the smoke-laden air.

Fiona was never sure afterwards exactly what it was that woke her. The distant yells or the appalling heat. She started up in alarm as the voices grew louder. She could hear no words, but there was no mistaking the terror in those voices.

"What's going on?" James muttered sleepily.

Gideon and Esther were already on their feet. Gideon reached the door and flung it wide. An acrid stench assailed their nostrils and hit the back of their throats, and with it, came the words the people were screaming.

"Fire! The ships are on fire!"

He and Esther turned and raced for the ladder to the upper deck.

"Come on!" Gideon shouted. "We must get off the ship."

Fiona knew she should follow, but she was too numb and shocked to move. She stood frozen in disbelief. The *Dolphin* on fire? But how could that happen? Where were the sentries?

"Come on! Move!" James yelled. Seizing her hand, he began dragging her after him.

People were fleeing the ships, swarming up the ladders that led above. Children were crying. People called desperately to their loved ones as they threw themselves at the ladders.

Fiona and James reached the nearest one. It was swaying alarmingly as people scrambled up, all terrified at the thought of being trapped below. Fiona was no less petrified, but as she grasped the rope and hauled herself to the first rung, it snapped, lurching crazily to one side. Fiona cried out as she scrabbled desperately for something to hang on to. She heard screams above her. James's voice.

"Fiona, what—" but then the rope gave way and Fiona was thrown backwards into James. They fell in a heap as others crashed down on top of them, along with the lower half of the ladder. For a moment, all was a confused tangle of arms and legs as people struggled to get up again. The fire was coming closer, like some stalking beast of prey. The smoke made Fiona's eyes stream as she gasped for breath.

"We are trapped!" shrieked a woman. Her husband, who had obviously only just made it to safety, looked helplessly down at her. Fiona saw him tense, preparing to leap down the hatch, but a voice stopped him.

"No! Stay where you are!"

It was Christophe. His voice was raw from smoke inhalation, but he just managed to make himself heard.

"We need a chain. Wait there and we will boost her up to you."

The man stayed put, though he looked as if it was costing him everything he had. The sobbing woman was lifted up to his frantic arms. As soon as he had her safely, the man turned to run with her, but Christophe's shout stopped him.

"Wait, we will need your help! The children must go next."

Two other men were sent up also to lend a hand. Everyone formed a line. The tallest men made stirrups with their fingers, while those above leaned perilously over the edge, reaching. The children were handed up, then the women, who fled with them. The men would be last. They reached up as high as they could, grasping at rungs that were still intact, hauling themselves up within reach of their comrade's outstretched hands.

Christophe called to Fiona as she was lifted to safety. "Make for the lifeboats. Get to shore!"

"I won't leave James!" She tried to reach for him as she was lifted, but her fingers fell short. Then she was on deck. The flames were bearing down on her. But Fiona couldn't leave. Where was James? Then she saw him rising ever so slowly into view. Darting forward she seized his reaching hands and yanked as hard as she could. He came slithering over the edge to fall at her feet.

"Are you alright?" He got to his feet.

"You idiot, why didn't you run?" Without waiting for an answer, he grabbed her and ran for the ship's rail.

"Up and over!" he choked.

The wood was hot beneath their fingers. Fiona thought she felt her fingers blistering as she hauled herself over. Then she hit the water and went under. She surfaced quickly and was relieved to see James treading water beside her.

"Where now!" he spluttered.

"We've got to get to the next cove!" Fiona looked around frantically. Please don't let us have to swim for it! She might just manage it, but James wouldn't. He wasn't a good enough swimmer.

Then, to her disbelief, she saw a dingy tied to the Dolphin's side. It was just big enough to hold the two of them.

"Get in!" she yelled, pulling desperately at the rope. After an awkward struggle, James managed it and held the boat steady as Fiona loosed it and scrambled in after him. The ends of the rope were cut. Another few seconds and it probably would have given way of its own accord. Fiona took up the oars and began rowing as hard as she could. Only one thought was in her mind. To reach land and run to the city for help.

The fire pursued her. Reaching out for her with greedy fingers. It seemed as though every ship in the harbour was ablaze. Men were vainly trying to douse the flames with buckets of sea water, while other boats, mainly filled with women and children, raced for shore.

"This boat's filling up!" James shouted.

"Look in the bottom. There might be a bailer."

James rummaged around for a moment under the seat until he found it and began bailing frantically. But as fast as he emptied it, the boat filled up again. Fiona could feel the water's cold fingers curling around her bare legs and feet. The boat was settling lower and lower in the water.

"I think we're sinking!" James yelled, redoubling his efforts. The water was rising now. It was to their thighs. The shore was tantalisingly close, but she knew with a sick certainty that they would never make it in time. Around her she could hear panicked screams and shouts as other boats also began getting into difficulties. Fiona felt tears fill her eyes. The bastards! Wasn't burning them in their beds enough to satisfy them? There was no choice.

"We'll have to swim for it!" she said. The water was already above their waists. Without further ado she scrambled over the side. James followed her. Their movement capsized the boat completely. It sank like a stone. Fiona struck out for the shore, but she was nearing exhaustion. Her battle with the sinking craft had sapped much of her strength. For a moment she saw James's head bobbing near her, then it vanished.

"No!" she would have screamed, but she had no breath left. She reached down a hand and her fingers closed on hair. James rose gasping.

"I can't do this! Leave me, get out of here!"

"Yeah right!" Fiona panted. "T-turn on your back and g-grip my shoulders."

James was too tired to argue. She flipped onto her front as James took her by the shoulders. But with her first stroke, she knew she wasn't going to make it. Her arm muscles screamed at the strain. She nearly went under. Coughing, she made another effort. They were going to drown, both of them together. Salt water stung her already raw throat. Then, as her head broke the surface for what she felt sure was the last time, she saw movement nearby.

* * *

There was only him left now. He had been the last to reach the deck, whereupon his rescuers had fled, calling to him to follow. He could have gone before now. His fear had screamed at him to do so, but he had ignored it. Helping the others to escape had kept the fear at bay for a time, but now that he was alone, it was sneaking up on him. The terrible memories that he had kept buried for so long were rising to haunt him. He wanted to scream. As he hurried off in search of an escape route, his limbs seemed to grow increasingly heavy, as though resisting his efforts. He didn't know if the tears streaming down his cheeks were caused by the smoke that stung his eyes and burned his throat, or the images that chased him through the ship's store rooms and gangways.

His father's face, grim and set as he ordered Christophe into the cellar. His mother, her terrified face white and tear-streaked as she thrust his wailing baby sister into his thin arms. The roar from the flames of a past long buried, seemed to mingle with those of the present to triumphantly shout his despair. How many times had he woken from just such a nightmare as this, drenched in cold sweat, and clutched the battered book in his arms, as though it were his lost sister. But it was all terrifyingly real, and there would be no escape this time. The flames chased him relentlessly, always just behind, as though to taunt him.

He was stumbling down yet another corridor when his desperately groping hands blundered into coarse rope and wood. Thank the sea god, a ladder! He began to climb as quickly as he could, choking and gasping for breath. He was hampered by the sling about his still healing arm. A cruel knife of pain twisted in his side, nearly making him lose his grip. It dug deeper, causing him to pant rapidly as he hauled himself up. He was just two rungs from the top, when the ladder gave a sickening lurch and skewed violently to one side. This was it then. One more movement and it would give completely. He looked down. The flames had utterly consumed the passage he'd just run along, and were already licking hungrily at the lower rungs. He could just let go. It would be so easy. He could just let go now and get it over with.

"Christophe! Give me your hand!" He looked up through blurred, reddened eyes at Katie's soot-blackened face. She was lying flat on her stomach, one hand extended.

"Give me your hand!" she gasped. For perhaps two crucial seconds, Christophe could only stare at her in disbelief. She had come back for him? Why hadn't she fled with the other women? Then his scattered wits reasserted themselves. He reached for her hand with his good one and clung. Then let go with the other. The ladder broke free as Katie gave a colossal heave. Christophe's feet scrabbled desperately at the opening. Pain lanced through his arm and side. He screamed once. Then he was over the edge. Their combined momentum sent them both careening hard into the ship's rail which splintered under the impact, plunging them into icy water.

The shock revived Christophe like a slap in the face. He broke the surface spluttering. He was still gripping Katie's hand. He hauled her up with him.

"I cannot swim!" she choked.

"It's alright, I've got you!"

Cradling her shivering body in the crook of his good arm, he trod water. But he couldn't keep it up for long, he knew. His side hurt so that every breath was an effort. It was taking all of his strength just to hold Katie's head above the surface.

"A boat!" Katie gasped, pointing. Christophe looked and saw a small boat, probably belonging to one of the local fishermen. It was making a wide circle, its lanterns ablaze, plainly searching.

"Over here!" It was little more than a rasping croak, yet the fisherman heard him. Swinging the boat hard around, he began rowing over to them as fast as he could. Christophe saw Fiona and James's scared white faces as they reached out their hands to haul him and Katie aboard. Without a word, the fisherman swung the boat around again and headed away with his exhausted passengers. None of whom had the strength for so much as a greeting.

Fiona and James clung silently to each other. Katie lay utterly spent at Christophe's feet.

Then a small dark head appeared from somewhere near their feet.

"Christophe?" a tiny, frightened voice whispered.

"Lena!" Leaning forward, Christophe gathered the trembling body into his arms and held her close, muttering a fervent prayer of thanks. He only hoped the rest of her family had made it also.

Behind them, the *Dolphin* disappeared in a ball of orange flame.

# Chapter 13

## The Jolly Sailor

Not one of the Travellers' ships survived. The conflagration consumed the entire beach, and was visible for miles. Despite the heroic efforts of the locals, very little was salvaged, and it was well past dawn before the flames were finally brought under control.

The sabotage of the boats had effectively ensured that no one could reach dry land, and even though every able-bodied seaman in the city had rushed to save the survivors, they could not save them all. Many succumbed to exhaustion or the freezing waters, and the blood of the wounded soon brought the sharks in ever increasing numbers.

Fiona stood in a huddle with James and Katie, watching in numb silence as the surviving Travellers picked their way through the wreckage.

Christophe was among them, together with Esther and her family, all of whom had miraculously escaped. They had been picked up by another boat, but had feared Lena was dead. Fiona had watched their reunion when an exhausted Christophe had carried her ashore. It was the only good thing she'd seen all morning. She had watched with the rest as men battled with the hungry flames, and had followed everyone down to the beach when it was over.

In place of the lush sand, there was only ash as far as she could see. Many embers were still smoking hotly, and people repeatedly doused them with sea water to prevent them from flaring up anew.

The incoming tide brought its own grizzly offering. Fiona had never seen a dead body before. She watched with sick horror as people searched the dead for their loved ones. Here and there among the bloated faces, Fiona saw ones she recognized. But some were burned beyond recognition.

It was when she saw the bodies the sharks had finished with, that Fiona finally reached the limit of her endurance. With a strangled cry, she turned from the dreadful spectacle and vomited onto the ash-covered ground. She felt a shaky hand on her shoulder, and looked round to find James in an equally bad state beside her.

When her stomach was empty, she stumbled away. She had no idea where she was going. She only wanted to get away from that scene of ruin and death.

She no longer felt quite herself any more. The girl who had raced to glory in the swimming gala had died with the *Dolphin*. And in her place… Fiona really didn't know.

Her stomach still heaved occasionally, but it was empty. The bile burned Fiona's already raw throat. She sat down in the lee of a large bolder, and drew up her knees and rested her folded arms upon them. She bowed her head so that her hair veiled her face. It reeked of smoke. Behind her, a low keening began as women greeted the new day with their sorrow. Fiona wished she could join in.

The sound of approaching footsteps jerked her out of her reverie. She looked up and saw James, Christophe and Katie making their way towards her. Looking at them, Fiona wondered if she looked as bad.

Soot had made Katie's hair even darker and her clothes were stiff with salt.

James was pale beneath his covering of ash, and Christophe appeared to be walking with difficulty.

"We ought to leave now," he said quietly. "We cannot endanger these people any more. It is us they want."

Fiona nodded, then asked the question she already knew the answer to. "It was because of me, wasn't it? That's why they burned all these ships and all those people…" she swallowed hard.

"This wasn't your fault!" James said sharply, laying a hand on her shoulder.

Fiona gave a hollow laugh. "Oh come off it, James. Why else were they attacked? If it was just a grudge against them, they could have done it any time. It's because they were hiding me."

James opened his mouth to argue, but could think of no response.

"All the more reason for us to leave at once," said Christophe.

"But we have no food or anything," said James.

"We can pick some up as we go. Come, make your farewells."

Fiona and James set off in search of Esther and her family. Katie and Christophe followed at a slower pace.

"Will you be fit to travel?" Katie said quietly, so only Christophe could hear.

Christophe's hand unconsciously went to his side. It had been giving him trouble ever since his escape from the *Dolphin*. He thought he had hidden it well. But evidently not from Katie.

"I can manage. I've got to. The sooner The Appointed is away from here the better."

"Who do you think did it?" Katie said, gesturing at the wreckage all around them.

"Well, I doubt it was Alfredo. He would not want to risk The Appointed getting killed."

Katie looked startled, as though the thought had not occurred to her.

"Well, who then?"

Christophe sighed wearily. "It could perhaps have been Miguel, but with Alfredo's men out looking for him, I doubt he would risk drawing attention to himself."

Katie's expression darkened at the sound of Miguel's name. "What does he have to lose?" she said bitterly. "If he knows his time grows short, he would want to be remembered."

It was Christophe's turn to look surprised. "I never thought of that. You may well be right. My only sorrow is that Alfredo has got to him first."

Esther and her family were still among those gathered on the beach. Fiona and James hesitated, not liking to intrude on their grief. Many people were weeping as they moved among the debris. Others just stood motionless, staring out to sea with lost expressions on their faces.

Esther and Gideon stood in a small huddle with their parents and Jeremiah and a few friends who had lived with them on the Dolphin. Lena was holding her mother's hand and they were speaking quietly. Also in their group was Carlotta, grim and silent as usual, with a small group of children gathered closely around her. They were clinging to her, and she was caressing them absently as she stared out to sea. Fiona was shocked to see the pure hatred blazing in her eyes.

Christophe and Katie came up to them and led the way over to the group.

"We are leaving," Christophe said quietly.

They looked at him aghast.

"But what will you do for food?" said Josephine. "We have nothing to give you."

"That doesn't matter. We can find food as we go." Christophe turned to Gideon and Carlotta, who were among those he had chosen as their escort.

"You should stay with the others. You are more needed here."

Carlotta nodded without looking at him. Gideon looked torn. Fiona could almost see the struggle taking place inside him as his loyalties fought each other. Christophe must have sensed it too. He stepped forward and laid a hand on Gideon's shoulder.

"Do not fret, my friend. Where we have to go, weapons will not help us. It is magic that will be chasing us. Alfredo will soon learn of our errand even without Miguel. He is bound to come after us. Perhaps the four of us can evade him more easily than a large group."

Gideon still looked troubled, but there was relief in his eyes. "Safe journey, Christophe," he murmured, clasping his hand briefly, then doing the same with James.

Esther hugged Fiona tightly, tears in her eyes. "Take care of yourself."

"You too," Fiona said, blinking away tears of her own. Then Josephine was hugging her too.

"Come back to us soon, my dear. We will all be praying for you."

Fiona didn't know what to say to that. There was a large lump in her throat. She merely nodded.

Christophe was hugging Lena, who was biting her lip hard to keep from crying. Then he hugged Esther. Fiona thought Esther looked as though she wanted to say something to him, but he was already drawing away.

Katie stood alone, watching as the others exchanged their farewells. She felt awkward, as though she was witnessing something very private. She shouldn't really be here at all. Were it not for her father, she wouldn't be.

Other people had realised what was going on, and had come over to say their own goodbyes. Every one of them wanted to touch Fiona or hug her. She stood still and let them, though Katie could see she felt very uncomfortable. She herself longed for it to be over. She wanted to be gone from here, and it was with an effort that she concealed her impatience. She thought Christophe shared her feelings to some degree, though he made no effort to halt or hurry his people. He seemed to feel it was Fiona's due.

At last it was over, and amidst numerous shouted well wishes and some scattered cheers, the four unlikely companions set out with Christophe leading in the direction of the city.

The sun was well up by this time, and there were already many travellers on the road, hurrying to market with the day's goods.

"So where exactly is it we're headed?" James enquired as soon as they were clear of the harbour.

"The first thing to be done is to find some supplies," said Christophe. "We will not find much in the way of food this side of the desert."

He was looking very grave, Fiona thought. The shadow of the night's events was evidently still hanging over him. He had lost his home, and many people he had known. She wanted to ask how they were to buy food with no money, but something about Christophe's expression prevented her. Instead, she fell to imagining what a sight they would look to anyone they passed in the street. They would be lucky if anyone sold them anything.

"So where are we going?" James repeated. "Surely the first thing we have to do is find the—"

"Not here!" Christophe hissed. "You never know who might be listening. There is an inn owned by some friends of mine where we can put up for the night. We can lay our plans there."

They had reached the city proper now. The streets were already crowded and Fiona had to really concentrate hard on keeping Christophe in sight in the milling press. She felt strangely claustrophobic, and memories of her last trip into the city kept intruding into her thoughts, no matter how hard she tried to ignore them. She was grateful when James silently took her arm. He always seemed to sense intuitively what she was thinking.

As they were passing a brightly bedecked flower stall, the owner shot out a veined and knotted hand and grabbed Christophe's sleeve. Caught by surprise, Christophe whirled, his hand already reaching for the knife at his belt, but his expression cleared when he saw who it was who held him.

"You should take care who you waylay, Magda," he said. "That sort of thing could get you killed one of these days."

"Oh, bless you, my dear. Who'd harm an old woman like me?"

Christophe shrugged. The others had stopped also, and were watching with interest.

"What is it, Magda? I am in something of a hurry today."

"I heard about what happened last night down at the harbour," she said, her voice a hushed whisper. "A terrible shame, it was. Do you know who did it?"

Christophe's mouth set into a grim line. "No, but the Guardians will find out soon enough, and whoever it was will live to regret it. Now if that is all—" he turned to go, but Magda grabbed his sleeve once more.

"Stop a minute. My boy Yassin said as how you was looking for news of Miguel."

Christophe turned to face her, eyes suddenly alert. "Yes? What is it?"

"Well now, what was it he said?" She absently fingered a fragrant purple blossom.

Christophe masked his impatience with extreme difficulty.

"This would look lovely in the pretty girl's hair," she murmured, gesturing vaguely at Katie, who happened to be standing nearest to her. Katie blushed and opened her mouth, but Christophe interrupted. "Magda, what did Yassin tell you?"

"Alright, I'm getting there. No need to rush an old woman."

Christophe took a deep breath. Fiona and James fought hard not to catch each other's eye. The temptation to laugh was almost overwhelming.

"He said as how Miguel was arrested this very morning by Alfredo's men. Took him to the grey prison they did. He's to be executed publicly on Traitor's Hill two dawns from now. Alfredo's declaring a half holiday so the whole city can watch."

There was no mistaking the satisfaction in Katie's eyes at the news, but Christophe merely looked grim.

"Well, that's one less of Alfredo's men to haunt the streets. I only wonder who will replace him. It will be difficult to find anyone equal to him. He was a master of his craft, even though it galls me to admit it."

Katie made a derisive sound.

"Well, we must go. Thank you, Magda. Thank Yassin for me."

"Oh I will, dear, I will."

"Well, that's a stroke of luck," said James. "At least we don't have to worry about him dogging our heels the whole way."

"I wish I could be there to watch it." Katie muttered.

Fiona looked at her in surprise. "Do you really hate him that much?"

Katie nodded.

"I don't think I could ever wish anyone dead, no matter how much I hated them."

Katie made no reply to this.

"What did he do to you?" Fiona pressed.

Still silence. Then, so softly that the others could barely hear her over the noise around them, "It was not only what he did to me. But also what he did to Jessemine and the others, especially Jessemine. Now they are all slaves because of him."

Fiona and James looked uneasily at each other, not sure what to say.

Christophe laid a hand briefly on Katie's shoulder. "I promise as soon as this is over, I will do everything I can to free them."

Katie smiled at him. "I will hold you to that promise."

Fiona exchanged a quizzical look with James. This was an interesting development.

The inn that was Christophe's destination turned out to be a large rambling brick building that looked badly in need of decorating. The sign hanging over the front entrance and creaking slightly in the breeze, proclaimed the name of the inn as The Jolly Sailor in large, clumsily scrawled letters. Below was a rather badly drawn sketch of a fat, jolly-looking bearded man swigging appreciatively from a tankard of ale.

James cast the sign a dubious glance. "I'm not sure about this," he muttered to Fiona. But Christophe was already striding through the door, and they had no option but to follow.

The inside was somewhat more inviting. About a dozen tables with long wooden benches drawn up before them were stationed rather haphazardly about the room. All were spotlessly clean. Sunlight streamed through the three big windows, casting long shadows on the pale stone walls and floor. There were two other doors. One presumably leading to the upper storeys, the other, situated behind the long counter in the exact centre of the room, appeared to lead to the kitchen. As this door opened to admit a maid with a loaded tray, women's laughter sounded, together with the clatter of pots and pans. A large tabby cat was curled up by the hearth, snoozing peacefully in a patch of sun.

The common room was almost deserted except for a man sitting alone at a table, who began tucking into his meal with gusto the moment it was set before him and paid no heed to their entrance. A stout woman in early middle age was busily wiping the counter top.

She looked round as they entered, and her plump, good-natured face split into a wide smile.

"Well now, if it isn't our little runaway. Couldn't stay away, eh?" She hurried out from behind the counter, and to the considerable surprise of the others, seized Christophe in a fierce embrace that nearly knocked him off balance. Fiona saw Christophe wince slightly as the woman crushed him to her capacious bosom. But he returned her embrace with equal warmth.

"Well, it's a fine young man you've grown into and no mistake," she said, holding Christophe at arm's length and studying him critically. "I remember well that skinny waif who would come scrounging for scraps at my door. You could still do with a little more meat on them bones though," she added, jabbing a finger in Christophe's side.

Christophe hid a grimace behind a smile. "It is good to see you, Bess. How are Ephrom and the others?"

"Oh, they're grand. The boys are great strapping men like their father. They'd eat us out of house and home if I'd let 'em. Saul is to be married come next spring, and our Zeb is looking into buying himself a bit of land for farming. They'll only be our Caleb left when they're gone, and Elsa of course."

"How is Elsa?"

Bess twinkled knowingly at him. "Aye, she's a bonny lass right enough, and about your age too. She'll be needing a husband soon."

Katie moved forward to Christophe's side, her hand outstretched in greeting. She was smiling, but her eyes told a story that Fiona guessed only too well. Fighting down an urge to laugh, she nudged James and they moved forward. Christophe, seemingly anxious to turn the conversation away from Elsa, readily made the introductions.

"We need somewhere to stay, Bess. Do you think you could put us up for a night? Two at the most."

Bess stroked a finger down the bridge of her nose. "Aye, I do have a couple of rooms free as it happens. Reckon they'll suit you well enough."

She fixed Christophe with a suddenly beady eye. "You'll be paying your way? I don't mean to sound harsh but times are hard right now, especially with our almighty emperor raising taxes for the third time this month. And with the Travellers leaving, business is set to fall right off."

"You will have the patronage of the Travellers for a good while yet," Christophe said grimly. "They will need somewhere to drown their sorrows I expect."

"Eh now, what's that? And what may you be meaning by that, young Christophe?"

It was Katie who answered. "All the Travellers' ships were burned last night. They destroyed everything. My friends and I are in some trouble. We really need somewhere to shelter for a couple of days."

A look of shocked amazement spread over Bess's round face at these words. "The Travellers' ships burned? Why we never heard a thing about it! That explains why there's been no customers today. And you're in some trouble you say?" She ran an appraising eye over their bedraggled clothing and soot-stained faces. "Aye, I can see that. Here's what we'll do then. For two nights you can have a bed and hot meals and in exchange, you two girls can help Elsa and my women in the kitchen, and you lads can help my boys in the stable."

Christophe gave her a quick hug. "That would be fine, Bess, thank you so much!" The relief in his voice was evident. Bess pushed him away.

"Get on with you! I won't have you dirtying up my nice clean apron." But her sharp tone belied her smile of pleasure.

"Upstairs with you now. A bath and a change of clothes is what you'll be wanting. You girls can borrow some of my Elsa's frocks and you boys can make do with some of my lad's things."

An hour later, clean and dressed in one of Elsa's dresses, Fiona joined James, Christophe and Katie in the common room.

It felt odd to be wearing a dress after the clothing of the Guardians, and Fiona knew which she preferred. As Elsa was more of a size with Katie, the dress was a little tight in the sleeves and across the chest, and she had to keep remembering to hoist up her long skirts.

"You'll look great crossing the desert in that," James said with a grin.

"Shut up," Fiona grumbled, sliding onto the bench beside him.

"You will have different clothes when we travel," said Christophe. "For now you are a kitchen maid and must dress accordingly."

"Oh yes, how could I forget that?" Fiona muttered. Bess had already outlined the evening's chores, and her daughter was only too keen to show the new kitchen maids the ropes.

Fiona caught Katie's eye and they exchanged a commiserating grimace.

“What do we do now?” said Fiona. “We have a couple of hours left before Katie and I need to be back here.”

“I suppose we hunt for that key you mentioned,” said Katie. “The one in the poem that your father found.”

Fiona sighed gloomily. “God knows where we start looking.”

“Tell us what your father told you about the key. Everything you can remember,” said Christophe.

Fiona glowered at him. “He said, ‘First find the key that unlocks all doors except for those within’, whatever that’s supposed to mean.”

There was a pensive silence.

“What kind of key fits all doors?” James wondered aloud.

“That’s easy enough,” said Katie. “Smugglers used to use keys they made in secret that were designed to fit the locks on chests of goods. They were a sort of key and lock pick combined. You could break into almost anywhere with them.”

“Well that doesn’t sound very magical,” James commented. “How’s that going to help us find the sceptre?”

“You are forgetting the last line,” said Christophe. “The key unlocks all doors ‘*except for those within*’ – that must mean something important.”

“Yeah, but what?” Fiona muttered.

“That does not matter at the moment,” said Christophe. “What matters is finding who would be likely to sell such a thing. You said your father gave it to a merchant friend to keep safe?”

Fiona nodded.

Christophe bit his lip, brow furrowed. At last he said, “There are merchants who sell trinkets which they claim are talismans against evil magic. There is probably not a drop of real magic in any of them, but people are very superstitious, especially rich fools who believe their rivals for power are looking for ways to get them out of the way.” There was no mistaking the contempt in Christophe’s voice.

“Tobias did say that his friend used to cast illusions over his goods to make people think they were worth buying, and give the good stuff to the poor.”

Christophe laughed. “Very clever. Being magical himself, it must have been amusing to sell worthless junk to those stuck-up fools.”

“It was him who told Tobias that the key had an illusion cast over it,” said Fiona, remembering suddenly. “He said it would reveal itself to me.”

“Did he give you a name for this man, or tell you where to find him?” Christophe asked. Fiona looked crestfallen.

“No, nothing.”

Christophe got to his feet. “Well then, it seems we have quite a hunt ahead of us.”

It was a wearying business. Fiona soon lost count of all the twisting streets and alleys they wandered down.

The shops selling artefacts were easy enough to find, owing to the signs over their doors. *Make safe your slumber and ward well your waking. Charms to keep bad dreams and wishes away.*

“Oh, please!” Fiona muttered the first time she caught sight of one of these. But she dutifully followed the others in and examined the goods for sale. But no flashes of insight came to her. The feathers, pebbles and variously cut metals looked exactly the same when she picked them up. Nothing suddenly revealed its true shape.

A thought began to grow in her mind. What if she wasn’t The Appointed after all? What if she’d already handled the key, and its true form had stayed stubbornly hidden? What would the others do then?

It was a dispirited group that made its way back to The Jolly Sailor.

“Perhaps someone has it already,” Fiona suggested wearily. “In which case we could search for weeks and not find it.”

“We do not have weeks,” Christophe snapped. “We do not even have days. It is only a matter of time before Alfredo is on our trail.”

There was a long silence.

“I could find it,” Katie said quietly. Fiona and James stared at her incredulously.

Christophe clapped a hand to his forehead. “Of course! How could I have forgotten? I am sorry, Katie. Here we have wasted a whole day.”

Katie coloured a little. “Well, not really. Fiona did ideally need to find it for herself. She is The Appointed after all, but that’s why I am coming along with you. You may as well make use of me.”

“What are you going on about?” demanded Fiona.

Katie explained her talent.

“Wow! that’s amazing!” said James. “So you could tell us where the sceptre is?”

“Maybe,” Katie said doubtfully. “But somehow, I don’t think it would work.”

“Why not?” Fiona said hopefully. “Think of the time you could save us.”

“You are forgetting the rhyme,” said Katie.

“So? What of it?”

“The instructions are not straight forward. They are like a riddle or poem that you have to solve. What would be the purpose of a magic key if you can just walk up and take the sceptre whenever you like? Besides, the poem tells you where it is.”

“On an island I cannot see,” Fiona said bitterly. “I shouldn’t have any problems then, should I?” But she couldn’t help looking at Katie with new respect. Here was someone with magical blood, like her father and Alfredo. She wondered which parent Katie had inherited her talent from.

There were several customers in the common room. A warm buzz of conversation and a haze of pipe smoke greeted them as they entered.

Several men looked up curiously, but almost immediately returned to their ale. All except one. As his glance swept over them, his eyes lingered for a second on Christophe with a flash of recognition, before returning to a contemplation of the murky contents of his mug.

“Come along!” Bess’s voice called imperiously from the kitchen door. She pointed a beckoning finger at Katie and Fiona.

"There's more ale needs fetching up from the cellar and supper won't be cooking itself. You two," pointing at James and Christophe, "you're needed in the stable. Get along with you." They scuttled off obediently, but as they passed the table of the man who had looked at them, Fiona saw him flip Christophe a strange hand signal under cover of demanding his mug refilled. And she could have sworn she saw Christophe return it.

For the next three or four hours, Katie and Fiona were kept extremely busy, running backwards and forwards with plates and mugs for the customers and returning with dirty crockery to be washed. The few patrons of the afternoon had now risen to a sizable throng, raucous and demanding. Fiona quickly learned not to come too close to any of them. The men were all too ready with their hands. More than once Fiona had her skirts unexpectedly lifted as she passed. The first time nearly causing her to drop the tray she was carrying. More than one hand tried for a swift grope. One man grabbed her as she passed and pinched her bottom hard. Fiona's hands were free then, and she whirled, a hand raised to slap his grinning face, but as if by magic, one of Bess's sons was there and the moment passed.

"You'll want to be careful," he said quietly. "These men are freer with their hands than they are with their purses."

"I've noticed," Fiona growled. She quickly became good at dodging the various attempts to waylay her.

Bess's daughter Elsa moved about with an ease and skill that Fiona could only envy. She was a plump, cheerful soul with a mass of honey-coloured braids and a ready smile. She flirted outrageously with many of the customers, though she followed Christophe with her eyes every time he came to beg a mug of ale for one of the stable grooms. Fiona saw with some amusement that Katie had noticed too. She made a point of keeping Christophe within her sight at all times, and often it was she who served him, much to Elsa's frustration.

There came a point when it appeared to be time for entertainment. Two men appeared on a platform at the top of the room, one with a dulcimer and the other a penny whistle.

Servants from stables and kitchen alike came in, and the musicians struck up a lively tune. In no time at all people were pairing off to dance. Fiona, halfway to the kitchen, paused uncertainly, but at that moment one of Bess's sons accosted her.

"Would you care to dance?"

Fiona looked around. James was surrounded by two or three laughing girls who appeared to be half bullying, half cajoling him onto the dance floor, and another man had just approached Katie. Seeing her path clear for the moment, Elsa was making for Christophe with a determined look on her face.

"OK," Fiona said. "But I'm not very good."

Her partner laughed. "You'll learn fast enough. I never yet met a maid who couldn't dance."

He was right. The music was lively and the enthusiasm of the dancers infectious. At one point she noticed Christophe looking around distractedly, but she was soon too caught up in the dancing to care. It was the most fun she had had since leaving Earth.

* * *

Christophe was relieved when the evening's chores were over. It had been a stroke of luck seeing Carlos here tonight. Before he could get near him, however, Bess's daughter had swooped down on him, dragging him along with her with a zeal that he couldn't escape. He peered distractedly over the heads of the crowd while Elsa tried to press herself close to him, praying that Carlos was not about to leave. But he just sat in his corner, calmly sipping his ale and watching the dancers.

When the dance finally ceased, Christophe was about to excuse himself when a voice called loudly for a reel. The musicians struck up willingly as everyone hastily assumed their positions, and now, for the first time, Christophe gave his full attention to the dance. He knew this reel. The men and women formed inner and outer circles facing each other. Christophe was facing Elsa, but his eyes were suddenly fixed on Katie. He knew what was coming and his pulse began to quicken. He danced his first few steps automatically, passing Elsa around to the next man in the circle with barely a thought. He danced with each girl in turn before passing her on, but his eyes never left Katie. He started slightly as Fiona was spun towards his outstretched arms and only just managed to catch her. Her awkwardness was as great as his and she fumbled her steps, not looking at him.

Then came the moment that he had been waiting for, and Katie was in his arms. How light she felt in his grasp. Almost weightless. Her midnight black hair fluttered across her flushed cheeks and her bright black eyes laughed up into his. He had never seen her look so happy or so lovely. He felt her press closer and a deep ache started in his chest, but all too soon he was passing her on. As she left his arms he felt momentarily bereft. He was relieved when the dance finally ended and Bess was calling closing time. His stomach reminded him that he had eaten nothing all day and he moved gladly towards the kitchen.

Just then he saw Carlos rise to leave and his earlier desire returned. He raised a hand, beckoning the other man over, and gesturing in the direction of the kitchen.

Fiona and James entered the kitchen to find Katie and Christophe already tucking in to plates piled high with lamb stew, peas and boiled potatoes. But they were not alone.

A man was sitting across the table from Christophe.

He was rather unremarkable to look at. He had the type of face Fiona forgot even as she studied it, but Christophe was chatting animatedly to him as though they were old friends.

"Here you are, my dears," Bess said, placing two steaming plates in front of James and Fiona.

Christophe broke off in mid-sentence, looking round. "Oh, there you are. I need to introduce you to someone. This is Carlos, the best thief in the city."

“Among other things,” Carlos said with a chuckle. “There isn’t a trade I haven’t turned my hand to at one time or another, and I’ve known Christophe here since he was that high.” He gestured somewhere around his knee.

Fiona and James shook hands a little warily. Carlos didn’t appear like their idea of a thief, with his smart clothes and cheerful grin. But maybe that’s the idea, Fiona thought. It’s a great disguise. After all, who’d suspect someone like him?

“So Alfredo ordered them all to be destroyed?” Christophe was saying.

Carlos nodded sadly. “Aye, and very useful tools they were too. No thief or smuggler would be without one. Get you into anywhere, they could, and out again, what’s more.”

Fiona suddenly pricked up her ears. The key! What Carlos was describing sounded very like the key they had to find. And this man Carlos was a thief. Surely if anyone had one or knew where one could be found it would be him. She leaned forward.

“You wouldn’t happen to have one, would you? Or know where one might be found?”

Carlos gave her a shrewd look that she didn’t like at all, but she held his gaze.

“No, lass. Alfredo had them all rounded up and destroyed. Anyone caught with one in his possession lost a hand. I had one of them once, but I’m a thief. Hands are vital to my trade. I found it prudent to get rid of mine.”

Fiona sat back in her chair. Destroyed? All of them? They were stymied completely now. If Alfredo knew what he’d actually done or had he known? Had her father not been as careful as he had thought? Had Alfredo’s purge been more than just an attempt to end the smuggling trade?

She chanced a look at James. His face mirrored her own dismay, but Christophe’s face as usual showed nothing of his feelings, nor, for that matter did Katie’s. She didn’t even appear to be listening to the conversation.

“Will you be staying around, Carlos?” Christophe was saying now.

“Oh, I’ll be around a day or two. It’s Miguel’s execution the day after tomorrow and the pickings will be rich there, what with all the wealthy turning out to watch the downfall of one of their own. Mind you, I won’t be sorry to see the last of him. He’s nearly had my neck in a hangman’s noose a time or two.”

He pushed back his chair. “Well, I think I’ll be turning in. Luck to you, Christophe. You know where I am if you need me.”

They clasped hands warmly.

“Luck to you also, my friend.”

“Ah, we miss you, Christophe, You never ought to have taken up with those wandering folk. Good people I’m sure, but it was a sad day for the underworld when you left us. Well, goodnight to you all.”

There was a silence after Carlos’s departure. Katie was looking at Christophe with open curiosity, but Fiona pre-empted her.

“So what do we do now? If all those keys were destroyed, then we’re stuck before we’ve even begun.”

“Not necessarily,” said Christophe. He turned to Katie.

"Will you still agree to search for it?"
She nodded. "If you think there's a chance it is still hidden."
"If that key is in this city, Carlos will find it."

* * *

Katie lay in bed, listening to Fiona's gentle breathing. It was quiet below, the last customers having finally departed. Katie listened to the innkeeper and her family making their way up to bed.

The Jolly Sailor was in the heart of the city, yet still the cries of seagulls reached Katie's ears through the open window. A gentle breeze cooled the stuffy room, and Katie pushed back the covers to let it cool her hot skin.

Fiona stirred uneasily and murmured something, but did not wake. A nightmare, Katie thought, and no wonder. Barely twenty-four hours before, they had all been fleeing for their lives. Who had set the ships ablaze? Not her father, Christophe had thought. She was glad of that, though she didn't like to think about what her father would say if he knew she had saved Christophe's life when he was of no importance. The Appointed should have been her first and only concern.

Christophe. The boy who revealed nothing and whom everybody seemed to know. The boy who had held her to him only a few short hours ago and looked into her eyes. The memory of how it had felt to have his arms around her sent a delicious shiver through her. She was in over her head now, whatever her father thought, and there was no going back.

Propping herself on one elbow, she blew out the candle glowing softly on a table beside the bed, and lay down once more, forming the question in her mind, closing her eyes, shutting out the world, all thought and sound, concentrating solely on the words.

*Where is the key that will help guide The Appointed to the sceptre? Where is the key that will help guide The Appointed to the sceptre? Where is the…?*

# Chapter 14

## Breakout

"Miguel has it?" Fiona's voice came out an incredulous squeak.

Katie rubbed her eyes. Though she had slept the night through, her dreams had allowed her little rest. She had received the answer she sought, and had hurried to rouse the others immediately on waking.

"It is in Miguel's house," she corrected.

"Well, that comes to the same thing, doesn't it?" said Fiona. "What the hell is he doing with it?"

"The man your father gave the key to kept it in his shop for many years, but finally his business began to suffer. Alfredo's taxes were growing higher and there were not enough customers. The man's health began to fail and the decline of his business eventually brought on an illness that he never recovered from. His children were forced to sell off the shop and everything in it.

"Miguel bought the key for the strong box where he secretly saved the money he earned from smuggling. You heard Carlos say last night that those keys were highly prized among thieves and smugglers, and Miguel was no exception."

"Which leaves us right back where we started," said James. "We've got no chance of getting it now, short of searching the house."

"Out of the question," said Christophe. "Alfredo will have had Miguel's house watched in case of suspicious activity. We would never get near it."

"We could go through the passage," James suggested.

Christophe shook his head. "We would be caught sooner or later, even assuming we found the key. We would need to search for it undisturbed, without arousing suspicion."

"As I said," muttered James. "We're still as badly off as ever."

But Christophe was frowning, biting his lip. They watched him warily.

"What we need," he said slowly, "is to search the house by daylight without interruption."

Fiona snorted. "How do we do that then?"

"If we had Miguel with us…"

"He's in prison," Katie said sharply. "The only way Miguel is leaving there is in a coffin. No one would let him return to his home."

"They would if it was on Alfredo's orders."

"Yeah, and he's really going to do that," Fiona muttered, but there was a look of dawning comprehension on Katie's face, replaced almost at once by anger.

"Surely you are not suggesting…"

"We will ask Carlos to forge us some papers from Alfredo, ordering Miguel to be returned to his house under guard, as he has something of value to his master hidden there. It should not be difficult. Alfredo gets scribes to write for him, so we would not have to worry about disguising the writing. The only thing that must look authentic is Alfredo's seal. Most of those men will be unable to read in any case. It will be the seal they will check for. Carlos can steal James and I some guard uniforms and we can break Miguel out and have him back well before his execution tomorrow."

"No!" Katie said fiercely. "You want to set that man loose? After everything he has put us through? After what he did to Fiona? And it was probably him who set the Travellers' ships on fire. Not to mention the fact that because of him, many good people are now bound for the slave markets."

"We have no choice," Christophe said sharply. "We have no chance of obtaining the key otherwise. We could search that house for days and never find it, and we do not have days."

"Miguel will tell the guards who we are the moment we get back."

"We can be long gone by then. We will make ready to leave as soon as we have the key."

They sat staring at each other, eyes blazing. Fiona and James exchanged uncomfortable looks.

But when Christophe spoke, his voice was unusually gentle. "Katie, listen to me! If there was any other way, believe me, I would take it, but there is none! Even you must see that. We need that key! Without it, the whole quest would be useless. We are talking about our people's freedom."

There was a long silence. Katie stared into Christophe's eyes, anger and indecision warring within her. He gazed back calmly, implacably. He would do this, whether she approved or not.

"Alright," she said reluctantly. "But I must rescue Jessemine and the others."

Christophe frowned. "But—"

"I will not leave them to be sold as slaves. They were my family. If Miguel does get free, I will not leave them to be trampled under his boots again." It was Jessemine who was particularly in her thoughts. She would give Jessemine the freedom that had been so long denied her. "Besides," she added, "a diversion of some kind might prove useful."

"This is ridiculous!" Fiona snapped. "We'll never get away with this."

Katie made no reply, but she agreed. They would be extremely lucky to pull this off. She felt a mixture of fear and excitement.

It had not taken long to form a suitable plan once they had made Carlos aware of their plight. To Katie's surprise, he had asked few questions. He had returned at midday with a bulging sack containing two maid's outfits and two guard's uniforms. He had even acquired two daggers from somewhere.

While they hurried into their new clothes, Carlos took a small paper package from a pocket and emptied a fine stream of white powder into a jug of wine already prepared for them by Bess. She too had been extremely cooperative, not asking any questions, just providing what they asked for.

It was because of Christophe of course. That was the only reason these people were risking so much. Fiona stood and watched with the others as Bess stirred the powder into the wine until it had completely dissolved, leaving the liquid unchanged to outward appearances.

Katie, who knew something of herb law, had nonetheless never come across this particular medicine.

"What is it?" she enquired of Christophe.

"A simple sleeping draught, nothing more. Though it has the unusual property of allowing the drinker to breathe under water."

Fiona was suddenly glaring furiously at Christophe, but he continued speaking. "It will create the perfect diversion. The local inns often provide food and drink for the guards and slave traders, and one serving maid looks very like another. Once they are asleep, you take their keys and free the slaves and get out of there as soon as you can. Once the uproar begins, the prison guards will be too flustered to pay our request proper attention."

It seemed fraught with risk, but no one could think of a better plan.

Katie and Fiona had blackened their faces with soot from The Jolly Sailor's hearth. This served the duel purpose of adding to their disguise and making their features less distinct.

Fiona had been forced to hide her revealing hair beneath a head scarf, and Katie had done the same for appearances sake.

No one troubled them as they made their way through the busy streets. Christophe and James's guard uniforms saw to that. Even Fiona had been impressed the first time she had laid eyes on them. With daggers at their belts, they were utterly transformed.

They approached the prison by a back route.

The fortress was a forbidding sight. Armed guards patrolled every parapet and walkway. High walls surrounded it and huge wrought iron gates cut it off from the rest of the world. Atop a flagpole at least ten feet high, Alfredo's pennant fluttered in the slight breeze. The prison looked impregnable.

Behind it rose Traitor's Hill, where all public executions were carried out. It was there that Miguel would be executed come the dawn, and his corpse paraded, as was tradition, through the city streets.

Fiona shuddered and averted her eyes. Much as she detested Miguel, she was glad she would not have to watch the spectacle.

When they were as close as they could get without being seen, Christophe whispered to Katie and Fiona. "James and I will await your signal here. Get away quickly and make your way back here as soon as you can. We will meet you here."

Katie nodded, while Fiona gave a sharp jerk of the head.

Her throat was too tight for speech. She could not suppress the fear that this incredibly risky plan would go pear-shaped, and she dreaded to think what the consequences would be. She was walking voluntarily into the clutches of Alfredo's men. It was insane! But there was no other choice.

"Good luck," Katie whispered back.

"Be careful," said James with a worried look at Fiona. Katie saw it and gave him a reassuring smile. Fiona tried to do the same, but her teeth seemed locked together and she could only manage a grimace. Katie turned away abruptly and strode out into the open, Fiona following close on her heels.

A sentry thrust his bayonet into their path.

"Halt! Who goes there? Speak!" The last word was a snap. Katie shrank back as if terrified. Fiona imitated her, though it was difficult to cringe and balance a loaded tray at the same time.

"If you please, sir, Katie stammered. "We were sent with wine and cheese for the traders. They always have their meal around mid day, sir, and our mistress—"

"Yes, yes," the man cut her off impatiently. "Go on then."

He removed his bayonet and stepped aside, somewhat reluctantly, Katie thought.

"If you please, sir," she said diffidently. "We don't know where we should go, us being new, you see, and our mistress said—"

"That way!" the guard snapped, gesturing with his bayonet. "And if I were you," he added as Katie made to pass. "I would take a lesson from your friend there. Silence and obedience are good trade marks in a servant, especially a woman."

Katie curtsied. "Yes, sir. Thank you, sir," and hurried after Fiona.

"That was brilliant!" Fiona said with a nervous giggle as soon as they were out of earshot. "You're quite the actress."

Katie shook a fist at the sentry's back. "Great oaf! I have lived among servants all my life and he tells me how to behave?" She continued to glower, only rearranging her expression when they reached the wagons.

There were about half a dozen of them in all, ugly, ungainly things with the slave trader's symbol (a pair of shackles and a whip) painted on them in green. A small group of men were lounging at their ease nearby.

They looked up as the two girls approached, their eyes passing over them greedily. Katie and Fiona kept their eyes modestly down.

"Your midday meals, sirs," Katie whispered as Fiona mutely proffered the tray.

"Well now," one man said. "A tasty bit of profit you two fine wenches would make. Such a shame you are already spoken for." He had a lazy drawl that made Katie's flesh crawl, and he appeared to be the leader. His companions laughed appreciatively at his words.

Fiona set the tray on the ground, but before she could fully straighten, the man who had spoken seized her in a tight grip, forcing her to her knees. Fiona knelt there in the dirt, her face and body rigid, eyes fixed on her captor's face. Katie longed to help her, but she could not blow their cover now. She merely stood there, trying to look fearful. It wasn't hard. One of the men was eyeing her openly, and the way his eyes deliberately roamed over her body made her feel unclean. She longed to step back.

The man tilted Fiona's head, pressing her cheekbones and jaw with his fingertips.

"You are certainly of fine stock," he said musingly, his fingers sliding deftly down the column of Fiona's throat. Katie didn't know how much more Fiona could take. The tension was visible in every line of her body. The man's hand dropped to Fiona's arm, squeezing the muscle.

"Young and strong, I see. Ah, the use I could put you to." He pulled Fiona towards him in a single rough movement. Katie started forward, unable to stand it any longer, but before she got within arm's reach of her, Fiona had kicked out savagely at her attacker, breaking his grip. Bounding to her feet, she turned and ran. Katie ran after her. The men's laughter pursued them, but they did not give chase.

"That's the good thing about wenches with spirit," the leader called after them. "There is so much sport to be had with them."

Fiona did not stop running until they were several streets away. Finally she collapsed panting onto a low wall. Katie dropped down beside her.

"Are you alright?"

Fiona rubbed vigorously at her face and arms.

"I can still feel his filthy hands all over me."

"We have to go back," said Katie. "We need to be there when they fall asleep. We will not have much time before they are spotted."

Fiona's breathing was calmer now. "I know, but I wish it wasn't just a sleeping draught in that wine."

They crept back by way of the numerous back alleys.

The slave traders were well into their meal, laughing uproariously at some joke one of them had made.

Katie and Fiona crouched silently in a doorway, waiting. It didn't take long.

Suddenly one of the men put a hand to his head. They were not close enough to hear what he said, but he keeled over in the dirt. The men were evidently surprised. One of them got up to go to his fallen comrade, but collapsed before he was fully upright.

Katie allowed herself a slow smile of satisfaction.

Looking at Fiona, she saw that the other girl was grim-faced.

"What is it?" she whispered.

Another man collapsed. They were nearly all out now. Those who had had the wit to try and go for help were lying where they had fallen.

Fiona smiled, though it did not touch her eyes. "It's nothing, it's just that I remember that feeling all too well. They won't be waking up for a while." She climbed to her feet. "Come on, that's the last of them."

They left their concealment and hurried over to the prostrate men. They did not have much time to work. Any minute now the men might be spotted by a patrol.

Katie saw what they were looking for almost at once. There was a huge bunch of keys stuck into the belt of the man who had groped Fiona. Katie silently pointed them out to her.

Fiona gave a grimace of disgust. "You do it while I keep watch. Hurry!"

Katie extracted the keys and hurried over to the nearest wagon. It took three tries before she found the one that fitted. She hurriedly unlocked them all and climbed into the first one.

The stench of human waste hit her the moment she was inside. Katie gagged, then saw the reason.

Men, women and children were packed into metal cages. The interior of each was not much bigger than a small cupboard. There was barely room for any of them to move, let alone assume a comfortable position. Many of the children were curled up on the floor while adults tried to comfort them. The tallest men were forced to crouch where they were.

A low keening came from the cages, as though the occupants feared to attract attention by making any louder noise.

For a moment Katie just stood where she was, staring horrified at the humans packed in like animals all around her. Then she hurriedly pulled herself together and fitted a key into the first cage.

"It is alright, I am here to help you."

They looked at her, some with fear plain in their eyes, some with hostility and others with resignation. Somehow the resignation was worse to behold than their fear.

When she had the last cage open, she jumped to the road. There was little room in the cramped space.

"Come on!" she called softly. "You have to run now!"

"Why are you helping us?" a hard-faced man asked. "What trap is this?"

"No trap, now run!"

The man landed beside her. He was stripped to the waist, and Katie saw angry red welts on his chest, back and shoulders. He looked around, head turning like a hunted animal, then beckoned to the others.

They made a sorry sight. Many were half-starved and wore little more than rags. Nearly all the children were barefoot. But Katie had no time to spare for them. Leaving Fiona to point them in the right direction, she went to the next wagon. There were six in all, with at least twenty people to a cage. One by one Katie released them, watching as the young supported the sick or elderly, and the strongest carried the smaller children.

Then Katie reached the final cage and her breath caught. Here were faces she knew. Servants of Miguel's house. People she had grown up with her whole life. They gaped at her in astonished joy.

"Katie! Bless you, child, what are you doing here?"

But Katie had eyes only for one face.

Jessemine was crouched in her cage, clinging to the bars. The moment she was free, she clasped Katie tightly to her as the others squeezed past them.

"Where have you been? I've been nearly out of my mind with worrying about you."

"You know where. I took Fiona to the Travellers. She will be leaving on a journey soon and I will accompany her as my father wished."

They were alone in the wagon now. Jessemine gripped Katie's shoulders, peering earnestly into her face.

"Katie, listen to me. We are free now. Miguel has been arrested. You can go where you like."

"That is what my father wants."

"Katie, Alfredo does not—"

"Katie!" Fiona called frantically. "There's a patrol coming, we have to go!"

With a final squeeze, Katie extricated herself from Jessemine's arms.

"I must go. Go well, Jessemine, I will come and find you when this is over."

She leaped down, barely hearing Jessemine's reply.

"Go well, my dear one. The sea-god keep you safe."

Katie barely had time to wonder why Jessemine had sworn by the god of the Travellers before Jessemine was past her and running.

Fiona seized her arm and dragged Katie after her.

"Come on! Move!"

Katie ran, scrubbing her free hand across her eyes in an effort to wipe away the tears that were blurring her vision. She had done it. Jessemine was safe.

* * *

James could feel the weight of the dagger at his belt. It was a light blade, one that could be easily concealed in a pocket. But it might as well have been a six foot club. The same feelings that had plagued him when he had helped to rescue Fiona from Miguel followed him as he followed Christophe. But this time it was different. This time he did not have twenty armed Guardians at his back. This time he would have to play the hero. A boy who had done nothing all his life except play football with his friends and try to keep up in school.

Christophe was in his element. Christophe, the boy who consorted with thieves and roamed the streets, who looked as though he had been born with a knife in his hand.

For the first time, James found himself wondering if Christophe had ever killed anybody, and just as quickly pushed the thought away.

He had a sudden urge to be home again. Back doing all the things he'd taken for granted before. Almost at once he felt ashamed. He could never leave Fiona. He would protect her with his very last breath, he knew that.

But how? An inner voice mocked. What possible use could you be? You're helpless and you know it. He ignored the voice. He didn't know what he could do but he would try, and if he wasn't dangerous, there was no harm in letting people think he was.

He couldn't go home anyway, not alone, not now he knew what Fiona meant to him. He couldn't face Carolyn. He berated himself for his cowardice. He didn't know if Fiona even shared his feelings, and he would never ask her and risk ruining their friendship.

"James! are you listening to me?"

"What? Oh, sorry." James jerked abruptly out of his reverie to find Christophe regarding him closely.

"Sorry," James said again. "What did you say?"

Christophe continued to watch him for a moment, then appeared to decide to let the matter drop, to James's considerable relief. They had come to a halt in the doorway of a ruined building. James thought it might once have been a shop, but what was left of it was little more than a burnt-out shell.

"We can wait here," said Christophe, leaning against a charred timber beam. "We have a good view of the prison from here."

James squatted guardedly beside him, eyes trained on the hulking fortress across the street. Guards marched endlessly to and fro atop its walls.

"It's an army," he muttered. "They need that many men to guard a bunch of prisoners?"

"Alfredo likes to demonstrate his authority at every opportunity," Christophe said grimly. "I daresay he will order everyone to turn out to watch the execution tomorrow."

"He orders people to watch his executions?" James was incredulous.

"Not always. People are free to watch or not as they choose. But on occasion, when Alfredo wishes to make a particular example of somebody, he sends out his guards to round everyone up. Shops are forced to close and all business is suspended. Even the slave auctions. You can be sure Alfredo will want to have as many witnesses as possible for the downfall of his spy. It shows that no one is expendable." He paused, as if thinking. "I expect he would do the same for my execution too, if for different reasons."

James opened his mouth but could think of nothing to say. Christophe's apparent calmness when speaking of his own death was unnerving. To cover his feelings he said lightly, "Well, you aren't exactly planning on dying any time soon."

Christophe flashed a grin, though it did not touch his eyes. "Not if I can help it, though death comes to us all."

"Do you think the girls are in position yet? I can't see them."

Christophe scanned the street. "Neither can I."

They were silent for a while, then James said, "Where do all the slaves come from?"

"Most of them come from lands that Alfredo has conquered, prisoners of war. But there are also many people off the streets. Alfredo believes that everyone should be useful. If you have an occupation, you are spared the slave markets. Anyone who is homeless or loses their business is rounded up and put to work. It is the fate that will await the Travellers if they are caught."

"Sorry I asked."

Just then, the street erupted with sound. Men were shouting.

"The slaves have escaped! Seal the area." The orderly ranks of men scattered as they drew their weapons, responding to the alarm.

"Come on!" Christophe yelled, running for the opening prison gates.

"They did it!" James breathed. He hurried after Christophe, wishing that his guard's uniform was a better fit. He did his best to imitate their brisk stride, drawing his dagger as he walked, though he had no idea what he meant to do with it.

People were running everywhere. Ragged men, women and children fleeing in every direction. Then James saw two girls burst suddenly out of an alley. The headscarf of one of the girls was awry, and her coppery hair gleamed in the afternoon sun.

"Fiona! Katie!"

They turned.

"Meet us there!" James gestured back at the ruined shop where he and Christophe had hidden. "We'll join you."

"Hurry!" Fiona yelled back, as they were swallowed up by the crowd.

James caught up with Christophe.

"I told the girls to wait for us back at that shop." He muttered out of the side of his mouth.

Christophe nodded once to show that he had heard, but did not break stride.

His dagger was sheathed at his waist, and he held a roll of parchment with an official looking seal. James hastily sheathed his own dagger.

A squadron of armed guards appeared around a corner ahead. Christophe hung back until the guards were nearly upon them, then stepped out deliberately into the captain's path.

"The prisoner Miguel is to be handed over immediately on the emperor's orders. Take me to where he is being held at once."

James nearly started at Christophe's imperious manner. Was he crazy? Even in his disguise it was plain that he was young. James had expected that Christophe would waylay a minor officer who would not dare refuse, not a captain of the guards.

The captain frowned at Christophe.

"I was given orders that the prisoner should remain under lock and key until the time of his execution."

Christophe's face darkened. He brandished the seal under the captain's nose.

"You forget your place, Captain. It is for neither you nor I to question the master's orders. The prisoner will be returned before nightfall."

The captain's eyes flicked once to the seal, then he nodded.

"He's in cell 18." He fished a ring of keys from his belt and handed them to Christophe.

"I would send men with you but they're needed to quell this riot. Bloody peasants!" He fingered his dagger lovingly before rapping a curt order to his men. They continued on their way and were quickly lost from sight. The captain never looked back once as Christophe marched off in the opposite direction, James following behind him in wondering admiration.

"That was brilliant! I thought that captain was going to pull his knife on you."

"He would have if it had not been for the seal. It will have severely dented his ego being seen taking orders from a whelp like me. Particularly one so arrogant. I would wager there will be some men waiting to waylay me down some dark alley a couple of nights from now."

He chuckled mirthlessly.

They met several more guards as they made their way through the seemingly endless maze of passages, but a quick flash of the seal from Christophe and a curt order and they were pointed in the right direction. The seal prevented anyone from asking too many questions for which James was extremely grateful. The guards were also flustered owing to the uproar outside and had little time to stop and chat.

The dungeons were dark and dank. Torches set in sconces on the walls cast a pale sickly light over the grey stone. Droplets glistened in the cracks in walls and the floor was slippery underfoot. Their shadows flickered oddly in the pale light. It was cold too. James felt gooseflesh on his arms and legs. Though he didn't think that was entirely due to the cold. The smell of damp and caged men was heavy in their nostrils, and in the distance, James thought he heard weeping.

The walls on both sides of the narrow corridor were lined with row upon row of plain black doors, each with a grill set into them at roughly eye level. They peered intently through each one as they passed, using a torch Christophe took from its wall bracket.

"That's him!" James breathed suddenly. Christophe was beside him instantly. Handing the seal to James, he produced the keys the captain had given him and fitted them into the rusty lock, before shooting back the heavy bolts at the top and bottom of the door.

The door swung open with a rusty creek of hinges. The man inside turned quickly with a clanking of chains, his face thrown into clear relief by the torch Christophe held.

The cell was a bare room six feet by three feet with nothing but some mouldy straw on the floor. Miguel was manacled to the back wall, the heavy chain attached to a collar about his neck, with the other end looped through a ring driven into the stone high out of Miguel's reach. His wrists and ankles too were manacled, and the locks were sturdy. Miguel was helpless. The chains barely allowed any movement, yet he faced them without flinching.

His face, which had been wary at their appearance, relaxed into a sneer when he saw who his visitors were.

"Well, well, this is a pleasant surprise," he drawled. "Come to gloat over me in my final hour?"

His eyes took in their borrowed uniforms.

"Surely such pathetic disguises as these did not fool the guards?"

Christophe's eyes were glittering dangerously. Taking the seal from James, he brandished it in front of Miguel's face. Miguel's eyes widened fractionally, but he recovered his composure almost at once.

Miguel blinked. "You are full of surprises, Christophe."

"Indeed," Christophe said softly. "I imagine you are surprised to see me, considering you and your followers left me for dead."

"Sadly no. I have long since come to the conclusion that some mysterious luck protects you. How else could you have remained free for so long? Or survived the beating my men gave you?"

Christophe made no answer. With another of the keys, he snapped open the collar around Miguel's neck and released his ankles. Then, slipping his arm through a ring on the hand manacles, he jerked Miguel roughly to his feet.

Miguel swayed slightly, his muscles cramped from so long in one position, but he regained his equilibrium quickly.

"You will have to lead him," said Christophe, surrendering the arm ring to James.

James slipped it onto his wrist. The metal felt cold against his skin.

Christophe drew his knife and took up his position directly behind Miguel.

"Move!" he ordered.

James set off, drawing Miguel with him. Miguel turned his head slightly to look at Christophe.

"I am surprised that you would wish to rescue me, Christophe. I would have expected to see you in the front row at my execution tomorrow, if it was not more than your life's worth. Just how much is it you are worth now?"

Christophe's blade was mere inches from the back of Miguel's neck.

"You have a job to do before then. Comfort yourself that you will not die in vain tomorrow."

Miguel turned his attention to James. "I do not believe I've had the pleasure."

James clenched his free hand around his own dagger. "You may not know me," he growled. "But a friend of mine was a prisoner in your house a short while ago."

"Ah, yes, The Appointed!" There was derision in Miguel's voice as he pronounced the title. "You were part of her rescue party. Lucky for her that you came when you did. There would not have been much left of her by morning."

With a snarl, James pulled up so abruptly that Christophe bumped into them.

"Enough!" he said, grabbing James's arm as he swung it towards Miguel's maliciously grinning face. "Let him enjoy the sound of his voice while he can. He will not have it for much longer."

James expected Miguel to give them some trouble as soon as they were among the guards once more, but he walked along docilely at James's side. This puzzled James, until he reflected that the guards were not likely to help Miguel in any case, and perhaps he was hoping for a chance to escape. James felt a momentary thrill of apprehension, until he remembered that Christophe would never allow it. His confidence in the other boy had improved markedly this day.

Fiona and Katie were waiting for them. Their reactions on seeing the prisoner were different and instant. Katie's eyes flashed hatred which Miguel openly returned and her hand convulsively gripped the dagger which had appeared from somewhere.

Fiona's expression was a mixture of fear and fury. She stepped back from Miguel, fists clenched.

Miguel smiled maliciously at her.

"We meet again, Appointed."

Snarling, Katie and Fiona both took a step towards Miguel, but Christophe placed himself between them.

"There is no time for this. We must act quickly."

"And what, pray," said Miguel, as Christophe led them down a quiet back street, "Possessed you to break me out of my prison? I will not flatter myself that it was for the pleasure of my company."

"You've got that right," Fiona growled.

"You have something we want," James said shortly.

Miguel raised a polite eyebrow. "Indeed? And what may that be?"

"The key to your strong box," Katie snapped.

Miguel looked genuinely surprised. "And what could you possibly want with that?"

"That is not your concern," said Christophe. "All you need to do is show us where it is. Then you will be returned to your cell. After all, you will have no more use for it."

Miguel sighed. "Very well, it seems I have no choice."

They reached Miguel's house without mishap, largely thanks to Christophe's many short cuts.

Another flash of Alfredo's seal got them past the guards stationed near the door. Once inside, Christophe turned to Miguel.

"Where is the key?"

"And why would I tell you that?" Miguel said derisively.

Christophe moved the knife until the cold tip of the blade touched Miguel's skin.

"This should be reason enough." There was a silence. Then, "In my study," Miguel said simply. "A pity you didn't take it while you had the chance. It would have saved you a lot of trouble."

"Keep moving," Christophe said quietly. "You must lead; James, take off the ring but keep within grabbing distance."

Miguel led the way to his study with Christophe always immediately behind him. The others watched Miguel keenly too. None of them expected for a minute that Miguel would just hand them the key and allow himself to be escorted back to his cell.

The study had the stale musty smell of a room that has been abandoned some time.

"You will need to get these hand manacles off me so I can get at the key."

"Not a chance," Christophe snapped. "Point to where it is hidden."

Looking furious, Miguel muttered, "Top drawer of the desk. The key is on that ring there." He indicated a set of keys hanging on a hook by the door.

Christophe made a curt gesture to Katie, who immediately reached down the keys and fitted one into the lock. She succeeded on the first try and, tugging out the drawer, scattered the contents over the desk. The others crowded forward, even Miguel.

There were plenty of rolls of parchment and ink and sealing wax, but no key. Katie looked into the empty drawer.

"That is everything."

Christophe turned to Miguel with a warning glint in his eyes.

"The drawer has a false bottom," Miguel muttered. He seemed sullen and defeated, all his cocky self-assurance gone completely now.

Katie felt about the drawer's wooden bottom, gently prodding and pressing. Then, as her fingers touched a particular knot in the wood, there was a barely audible click, and an entire section swung back. Katie felt into the interior and gasped.

"You've got it?" said Fiona.

Katie slowly withdrew her hand. Clutched in her fingers was what seemed to everyone else to be a key of standard size, a little bent and dull with tarnish.

What Fiona saw was a silver key of superb workmanship, made in the shape of a mermaid, right down to the fins and curved fish's tale. There was some strange lettering carved into the metal, and it pulsed softly with a silvery glow. A low humming, nearly too low to hear, emanated from it.

Fiona could hardly believe it. She had never seen anything so beautiful. And it was clear that the others saw and heard nothing. The last of her doubts were shattered. The key had revealed itself to her as her father had said it would. She was indeed The Appointed.

"That's it," she breathed. Her voice seemed somehow lodged in her throat. Almost of its own accord her hand reached out for the key, and as her fingers closed over it, she felt a wonderful warmth spread through her arm into her body. The moment it was in her grasp, the cloaking illusion vanished, and the others saw it for what it truly was.

They gasped.

"It's beautiful!" James breathed.

"Look at the glow!" Katie exclaimed wonderingly.

"You are indeed The Appointed," Christophe said softly.

At that moment Miguel acted. He gave his wrists a sort of twisting jiggle and the manacles clattered to the floor. Without giving them time to recover, he snatched the knife from James's belt and in the same movement, seized Fiona's wrist with his free hand. Pulling her round to face him, he put the knife to her throat. It all happened so fast that no one had time to prevent it.

"Did you really think those pathetic manacles would stop me?" Miguel said derisively to Christophe. "I was a master at my trade long before you were even born."

Christophe's knife was in his hand, but he made no move to strike. He was well aware that Miguel would have ample time to cut Fiona's throat even as his own blade found its mark.

Releasing Fiona's wrist, Miguel draped an arm over her shoulder and reached unhurriedly behind her. He pressed a section of the wall and a trap door swung open.

Katie gasped.

"That's right," Miguel said softly. "You never knew every escape route from this house, my enterprising little spy. It's a shame I cannot spare the time to punish you for your disloyalty, but we may well meet again some day. Take care, Christophe. You never know who will stab you in the back." Though his words were addressed to Christophe, his gaze never left Katie.

Then in one movement, he flung Fiona violently from him and was through the trap door. It slammed behind him and there was the sound of a bar being shot home, and footsteps hurrying away.

James caught Fiona before she fell and held her tightly. She was trembling badly, but she had still managed to keep hold of the key. She raised her free hand to her throat, and was startled when her fingers came away clean. She could still feel the blade's icy touch against her skin.

Christophe swore loudly. He looked more furious than Fiona had ever seen him.

"That crafty son of a whore!" he snarled, kicking viciously at the wall. He seemed beside himself with rage.

"Christophe!" James said urgently. "We have to go!"

Christophe controlled himself with an effort. "You are right, we cannot stay here. It will not take long for the guards and slave traders to put two and two together and start looking for us, and Alfredo too, now Miguel is free."

"We will have to leave the city," said Katie. She looked nearly as furious as Christophe.

He nodded. "We will go straight back to the inn and gather some food. We leave tonight."

# Chapter 15

## Dreams in The Desert

The pony plodded patiently along, drawing the laden cart behind it.

Though the night was still young, a fog had begun creeping in from the sea around late afternoon. Caleb could smell the salt in it. Much more of this, and he would be forced to light the lantern.

The fog didn't worry him. Very few things did. He was placid and easy-going by nature. He listened contentedly to the rhythmic clip-clop of the pony's hooves and the soft rumble of the wheels over the hard ground.

It had been a bad year for crops. Even the recent storms had not been enough to counteract the damage weeks of blistering heat had wrought. He would help with the making of the beer soon. It would not be a good brew this year.

He whistled merrily as the cart bumped and jolted along.

The sound of galloping hooves made him look around. About half a dozen armed men, dressed in the uniform of Alfredo's guards were bearing down on him.

Caleb backed the cart into the side of the road and sat waiting for them to pass.

At sight of Caleb, the leader barked a command and the men drew to a halt.

"You there!" the leader snapped. "Where are you bound?"

"To the farm houses away yonder," Caleb replied placidly.

"What do you carry?"

"Just food and blankets and a few herbs. My mother's been sick some time and she's ailing fast, what with this heat we've been having."

"Search the cart!" The leader barked to three of his men. They complied, scattering the contents of the cart bed in the dirt. They found exactly what Caleb had told them they would find. Neatly tied parcels of food, some woollen blankets and a herb pouch, but the leader regarded Caleb suspiciously.

"Are you hiding anyone in your cart?"

"As you see, sir," Caleb said, gesturing at the empty wagon bed.

"Check for a false bottom," the leader rapped. To Caleb, "It wouldn't be the first time you peasants have tried to smuggle people from the city. You should know that as of today, anyone caught harbouring or sheltering criminals or fugitives will be sentenced to death by execution."

"I understand, sir," Caleb said respectfully. A lot better than you think I do at any rate, he added silently.

The men prodded and poked the wagon bed but found nothing out of place. The leader was evidently still suspicious. It was clear to Caleb that he hoped to catch someone that night, and it did not really signify who. Still, the men had little choice but to go on their way, leaving Caleb to gather his scattered provisions. He took his time about this, in case anyone was watching, then clicked his tongue at the pony and set off once more.

He travelled on for another two hours without incident. He met no one else on the road. No one wished to be abroad this night if they could help it. By the time he eventually drew the pony to a halt, the city was a barely discernible speck at his back, and the fog had risen in earnest.

Caleb got down, stretched his stiffened limbs and reached beneath the seat of the cart. His fingers found a lever. He pressed, and the entire underside of the cart dropped down to the road with a thud.

Four dishevelled figures tumbled out in a heap, struggling painfully to their feet as cramped muscles protested.

"That was close," Fiona breathed. "I thought we were goners back there."

"If he'd made you get off your seat…" James left the sentence unfinished.

"We were lucky those men were not too bright," said Christophe. He and Katie began unloading the cart.

"I really appreciate this, Caleb. Thank your mother for me, will you?"

Caleb merely nodded as he remounted the cart.

"The fog should hide you well. There's no one going to find you easily in this. Good luck to you." He and Christophe clasped hands, then Caleb turned the pony in the direction of the city.

"We will sleep here tonight," said Christophe. "This fog will prevent Alfredo's men from searching very far tonight, but we will need to be away by dawn."

No one raised any complaint. None of them had had much sleep since the fire.

They had somehow managed to return to The Jolly Sailor unseen. When Christophe had explained their plight to Bess, she had not wasted time asking questions.

"You'll need to escape the city sharp then. I'll rustle up some food for you and have Caleb drive you in the wagon."

"We have a long journey ahead of us," Christophe had begun hesitantly, but Bess had waved his words aside.

"Never you mind about that. You can work off your debt on your return."

Carlos, who was still at the inn, had somehow managed to provide them with Guardian's clothes, which they had all slipped into gratefully. They all went armed, but Christophe carried the full collection of a Guardian's weapons. A dagger, a bow and full quiver and a quarterstaff. At Katie's directions, Carlos had also visited an apothecary, and returned bearing various herbs and salves in different coloured pouches. Bess had also provided woollen blankets and cloaks.

"You'll be grateful for them in the desert. The nights are chilly when the sun goes in."

Every minute, Fiona had expected to hear fists pounding on the inn door. It would soon be common knowledge who it was behind Miguel's escape. But within a couple of hours of their arrival, they were on the road.

Fiona supposed she should be grateful for the fog's concealment as she rolled herself in her blanket. The very air felt damp, and it seemed to have seeped into their clothes too, making her shiver.

"Do you want me to find out what direction we need to go in?" Katie asked.

"If you can," said Christophe. He was the only one who hadn't settled down to sleep, but was sitting with his blanket wrapped around his shoulders, face turned towards the city.

"I'm sorry, Katie," Fiona murmured sleepily. "Jeremiah gave me a map, but it was lost in the fire. Now you're stuck with being our guide."

Katie yawned sleepily. "If I can help I will. That's why I'm here, after all."

Christophe smiled down at her as she lay curled up on the ground near him. Fiona and James lay close together for warmth.

Christophe kept up his lonely vigil well into the night, listening to the steady breathing of his three companions. At one point, Katie stirred and murmured something. Christophe resisted the urge to wake her.

Time passed and still he neither saw nor heard any sign of pursuit. Try as he would, his eyes grew heavier until he was struggling to keep them open. Finally conceding defeat, he lay down.

Birdsong woke them at dawn. Not the usual cry of seagulls, but the lilting call of blackbird and song thrush.

Fiona sat up and stretched, stiff from her night on the ground. Though she suspected she would be feeling considerably worse in the days to come. She felt the key's reassuring touch against her breast where it nestled beneath her tunic, tied with a leather cord around her neck. It felt warm against her skin.

The fog had largely dissipated. A few stray wisps rolling back towards the sea. The sun did not appear to have made up its mind whether to appear or not.

They made a breakfast of flat corn bread and dried fruit, washed down with water from a nearby stream, as they wanted to preserve the contents of their water bottles as much as possible. When they were finished, Christophe turned to Katie.

"Were you able to find out which direction we should take?"

"North," Katie said pointing. "We should reach the fringes of the desert by sunset if we walk all day. After that, we keep north to the mountains."

They divided their food between them and took a water bottle apiece. Making bundles of their blankets, they tied them to their backs. Christophe wore his quiver at his waist and carried his bow and staff. Katie's many herb pouches were tied to her belt. Katie led them, with Christophe at the rear, ever alert for signs of danger.

"I hope Caleb returned to the city safely," he said grimly. "Alfredo's spies will soon learn where we were staying, and it will not take long for them to discover our true identities."

No one made a reply to this. Fiona didn't like to think what would happen to Bess and her family if they were found out; particularly after everything they had done for her. She opened her mouth to ask, but decided upon reflection that she was better off not knowing.

Wishing to divert her thoughts, she fell in beside Katie.

"Where will you go when this is over?"

Katie shrugged. "I have not really given it much thought. I am free of Miguel now, so I suppose my life is mine to do with as I please. Jessemine taught me some herb law. Perhaps I could make a living as a healer. Although, as Christophe says, I'm probably an outlaw now. What about you? Will you stay here? Or return to the world you came from?"

"Like you, I haven't thought beyond this journey. I don't even know if I'll make it back, but if I do, I'd like to return to Earth."

"You don't think you could get used to living here?"

"Maybe in time I suppose I could, but Earth was my home for sixteen years. It's the only life I've ever known. And there's my parents. They probably think I'm dead by now. The police must have given up looking for me ages ago."

She cast Christophe a reproachful look. "I tried so hard to disbelieve everything my father and Christophe told me, but this key… I suppose I can't doubt any longer now."

"Would you go back?" Katie asked James.

"If Fiona returns to Earth I will go too, though I have no real place in either world, and I suppose I never will."

"That's not true!" Fiona said hotly. "What about everything you've got going on back home, and what about Carolyn? She must be mad with worry by now."

James shrugged, but made no response.

Fiona regarded him thoughtfully.

"And yet it might have been different," she murmured. "What if our roles were reversed?"

James punched her lightly on the arm. "Then it would be up to you to make sure I didn't stab myself in the foot with this sceptre."

"It is no joking matter," Christophe said sternly. "We are talking about a highly dangerous weapon. I hate to think what Alfredo would do with it if it fell into his hands."

"Oh, lighten up!" Fiona said irritably. "We all know it's dangerous. Why else would I be risking my neck? But even if I do manage to destroy this thing, that hardly puts an end to your troubles, does it? After all, Alfredo's managed to do quite a lot of damage without the sceptre's help."

"He certainly cannot be crushed overnight," Christophe acknowledged. "But the loss of the sceptre will be a real blow to him. He has coveted it for so long."

"That's what I don't understand," said James. "I mean, where are Alfredo's friends? The warlocks or whatever they call themselves. Have they all died out? Why would they be in hiding now that one of them is in charge? They've got nothing to fear."

"Little is known about the warlocks," said Christophe. "Once, they fought actively against the merpeople and, according to what Fiona's father told her, the sceptre was meant to be their ultimate guarantee of victory, but they have been little more than legend to our people for years. There were rumours of children with magical potential disappearing and never being heard of again, but that was all most people took them to be. We none of us knew what Alfredo truly was, though perhaps we should have suspected something of the kind. No normal man could conquer and subjugate a nation virtually single-handed."

They walked most of that day, with only a short rest for a meal. By evening, they were all footsore and weary. Though there had been no sun to speak of, the air had felt uncomfortably warm.

They walked until the sun was well down, before Christophe finally called a halt.

As they had met no one, Christophe allowed them to make a fire to ward off the night's chill, which was apparent as soon as the sun was down. They huddled around it and ate their meagre supper. Fiona suspected that she would soon be heartily sick of bread and cheese and dried fruit. Once more they left their water bottles untouched and satisfied their thirst at a little bubbling spring.

"This is probably the last water source for some miles," said Christophe.

"And it's drying up," said James. "If this weather carries on, there'll be nothing left of it."

"I will stand the first watch," said Christophe. "We ought to take it in turns. I will wake one of you in a couple of hours."

The others rolled gratefully into their blankets and were soon asleep.

* * *

"Katriana!"

Katie started as though she had been struck. She knew that voice, but it couldn't be. It wasn't possible.

"Katriana!"

"Father?"

"Yes."

"Where… where are you?"

"I am close. I have been tracking you since you left the city. Your excellent guidance will no doubt lead me to the sceptre."

"I don't understand."

"I am able to communicate with anyone if I have seen their face. For one of magical blood such as yourself, I can communicate with you both waking and sleeping. I can access all your thoughts and memories. I can find you wherever you are, even in your dreams."

There was a certain smugness in the way he explained it, and it nettled Katie.

"Why didn't you tell me of my heritage?" she demanded. "You never told me you were a warlock either."

"There was no need for you to know. Your gift developed naturally of its own accord, and I watched you from afar."

"Until I was ready?"

"Yes."

"What will you do with the sceptre once you have it?"

"That does not concern you."

Katie was furious. First he had asked her to spy on his enemies with very little explanation, then he had casually admitted that he was now spying on her in turn without telling her, and he still wouldn't tell her what it was all for.

"Was it you who set the Travellers' ships on fire?"

"That was a parting shot from Miguel. I believe he thought he would go out in style, so to speak."

"But it was you who ordered Jessemine and the others to be given to the slave traders?"

"Of course. Their position with Miguel was terminated. They needed to be usefully employed."

"But they had done nothing to you. Why take away their freedom?"

She felt a change in the atmosphere. A weight or presence crushing in on her. When her father next spoke, his voice had an ominous quality.

"I do not appreciate being second questioned by you, Katriana. You are young in the ways of this world, and can have no opinion on things you do not understand. Do not think that because you are my daughter, that I will allow you to take any special liberties. Now tell me everything The Appointed has told you."

Cold fear filled Katie throughout this speech. She wasn't sure if it was her own or what her father wanted her to feel, but she felt unable to resist his command. However, a small bit of her anger remained. Enough to make her only tell her father the facts that Fiona had given and nothing more. Nothing about Christophe. She could imagine her father sifting through her memories the way Miguel did papers on his desk. She did not care for the feeling. It was an invasion where no one had a right to be.

At last her father's voice spoke again.

"An extremely resourceful spy, this Tobias. It is a pity he was not in my employ. A key that unlocks all doors except for those within. I have heard of such talismans, though I had no idea that any still existed."

He was musing to himself, Katie realised. She was nothing but a collector of information. Another of his spies. The realisation cut her to the quick. She longed to be free of his voice.

"You have done well, Katriana. I am pleased with you. You will continue as you have been and lead The Appointed to the sceptre. I will follow. We will speak again soon."

The presence departed and Katie awoke.

She lay where she was, waiting for her emotions to settle. What am I doing here? She wondered unhappily. Alfredo was following them. She was leading him to the sceptre. The thought did not please her as it once would have done. She could no longer fool herself that he would simply let the others walk away. Would he sell them to the slave traders? She remembered the indifference he had shown when speaking of Jessemine and the others. He had not even tried to deny it. And what would become of her when this was over? Had he thought that far?

Or could he not look beyond acquiring the sceptre? And the worst question of all, did he even care?

All her life she had wanted her father's approval, but did she really want the approval of such a man? She had hoped that this business would bring them closer, but he seemed more a stranger to her than ever.

Katie weighed up her options. She could run now, just sneak off in the night, and Alfredo would lose his guide. She could tell the others that he was following them. She could claim she had had a vision. It was true in a sense. But they would ask how he was able to follow them, and Katie did not feel able to explain that. Besides, it would not deter them. Christophe was expecting pursuit. No, she decided, the best thing to do was remain with them and worry about her father when they were nearer their goal. She would think what to do then.

Katie knew that sleep would never come to her now. Still with her blanket wrapped around her, she got up and walked over to where Christophe sat by their dying fire.

He looked up in surprise. "You can sleep a bit longer. I was going to wake someone in an hour."

"I can't sleep."

Katie threw a couple of pieces of wood on the fire and huddled close to the blaze.

In the sudden light, Christophe saw her face clearly.

"You are pale!"

"I'm alright. It was just… just a nightmare, that is all. I will feel better in a little while."

Christophe nodded and they sat in companionable silence for a time.

Katie was very aware of how near he was to her. Close enough to touch if she cared to. The idea filled her half with fear, and half with a reckless daring. But then Christophe spoke softly.

"I fear to sleep. There are dreams awaiting me as soon as I close my eyes. I thought I was finally free of them, but since the ships burned…" he broke off with a weary sigh.

Katie was taken aback by the sadness in his voice. "What do you dream about?"

Christophe did not look at her. Staring off into the distance he said, "I am trapped in a burning room with my family. Everything around us is in flames. I can save them, but I just stand there. They try to escape but everywhere they turn there is a wall of flames hemming them in. They call out to me, begging me to help them, and I know I can, but I stay frozen where I am. I watch as they are consumed along with everything else in the room, everything except me. I remain untouched. I see their faces, the hurt and bewilderment in their eyes."

Katie stared at him, appalled. When finally he turned to look at her, she saw such an expression of desperate unhappiness in his eyes that it tore at her heart.

"When I was five," he said. "Alfredo's men set fire to my family's home. My parents had been actively resisting Alfredo's rule for many years, and it was well known that my father and Tobias were friends. When Tobias disappeared and no trace could be found of him or his child, Alfredo took his revenge.

"It was at night in the middle of winter. Some sixth sense woke me. I could hear a roaring, crackling sound and it was difficult to breathe. Then my parents burst into my room. My mother was carrying my baby sister who was crying. She looked terrified. She thrust her at me. 'Take her!' she screamed. 'Take her and run!'

"Then my father pressed a book into my hands. 'Take this and guard it well,' he told me. I knew what the book was. My father had told me the story. He said we had a very important job to do. My father told me that he and my mother would look for me. I took my sister and the book and ran. I ran while my parents perished."

There was no mistaking the bitter recrimination in his voice.

"You were a child!" Katie protested. "You cannot blame yourself for your parents' deaths."

It was Alfredo, she thought in anguish. Heaven help me, my father did this.

"What happened to your baby sister?" she asked gently.

"We lived on the streets. But it was mid winter and I had no idea how to care for a baby. We both fell sick. An old woman took us in. I recovered but Ruth died. One night I heard the woman planning to hand me over to the slave traders, as I was costing too much for her to keep. So I ran away. I spent the next five years on the streets. I stole to survive. One day I stole from the leader of a street gang. His boys chased me and caught up with me in a back alley. But instead of attacking, they took me under their wing. They taught me burglary skills and how to fight with knife and quarterstaff. When I had learned from them I went on my way.

"Then one day I got in a fight down at the docks. I cannot even remember the cause now. I was hurt badly. They left me on the wharf and who knows what would have happened if Josephine had not found me. The *Dolphin* was taking on fresh cargo. They were leaving that very afternoon. What I remember most about that first meeting was the baby that Josephine had strapped to her back. It was Lena, newly born. But she looked so much like Ruth, I suppose that was what made me stay with them. Josephine nursed me back to health and my various skills soon earned the respect of the other Travellers.

"All these years I had kept my father's book with me. I was determined to carry out the charge my father had been given. So I bided my time, waiting for the time when Tobias's daughter would come of age. I learned all the particulars from Jeremiah, who had been instrumental in her escape. It was he who told me how to reach her and return with her. And I will make sure she succeeds. I will not let my father's death be in vain."

The unhappiness was gone, replaced by a fierce, implacable determination. It made Katie's heart glad to see it.

"You will succeed," she said softly. "We will do it together." Very deliberately, she leaned forward and kissed him on the mouth. She saw his eyes widen for a moment in disbelief, then his arms reached to draw her close and he returned her kiss.

Christophe was caught completely off guard by the sudden physical contact, but his surprise changed almost instantly to delight. A fierce joy more powerful than anything he had ever known rose up in him. He felt her relax into his arms, her lips opening gladly to his. It felt as though she belonged there and had always done so. He felt whole as he had not been for a long time. Her long hair swung forward, brushing his face like a gentle caress.

When at last he raised his head, it was to see her looking at him with eyes that expressed everything he could have desired. She was a little breathless, but she still clung to him, pressing close, until he was no longer sure where one ended and the other began.

She gave a small laugh. “I have wanted to do that ever since I first saw you. Even when I thought you wanted to kill me.”

Smiling, he pushed the hair behind her ears with gentle fingers. “I know.”

Fiona and James exchanged surreptitious glances during breakfast. There was something different about Christophe and Katie. It was in their eyes, the way they were never far from each other. For the first time since she had met him, Fiona actually thought Christophe seemed happy. He was definitely more relaxed. Something had evidently happened last night. It hardly took a genius to figure it out. Fiona was glad for Katie. She liked the girl, and Christophe had shown a marked preference for her from the first. Though she couldn’t help but feel a pang when she thought of Esther. She would get an unpleasant shock on their return, though Fiona had to admit that Christophe had never shown anything other than friendship towards her.

They turned their attention to the vast, featureless expanse that stretched before them away into the distance. Sand, brownish beige in colour, as far as they could see.

Fiona eyed it dispiritedly. It looked endless. Did they have enough food and water to get them across? She suddenly found herself wishing her bundle was a good deal heavier.

They set off before the sun was fully up. At first it was not too bad. They passed great dunes and low outcrops, with here and there a stunted bush or tree. The rustlings, chirpings and scrapings of the various insects were incessant.

But when the sun came up it was another thing entirely. The heat was intolerable, and the sand gave off a ferocious glare that forced them to squint against its fierceness. Flies buzzed around them continuously, tasting their sweat. Even when the sun eventually sank below the horizon, the heat the sand gave back was fierce. They could feel it through their boots.

By the time they lay down to rest, their heads were throbbing and their throats were parched. Fiona would never have thought water could taste so wonderful. Those few sips from her water bottle were almost heavenly and it was a torment almost too cruel to bear to put it away again. She longed to drain its contents. What she had drunk did not seem nearly enough.

The next day was no better, or the two days after that. The nights gave them little rest either. The heat of the day replaced by a cold that chilled to the bone. Katie gave them a salve to rub into their skin that kept the worst of the insects at bay, but there was not one of them that didn't have a few angry red welts on their bodies. At first they tried talking to keep their spirits up, but as the days passed, they found they needed all of their rapidly eroding strength just to keep going.

At night Fiona and James slept close together for warmth, and Katie and Christophe held each other tightly.

By the end of their first week, things were looking grim. Despite all their care, their food and water was getting low. They were all close to exhaustion. Fiona was finding it harder to stave off her fear that she would not leave this terrible barren place alive.

Then suddenly Katie stopped. She was in the lead as usual, Christophe at the rear. The others came to a halt too.

"What is it?" James asked wearily.

Katie was looking up at the sky, a worried frown on her face.

"The sky, it is so dark all of a sudden."

"A storm?" Fiona said doubtfully.

"We should keep moving," said Christophe. "If it is rain, it will be welcome."

The wind was picking up, letting out an eerie moan as though in warning. It grew in intensity until it was lifting the sand.

"Christophe!" Fiona said uncertainly.

"Keep going!"

The wind rose to a shriek. The sand whirled round them in a frenzy, dashing into their mouths and eyes, striking exposed skin with stinging force. They blundered on, arms over their faces to protect their eyes from the flying sand, heads down against the ferocity of the wind, but the storm intensified.

Soon James had lost sight of the others completely. He could see nothing but the whirling clouds of sand. He tried to call out for Fiona, but his feeble voice was snatched away by the howling wind. He could barely keep upright, yet he knew that if he gave in to his exhaustion, he would be buried.

Quite by chance he spotted a huge boulder, looming suddenly out of the maelstrom. With the last of his strength he made for it. Crouching beneath it, he waited out the storm.

It seemed to go on for hours, but at last, the wind dropped, the clouds rolled away, and the flying sand settled gradually. He stayed where he was for a long time. Finally, when he was sure it was safe to do so, he came out from his shelter and peered cautiously about. Everywhere seemed quiet after the howling gale. The landscape was as flat and featureless as before. He had no idea where he was. He had lost his sense of direction completely. He brushed sand from his hair. It had got inside his clothes and he longed to scratch. He needed to find the others, but he had no idea which direction to take. Picking one at random he set off. Now and then he called.

"Fiona, where are you?"

“Katie, Christophe, can you hear me?”

His throat was raw and dry. It sounded weak even in his ears. They’ll never hear that, he thought despairingly.

Then, to his disbelief, he thought he heard an answering shout. He froze where he was, straining to catch it again. Yes, there it was. He set off in the direction of the sound.

“I’m coming, where are you?”

The answer came back, guiding him, two voices, he thought.

Eventually, coming down into a narrow gully, he saw the faces of Katie and Christophe peering out from behind a boulder very similar to the one he had sheltered under. They looked extremely windblown, but none the worse for their ordeal.

“Thank goodness you are safe!” said Katie.

“Where’s Fiona? Have you seen her?”

They both shook their heads.

“We hoped she was with you,” said Katie.

“We must look for her,” said Christophe. They searched all around where they had sheltered. They called and called but there was no answer.

James was growing frantic. Where was she? She couldn’t have just disappeared.

Then, as they were passing a partially collapsed sand dune, he thought he heard a low moan. He stopped where he was.

“Fiona?”

The cry came again, weak, barely audible. James cast about wildly, but couldn’t see her anywhere. The realisation struck him like a punch in the stomach. The mound he had taken to be a partially collapsed sand hill.

“Christophe, Katie, get over here!”

“What is it?” Christophe said sharply.

James was white. “She’s buried under that. We must get her out!”

So saying he dropped to his knees and began frantically digging at the sand.

“Stop it!” Christophe snapped. “You will only bring more down on her!”

Crouching down beside James, he began scraping away at the sand.

James could hardly bear it. What if they didn’t get her out in time before she suffocated?

“We’re coming, Fiona,” he called. “Just hang on!”

* * *

Darkness, complete and impenetrable. A feeling that her mind was slipping away from her. A voice speaking.

“You cannot hide from me, Appointed.”

“Who are you?” Did she speak the words out loud?

“Your worst nightmare. The thing you can neither escape from nor defeat. What chance do you think you have?”

Alfredo! But he couldn’t be speaking to her.

The voice laughed, a cruel mocking sound that chilled her soul.

"You pathetic little fool! You can have no concept of what I can do to you. The power I have at my command could have you screaming your despair for a hundred years with no one to hear you. Know this and tremble, Appointed. It is what awaits you."

"No!" she whispered. It was an effort to speak at all. The fear was numbing her, paralysing her, body and mind. It took all she had to go on.

"I will destroy the sceptre and see you crushed!"

The laughter came again, long and loud. She longed to put her hands over her ears, to shut it out. But it was in her mind, filling it until she thought she would be driven mad with it.

"Nurture that illusion while you can, Appointed. You will learn the truth soon enough."

Black dots seemed to dance before her eyes, then her mind blacked out.

"I can see an arm," James cried.

Christophe dug more frantically, uncovering part of a torso, then another shoulder.

James and Katie seized the still half-buried form and heaved with all their might.

Fiona lay on her back, her face pale, sand in her long hair.

Christophe bent close.

"She still lives. Another few minutes and we would have been too late."

Fiona stirred and moaned. Katie hurriedly turned her onto her side as she began coughing up sand, chest heaving violently.

An unpleasant memory rose unbidden to James's mind. Drowning, his lungs filling with water.

Fiona's eyes flew open. They were wide and terrified.

"No! Leave me alone! Somebody help me!"

"Fiona, it's alright. You're safe!"

Fiona's eyes focused on him, and the fear gradually left them. James helped her to sit up and Katie offered her some water. She drank greedily.

"Thanks!" she rasped finally. "I thought I was finished!"

"What happened?" said James.

"When I realised I was lost, I tried to dig myself a sand cave to shelter in. The whole hill came down on me. I couldn't get free. More sand kept falling on me every time I tried."

James shuddered. "How many times do I have to almost lose you?"

"I'm sorry," she said meekly.

"We can rest here for tonight," said Christophe. "We are all too exhausted to go any further."

They lay down where they were, and Christophe and Katie were soon asleep.

"James?" Fiona whispered softly.

"Yes?"

"While I was under the sand, Alfredo spoke to me."

James lifted himself on one elbow, startled.

"What do you mean?"

"I don't know, it was like he was in my head. He certainly wasn't there with me. It was horrible! I've never been so afraid. He said he would drag out my torment for a hundred years. He said I couldn't hide from him and I could never defeat him. I felt so worthless. So insignificant. And he laughed at me."

She was shaking. James pulled her close.

"It was a dream. You were unconscious when we pulled you out and short of oxygen. It was probably a hallucination or something."

"But it felt so real. It didn't feel like a dream. What if he is keeping track of us somehow?"

"We'd have seen him if he was following us."

"He could be using his magic to hide."

"It was a dream, Fiona, just a dream. You're safe, I promise!"

They lay down again, and he put an arm around her.

"Go to sleep," he said gently. "You're exhausted. It was only a dream."

"I hope you're right," Fiona murmured.

# Chapter 16

## The Right Words

The stew was getting cold, but Gideon ignored it. Around him the talk was quiet and subdued, even though the common room of The Jolly Sailor was full.

His table companions were equally silent. His father was tucking into the plate of food that Bess had set before him, but Gideon doubted he really tasted it.

Carlotta stared moodily into her mug of ale, as if she hoped to find answers there.

It was risky being here at all. Since the fire, he and his people had been in hiding, forever on the lookout for the slave traders. Alfredo had given his orders quickly. Any Guardians were to be rounded up and executed, the rest were for the slave markets. So far, they had managed to stay one step ahead of their hunters, but that would not last for ever.

There had been hardly any food since the fire except what could be begged or stolen. Many had nothing but the clothes they stood up in. The Guardians had few weapons with which to protect their fellow Travellers. They had rarely been in a more serious predicament.

The Jolly Sailor had always been a haven for the Travellers when they came ashore, but that was no longer the case. Gideon shot continuous glances towards the door, poised to bolt should any of Alfredo's men show themselves. The Guardians had to stay free at all costs. They were the only protection their people had. Gideon fidgeted restlessly.

"Patience, son," Antonio said quietly.

"We cannot wait much longer!" Gideon snapped. He cast another meaningful glance at the street door. Antonio went on placidly eating his supper.

Gideon resisted the urge to get up and pace the room. He was sick of running and hiding. Sick of the tyranny he'd been forced to suffer all his life. The fire was the final straw for him. The urge to strike back at his oppressors in any way he could was almost overwhelming.

Carlotta looked up from her ale and briefly met his gaze. The burning fury he saw there matched his own. Here was at least one ally, but they needed a good deal more than two people to make any kind of difference.

At last, after what seemed an interminable length of time to Gideon, Bess announced closing time. The patrons grumbled at this.

"What are you about, woman?" a drunken lout at the bar shouted. "The night's still young yet, bring me more ale!"

"I'm sorry, sir, you'll have to come back tomorrow," Bess said firmly.

The man advanced on her unsteadily, but before he got within an arm's length of her, Caleb and his brothers had appeared as if by magic, and were propelling the startled man towards the door.

"I won't come back here again!" he bellowed. "The Wanderer's Haven stays open till decent hours, and their ale's better too. Your ale tastes like—" the rest of his words were mercifully cut off as Caleb slammed the door in his face. Gideon exchanged rueful glances with his father. The Wanderer's Haven was the most notorious brothel in the city.

"The whores are welcome to him," Antonio muttered. "No decent woman would look twice at him."

Bess lowered the ladle she had taken up to defend herself with a sigh. "Still, we could do with his custom."

"Oh come, Mama," said Zeb. "That lout was responsible for nearly every brawl this place has ever seen."

"Aye, but he kept the coffers full," said Bess. "Goodness only knows we could do with the money."

The remaining patrons left without much fuss. Some of the Guardians had risen also and made for the door. They slipped out with the rest to station themselves where they could get a good view of the street.

Most returned to their seats once the coast was clear. Bess's husband Ephrom locked the front door and threw the bar across. Caleb did the same with the door to the yard while Bess's daughter Elsa pulled down the shutters. Together, they numbered about thirty including Bess and her family, and a stranger Gideon had never met until this evening. He had introduced himself as Carlos, a friend of Christophe.

"What has become of Christophe and The Appointed?" Antonio asked without preamble. "Were they able to leave the city?"

"They sheltered with us for two days," Bess replied. "Then we sneaked them out in the wagon." She nodded at Caleb.

"I was stopped on the outskirts of the city and the men searched the wagon, but they found nothing. I took them well clear of the city's boundaries. It was a foggy night, so pursuit would have been nigh impossible. I reckon they got a good start. Those men were more concerned with hunting Miguel."

"I would give a good deal to know how he managed to escape," Gideon muttered. It was extraordinary. The man had somehow escaped from the most secure stronghold in the city. Even stranger was the escape of nearly a hundred slaves. A coincidence? The slaves had had help. Men had been found drugged and the keys were missing. If Gideon didn't know better, he would have suspected Christophe's hand, but Christophe would never help Miguel.

"That is not important right now," said Antonio. "We need a way of smuggling our people out of the city, or the women and children at least. Every entrance is guarded. Alfredo's men stop all who enter or leave."

There was a subdued silence.

"Where would we go if we left?" a man sitting at a corner table asked dully. "The travellers are welcome nowhere among land folk." There was a murmur of agreement. The Travellers had moved from place to place for so long that they had no land or settlement to call their own. Everything they owned they carried with them. Their homes were the ships they built and crewed. Or had been, Gideon thought bitterly. In one night, they had had everything stolen from them. Their homes, their livelihood, their freedom.

The anger that had been boiling just beneath the surface of his mind for days, suddenly burst its dam.

"Why should we leave? This land was ours long before the city was built."

"Hush, lad, you do not know what you're saying," someone murmured, but Gideon was on his feet. He wasn't even aware of rising. Every eye in the room was fixed on him. Some showed irritation, others only a weary resignation. Their expressions only fuelled his anger.

"All our lives we have been treated like criminals, forced to be forever on the run, never settling anywhere. We never harmed anyone. All we have ever done is try to survive. Now Alfredo's men take everything from us, and your response is just to slink away with your tails between your legs like beaten dogs? How much longer will you allow people to rule your lives? To say where you can go, to label you a criminal, a parasite! The parasites are out there!" He gestured at the darkened windows. "In their comfortable houses while their fellow human beings break their backs to keep themselves and their families fed. I say we stop running. I say we take back the land that is rightfully ours and drive out Alfredo and his kind once and for all!"

There was a ringing silence. Gideon realised he had been shouting. He felt his cheeks grow warm, but he refused to back down. He knew he was right.

Antonio rose quietly and laid a hand gently on Gideon's shoulder. "We hear you, son, but consider what you are saying. We are not nearly enough to destroy Alfredo. He has an army at his command. What do we have? A few men with knives and arrows. A mere nuisance that Alfredo can crush whenever he chooses. We do not wield his power, nor do we know anyone who can. You know what The Appointed was told. Alfredo is of the blood. He has gifts we cannot even begin to comprehend. If we still had the merpeople with us we might have some chance, but they have been gone almost twenty years. Without them, we are virtually helpless."

Gideon brushed his father's hand aside impatiently. "So you would let an unarmed woman save your skin?"

He turned away, disgusted, and strode out of the inn, letting the door bang behind him. The hubbub of voices was instantly cut off. He stood for a while, breathing deeply, waiting for his anger to subside.

What could he do to make them see? Running did no good. If you ran, sooner or later you were caught. They were depending on The Appointed, but was she expected to liberate them all on her own? Why shouldn't they take back what was rightfully theirs? Gideon put his head in his hands. He had to convince them that what he was proposing was right. He felt it more deeply than anything he had ever known, a conviction as strong as his certainty that Alfredo's rule was unjust and cruel. But he needed help. He could not fight a war alone. He needed words. The right words. But he had no idea what they were.

The door of the inn opened and the Guardians flooded out, all looking around guardedly for signs of danger. Gideon saw his father and pressed into the shadows. He didn't want to speak to him or anyone else just yet. He felt let down, but by his father most of all. While he acknowledged the sense of his father's words, he had nonetheless hoped for his support if no one else's. His father looked around for him, then set off in the direction of the docks. He prepared to follow, when a voice beside him made him start violently.

"That was well spoken in there! If only those fools had the wit to see it."

It was Carlotta. He had been so caught up in his own bitter reflections that he had neither seen nor heard her approach. He recovered quickly.

"Will you walk with me?"

She wordlessly fell into step beside him.

He found himself studying her surreptitiously out of the corner of his eye. She was even more of an enigma than Christophe. She was the most deadly fighter he had ever seen. She was reserved to the point of being unapproachable most of the time. She was fearless and implacable. She both intrigued and puzzled him. Yet for all that, she was attractive. He admired her courage and loyalty. She and Christophe might have been brother and sister.

"What will it take to convince them?" he said unhappily. "What will it take before they finally decide enough is enough? There is nowhere else for us to go, unless we try to cross the desert."

"You know they would find us," she said bluntly. "They will hunt us for as long as they have breath. This will never stop until one side or the other is killed. I say it should be them."

"My father is right though, Alfredo would crush us with barely a thought."

She smiled at him mockingly. "Giving up already? Was that only talk in there?" He bristled.

"I want Alfredo destroyed as much as you do, but we are badly over matched, and we have no magic to protect us."

"Alfredo is preoccupied just now with The Appointed. She is his primary concern. He will be bent on tracking her movements. It will mean his doom if she succeeds. That must frighten him even if he will not admit it. What better time to strike, while he is insecure?"

"You mean, distract him to buy The Appointed some time?"

She grinned at him, a fierce look that made his pulse quicken.

"I have been making enquiries around the city. The mood for revolution is ripe. Many would be only too happy for a chance to fight, but they also fear to act alone. But if enough of us band together, we can certainly give Alfredo's men cause for concern."

She gripped his arm, pulling him up short and swung him round to face her. Her usually expressionless face was intense and her eyes had a light of passion that he had never seen before. He was very aware of her at that moment. The way her Guardian's uniform moulded to her supple form. Her dark hair which, in defiance of the usual Traveller's style, she wore cropped short, was now windblown and tussled. The fine strong features of her face, not beautiful in the common sense, but a face not easily forgotten once seen. But most of all her eyes, deep and dark, two pools of fire pulling him in, giving him hope.

"We will find a way to convince them, Gideon," she said softly. "The Appointed depends on us!" Her face was barely inches from his own, and she still hadn't released her hold on his arm. His senses were confused, yet he felt more alive than he ever had before.

What would have happened next was not hard to guess, but Carlotta suddenly let go of him and whirled, knives appearing from nowhere in her hands.

Gideon was almost as quick, as his Guardian-trained senses screamed a warning, but even so he barely managed to get his quarterstaff up in time to deflect the blow of the wicked-looking cudgel aiming directly for his head.

Five men, tall and powerful, all with Alfredo's personal insignia emblazoned on their tunic fronts. They fanned out with practised efficiency, blocking all escape routes.

"In the name of high emperor Alfredo the one and only," one of them intoned in an expressionless drone. "You are under arrest on a charge of evading the emperor's justice and perverting the law."

Gideon's eyes flicked this way and that, seeking a way out, but they were trapped. They would have to stand and fight. Even as the men stepped forward to apprehend them, one of Carlotta's knives buried itself in the chest of the speaker. He fell with a startled grunt. Before the men could recover, she had leapt for her closest attacker, while Gideon swung at another, the man with the cudgel. The man deflected the blow and once more swung for Gideon's head. Gideon sidestepped. Out of the corner of his eye he saw another man leap on Carlotta. She was now fighting two men at once. The momentum of the second attacker and Carlotta's fury quickly bore them all to the ground, Carlotta disappearing from view under the larger men's bulks. Gideon fought to reach her, but the fifth man now joined the fray, and Gideon suddenly found himself simultaneously trying to fend off a cudgel and a long dagger. He was pressed back towards the wall of a building, unable to launch an attack of his own, forced to continuously defend. His own harsh breathing sounded loud, mingling with other grunts and cries. He was tiring, he knew. He was badly over matched, only his lighter, more agile movements saving him.

Then the man with the cudgel abruptly tottered where he stood, the weapon falling from suddenly useless fingers. He toppled to the ground without a sound. Gideon and his remaining assailant stared in surprise. A knife protruded from the man's back. Carlotta was in a half sitting position on the ground, the bodies of her two attackers lying beside her. She was clearly hurt, streaked with blood and mud, but she raised another knife, cocking her wrist to throw. The remaining attacker fled.

Instantly Gideon hurried over to her. "Where are you wounded?"

She grimaced. "It is nothing serious. We should go before more of them come."

"Let me bind your wounds first." Without waiting for her consent, Gideon gently pushed up one torn sleeve to reveal a shallow cut on her forearm. That wasn't too serious. The bleeding was already slowing.

One of Carlotta's leggings was also soaked. Gideon pulled back the cloth gingerly to reveal a deep gash in her thigh. Without a word he tore strips from his tunic and bound the wound as tightly as he could.

"Can you walk?"

Carlotta wordlessly retrieved her knives and struggled to her feet. Her face was twisted with pain but she was upright. Gideon threw her arm over his shoulder, taking most of her weight.

Their progress was painfully slow. Gideon kept expecting any minute to hear sounds of pursuit. The murder of any of Alfredo's guards was a killing offence on sight.

Carlotta made no complaint as they walked, but suddenly she turned to Gideon, her gaze intense.

"If they come, leave me! Get back to the others."

"What do you take me for?" Gideon said firmly. "A Guardian never abandons a comrade."

She made no answer, but her look said all too clearly what she thought of that. He knew she would slow them down if they were caught, but he knew equally that he could never run, leaving her behind, virtually defenceless.

Somehow they reached the docks without incident. Gideon hurriedly sought out his mother and handed Carlotta over to her, but as he turned to leave, Carlotta called his name.

He turned back at once, hardly knowing what to expect. She was already lying on a makeshift pallet of cloaks while Josephine applied a poultice to her leg with a sure, gentle touch.

She met his gaze squarely. "Thank you."

Two simple words, but Gideon fell asleep that night with them ringing in his ears.

* * *

Bess carried the tray of mugs over to the table where her husband and sons were tucking in to a belated supper. She felt a smile of affection spread across her face at the sight. How many evenings had they sat around the exact same table after everyone was gone? In the past the old cradle had sat by the hearth, doing service for one baby after another as the family grew. The hustle and bustle was over and the freshly scrubbed kitchen free of clutter and noise. How long would it be before they got the old cradle out again? She eyed her boys. Handsome lads all of them; healthy and strong. Saul would fly the nest first, but Elsa would not be far behind him unless Bess missed her guess.

Her daughter was in her usual place next to her father. She had been the apple of his eye from the moment she was born, never able to do anything wrong, and with her father wrapped around her little finger. He had been pleased to have a daughter.

"With three big lads clumping about, it'll be nice to have a lass about the place."

Bess was wiser to her daughter's activities than her husband, or indeed her brothers, all of whom were fiercely protective of their little sister. Bess sat down with a weary sigh and accepted the plate Elsa passed her.

"Another day gone. I don't think I've paused for breath."

"Maybe we're getting too old for this," Ephrom said innocently.

"You speak for yourself!" Bess waved the stew ladle threateningly. "I could give you a good chase with this to spur you on."

Elsa giggled. "You'd be caught too, Papa. There's none can escape Mama when she has the mind."

"Aye, lass, that's true enough. Pass me my pipe like a good girl."

Elsa obeyed. Her father always took a pipe after dinner. It was the last thing he did before going to bed. Bess watched as he filled and lit it from one of the candles on the table. He sat back with a contented sigh.

"It's time you gave that up," she said sternly. "That cough of yours is getting worse. Don't think I haven't noticed!"

He blew a smoke ring as high as the ceiling. "Nothing escapes your notice, my love."

"Don't you try getting around me with flattery, Ephrom. You'll send yourself to an early grave, so you will, and where would we be then?"

"Oh, give over, woman," Ephrom said mildly. "If a man can't have a few simple pleasures in life, then it's not worth living. Goodness knows we've precious little to enjoy these days."

Their children exchanged pointed glances. They had listened to their parents have this argument every day of their lives for as long as they could remember. It was as much of a ritual as their father's pipe.

"You're even quieter than usual tonight, Caleb," Elsa observed, giving her brother a playful nudge in the ribs.

"I was just wondering how Christophe and the others were faring."

"Aye, that boy's always gone his own way," said Bess. "Never tells anyone what he's about. I fancy he's in deep water this time."

"Those others didn't look like they were from round here," said Ephrom. "I wonder where he can have picked them up from. He was never the sort to take in strays. Not when he's one himself."

"I'm worried for him," said Caleb. "Those men on the road were looking for him or I'm much mistaken. They probably think he's behind all those poor people escaping."

"I shouldn't wonder if he was," said Bess. "He was always a hero to those in need, even after he took up with the Travellers."

"It's a shame what happened to them," said Ephrom. "Losing everything in one stroke like that, and their women and children forced out on the streets like beggars. You can say what you like about the Travellers, they never asked for anything, and they always paid their way."

"Aye, they're a proud race. They won't take this lying down." Bess shook her head. "You should have heard them tonight. One young lad was all for storming in and snatching Alfredo's throne out from under him. He was shouted down though, and a good thing too. Talk like that will only get you killed."

"I'd join them," Caleb said suddenly. "The best way to deal with a bully is to stand up to him or he'll crush you beneath his boot heel. Many would flock to the Travellers if they chose to make a stand."

"You'll do nothing of the sort!" Bess said sharply. Hearing quiet, easy-going Caleb talking of going to war had unnerved her badly. "This family's always managed to keep out of trouble and they've left us alone by and large. We don't need trouble brought down on our heads."

"I'm just saying that sometimes you have to fight for what is right."

Bess opened her mouth furiously, but Ephrom's gentle hand on her arm stopped her.

"Time for bed, I think. Early start tomorrow as always."

Alone in their room, Bess turned to Ephrom with a worried frown. "You don't think Caleb will do anything silly, do you?"

He considered, "A man can only take so much before he decides enough is enough."

Seeing her stricken face, he added hastily, "Our Caleb is a sensible lad. He would never do anything that would endanger his family."

Bess lay awake for a long time, listening to her husband's steady snores. She hoped he was right about Caleb. She understood his frustration, but she saw little point in fighting a battle you had no chance of winning. Best just to keep your head down and get on with it. Stay out of your enemy's way and they'll likely stay out of yours. The philosophy had worked up to now.

She thought of the legend of The Appointed. The saviour who would free them all from Alfredo's rule and help build the world anew. She had never given much credence to the story. How could one girl, with no reported powers of her own, defeat the worst tyrant the land had ever known? Would she command a mighty army? Would she return the merpeople to them? That would be something at least. Bess didn't recall the story saying exactly how The Appointed would bring about their liberation. It was a fool's hope.

Unbidden, the image of Christophe and his strange friends returned. He had proved remarkably close-mouthed about them. On the day they had left, he had said nothing of where he was going, only that they were being hunted and haste and secrecy were needed to get them away. She had obliged of course, but now she found herself wishing she had tried to learn more. She pictured again the three strangers. The dark-haired girl with the watchful eyes. The tall fair-haired boy and the pretty red-haired girl with the pensive expression. She certainly was not from anywhere local. Bess had never seen a person with her colouring before. She might almost be from another land. Bess felt a sinking sensation in her stomach. Didn't the stories all say that the girl saviour had been sent to a safe place for her protection, and would return one day to free her people? Surely Christophe couldn't be so stupid as to think that… no, it was impossible. But the secrecy, and the fear of being hunted? Oh, Christophe, she sighed inwardly. My lad, what have you done? It was a long time before she fell asleep.

The heavy pounding on the door of the inn woke Bess with a start. She sat up, reaching for the poker she always kept near to hand and digging her elbow into her husband's ribs.

"Ephrom, wake up you big lummox. Someone's trying to break in!"

He sat up with a grunt. "What's that you say?"

The pounding broke out anew. Ephrom was out of bed in a flash, grabbing up a candle and his heavy cudgel.

"Drunken layabouts. I'll teach them what it means to get a fellow out of bed at this hour." Still muttering to himself, he barrelled out of the door and down the stairs.

Bess followed, trying to ignore the sensation of fear in the pit of her stomach. Something told her this was far more serious than a man with too much ale inside him. She had been dreading something like this, though she hardly knew when the feeling had crept up on her.

Her three sons appeared, also clutching weapons. Caleb had also had the presence of mind to bring a lantern. Bess saw Elsa's scared white face peering furtively around her bedroom door.

"Stay in your room, lass," Bess ordered sharply. "And don't you stir a finger till I say, understand?"

Elsa nodded, wide-eyed, and her door closed with a snap.

The pounding was louder now, and Bess could hear raised voices too.

"In the name of the Emperor, you are under arrest. Open this door at once!"

"Something heavy smashed into the door. They were attempting to force their way in. Bess felt a wave of nausea. The door was stout wood, but it would not hold for long under such an onslaught.

She turned to Ephrom. "Maybe we can escape out the back way."

"No good," he said tersely. "They'll have men waiting. Get back to Elsa, stay with her. Maybe you can hide and go for help while they're busy with us."

She hesitated, torn. Elsa was alone up there, defenceless, but she couldn't stand by and do nothing while her husband and sons were stolen from her. Ignoring Ephrom's pleading look, she stood her ground, poker raised, as Ephrom threw back the bolts.

A dozen men stood framed in the doorway, all wearing the black uniform of Alfredo's guards. They were big men, and every one of them was armed.

Ephrom glared at the leader. "What do you mean by making such a racket at this hour?" he demanded angrily. "Can't you let hard-working citizens rest?"

The leader stared back expressionlessly. "You and your family are under arrest for sheltering and aiding in the escape of known criminals."

At this, Bess began cautiously moving back the way she had come. Her mind was made up. She would take Elsa and run. If they were free, there might be a chance of rescuing her husband and sons. If they took them all, they were lost. Caleb saw her, and immediately moved to screen her from view. His brothers joined him, forming a solid wall of bodies between their father and the intruders. Bess heard Ephrom's voice. It sounded remarkably calm.

"People come and go from our inn as they please. I don't enquire into their concerns so long as they pay. Who might these criminals be?"

At the top of the stairs, Bess froze, hardly daring to breathe. Please, let them have made a mistake. Let it be somebody else.

"Can you deny that the fugitive Christophe was a guest at your establishment a few nights back?"

"Well, what of it? I never knew as how he'd done anything wrong."

A tinge of scorn crept into the other man's voice. "You were not aware that this boy is possibly the most wanted outlaw in the entire city? That there is a price of five thousand gold crowns on his head, dead or alive?"

"Aye, I knew that, but I never knew why. I don't think it was ever explained."

"Enough of this!" the leader was finally losing patience. "A few days ago, Christophe and three accomplices posed as prison guards and freed the spy Miguel. They also succeeded in freeing several slaves bound for market before fleeing the city. We have reason to believe that they were aided in this endeavour by a man named Carlos, a known spy and thief, who was also resident at this inn."

Bess's head reeled. They knew everything. There was no way to talk themselves out of it. But Christophe freeing Miguel? Impossible! Christophe would never free that monster.

"You will tell us where they were bound," the leader ordered.

There was a long silence. Bess tensed.

"I'm afraid I can't do that," Ephrom said quietly. "Because I have no idea where they were headed, and I wouldn't tell you even if I could."

Even in the midst of her fear, Bess felt a surge of pride. She would never have thought Ephrom could be so composed and calm, but the man's next words chilled her to the bone.

"Is that so?" the leader drawled. "You have remarkable spirit. But spirits can be broken. You will soon wish you had told us everything when we asked. You will in the end, you know, but this way would have been quicker." Then to his men, "Take them!"

Cries broke out and the sound of weapons. Bess ran. She hammered on Elsa's door with her fists.

"Elsa, open this door right now!" There was the sound of a bolt being drawn back, and Elsa's pale face peered through the crack.

"Mama, what—"

Bess shouldered the door open. "Run, girl, if you want to save your skin. The back stairs!"

She wheeled away, Elsa at her heels. The shouts grew louder, then someone uttered a shrill scream. Elsa was sobbing as she ran.

"Where's Papa? What are they doing to him?"

"Run!" Bess shouted. She sprang down the last few steps and hurtled past the half open kitchen door, but a piercing shriek made her spin around, poker raised. A man stood framed in the doorway, a knife to Elsa's throat. Another stood grinning beside him. A draught wafted in from the open kitchen window. They must have forced it while her family were all busy at the front. But as the small portion of her mind that could still think rationally reached this conclusion, the man who was not holding Elsa pointed his own knife at her.

"Lower your weapon, or we kill the girl."

Bess let the poker clatter to the floor and raised her hands to show she was unarmed. Elsa's captor seized Elsa by the hair with his free hand and began dragging her back the way they had come. Elsa was sobbing hysterically, almost incoherent with terror. Bess instinctively moved to go to her, but a dizzying blow to the side of her head sent her staggering backwards. She righted herself, blinking the stars from her vision. Her head spun.

"Will you come quietly?"

She nodded weakly, still struggling to gather her dazed senses.

The struggle was almost over when they reached the hall. Ephrom and his sons were outnumbered three to one. Bess's sons were in a line, their hands shackled behind them, their faces sullen. But Ephrom lay motionless on the ground, his bloody cudgel in his hand, and more blood matting his hair and trickling down his cheek.

Elsa let out a scream and fainted. Bess froze where she stood, her blood turned to ice. No, not Ephrom!

"What have you done to him?" She breathed at the leader. For answer, he motioned to her captor, who produced a pair of manacles and shackled her wrists behind her back. She barely noticed. She had eyes only for Ephrom. The leader eyed her with evident satisfaction.

"He still lives, for the moment, but that could change of course if you give us any more trouble, but you won't, will you?"

She shook her head dumbly.

Two men lifted the motionless forms of Ephrom and Elsa, handling them as if they were sacks of grain. Bess and her sons were each taken charge of and led outside to where a cart waited, but some of the men disappeared back inside the inn. Bess wondered why, but didn't dare ask. She was manhandled into the cart and pushed down between Caleb and Ephrom. With her hands shackled, she could not check for a pulse, but she bent her head to his chest, and felt a wave of relief as she heard his quiet breathing. The cart set off, bumping and jolting over the uneven cobbles. At the end of the street, Bess looked back, and saw the first tendrils of smoke already beginning to rise from the inn's windows.

* * *

Gideon was awake early. Most of his life he had been soothed to sleep by the gently rocking motion of a ship. He never slept well on land, and their recent difficulties had meant even less sleep than usual. He hurried out in search of breakfast. Most people were up and about. Some of those who had been at The

Jolly Sailor the night before cast him wary glances, but he ignored them, choosing to sit with Esther and Lena.

Somewhat to his surprise, Carlotta was there too, with her younger brothers and sisters. She was the closest thing to a parent they had left to them now. Her leg was bandaged, he saw, but other than that, she seemed none the worse for the previous night's skirmish. She nodded to him, but gave no other sign of greeting. He was hurt, but he didn't show it, sitting down and accepting a slice of stale bread and cheese and a cup of water from Esther.

Looking at her, he thought she looked even more weary than he did. There were dark circles about her eyes, and there had been a strained quality about her of late, though she had seemed as cheerful as ever, and had done more than her share of taking care of the children and the wounded. But she was quieter than usual. There was no hiding it from him. He knew the reason of course. She was worried about Christophe. She had loved him for years, though Gideon had never seen evidence that Christophe returned her feelings or was even aware of them. Personally, Gideon thought that Christophe was not the right man for his sister. She was gentle and quiet and liked the comforts of home. Christophe was restless and hard and loved action. Still, for Esther's sake, he hoped Christophe would come to care for her eventually.

"I hear there was quite an argument at The Jolly Sailor last night," she said now.

He shrugged. "The whole meeting was a waste of time. All they do is sit and talk, as if that will solve anything."

"You would have us fight?" she said.

"We cannot run for ever. It is time we took back what is ours, but no one will listen."

"Can you blame them?" she said gently. "The loss of our ships has shaken people badly. Many feel they have reached the limit of their endurance. You cannot ask any more of them."

He let out a growl of frustration.

At that moment, Carlos rushed up to them, his face ashen.

"There was a fire at The Jolly Sailor last night," he panted. "It's a ruin, burned to the ground!"

Gideon and Carlotta were on their feet at once.

"Are you sure?" Gideon snapped.

"I saw men leaving the place with buckets. They've been fighting the blaze for half the night."

"Where are the family?"

"No sign of them. Take me to your elders. They should hear of this, and I need someone to help search the ruins."

"I'll come with you," Gideon said at once. Carlotta nodded.

"Watch the children!" Gideon called over his shoulder to Esther.

The Jolly Sailor, when they finally arrived was a sorry sight. The ground all around was blackened and scorched and slick with water. The building itself was little more than a shell of still smoking timbers and half collapsed beams. There was no one else there now, the fire carriers having done all they could.

"Be careful," Gideon muttered. "This could collapse at any moment."

They ducked in cautiously. Shards of broken crockery crunched beneath their feet, and the stench of smoke and charred wood made them cough.

They scanned the debris, looking for any sign that would indicate what had become of the family.

Carlotta suddenly let out a sharp hiss and beckoned to the others.

They picked their way cautiously over to her. Wordlessly, Carlotta pointed to some smears showing through the ash covering the floor. They were almost invisible beneath the soot and grime, but once seen, it was impossible to mistake them.

"Blood!" Gideon breathed. "They are dead then?"

"Or taken," said Carlotta.

Gideon felt a lead weight settle in the pit of his stomach. "But why?"

"They were sheltering Christophe and the others," Carlos said dully. "They helped them flee the city."

Gideon put his head into his hands. Those poor good people. Friends to the Travellers for nearly twenty years. To come to this.

"What about the upper floors?" he said tonelessly.

"Fallen through completely," said Carlotta. "We need to inform the elders."

Gideon nodded and they left the inn.

As they returned to camp, Gideon felt such a rage building up within him that he thought it might burn him up as completely as the inn. Someone would pay for what had happened to Bess and her family if it was the last thing he did.

They burst into the makeshift hut fashioned from discarded timbers where the elders were congregated. His father was there, and Jeremiah as well.

They looked around in surprise at the intrusion, but Gideon did not give them time to speak.

"The Jolly Sailor has been destroyed, burned to the ground last night."

There was shock and outrage on every face. Everyone began exclaiming at once, until Antonio held up a silencing hand.

"Are you sure, son? After all, we were only just there—"

"I saw the ruins myself," Gideon interrupted. He indicated his two companions. "We have searched the building. The family are gone. There is no sign of them. Either they are dead or taken prisoner."

There was a heavy silence.

"Well," one man began awkwardly. "I do not know what we can—"

"You do not know what we can do about it?" Gideon fumed. He'd had enough of this. Enough of their dithering and pointless delays. Enough of running and hiding like hunted animals. Now was the time to act. If not now, then never.

"How many people have to suffer and die for our sake? How long are we going to just sit and watch while Alfredo takes everything from us. He has taken everything we have ever worked for. Our loved ones and our homes, but most of all, he has denied us the right to live as free people, to choose and govern our own lives. He has taken away all justice and mercy and given only fear and cruelty in exchange. And what have we done about it? Just sat back and let him! We pretended to be resisting him, but all we have ever done is cowered in our ships. Now that they are gone, we are still running!

"A family were taken last night. Probably killed. Their home and livelihood destroyed. And all because they chose to help some of our own in a fight that was none of their concern. How many times have they given us food and shelter and never once complained of the risk? Now one of our own leads The Appointed in a quest to conquer an enemy whom she has never known. She has taken up our cause for us. We have some of the best fighters in the land, and yet we allow our people to live in squalor and to be sold as slaves. We are in a position to help and we do nothing, and we run and hide like cowards. I say let us act now. Let us buy The Appointed the time she needs to fulfil her quest. Let us give her a free land to return home to so that her work will not have been in vain.

"I ask you this. If we do not fight for them, who will?"

A ringing silence followed. Gideon stood there, breathing rapidly. He had dared to challenge the elders, a Guardian barely a man grown. He suddenly felt extremely alone. Carlotta stepped up to stand beside him, and Carlos joined them. He took comfort in their presence.

Then Antonio rose slowly. Walking across to where Gideon stood, he placed a hand on his son's shoulder.

"The boy is right," he said loudly and clearly. "He sees with wiser eyes than ours. I stand with him."

Gideon flushed with pleasure.

There was another pause. Then Jeremiah also rose.

"I too stand with him. Who else will join us?"

There were a few more murmurs. They grew louder, until suddenly every man was on his feet, shouting their assent in a roar that made Gideon's ears throb, even as it made his heart soar. It seemed he had found the right words at last. He only wished it hadn't taken so long.

He felt his father squeeze his shoulder gently.

"Well done, son," he said close to Gideon's ear. "Come, we have work to do."

# Chapter 17

## The Mountain's Heart

Fiona sat up groggily at James's light touch on her shoulder.

She hadn't really been sleeping. She couldn't remember the last time she had had any proper rest. She was losing track of the days, which all seemed to pass in a haze of heat and exhaustion and terrible thirst. That was the worst of all. They had been as careful as possible with their water, but their supply was running dangerously low, and they had come across no fresh water source. It had rained briefly two days ago, or was it three? They had done their best to collect some of the water. But it wasn't their only concern, though the most serious one. Their food rations were also running low.

Walking in the heat of the day sapped them of their already dwindling energy. At every halt, Katie applied salves to their blisters and sunburn. Fiona suffered particularly from the latter. Her fair skin had always burned easily, and with nothing to protect it, it quickly grew angry red and sore. But Katie's ointments were also diminishing.

Even at night they were not spared. Biting insects, drawn by their sweat, attacked constantly.

Fiona couldn't remember the last time she had felt clean. Sunstroke made her feverish and delirious at times, so that sometimes she was not always aware of her surroundings.

Christophe was suffering too. He had begun their journey before he had fully regained his strength, and lack of nourishment was rapidly eroding what was left of it. He had dispensed with his sling, despite Katie's protestations that his arm was not yet fully healed, and his side still troubled him, though he never complained. More than once Katie made him strip off so she could examine the wound. She reported that it was healing well, though she doubted it would ever cease to trouble him completely.

Katie's visions kept them on the right course. Fiona frequently found herself wondering how they would have managed without her. She was their guide and healer, often putting their needs before her own, always treating herself last. Her constant checks to keep them in the right direction kept her from getting much real sleep, and she was looking increasingly pale and hollow-eyed.

Surprisingly, it was James who was holding up the best. His naturally robust nature seeming to cope better with the forced conditions of the crossing. But even he could not go on for ever, and Fiona had noticed that he was beginning to flag, though he said nothing of it, always pressing Fiona to eat and often giving her half of his share in an effort to boost her rapidly failing strength. She knew what he was doing, but couldn't think of a way to refuse.

She accepted the water bottle from James gratefully. She suspected he was going without, and while her guilt was acute, her thirst was such that she could never refuse it when offered. She forced herself to take just a few sips, all the while fighting the ever growing temptation to drink it all and ease her parched throat.

Though they travelled when it was relatively cool, the burned skin of her face and arms throbbed unrelentingly and she ached in every one of her joints. Her muscles were weak from hunger and her wits dull and lethargic. But every day she took her accustomed place in their little procession and shouldered her considerably lighter pack.

They walked for the most part in silence, concentrating their remaining energy on placing one foot in front of the other and watching the landscape ahead of them. The yellow sand stretched on endlessly, a flat, featureless expanse that showed no sign of coming to an end. There had been at least two more sandstorms since the one that had nearly killed Fiona, but they were better prepared. They knew what signs to look for and sought shelter behind boulders or beneath rocky outcrops. The early morning sky indicated another scorching day.

Fiona had been walking in a semi-exhausted haze for some time, when a noise made it through her befuddled consciousness and roused her a little. She strained to catch it, but all she could hear was the incessant chirping of crickets. Just a hallucination, she thought. But she was more alert now, and a short while later, she caught it again. She stood still, turning her head from side to side, trying to pinpoint it.

"Fiona!" James called hoarsely over his shoulder. "What are you doing?"

"Water," she croaked.

"I know, but we can't have any more just yet. We're running low as it is."

"No, I mean I think there's a spring or something nearby. I can hear it."

James fell behind the others and came to stand with her.

"Are you sure? It's often possible to imagine things stuck in a desert."

"Just listen, will you?"

James dutifully fell silent, trying to hear anything over the usual noises, and failing.

"I don't hear anything."

"What are you doing back there?" It was a sign of Christophe's exhaustion that he had only just noticed they had fallen behind. Not having the strength to shout, Fiona waved frantically to him. Christophe and Katie hurried over.

"What is it?" Christophe demanded urgently, casting about everywhere for signs of danger.

James hastened to reassure him. "Nothing's wrong, it's just that Fiona thought she heard a spring nearby."

"Where?" Katie said quickly.

"I couldn't really tell, I probably imagined it," Fiona said reluctantly.

Christophe cupped both hands behind his ears. As though to oblige him, the crickets momentarily ceased their chirping.

"I do believe you are right," he said slowly. There was another pause. Katie and James imitated Christophe, but Fiona remained motionless. She did not think she could bear the disappointment if she didn't hear anything. But then Christophe was pointing.

"This way!"

He led them more or less in the direction they had been headed, though bearing a little to the right. Soon the noise of running water became audible to everyone. They broke into a lurching run, eyes straining for a sight of it, mouths greedy to taste it. And then, there it was, a fast little cataract tumbling down a small gully. With cries of delight they clattered down to it, their feet dislodging pebbles and loose scree. The ground was still sandy, but at the water's edge, it became stony, hard-packed earth. Fiona dropped to her knees and bent her head, taking huge, greedy gulps. Happiness such as she had not felt in days surged through her. When she had drunk her fill, she plunged her entire head under, running her fingers through her hair to dislodge the worst of the sand. She came up dripping, but grinning. The others lost no time in following her example.

"Isn't this wonderful?" James called, flicking water at Fiona. She splashed him back, laughing.

"We should fill the water bottles," Katie murmured.

Christophe nodded. Straightening, he shook the wet hair out of his eyes, and froze.

"What is it?" Katie said quickly.

Christophe said nothing, but placed a warning finger to his lips. Fiona and James looked up, catching the sudden tension. Christophe had dropped into a guarded crouch, one hand on his long knife. He whispered, so quietly that they could barely hear him, "There is someone watching us."

"How do you know?" Fiona breathed, staring about everywhere.

"I sense their presence. Be ready to run if I tell you."

They waited, holding their breath, all the gaiety of a moment before vanished completely.

James, peering around guardedly in every direction, thought he saw a furtive movement in the sparse scrub on the far side of the little stream. Taking care not to make his movements too obvious, he shifted his position so that Fiona was partially screened from view. Christophe nodded once at him.

Katie was crouched, her body tense as a taut bow string, eyes blazing. "Is it an ambush?" she muttered.

Christophe shook his head. "If so, then why do they not attack? Get behind me!" She ignored him. Christophe gave her a look, then rose cautiously to his feet. He made as if to step round in front of her crouched form, but she was up beside him in an instant. He glared at her, but it was too late to hide. They would surely have been seen. She returned his gaze stonily. She meant to stand and fight with him, and though he feared for her, he couldn't help but love her for it. He pointed at the opposite bank.

"You there, show yourselves!" There was a brief pause, then as if from nowhere, half a dozen men rose suddenly into view. They were bare-chested, their ebony skin painted with many intricate signs and symbols. Their arms were similarly decorated and corded with muscle. They looked lean and fit. Below the decoration they wore baggy pantaloons that flared wildly above the ankles. On their feet they wore open-toed sandals. Turbans encircled their heads, and they carried spears and two-handed swords. James didn't care much for their chances. They were outnumbered two to one. He and Fiona began edging slowly backwards away from the confrontation, poised to make a break for it at Christophe's signal. Christophe stepped forward to the water's edge, his knife flashing in the midday sun, Katie at his side. A man who appeared to be the leader stepped forward too until they were directly facing each other, only the thin ribbon of water separating them.

"Who are you?" he called across to them, his voice clear and strong. "What is your business here?"

"I might ask you the same question," Christophe replied evenly. "I was not aware that this land was even inhabited, or that it was common practice to waylay strangers."

"You are in the territory of the desert clans," replied the other. "We have a right to challenge anyone seeking passage through these mountains. I ask once more, tell me who you are and state your errand."

Christophe hesitated fractionally. "We are travellers. We seek safe passage through the mountains. We mean you no harm. Let us go on our way and we will trouble you no further."

The man's face darkened. "Still you refuse to answer my questions. It is our law that none shall pass freely unless we are satisfied of their intentions."

"A law known only to yourselves, it seems."

The man took another step forward. "Enough of this. Since you will not answer freely, you will come with us now to answer to our chief. He is a just man. Be truthful with him, and you will be treated fairly. Come with us willingly, and you will not be harmed. What is it to be?"

Christophe turned swiftly to the others, reading the mix of fear and apprehension on their faces.

"Do we try to run for it?" James whispered.

Christophe shook his head. "They would cut us to pieces before we had gone fifty yards, and there are too many to fight."

"You're saying we have to let them take us?" Fiona demanded incredulously.

"I do not know of these people. They may be friendly or not, but until we know, we had better cooperate with them. They may be able to offer us fresh food and water, which we need if we are to continue, and I doubt we will be able to get far if they do not wish it. Better to earn their friendship if we can."

The others nodded reluctantly, bending to pick up their discarded packs.

Christophe turned back to the leader, waiting patiently on the opposite bank.

"We accept your terms."

The man nodded. At his signal, his men lowered their spears.

"Cross."

Christophe led the way, his knife sheathed, but within easy reach.

The man who had done all the talking eyed Christophe's knife, bow and quiver.

"You are no stranger to combat," he observed.

"I get by," Christophe replied.

The men formed a silent ring around them as they set off. They made no threatening gestures, but it was clear that they were under guard.

Christophe did not concern himself with their escort. As they walked, he mulled over what he should tell this chief they were being taken to. He would have to give him some story. They would have a very slim chance of getting through the mountains alive if they attempted to pass without permission. He had no memory of any people inhabiting these remote regions, but his knowledge of life beyond the city was sketchy. Since joining the Travellers, he had spent the greater part of his time at sea.

Still, the fact that these men hadn't simply killed him and his companions outright, said something about them. They reminded him somewhat of the Guardians, and he felt reasonably confident that he could handle the situation. The trick was in finding a plausible story that would let them go unmolested. He was under no illusions about what would happen to them if it was suspected that they were lying. At best they would be made prisoners and they could not afford to dally here.

It bothered Christophe that there had been no sign of pursuit since they had left the city. Surely Alfredo would know of their disappearance by now and sent someone to track them. Yet he had seen no evidence of anyone following them.

If Christophe took some measure of comfort from their situation, Fiona's spirits were at their lowest point. She looked at the men with their spears and their guarded expressions and saw yet another attempt to capture and interrogate her. Once again she was someone's captive and her freedom depended solely on the whim of others. It had been so ever since she had arrived in this wretched land and the knowledge infuriated her. Worn down by her ordeal at Miguel's hands and their nearly fatal crossing of the desert, she wanted more than anything for this to be over, for the task to be completed and to be safely home again. And here was another delay.

She looked at James. He seemed deep in thought, taking no notice of their surroundings. Katie's eyes watched alertly. She wasn't letting her guard relax for an instant. Fiona smiled bitterly. She would have liked to know what Katie thought they could do against a dozen armed men, particularly when Christophe was the only experienced fighter among them, and he was not at his full strength. For the first time, Fiona found herself wishing they had brought along a Guardian escort with them after all.

They were leaving the desert behind now. The sand giving way to short, coarse grass, turned brown by the sun. The sparse scrub was giving way to trees and bushes, with here and there patches of heather and bracken. The ground rose in many small hills and tussocks, a clear sign that they were entering mountainous country. The sun was as relentless as ever, but the trees provided some welcome shade.

They walked for what felt like hours. Their guides did not seem much inclined for conversation, and Fiona and her companions were too weary to make the effort.

At last the hilly country gave way to tilled fields and signs of habitation became evident everywhere they looked.

Corn and what might have been maize or barley grew tall, almost on a level with their heads. Goats and sheep cropped the short grass. The settlement itself was made up largely of huts built of wood and thatch, often with a dog or a donkey tethered outside. Children ran about everywhere and women were gathered around cooking fires or else laughing and gossiping as they washed clothes in a nearby spring and draped them over low-hanging bushes to dry. The scene was one of busy contentment, though that quickly changed as the newcomers were sighted.

The dogs sent out the warning cry first, their deep-throated barks causing men, women and children alike to cease their activities and begin searching for the source of the disturbance. Men appeared from all directions, spears in hand, but fell back when they saw their comrades. One hailed the leader with a wave.

"Ibrehem! We had nearly given you up for lost. Who do you have with you?"

"Strangers!" Ibrehem answered curtly. "Tell someone to quiet those dogs and then send a message to the chief at once. He will need to speak with them."

Ibrehem led them on, wending through the huts, which were dotted around in a rather haphazard fashion. He was making for a grassy stretch which was clear of any dwellings or crops. Blackened bare patches of earth here and there showed where fires had been made. It was plainly some sort of meeting ground, Fiona thought, looking around warily.

They had drawn a sizable crowd by this time. People abandoned their pursuits and fell in with their procession, gaping openly at the newcomers. Fiona in particular generated more stares than the others. She didn't understand this and it unsettled her even more. She felt very exposed on this open grassland. There was no cover, no place to hide. She felt James come up beside her and draw her arm through his. As always, he seemed to know when she needed comfort or reassurance. She moved closer to him and gave his arm a squeeze. Grateful for his nearness.

Katie seemed to be having similar misgivings.

"You do not get many visitors, do you?" she commented dryly.

"We are an isolated people," was the non-committal reply.

Their guards led them to the very centre of the meeting ground, where the grass had been chopped back to reveal a bare patch of earth on which large boulders had been arranged to form a circle. Ibrehem gestured them into the circle and fell back with his men, still ringing them, but not standing in the circle itself. Fiona was put uneasily in mind of a sacrifice and banished the thought hurriedly.

At that moment the crowd fell silent, the low buzz of chatter dying to nothing almost instantly. They parted like stalks before a breeze, and a single figure made his stately way through them to where his four visitors stood waiting.

Christophe was surprised by this turn of events. He had expected that the chief would see them in his hut. He had been half-hoping to gain a private audience so that he could speak to the chief alone. This hope had been increased by the fact that Ibrehem and his men had not troubled to relieve him of his weapons, suggesting that they were not being considered prisoners. But this, it was like a trial, a judgement. He didn't like it. He saw the chagrined looks of the others and motioned them behind him. He was the best source of protection they had. If they were going to get out of there alive, it was up to him.

He stood watching the man as he approached and took his place in the circle. He stepped up onto a slight grassy hummock, placing him slightly above his guests. But even without the added advantage of height, he was impressive.

He was a tall man with broad shoulders and a dignified bearing. He was bare-chested like his men, with the same pattern of symbols painted across his chest. The face beneath his turban was bearded and lined, though still quite young, and he exuded an air of calm authority that demanded respect. For the first time, Christophe began to seriously wonder what they had got themselves into, and, more importantly, if he would be able to get them out of it. While there was nothing threatening about the man, he had a direct, intense gaze that made Christophe certain that any outright lie would be spotted at once, and the man's face, though not cruel, was nevertheless stern.

"My name is Sulaiman Muhammed Al-Jaffarin, Chief of the Desert Clans. How do you come to be here in my domain?"

He had the most beautiful voice Fiona had ever heard; deep and low with a soft musical lilt that flavoured the pattern of his speech. It took her aback. She had expected him to sound hostile and commanding, rather than politely curious. A voice like that made you want to answer it. She felt completely undone. She saw that Christophe too had been taken by surprise. He pulled himself together with a visible effort.

"We are simple travellers, Sulaiman Muhammed Al-Jaffarin. Our errand is pressing and we hoped by crossing the desert to shorten our road. We meant no offence to you or your people. We wish only to be allowed to go peacefully on our way."

"And if I grant your request, where would you go then?"

"Our way lies through these mountains."

Sulaiman Muhammed Al-Jaffarin gave Christophe a searching look.

"Our people own and farm all the land between the desert and the other side of the mountain pass. These mountains provide natural and formidable barriers to anyone wishing to take us by surprise. No one may pass through our territory without first giving reason for their passage. You have not done so. You say your errand is pressing. Tell us of it."

His voice was so gentle and reasonable, that Fiona was feeling a mounting need to tell him everything. The aura of calm strength that seemed to surround him was palpable. A glimmer of fear and suspicion arose. This feeling was not rational. Was this magic of some kind? Was it Alfredo himself? Had he got ahead of them somehow and been lying in wait for them? She remembered his sneering voice, his taunting words. This was a trap. She prayed Christophe would get them out of it soon.

"We are no danger to you," Christophe was saying. "There are only four of us as you can see. How can we be a threat to you?"

"Yet you are a skilled fighter, and skilled too at avoiding questions. Your behaviour suggests you have something to hide."

Christophe was silent. He could not refuse outright to satisfy this man's curiosity, and he had no intention of telling him the truth. He searched quickly for a convincing lie. The chief was right. He was a practised liar. It was impossible to survive on the streets otherwise. But before he could speak, the decision was taken out of his hands.

"We're looking for the secret of the mountain's heart," James said suddenly.

All eyes turned instantly to him. A low murmur broke out among the watching crowd. Katie and Fiona stared at James in disbelief. Christophe was instantly wary. What was the boy planning? He had just given them away. Why?

Sulaiman Muhammed Al-Jaffarin held up a finger and the muttering subsided at once. He regarded James thoughtfully.

"What is your interest in this secret, boy?"

James stepped forward. He looked nervous, but he faced the other man steadily.

"Our city is in danger. A prophecy speaks of a magic found here that will help to save our people. We don't want to attack your people. We only want to help our own. My friends and I came searching for this magic. If you are native to this area, perhaps you can help us?"

Christophe stared at James in speechless admiration. James's tone was deferential and his manner respectful. He had given the chief enough of the truth without revealing anything important, and what was more, he had managed to switch the roles so that he was now the one asking for information.

I should have met you years ago, Christophe thought wryly. I fancy you could have taught me a thing or two.

Sulaiman Muhammed Al-Jaffarin seemed equally impressed. After considering them a moment more, he addressed his people.

"I sense no lie or threat. We will make our guests welcome!" There was a resounding cheer. In the blink of an eye, all weapons were sheathed and hostile scowls melted in an instant to ready smiles. The chief's word, it seemed, really was law in all matters. Sulaiman Muhammed Al-Jaffarin himself turned to them with a gracious smile.

"You have travelled far, my friends. For four youngsters barely full grown to cross the desert alone is a feat indeed. You need food and rest. Come and take what you can of both. We will talk more later." He clapped his hands twice. Instantly Ibrehem appeared with a young woman whose face was completely hidden beneath a layer of fine white gauze.

"I will leave you in my children's care," Sulaiman Muhammed Al-Jaffarin said cheerfully. "They will show you where you may bathe and have your clothes cleaned. There will be a feast tonight in your honour. Rest well until then."

Ibrehem and his sister, who introduced herself as Meryam, led them to a small fenced-off enclosure where huge kettles of water heated over fires and they were presented with bowls of fine sand. Fiona eyed hers dubiously, having seen more than enough sand to last her a lifetime.

"The water will be ready shortly," Meryam told them. "Who wishes to go first?" she indicated a large sunken depression in the ground that women were already filling with water. They looked at each other.

"I will," Katie said at last. The women withdrew and Meryam handed her a pot of sand and directed her to the pit.

"Leave your clothes in a pile and they will be washed for you," she said. Having no other choice, Katie turned her back to the others and began to undress. Ibrehem handed Meryam a blanket which she passed over her shoulder to Katie with instructions to wrap herself in it when she was done. Ibrehem then handed blankets to the others. When they looked at him, puzzled, he grinned and with a sweep of his arm, indicated their soiled clothes.

"No need to sit dirty while you wait your turn. Meryam will have them clean very soon."

All his guardedness had vanished along with his weapons and he was as open and friendly as his sister. There was no denying such hospitality, so they each accepted a blanket and moved away to undress.

Fiona had her own reasons for not wanting to be observed. She could feel the key against her chest. How was she to keep it hidden? Meryam was still waiting patiently for her clothes. She hurried to undress and wrap herself in her own blanket, clasping it close to her body as though embarrassed. This was not entirely faked, but her main object was to conceal the key from view. She was not entirely sure of her success, but if either Meryam or Ibrehem saw anything, they gave no sign.

They seemed surprised by such modesty, but they politely turned away and talked together until their guests were all seated on the grass with their blankets pulled tight around them. Meryam gathered up the discarded clothes and bustled off. Ibrehem said he would leave them in peace and departed also.

They took it in turns to bathe in the rapidly cooling water. Fiona was last. She scrubbed her body with the fine sand until her skin tingled pleasantly all over, and wet her hair thoroughly. Though she did her best to screen her movements, it was a very public area, and it was impossible to hide entirely. This made her hurry through her ablutions. She tried not to look at the others, whose blanketed forms lay stretched on the grass.

When she was done, she joined the others on the grass. She was soon sweating again in the hot sun, and longed to take the blanket off again, but refrained with a guilty blush. It felt good to be clean again.

"That was quite a chance you took back there," Katie observed, raising herself on one elbow to look at James's prone figure.

He opened his eyes sleepily. "Well, the other way wasn't working. No offence," he added to Christophe.

Christophe grinned. "None taken. How did you know it would work?"

"I didn't. But I figured we hadn't much to lose. We weren't going to get anywhere without their say-so, and I thought if we could make them believe we needed their help, they'd stop thinking we were a threat and be less suspicious. Besides, we need more food and water, and the secret of the mountain's heart is the next bit of the poem that we have to worry about, now that we have the key."

"I wish we knew what that actually meant," Fiona muttered.

"Well, it evidently meant something to them," said Christophe. "It was impossible to miss their reaction."

"You think they know the secret?" Fiona said hopefully.

"Maybe. Perhaps the chief will tell us over dinner if we can continue to make him believe we are no threat."

"Well we're not," James pointed out.

Meryam returned for them an hour later.

"I am to take you to a place where you may rest," she said shyly.

They fell in behind her, not sorry for the opportunity to catch up on some much needed sleep.

"Why do you keep your face hidden?" Fiona asked Meryam, vainly struggling to hide a yawn.

"It is the law," Meryam said simply. "No man except those of her immediate family may look upon the face of a woman before she is wed."

Fiona opened her mouth to ask how a man would know he wanted to marry a woman if he couldn't see what she looked like, but decided she didn't have the energy. Probably neither party had any choice in the matter. She yawned again. She was nearly asleep on her feet, and it was all she could do to place one foot in front of the other and keep her blanket wrapped firmly around her. She had been rather dismayed when Meryam had not returned with clean clothes for them, promising that their own clothes would be ready for them to put on for the feast tonight. Fiona's cheeks burned as she walked. Though she was swathed from head to toe in heavy fabric, she still couldn't shake off the feeling that she was walking through a very bright spotlight. Though no one looked twice at her that she could see. The people of this world seemed to set very little store by modesty at all, yet here, the women were forced to keep their faces covered.

She suddenly realised that Meryam was conducting them into a hut that seemed to have been set apart for them. Four pallets of bracken and gorse were neatly arranged against the walls. Meryam bid them farewell for the present and quietly withdrew, drawing a raw-hide flap across the mouth of the hut to screen them from view. At least there's some privacy here, Fiona thought wearily, stretching out thankfully on the nearest pallet. The others were quick to follow her example. Even Christophe did not go back outside to keep watch, but lay down too. In no time at all, they were asleep.

It seemed to Fiona that she had barely closed her eyes when she was jerked abruptly awake by a deep, booming gong that reverberated through the entire encampment. She saw Christophe's outline crouched in the hut entrance, the flap pulled aside. She sat up and saw that he was fully dressed once more. Looking down, she saw her own clothes in a neat pile at the foot of her bed. James and Katie were also sitting up.

"What is it?" James asked groggily.

Christophe turned back to them. "It appears the feast is about to start. Hurry and dress. I expect someone will be along to fetch us shortly."

He and James stepped outside while Katie and Fiona dressed. Fiona was glad to be able to cover the key up again. Had it been seen? She felt a brief twinge of apprehension. Would they try to take it from her? No, they would have done so by now, surely.

Ibrehem came for them a few minutes later. He led them once more in the direction of the communal meeting ground. The cleared space was alight with cooking fires and what appeared to be the entire settlement was already gathered around them. Women turned meat on skewers over the flames, with one eye kept on the children who darted here and there. Many people cast curious looks at Fiona and the others, and several hailed them or gave them small waves of greeting.

Fiona watched this with a certain amount of suspicion. These people's behaviour had transformed in the blink of an eye. One minute they were unwelcome strangers, the next they were being greeted like old friends. A surreptitious glance at the others showed the same doubt reflected in their eyes.

"I sense a trap," Christophe whispered out of the side of his mouth. "We must tread carefully."

They were conducted to the place of honour with the chief and his family. Once they were seated, Sulaiman Muhammed Al-Jaffarin got to his feet and raised a hand for silence. Everyone bowed their heads as he began to speak a ritual prayer. Fiona and the others bowed their heads dutifully, but the prayer was a long one and Fiona had a crick in her neck by the time it was over.

There was none of the informality of the Travellers' feasts. Meryam presented her father with a platter of meat that looked to Fiona like goat, still skewered and lying on a bed of leaves. There was also flat bread flavoured with herbs and a goblet of wine. Her father sampled everything, pronounced himself satisfied and was served, followed by the guests and the rest of the men. The women and children were served last and the bones were thrown to the dogs.

Once everyone was served, chatter resumed once more and Sulaiman Muhammed Al-Jaffarin turned his attention to his guests.

"Forgive me for asking," Katie said. "But you have not told us how we should address you."

The chief looked surprised. "By my name." He saw the horrified expressions on the faces of James and Fiona and raised an eyebrow. "Is that not allowed where you come from? I am chief of this village, but I am no more immortal than the rest of my people."

"It's not that," said James awkwardly. "It's just that your name's such a mouthful, if you don't mind me saying so."

"Really? And what may your names be?"

"I'm James and this is Fiona."

The big man laughed. "I see now why my name daunts you so, but what would you call me then."

"Could we not just call you Sulaiman?" Fiona asked tentatively.

Meryam and Ibrehem looked terrified and Christophe shot Fiona a warning look, but the chief merely smiled, a wondrous, dazzling smile that lit up his entire face and made his eyes twinkle.

"Sulaiman. I like that. Much simpler. You shall call me that as long as you are here."

Fiona and James looked extremely relieved.

"You will forgive me for saying so," Sulaiman continued, looking at Fiona. "But we have never before seen anyone with your looks and colouring."

Fiona sighed wearily. "I'm not from round here. James and I live far away."

Sulaiman's eyes sparkled with interest. "Indeed? And what of you, my silent companions? Will you not give your names?"

"I am Christophe and this is Katie. We are of the sea folk. The Travellers. Perhaps you have heard of us?"

"Ah, the wandering people. Indeed I have heard of them. Merchants and traders. You are far from your native shores and from the look of you, your journey has been a difficult one. Will you not now speak more of it?"

"No," said Christophe before any of the others could answer. "Not until you explain what it is you want with us."

Sulaiman regarded him levelly. "What makes you think I require anything from you?"

Christophe returned his gaze unflinchingly. "When we were brought to your village we were little better than prisoners. Now all of a sudden we are honoured guests. Something happened to change your minds. I fancy it has something to do with our errand. You know something about it, or you believe that by helping us you stand to gain something, perhaps for the benefit of your people."

Ibrehem was on his feet instantly. "You presume too much, Christophe!" he snapped, but his father motioned him to silence. Ibrehem resumed his seat, glaring at Christophe, who had not moved during the outburst.

Sulaiman got to his feet until he was standing over them. Everyone fell silent at once, looking to their chief.

Christophe tensed, feeling sure that a reprimand or judgement was coming. But to his surprise, Sulaiman made him a short bow.

"Behold, my people. Here is a boy wiser than his years. Young though he is, he has already mastered the tools of cunning and discretion, and re-taught a chief a forgotten lesson; humility. Something no man should lose, especially when he is head of a village."

He sat down, and gradually the eating and chatter started up once more. Evidently the people were used to such speeches, though a few shot puzzled glances in their direction. Fiona, James and Katie exchanged bemused glances, but Sulaiman was already turning back to them.

“You are correct, Christophe of the wandering folk. Your errand did mean something to us, and it is possible that you may be able to help us, but we wanted to be sure of you first, and I beg your forgiveness if we caused any offence.”

“What is it you think we can do for you?” Katie asked.

Sulaiman looked directly at Fiona.

“My daughter Meryam informs me that you possess a magical talisman. Is it so?”

Fiona felt her heart sink. It was what she had feared. But there was no help for it now. Reaching into her tunic, she withdrew the key on its leather chord.

Sulaiman leaned forward, examining it closely, but making no move to touch it.

“This is a superb piece of craftsmanship,” he said at last. “What is the nature of its magic?”

“It will help me find the secret of the mountain’s heart,” Fiona said, then added for good measure, “and only I can use it. It’s useless to anyone else.” She slipped it out of sight again and waited.

“It seems,” Sulaiman said thoughtfully, “That you are the one the legend speaks of.”

“What?” Fiona said sharply. This road sounded all too familiar. “What do you mean?”

“Just under twenty years ago, a vision was sent to our seer in a dream while he slept. It showed him a holy shrine hidden deep in the foothills, and he was told that it held a secret of great magic. This shrine was to be kept safe and warded until the time when one arrived bringing magic to unlock the shrine and learn its secret. We were to aid them in any way they asked, for if this secret was discovered, it would serve mankind and lead to a brighter future. We saw this vision as a divine sending and have carried out the charge faithfully. When you first mentioned the secret of the mountain’s heart, we began to wonder if you were the one the prophecy spoke of. When my daughter came and told me of the strange talisman you carried, I became certain. My people will help you in any way we can.”

Fiona felt a great weariness settle over her. It was The Appointed nonsense all over again. Would she never be free of it? With a silent sigh of resignation, she said, “I am the one your prophecy meant. Can you show us to this shrine?”

“We were given this guardianship by a divine power,” Sulaiman said gravely. “If you are indeed the one whom the prophecy spoke of, then it is our duty to aid you in any way we can.”

“I’m not a divine anything,” Fiona said tiredly. “Just show us where this shrine is.”

“It will be as you wish,” Sulaiman said with a bow. “We will leave tomorrow, but tell me if you would, what this danger is that threatens human kind?”

“Do you know of the man who rules the city on the other side of the desert?” said Christophe.

Sulaiman nodded. “We have heard of him. By all accounts he is a cruel tyrant who rules with an iron hand. They say his reach is long, though thankfully, it has not yet found us here.”

“He will!” James said emphatically. “He won’t stop until he rules the world.”

“He’s very powerful,” Fiona explained. “He’s got magic of his own, but he needs a weapon to make his power complete. We want to destroy it, and whatever is in this shrine of yours is a clue that will help us find it.”

Sulaiman looked serious. “My people know how to fight, but we have no defence against magic. Against such a weapon as you speak of, we would surely perish. Such a thing must be prevented at all costs. It will be an honour to aid anyone in such a cause. We will leave at first light. Go now to your beds and get what sleep you can.”

It was late when they eventually returned to their hut. Fiona, who was leading, pulled back the raw-hide flap, and screamed as a loud cackling issued from the corner.

“What’s up?” said James, as Fiona let the flap drop and took a hasty step back.

“There’s something in there!”

James blinked. “Did you see it?”

“No, I just heard it. It was laughing.”

James grinned. “How much wine did you drink?”

“See for yourself!” Fiona said indignantly. “It scared the hell out of me!”

Katie stepped forward and lifted the flap. The sound came again, a mad laugh that raised the hair on the back of their necks.

“Sounds like a chicken,” James said with an attempt at a laugh.

“What?” Fiona hissed back. “There’s no way that’s a chicken!”

“Well, we won’t find out standing out here.”

“Be careful,” said Christophe. “Let me go first.”

Drawing his knife, he moved past Katie.

There was a sudden squawk, then Christophe’s voice.

“Come in, all of you.”

They ducked inside. The hut’s interior was dim, but their eyes soon grew accustomed to it, and they saw that Christophe was crouched by one of the pallets, one hand firmly gripping the shoulder of what appeared to be a bundle of sticks and dirty rags.

The man’s form was so emaciated that he looked as if his limbs would snap if handled too roughly. He was wearing a soiled jerkin covered with food stains and his bare feet were crusted with grime. His face was mostly hidden by a long beard that fell down his chest, but for mad, roomy eyes that glinted at Christophe.

Christophe looked completely nonplussed. Katie came instantly to crouch on the man’s other side, her expression wary. Fiona and James backed away with expressions of revulsion. The stench of the man’s unwashed clothes and body was foul.

“What are you doing here?” Christophe demanded.

"Abou meant no offence," his captor replied in unctuous tones. "Abou will not harm noble warrior, no, he will not!"

Christophe released him, but remained within grabbing distance.

"What is it you want?"

Abou's eyes roved around the hut. When they settled on Katie, crouching next to him, he uttered a blood curdling shriek and lunged for her. Long blackened nails clawing at her face.

Katie screamed and reared back. Christophe caught her with one arm and held her against him. With the other, he held his knife inches from the man's popping eyes.

James moved forward and gripped the man's thin arms. "I've got him, Christophe."

Christophe lowered the knife and drew Katie close. She lifted her face from his shoulder, staring at her attacker with a mixture of shock and bewilderment.

"Shall I get help?" Fiona asked from her place by the entrance.

Christophe shook his head. He pushed Katie behind him, while still keeping one protective arm around her. Then turned his cold gaze on the little man, twisting frantically in James's grip. He kept it up a little longer, then, seeming to realise that he could not break free, he fell still, returning Christophe's gaze balefully.

"If you ever try that again," Christophe said quietly. "It will be the last thing you ever do. Do you understand?"

Abou glowered sulkily back at him, lower lip thrust out like a child's.

"Brave warrior foolish to protect her. Abou knows who she is."

"And what is that supposed to mean?" Katie spat furiously, still pressed against Christophe.

Abou let out a mad cackle of laughter. "Abou sees everything. His dreams tell him many things."

Katie gasped. "You are a seer?"

"Abou knows what you are," he cackled gleefully. "You can never run. You can never hide what you are." He let out a shriek of delighted mirth. "It will come back to haunt you," he said in a singsong voice.

James saw that Katie had gone white. She dropped her face back into Christophe's shoulder. Christophe tightened his arm around her.

"For the last time, old man," he said between gritted teeth. "Tell us what you want or I will throw you out!"

Abou's eyes wandered vacantly around the hut once more, before finally settling on Fiona, who flinched. James tensed, ready to restrain Abou if he showed any sign of wanting to attack Fiona. But Abou made no attempt to reach her. He merely gazed at Fiona with a calculating look in his eyes.

"Abou knows who you are too. He knows what you have been sent to do, Appointed."

Fiona froze. So did the others, but Abou continued speaking. He was no longer looking at Fiona. His eyes were not focused on anything in particular. He no longer even seemed aware that they were there.

"Abou knows what she must do, but can she do it? Will the sacrifice be too great? Will she save poor people? Abou does not know. He wonders, but he does not know. He cannot know. The dreams will not speak to Abou. Why have they abandoned him? Why have they abandoned Abou? What has he done to them? He has done nothing! Abou always listens to them. He repeats what they tell him. So why will they not talk to him?"

Fat tears leaked from his roomy eyes, making tracks down his grimy cheeks.

"Abou is alone!" he wailed shrilly, throwing back his head.

James stared at the others, utterly bewildered.

Just then, the raw-hide flap lifted, and a woman with a harried, anxious face looked in.

"Oh, Father, there you are! I thought I had lost you."

She gave them an apologetic nod.

"You must not mind him. He is quite mad, you know, but he means no harm. I am sorry that he disturbed you. Come, Father."

She offered her hand and Abou took it, allowing himself to be led from the hut. He was still crooning softly, though the words were unintelligible.

There was a silence after he had gone.

"Well!" James said with a nervous laugh. "What the hell was all that about?"

"Do not think on it now," Christophe said grimly. "We should get some sleep. We leave early in the morning."

They began their journey before the sun had properly risen.

Fiona felt poorly rested. It had taken her some time to fall asleep, and judging by the faces of the others on waking, she had not been the only one.

Christophe was up front, deep in conversation with Ibrehem, who, as the best scout and tracker in the village, had been placed on point. Katie was with them but, even from here, Fiona could see that she looked distant and preoccupied. She had been that way ever since they'd woken. Not speaking a word through breakfast, and she looked as if she had not closed her eyes all night.

"What do you suppose is wrong with her?" Fiona murmured to James.

James, who had also been looking in the same direction, frowned. "I suppose she's still a bit upset about what that lunatic said last night."

"He did seem to have it in for her, didn't he?"

James shrugged. "Christophe will sort her out."

"I was a bit freaked out by what he said to me," Fiona admitted.

James looked at her sharply. "What do you mean?"

"That stuff he said about a sacrifice being too great. It got me worrying."

"About what?" James said with a laugh.

"Well, what if there was something in it? A warning of some kind?"

James's expression grew serious. "He was mad, Fiona, a nutcase. You saw the way he went for Katie. I reckon he'd have throttled her if Christophe hadn't stopped him. And you saw him, one minute he's cackling like a maniac, the next he's blubbering like a baby."

"I know, but he's a seer, like Katie. He has dreams like she does. That's probably what's bothering her."

"He may have been a seer once, but not any more. You heard him, the dreams abandoned him. I really don't think you should take him seriously."

"Yeah, you're probably right."

"Of course I'm right, aren't I always?"

Fiona grinned, but she still couldn't quite shake off the faint sense of foreboding she'd felt at Abou's words. Was it a coincidence that he'd called her The Appointed? She hoped so.

They were ascending into the foothills. It was a long and arduous climb, and despite weeks of hard travel, Fiona's legs soon began to ache. They kept at it for most of the day with very little rest, eating their meals on the go. Sulaiman and his selected men loped along tirelessly, leaving Fiona and the others to trudge wearily along in their wake.

Night had well and truly fallen by the time Sulaiman called a halt. His men built a fire, and they made a meal of roasted goat, bread, cheese and wine. Once this was over, everyone rolled in their blankets but for a lone sentry on watch. Sulaiman had informed them when they stopped for the night that they would reach the shrine early the next morning.

Katie did not lie down with the others. The restlessness that had plagued her all day would not permit her to find solace in sleep. She soon got up and walked out of the encampment and into the shelter of the trees beyond. The sentry gave her a cursory glance, then returned to his vigil. She kept walking until she was beyond sight of the fire, then sank down in the grass, arms clasped tightly around her drawn-up knees.

Abou's words replayed themselves endlessly over and over in her mind. And no matter how many times she told herself that he was deranged and had no idea what he was saying, his words had too much of the ring of truth about them to be ignored. What else had she been doing all this time if not running and hiding? First hiding her mission from her companions, then trying to run from her father. But he was tracking them by means of his connection to her. Sooner or later the truth would come out, just as Abou had said. She had a sudden image of Christophe flying at her as the mad seer had done, the same feral glint in his eyes, knife held at her throat. Who would protect her then?

"Katie?"

She looked up with a start. She hadn't even heard him approach.

"You have not been yourself all day. What are you doing out here alone?"

The gentle concern in his voice tore at her. She turned to look at him, and try as she might, she could not keep the tears from sliding down her cheeks. He was beside her in an instant, reaching to pull her close, but she held herself stiff.

"I'm not a bad person, Christophe," she managed, swallowing hard to control her tears. She saw the bewilderment in his face.

"What are you talking about?"

"I have made a lot of mistakes, but I would never hurt you or Fiona or James. You do believe me, don't you?"

“Katie, what…?” Then understanding suddenly showed in his eyes. To be replaced an instant later by a dark look.

“This is because of what that madman said to you, isn’t it?”

“He is a seer, Christophe. Like me.”

“He is out of his mind.”

“But what do we really know about him? Come to that, what do you know about me?”

“You ask me that after everything that has happened between us?”

“I need to know that you trust me! I need to hear you say it!”

“I love you,” he said simply. “Is that enough?”

It wasn’t, and never would be as long as she kept the truth from him. But the thought of losing his love was more than she felt able to bear, so she supposed it would have to do.

He reached for her again, and this time she came willingly, returning his kiss with an urgency she could neither hide nor explain.

Christophe held Katie as she clung to him fiercely. He could feel her nails digging into his back through his clothing. Her mouth was firm and insistent on his, and he felt a rush of desire that took him by surprise with its force. He had meant what he said. He loved Katie, loved her with an intensity that continued to startle him. He knew that whatever happened between them this night, it would move them into a new phase altogether. A tiny part of his mind tried to warn him. It was against the law of his people for any sort of physical bonding to take place outside marriage. It risked being made outcast. But Christophe was not entirely inexperienced, and he knew that what he felt for Katie in that moment was more natural and right than any law. He knew she felt it too. He could feel it in her quickened breath on his cheek and the way her body trembled slightly beneath his hands. He eased them both gently backwards until they were lying together on a soft bed of grass and bracken.

Much later, sleeping peacefully in Christophe’s arms, Katie felt a touch in her dreams, an intrusion that was all too familiar. She had hoped she would never hear that voice in her mind or feel that presence again. He would find out soon enough that she had betrayed him, and gone over to the side of his enemies, but she had hoped it would be too late for him to do anything about it. She did not feel ready for this confrontation, but perhaps it was better to get it over with. She could worry about repercussions later. Even sleeping, she felt dread settle on her like a heavy weight.

“Katriana!” She ignored the voice, wanting desperately to return to the blissful dream of a few minutes before.

“Katriana, answer me!”

Reluctantly, Katie opened her mind. “I hear you, Father, what do you want?”

“Have a care, daughter, it is unwise to refuse my summoning.”

She took a deep, inward breath “I will not help you any more,” she said firmly. “I am through being used by you.” She felt a probe of white hot fury burrowing into her thoughts, seeking what lay hidden there. She opened herself up to it willingly, wanting to show her father the extent of her betrayal. She concentrated on an image of Christophe as she had seen him before closing her eyes. His dark head resting against her shoulder. She felt a pleasurable tightening of her stomach with the memory of what had passed between them a few short hours ago.

She felt her father's rage bearing down on her like an implacable force, crushing her will. She met it with her own fury.

"I know what you are, and I know what you have done. I tried to make excuses for you because you were my father, but not any more. You never cared about me except when you thought you could make use of me. That was all the interest I had for you. Well, now you can find yourself a new tool."

His voice was as cold as winter.

"You forget that I can track you wherever you go. My connection to you is strong. You may have gone over to my enemies, but it is them you will betray in the end."

With a scream of rage, Katie forced the voice from her mind, erecting a wall of denial against what it was telling her. To her astonishment, the voice receded. She could feel the might of his will pushing against her defences, but it was oddly distorted, rippling like water. Hardly knowing what she was doing, she pictured gates falling into place, bars, locks and bolts snapping into their fastenings. All at once, she felt the mental link snap like a broken thread, and with it went the feeling of oppression that she now realised had been weighing on her ever since her father's first contact. Somehow, she knew, the connection was severed, at least for now. Her father's main source of guidance was gone. He might still try to track them, but it would be through no doing of hers. She was free of him, providing she kept her wardings in place.

She opened her eyes. Her head ached dully, but apart from that, she felt better than she had in days. She lay there for a few minutes, savouring her new-found freedom. How she had driven her father from her mind, she didn't know. It had been mostly instinct and rage that had led her. Did her magical heritage have anything to do with it?

She pulled Christophe closer, drinking in his warmth. A lock of hair had fallen across his face. She gently lifted it away. Her last thought before sleep claimed her once more, was that she wished Abou was there, so she could tell him how wrong he was.

The next morning saw Fiona and her companions on the final leg of the journey to the shrine.

They had only been walking for a couple of hours through country that grew greener and steeper by the minute, when Sulaiman, who had been conferring quietly with Ibrehem, fell back to speak with them.

"We are nearing the shrine now. What is your plan from here?"

Fiona blinked. "No idea really. I'll just take out the key and hope inspiration comes."

The key had been growing warmer all morning. It was not painful, but Fiona could feel its heat even through her clothing. She wondered uneasily what that meant.

They topped a final rise, and Sulaiman brought them to a halt.

"There," he said pointing, "is the shrine we have guarded these near twenty years."

James stared around in bemusement. "Where? I don't see anything."

They were standing on a bare plateau. To one side of them, the wall of the mountain rose smooth and sheer. To the other, the ground dropped away in a steep precipice that ended in a stony gorge, at the bottom of which a stream rushed noisily. There were no buildings or ruined temples. No sign whatsoever of habitation. Fiona stared from James to Christophe, utterly perplexed.

"Use the key," Katie suggested.

Fiona opened her mouth to say that she had no idea how, then shrugged and pulled out the key.

It was warm in her hand, and as it emerged, she saw with amazement that it was pulsing with a soft silvery light. She could feel it throbbing against her palm, as though it were a living heartbeat. She stared at it in wonder, hearing the awed gasps of those around her.

"Wow!" James breathed softly, peering over her shoulder.

"It's never done that before," Fiona said a little shakily. "I could feel it getting warmer as we walked, but I had no idea what it meant. It must be acting to something, but what?"

"Other magic," Christophe said promptly. "This is a magical object. It stands to reason that it would respond to other magic. All we have to do now is pinpoint its source."

"Oh, is that all?" Fiona snapped irritably. "And how do you suggest we do that?"

"Search the area," he replied with infuriating calm.

Scowling, Fiona held up the key and swept her arm in a wide arc that took in the whole of the little plateau. Sulaiman and his men fell back a pace, making a clear space for her to work. Fiona didn't really know what she was supposed to be looking for, but the effect was immediate. As her arm took in the precipice, the key's light instantly dimmed, but as she pointed at the mountain, it brightened, tiny sparks raining from it like silver fireflies. They left a blazing trail on the ground.

Excited in spite of herself, Fiona followed the trail. James, Christophe and Katie at her heels. Sulaiman's men made to follow, but he waved them back.

"Watch, my friends," he said quietly. He was watching Fiona with a kind of reverence in his clear brown eyes, but she barely noticed, her whole attention focused on what the key was showing her.

The sparks seemed to be disappearing into a small grassy hollow in the lee of a large boulder. They sank into it and were soaked up like water, though the key continued to pulse with light. Fiona bent and saw a large flat stone slab, almost hidden by bracken.

"Help me clear this," she said.

James and Katie dropped to their knees with her and together they began pulling up clumps of bracken. The stone that eventually lay exposed was a slab of grey granite. Intricate symbols had been traced over it, with diagrams that Fiona couldn't even begin to fathom, but as she bent closer, the key swinging on its leather cord round her neck, the symbols blazed into life, gleaming with the same silvery light as the key.

"Sulaiman!" Fiona called to the clan chief. "What do you make of these symbols? Can you read them?"

He was beside her at once, bending to examine the curious writing.

"This is not a tongue I am familiar with," he said at last. "The script is clear and flowing, but the characters appear ancient. They have no resemblance to the lettering we use today."

"And these diagrams?"

Sulaiman shook his head.

Fiona suddenly noticed an arrow on one of the diagrams, pointing clearly to a long groove cut deep into the slab. It was impossible to tell whether it was natural or man-made.

Moved by an impulse she could never afterwards explain, Fiona fitted the key into the groove. There was a brilliant flash of light from key and symbols alike, and an audible click, and the slab swung upwards and over, landing in the bracken with a dull thud. A shallow tunnel was exposed, plunging steeply downward into darkness. Fiona knew with absolute certainty that the secret, whatever it was that she had come to find, was hidden down there.

She turned to Sulaiman.

"Thanks for all your help. I guess we're on our own from here."

He stepped forward and placed gentle hands on her shoulders.

"It has been an honour to guard such a wondrous magic. Whatever danger threatens our land, I am confident that you are the chosen one who will save us from it. I and my people are for ever at your disposal."

Fiona blushed furiously. "There's no need…" she began awkwardly, but then a thought suddenly struck her. She turned to Christophe.

"Am I right in thinking that there are those in the city who will fight when the time comes?"

He nodded at once. "If I know the Guardians, they will not allow the burning of their ships to pass unchallenged."

Fiona turned back to the clan chief.

"If you would, please take the best of your warriors and go to help them. This danger affects all of us, and Alfredo and his men won't be defeated by just the four of us. We're all in this fight whether we like it or not," she added with a trace of bitterness.

"It shall be as you ask," he replied solemnly. "We will see this tyrant crushed into the dirt where he belongs." He beckoned to his men, and with only a parting wave, they turned their backs on the four travellers and were quickly lost from sight.

"Come on," Fiona said heavily. Holding the still glowing key before her like a torch, she led the way into the tunnel.

They walked for what felt like hours. Everything outside the pool of light cast by the key was inky blackness. Every time they reached a fork, Fiona pointed the key in all directions until it indicated which path they should take, its dancing sparks clearly blazing a trail for them.

It bothered Fiona a little that the key was their only guide. The passages that honeycombed the mountain were a veritable maze, and if the key's magic were to somehow fail, they would be hopelessly lost.

They passed through many natural chambers, and Fiona would stop and search with the key. But it did not flare as it had done with the slab or the forks, and they were forced to carry on.

It was getting colder too. They soon found that they were shivering.

Then, as they rounded yet another corner, the key suddenly erupted with silver sparks once more. Following where they led, they came out in a chamber larger than any they had yet seen.

It was like a huge underground cavern. Its ceiling stretching immeasurably high, so that not even the light of the key could pick it out.

James's audible gasp echoed around the vast chamber. Huge stalactites and stalagmites decorated the walls, glowing with their own phosphorescence. The key flared again, the sparks sinking into the opposite wall.

Crossing to it, Fiona saw a huge stalactite, the ice as smooth as polished marble. Guessing what was needed this time, Fiona touched the key to its polished surface. There was another brilliant burst of light as the ice flared at the point of contact. They watched in amazement as symbols appeared, snaking their way over the stalactite as though they were being traced with an invisible brush, until what was revealed was a glittering mosaic in perfect detail. They all stared at it, hardly knowing what it was, then at last Katie said in a hushed whisper, "It's a map!"

"What?" said James.

"Are you sure?" Fiona said at the same time.

Katie could hardly contain her excitement. "Look for yourselves! I tell you, it's a map of the island. The one we have to cross to, where the sceptre is hidden."

She was right. The mosaic showed a small island, covered by a dense jungle of vines and creepers. A clear passage had been drawn through the snaking vines to what looked like bog or marsh land. Beyond that, a vast chasm stretched, and on the far side of it, a long winding path snaked its way off the map, and at its end… "The sceptre!" breathed Christophe. "We have found it!"

"Only one problem," said James. "That poem says the island is invisible, remember? '*Cross to the island you cannot see*'. How will we find it?"

There was a gloomy silence.

"We're so close," Fiona wailed. "There must be a way—"

"Quiet!" Christophe said suddenly. "I hear something."

They all fell silent, listening. A distant rumbling reached their ears. Even as they stood there, undecided, it intensified, until they could feel it vibrating through their feet.

“The ceiling!” Katie cried sharply. Looking up, they saw, in the bit of roof visible by the key’s light, thin hairline cracks appearing. They widened even as they watched. The key flared brilliantly once more, silver sparks flickering wildly off the walls.

“Run!” Christophe yelled.

# Chapter 18

## The Travellers Return

The room stank of blood and infection. Gideon wanted nothing more than to leave quickly, but he forced himself to remain still as Esther finished applying dressings to the gash in his thigh.

"I wish you would not make such a fuss," he said irritably. "It was barely a scratch."

Esther rubbed her free hand across tired eyes.

"That scratch might have caused you to bleed to death if it had been any deeper. Any higher, and that knife would have punctured an artery."

Gideon forced himself to swallow his irritation. It wasn't his sister's fault. She was as exhausted as he was. Right from the start she had offered her services to the wounded. One of the ruined shops had been transformed into a sick room. It still retained the living quarters above where the more seriously wounded were taken, and its back room was a store house for herbs and dressings, though they were in short enough supply.

Men and women had flocked to the Guardian's banner when it was put forth, more than Gideon could have hoped for. He had felt certain that people would take a lot of convincing, and had been overjoyed when people turned up in droves.

Farmers wielding pitchforks and stout axes, merchants' guards and members of street gangs, as proficient with knife, bow and quarterstaff as the Guardians themselves, blacksmiths wielding hammers. Even women with long kitchen knives who had proved remarkably adept at using them, a lifetime of pent-up rage and helplessness watching their families starve and suffer finally bursting free of restraint. They had all put on the Guardian's uniform and taken the Guardian's oath.

The Appointed was largely responsible for the people's mood. Gideon and his fellow Travellers had wasted no time in spreading the news that The Appointed had returned to lead the battle to save her people. People had grown up hearing the legend and having it come true had rekindled their determination and desire for freedom.

But it wasn't enough. Even with new recruits pouring in daily, Alfredo's men still controlled the city. The Guardians held isolated areas which had been dearly won, but they simply were not enough to challenge Alfredo's army.

One thing no one had foreseen was that the ranks of Alfredo's men would also swell. Perhaps it was fear for their families, or a desperate attempt to gain some power and security, or the belief that the Guardians would never triumph and it was safer to support the winning side. Gideon didn't know, and to him it didn't really matter. All he cared about was that the Guardians were still largely outnumbered and had limited resources.

There were daily riots in the streets, as shops and businesses were looted and the houses of notable followers of Alfredo were burnt. But Alfredo's men retaliated with a swift, ruthless efficiency that was horrifying. They raided many of the outlying farms and villages, slaughtering the women and children who had fled there to escape the fighting. When a master bow maker went on strike, his business was burned to the ground with him and his helpless workers trapped inside. Many cursed the Guardians, blaming them for the deaths of their families and cursing them for not leaving well enough alone. It was ugly. The city had become a war zone in a matter of a week.

Gideon felt tired to his very bones. Taking pot shots at their enemies was accomplishing nothing, except the loss of fighters they could ill afford to spare. They were losing. It would not be long before they were all ploughed into the mud.

"You are troubled, brother," Esther observed quietly, washing her hands in a basin at her elbow.

Gideon flexed his leg gingerly. It hurt, but it wasn't too serious.

"We are losing, Esther. Father's command has already lost a third of its number. We need to turn things around and quickly."

"Have our scouts learned anything yet?"

"They have not returned."

A groan came from one of the other occupied pallets. Esther went to him at once.

"There is nothing more to be done for you," she said over her shoulder with uncharacteristic briskness. "That pallet will be needed. Go and get some rest."

Gideon shot her a puzzled glance. She was bent over the wounded man, coaxing some water between his cracked lips. Her eyes looked oddly bright.

Gideon left quickly. He had forgotten what it must be like for her, to see all those she cared for risking their lives and being able to do little but sit and watch. Also, there had been no word of Christophe and The Appointed since their departure. Esther never mentioned Christophe's name, but he knew she feared deeply for him.

He had barely taken one breath of the welcoming fresh air outside the makeshift hospital, when running footsteps made him turn sharply. A young woman in Guardian's uniform was racing towards him.

"Gideon, I have been looking everywhere for you. The Commander needs you right away. Carlotta has returned!"

Gideon felt his heart leap. Carlotta had been missing for three days, scouting around Alfredo's house and grounds, hoping to learn something of the emperor's plans for dealing with the revolution. He had been worried for her, but she had been eager for the challenge when Antonio had assigned it.

Gideon had applauded his father's choice, even while a knot of dread tightened his chest. Carlotta was as good a scout as she was a fighter, and had proved herself on numerous occasions.

They were all directly answerable to Antonio as leader of the Guardians, and Gideon no less than anyone else. Antonio had more than proven his worth since the revolution began. He was just and wise, a brilliant tactician. His kindness and encouragement were a real source of strength and confidence to the newer fighters, and his experience had helped his command to stay together even as their numbers had dwindled. He somehow managed to instil a sense of hope and belief in all of them, that what they were doing was not only right, but necessary for the survival of themselves and their families. No man in the history of the Guardians had ever managed to forge such a united front. They were all, from the youngest recruit to the eldest veteran, utterly committed to their cause, and there had not been a single desertion, despite the numerous casualties. Gideon was proud to serve under him.

They found Carlotta huddled before a brazier with several others, Antonio among them. He spotted Gideon and waved him over.

"Ah, there you are, son, how is the leg?"

"It will heal. Esther bandaged me up." His father gave him a relieved smile.

Gideon's eyes strayed to Carlotta. One of the Guardians had just handed her a bowl of broth and a hunk of bread which she was devouring ravenously. Her clothes were torn and splattered with mud and her face was bloody. She returned Gideon's questioning gaze with a feral grin.

"Eat your fill, then give your report," Antonio said to her.

Gideon himself passed her a cup of water which she accepted, taking great, greedy gulps. At last, she scrubbed the back of one hand across her mouth and said, "Alfredo is gone."

Surprised murmuring broke out among her listeners. Antonio raised his hand and it ceased.

"Are you certain of this?"

She nodded. "It seems he has been gone for some time. He told no one where he was going or when he would return."

"He has gone after The Appointed!" Gideon said at once.

Carlotta shrugged. "Probably, but the important thing now is that his disappearance has thrown his men into confusion. They are desperately trying to crush the rebellion before he returns and they fear that every day will bring him back to the city."

There was a silence as everyone mulled over this news.

"It is a pity we cannot capitalize on their fear," one man muttered. "If only we could take the prison. That is their biggest stronghold. If we managed that, then many men would likely flee rather than brave Alfredo's displeasure. The city would be as good as ours."

He was right. The prison had been both fortress and sanctuary to Alfredo's men. It was their main source of power within the city. It was also extremely well defended. It was galling. Many of their best fighters were in those cells. With them freed, the odds would be evened up considerably.

"We do not have enough fighters to attempt that," Antonio said, echoing his son's thoughts.

“We must do something to break their spirit,” the same man countered hotly. “Otherwise they will continue to crush us like ants beneath their boots. We are losing, in case you had not noticed, and while they sit safe and sound behind their protective walls, our women and children are being slaughtered before our very eyes.”

Gideon remembered the man now. His wife and children were among those killed when a village was ransacked. It was a classic move. Kill the loved ones of your enemy, and he will be forced to back down. But far from backing down, it had only fuelled the man’s desire to hunt down and wreak revenge against his family’s killers.

“I have an idea,” Carlotta said quietly. All eyes turned to her. She stretched in the manner of a lazy, well-fed cat.

“The best way to defeat your enemy, is to take away what they fight for.”

“Are you suggesting we hunt Alfredo down?” someone asked derisively.

“Alfredo is beyond our reach,” she replied coldly. “But his symbol is not.”

Gideon stared at her blankly for a moment, then understanding dawned.

Alfredo’s house. The most important and feared building in the city apart from the prison itself. The place where laws and judgements were made. The place associated with more horror stories than anywhere else. It was to Alfredo’s house that prisoners were taken for special interrogation. When a sentence of death was to be pronounced, it was done in Alfredo’s house. It was from the balcony of that same house that Alfredo would stand to make the pronouncements that were guaranteed to heap still more misery on the heads of his people. And it was into that house that people disappeared, never to be seen again. Alfredo’s house was, in the eyes of many, the symbol of his rule, perhaps more so than the man himself. The physical form of all the fear, anger and suffering that dominated their daily lives. To destroy it would be a great coup indeed, and what better time than now, when its master was absent from home.

There was a silence as Antonio considered the proposal. Gideon waited with baited breath, thinking that if his father said no, he would do it himself. They couldn’t pass up such an opportunity.

“This will need some careful planning,” Antonio said slowly. There was another pause, then, “We will do it.”

* * *

Gideon straightened his unfamiliar cloak, repressing a shudder of distaste as he did so. Though he knew it was for a good cause, he still felt like a traitor.

Carlotta and a gang of helpers had stripped uniforms from the enemy dead. They had toured the houses where the dead were taken until their families claimed them for burial or cremation. It had been hard, Carlotta had told him matter-of-factly, to find clothing that was not too heavily stained with blood, though he knew women had been busy washing all afternoon. It was at times like this that Gideon reminded himself how ruthless Carlotta could be, and he sent up a silent prayer of thanks that she was on their side.

Yet she attracted him. There was no denying it, and days of close intimacy with her had made him aware of his feelings as nothing else could have done.

As though in answer to his thoughts, the door opened, and she entered, fully dressed for the evening's work. Gideon hastened to tuck in his shirt and reached for his belt knife, sliding it into its sheath and settling it in its accustomed place at his waist.

The Guardians had commandeered several of the city's abandoned buildings and transformed them into temporary barracks. Men and women were housed separately.

"You should not be here," he said, still a little flustered.

She smiled. Her face was flushed with the anticipation of their night's work.

"I just came to wish you luck." She approached him, looking him over critically. Reaching up one hand, she tugged his shirt collar straight, then surprised him by seizing him roughly and kissing him hard on the mouth.

He tried to pull back, startled, but her arms were tight around him and his body would brook no denial. His arms came up to hold her. Desires such as he had never felt before flooded through him. He wasn't even sure what he was doing any more. He returned her kiss, feeling the heat of her body through her clothing and the strong beat of her heart against his own. Her eyes were alive in a way that he had never seen them before. It was almost a hungry look.

She pulled away abruptly. "They will be waiting for us," she said with a throaty laugh, and then she was gone.

Gideon stood for a moment exactly where she had left him. He felt dazed, disorientated. He was not sure what had just happened, but he knew what it meant, what it had to mean. A surge of elation filled him as he hurried to join the others.

"You are late, son," his father said reprovingly.

"Sorry, Father, I was… distracted." He felt a guilty blush rise to his cheeks and hurriedly turned away.

He looked for Carlotta, spotting her almost at once. He hoped she would look his way, but she was absorbed in testing the blade of a knife with a thumbnail.

Gideon took his place among his fellow Guardians. They were scarcely recognizable in their borrowed uniforms. Many of them had the hoods of their cloaks pulled up to obscure their features. Gideon hastily followed suit. It would never do for him to be seen. He was far too well known.

There were twenty of them in all, plus half a dozen others got up to look like prisoners. Men were just finishing tying their hands behind their backs. When they were ready, they set off into the night. Each captive had a handler who tugged them along by their rope leashes while the rest flanked them.

It was relatively quiet in the city tonight. There had been a lull in the day's fighting. News of the intended attack on Alfredo's house had spread quickly. There had still been riots in the streets, but little open combat. The Guardians had remained largely hidden, creating the tempting illusion that they were perhaps losing heart.

They had taken care to choose well-known faces as their prisoners. Antonio himself was one, and it was Gideon who had charge of him. There were no women among Alfredo's followers, so Carlotta was consequently a captive as well. Her knife, along with many others was hidden in various pockets inside her clothing.

Alfredo's house was swarming with activity when they approached. The captives took care to bow their heads in submission as they came within view of watching eyes.

"You there," Gideon called loudly to the nearest sentry. "Open the gate!"

"Who goes there?" the sentry demanded, trying to make out the face beneath Gideon's hood.

"Open the gate, man," Gideon barked. "These prisoners are to be held inside to await the master's return. He is on his way back to the city. He sent word that he wants to question this lot personally."

"Speak the password," the sentry said suspiciously. Gideon spoke the password Carlotta had given them and the man gave a nod of relief.

"No one tells me anything these days," the man muttered, opening the gate and calling to his fellows.

"It's about time the master returned, that's all I can say. The city's overrun and there's too many of the vermin for us to control 'em all."

"Our luck's about to change," Gideon said, thrusting his father forward and jerking his head up so that his face was visible. "We've nabbed ourselves some of the ring leaders."

The other prisoners were also pushed forward and their faces revealed. The man's eyes took on a hungry gleam when they saw Carlotta.

"Well now," he said approaching her. "What's a wench like you doing falling in with such company?"

He called out to his colleagues, some of whom had gathered to eye the newcomers. "We could have some sport with this one, eh, lads?" There was appreciative laughter at this.

Carlotta jerked herself free of her captor's grasp. "You just try it!" she spat. The look in her eyes was so ferocious that her would-be tormentor took an involuntary step back. A chorus of jeering catcalls rose from his audience.

"Ooh, she's got spirit, that one has. What's the matter, Jared? You afraid of a little girlie?" The man flushed a dark crimson as Carlotta let out a snarl of rage that Gideon felt sure was genuine. He affected an air of boredom.

"Save your amusements for another time and step aside. These prisoners need their quarters and we need our beds."

"It's a shame you didn't nab that fellow Christophe," the sentry at the gate said sadly. "That'd be a real feather in our caps."

"That would be too much to hope," Gideon gave an expressive shrug.

Then he whirled, swinging his quarterstaff at the head of the sentry. The man dropped like a stone. Before his stunned comrades could gather their wits, the other Guardians drew their weapons. The prisoners shook off their loosely tied bonds and plunged into the fray, daggers cutting.

But the element of surprise was short lived. Alfredo's men were highly trained, and once they realised that their attackers were enemies and not their own men, they were swift to retaliate. One man let out an alarm call. A Guardian's dagger silenced him in mid cry, but the damage was done. Another broke away from the press and fled, calling for reinforcements. Several Guardians tried to give chase, but they were forced to turn and fight as more of Alfredo's men appeared, drawn by the commotion and the cries of their comrades. Men fell on both sides, but the Guardians were rapidly becoming outnumbered.

Gideon caught a brief glimpse of Carlotta, blades appearing as if by magic in her hands one after the other, cutting down those in her way as the Guardians were pressed back towards the front door of the house.

The fighting was fierce and intense, but Alfredo's men were falling, and now none were coming to replace them.

They had almost reached the open front door, when Gideon saw his father go down.

"Father!" he tried to force his way through to him, and just managed to deflect a wicked-looking cudgel aiming straight at his head. He took the blow on his quarterstaff and it sent a painful jar up his arm. He turned to meet his attacker and felt a searing pain down his other shoulder. A man had taken a savage swipe at him with his dagger and caught him turning. It had narrowly missed his chest. The slash was deep. Blood soaked the torn sleeve of his tunic and ran down his arm. He was now fighting for his life against two attackers and he was tiring. He was trying to counter the knife-man's thrusts with a damaged arm, and the man with the cudgel was a lot stronger than he was. He could do nothing but deflect his savage swings and every blow he stopped sent an agonising jolt up his arm.

Then the man with the knife stumbled on the slippery ground and Gideon was able to plunge his own blade deep into the other man's side. The man fell with an agonised cry, wrenching Gideon's knife from his hand as he did so, at the very moment that Gideon's quarterstaff deflected another vicious blow and snapped cleanly in two.

Gideon was defenceless. He had no time to draw another dagger. The man with the cudgel was already swinging for the death blow, a look of savage triumph on his face. Gideon threw himself desperately to one side, and the man hit the ground with a loud grunt, Carlotta's blade in his back.

Gideon looked up, dazed. Those of Alfredo's men who were still alive had surrendered. He had been the last one still fighting. The dead and wounded lay nearby, fighters from both sides, but Gideon was relieved to see that his father was not one of them. He was upright, blood crusting around a gash above his right eye. Alfredo's men stood in a sullen row, about a dozen in all.

Antonio rapped out quick orders.

"Two of you stay and tend the most seriously wounded and bind the prisoners. The rest of you come with me. There is work to be done."

"What do you intend to do now?" one man jeered. "Move in and make yourselves at home?"

"You will see in a moment exactly what we intend to do, and I am not sure you will like it," Antonio replied quietly. "It would have been better for you if you had died just now. Your master will not be pleased with you on his return, if you live that long."

The man spat on the ground and received a fat lip from his nearest captor. But others looked apprehensive.

"What are you going to do?" Carlotta's tormentor demanded, voice shrill with fear. "We've surrendered. You've won."

Antonio made no answer as he led his comrades towards the house.

Carlotta paused as she passed the sentry, disgust on her face. "Be thankful I have let you live long enough to see," she hissed in his ear.

Several frightened-looking servants were congregated in the hall, their wide-eyed gaze trained on the door as Antonio led his company in. Antonio addressed them.

"You are free to go on your way. In a short time this house will be no more. Return to your families."

"He will surely come after us," a woman said fearfully.

"Leave the city. Get as far away from here as you can. You have been given a chance to start your lives afresh. Take it while you may."

"What of the men?" a haggard-looking man demanded.

Gideon stepped forward. He could see that his father was feeling the effects of the blow he had taken and he was anxious not to prolong this any further.

"See for yourselves." He gestured to the gates where the remainder of Alfredo's men stood bound and helpless, their weapons in a pile at their feet. Even as the astonished servants watched, a Guardian moved from one captive to another, conducting a search for any hidden weapons.

"You see the way is safe," Gideon said. "Now go!"

Without a word, the procession filed out past him one by one and was quickly swallowed up by the night. None of them looked back.

Antonio was instantly business-like.

"You know what to look for. Hurry! We must be away from here before reinforcements arrive. We will assemble here."

Gideon lagged behind the others. "Are you alright?" he asked his father anxiously. "I tried to reach you."

"It looks worse than it is," Antonio assured him. "I am just a little dizzy, that is all. Besides," he added, eyeing the caked blood that made Gideon's sleeve stick to his arm. "Your injury is much more serious. You must let your mother or Esther look at that as soon as we get home."

Gideon hurried to catch up with Carlotta.

It did not take long to find what they needed. They took care to search the house for people hidden or imprisoned, but all the rooms were empty.

Watching Carlotta as she methodically went about her task, Gideon was amazed to see that she hardly bore a scratch from the fighting. One of the few who could boast as much. He eyed his own arm ruefully. It was nasty, but he had sustained his fair share of wounds of late, and he suspected he would acquire a good few more before this was over.

They duly assembled once more.

"It is time," Antonio said quietly.

Several Guardians produced canisters of oil used for filling lamps. They spread it liberally on rugs and furniture and anything else that would readily burn. Not a single room on the ground floor was spared and a slick coating covered the stairs to the upper floors. Emerging once more into the open, they proceeded to light torches of dry wood and twigs which were hurled through the door into the oil-soaked hall, and also into some of the upper rooms whose windows were open. They then hurried to safety.

The flames caught instantly. A few tendrils of smoke rising lazily from an upper window.

More than one of Alfredo's men had realised by now what was happening. They struggled, screaming alternate threats and invectives, though the effect was spoiled somewhat by the naked horror in their eyes. It was all their captors could do to restrain them. They were savage, hysterical, desperate to save their master's home. But their bound hands made it impossible for them to put up any real fight. They were quickly subdued and hustled off to a safe distance.

Acrid smoke was pouring through every window and the open front door. As captors and captives alike watched, a muffled boom seemed to shake the building to its foundations, and the whole was suddenly engulfed by a wall of flames.

"We must leave," Antonio said sharply. "Bring the prisoners."

As he fled with the others, Gideon remembered another night and another fire. He wondered if any of those responsible were with them tonight, or lying on the funeral pyre that would soon be Alfredo's home. He found himself hoping so. Revenge was indeed sweet.

People were already pouring out into the streets. Alfredo's house was the highest landmark in the city. He had made sure that it could be seen anywhere. The house had become a beacon for all to see, and their anxious cries filled the night. But these quickly turned to cries of wonder and elation as people realised the truth. People passed it on to their neighbours. The message was filtered like water through every street and alley. At first it was hushed murmurs.

"Alfredo's house is on fire."

"Alfredo's house is burning!" But the murmuring quickly grew to an excited babble, and finally swelled to a full-throated, jubilant roar.

It seemed to Gideon that every man, woman and child was out on the streets to witness the destruction. As he and his fellow Guardians entered the main square with their prisoners in tow, the cheer that greeted them was deafening. The vast crowd surged forward and Gideon soon found himself, along with his comrades, hoisted onto their shoulders.

But at the sight of the hated enemy, with hands bound behind their backs, trying to sneak away unseen, the mood turned ugly in an instant.

A woman began it. Spotting one man trying to squeeze his way through a press of people to escape down an alley, she let out a warning cry. Others took it up, surging forward in a rush to block off escape routes. The roar rose to a crescendo. In a moment, years of pent-up fear and rage finally burst its banks to flood the square. The hapless victims had no chance. Like a final judgement the crowd descended on them until they were swallowed in the crush.

"Gideon, move!" It was Carlotta. She had seized his arm and was tugging him along. He had stood in horrified fascination as the crowd swarmed. He was not quite able to take it in. All at once ordinary citizens become savages thirsty for blood.

"They will tear them to pieces!" he gasped.

"They will do the same to us too. The blood lust has seized them. This is the outcome of Alfredo's rule. They will not stop to distinguish friend from foe. Now run!"

Her words jolted Gideon out of his daze. Their disguise had all at once become a death warrant. When they had first arrived, many of them had been recognized for who they were, but in the fury-blinded rabble, one uniform was the same as any other, and the uniform would get them killed as surely as a knife in the back.

Gideon ran, making as fast as he could for the Guardians' barracks. Looking back once, he saw a group of young boys and girls swarming like ants over one of the many statues of Alfredo that dotted the square on magnificent columns. Even as he watched, the statue swayed, then toppled to fall in ruins to the street below, its destroyers jumping clear at the last moment.

"Gideon!" Carlotta's furious shout sounded right in his ears. He had come to a complete stop without realising it. Hastily he tore his eyes away and ran on.

They reached the comparative peace of the barracks. The rioting was distant now, all having been drawn to the main square.

A bright orange glow filled the sky. Gideon stood staring up at it, his spirits soaring. He longed to tear off this hated uniform and rush to join his fellow countrymen and women. Carlotta's practical tone broke in on his raptures.

"You should go to the infirmary. That arm needs seeing to."

He turned to her, his eyes shining. He had never felt so truly alive as he did this night.

"We did it, Carlotta, we actually did it!" Suddenly he pulled her to him and kissed her on the mouth. It was forward of him, he knew, but at that moment, he felt he could dare anything.

She returned his kiss, and his senses sang with the promise of all that was yet to come between them.

"Marry me?" he whispered in her ear. He felt her stiffen in his arms. She drew away.

"It is late. You should get some rest and a proper dressing on that arm."

"You will give me your answer tomorrow?" he called after her as she made to enter her own quarters. She didn't reply, but it hadn't really been a question. They were as good as betrothed now. It only took the formal words of the marriage ceremony to make it official. He stood a moment longer gazing at the door through which she had disappeared, then set off for the infirmary.

By morning, all that remained of Alfredo's former home, the symbol of so much fear and oppression, was a gutted, blackened ruin.

* * *

The next few days saw some of the most savagery and bloodshed that the city had ever known. The loss of their master's seat of tyranny seemed to have pushed Alfredo's supporters over the edge of a precipice from which there was no return. The city streets had become one large killing field. During the night of the fire, every personal monument to Alfredo's reign had been reduced to rubble. Many Guardians had hoped that Alfredo's followers would flee the city, but they had done the opposite. At dawn, the butchery began. Alfredo's men abandoned all restraint, killing anyone who happened to cross their path or who dared to venture out alone. It made no difference who they were.

The Guardians patrolled the streets in a vain attempt to protect the people, and more were lost each day. Alfredo's followers fought with the desperate abandon of men who had nothing to lose. They no longer even attempted to capture any Guardians they met, but simply killed them on sight. It was courting death to even step out of a front door, and the raids and pillaging of homes and businesses still continued, so that nowhere was safe. Even refugees seeking to leave the city and escape the madness were cut down as they fled.

The Guardians were fighting a losing battle. The one remaining stronghold, the prison fortress, remained as unreachable as ever. Gideon and his fellow comrades knew that if those walls could be breached and their companions set free, then the odds would swing greatly in their favour. But they lacked the numbers to even attempt such a thing, and the fortress was defended more fiercely than ever since the fire.

But these were not the only reasons for Gideon's despondency. Ever since the night of the fire, he had hardly seen anything of Carlotta.

He had woken early the following morning, and had immediately set off in search of her, intending to bring her before his father and announce their forthcoming marriage. It was still a distant event. They could not hope to marry until the revolution was over and normal work had resumed. He had no way of supporting her or the younger siblings that were under her care. When he enquired after her, however, he was told she had already left on patrol. Whenever he tried to speak with her, she was always in a hurry to be gone and she made a point of never being alone. Eventually, he was forced to the unwelcome conclusion that she was avoiding him, though he was at a complete loss as to the reason.

"Gideon! Are you well?"

Gideon started. He hadn't even heard the other man approach, and judging by his manner, this was not the first time he'd been addressed.

"Yes? What is it?"

The man was still looking at him in some concern. He was one of the younger recruits.

"Are you well?"

"I am perfectly well. What do you want?"

"Your father Antonio is asking for you. Something has come up. All the Guardians that can be spared are to come."

Gideon wasted no more time but hurried after his young guide, praying that they would meet none of Alfredo's men spoiling for a fight on the way.

His mind was in turmoil. Surely only two things would warrant calling Guardians from their duties when they could not easily be spared. Perhaps Christophe and The Appointed had returned already, though that did not seem likely. Christophe had expected to be away for some time, especially as no one knew where the sceptre was hidden, or how it was to be destroyed.

No, the more likely reason was that Alfredo had returned to the city, or was on his way. Their fortunes would take a dire turn then. Gideon didn't even like to consider it.

Gideon's guide led him to the largest of the barracks, formally a bath house used by those who could afford it. Until the uprising had begun, Gideon had never set foot in it.

The place was crowded. The floor was covered with pallets made of straw and blankets on which several people were squatting, while others perched on upturned bath tubs. Most were packed in along the walls, leaning shoulder to shoulder. It was uncomfortably hot. Gideon squeezed in as best he could.

He saw his father standing near the door. He and the other leaders were grouped together a little apart. Antonio did not move from his place, but on Gideon's entrance, he raised a hand. Silence fell instantly.

"Friends, a strange report has reached us. One of our scouts returned this morning to say that a large company of men has encamped on the outskirts of the city. It seems that they arrived overnight. They do not wear the uniform of Alfredo's men, nor do they wear Guardian's dress. Their clothing and appearance are altogether strange, as are the weapons they carry. They bear none of the traditional fighting weapons. So far they have made no threat or made any attempt to enter the city. I propose to lead a group of volunteers to their encampment to learn of their intentions if we can. We must act swiftly. Alfredo's men will discover them soon if they have not already. They will try to win them to their side or destroy them. We must reach them first. Who will go with me?"

Gideon raised his hand at once, along with several others. His father gave him a swift nod.

About thirty made up the group. Gideon was pleased to see Carlotta among them. Perhaps now he would be able to speak with her. But she did not even look his way, and before he could approach her, his father was at his side.

"This troubles me," he murmured softly. "These men are foreign to these parts. They have come far and their weapons suggest that they do not come in peace. This could be an ill day for us. If they join Alfredo's followers then the city is lost."

"Then why have they not yet attacked the city if that is their intention?" Gideon countered. "If they are Alfredo's men, what are they waiting for?"

Antonio said nothing. Gideon knew what he was thinking. It was in his heart too, a tiny spark of hope. If these men could be persuaded to fight on the Guardians' side, then there might be a chance of ending this revolution. They needed to gain control of the city before Alfredo's return.

The encampment was large, much larger than Gideon had expected. Campfires blanketed the plain and makeshift tents (little more than cloaks propped on sticks) were dotted everywhere. Donkeys and mules grazed nearby and men were unloading food supplies. Gideon stopped where he was, staring. It looked so homely, more like a settlement than an army. Only the absence of any women or children suggested that this was no normal migration. The rest of the party had also halted. Some rested hands on weapons but there seemed no need. There had been no outcry at their approach. Gideon wasn't sure that the newcomers were even aware of them.

Without warning, twenty men rose up, all clutching long spears. They seemed to appear from nowhere, rising out of the scene of domestic bliss around them. The Guardians were all caught by surprise, but they recovered at once. Nearly everyone had a weapon in their hands. Gideon unconsciously assumed a battle-ready stance. He saw Carlotta poised like a taut bow string, ready to leap at the first provocation. Only Antonio had not drawn a weapon. He stood facing their opponents, palms held out before him in the universal gesture of friendship. He stood perfectly still. Gideon hesitated for a moment, then sheathed his dagger and imitated his father. The rest followed suit, some more reluctantly than others. Carlotta was the last to do so.

"We mean you no harm," Antonio's voice was calm and clear, carrying easily around the encampment. "We wish only to know who you are and what your business is here. You must know that you are encamped on our ground."

A boy stepped forward. He was barely older than Gideon.

"My name is Ibrehem. We are men of the desert clans. Our chief wishes an audience with you. We also come in peace."

"Will your chief not speak with us himself?" Antonio asked pleasantly.

"If you can guarantee his safety, we will take you to him."

"It was you who drew weapons against us," Carlotta snapped. "And on our own ground too. You expect us just to follow you?"

Antonio silenced her with a warning look. Ibrehem and his companions had bristled noticeably.

"We will gladly meet your chief, but as a show of good faith, you will leave your weapons on the ground where they are. We will do the same."

Ibrehem held a quick consultation with his comrades.

"We accept," he said stiffly, suiting his words by laying his spear on the ground at his feet. His men did the same. At a nod from Antonio, the Guardians followed suit, though with obvious misgivings. Gideon thought they were taking a terrible risk marching unarmed into a stranger's camp. Their escort might appear weapon-less, but they had a hundred or more companions they could call on at a moment's notice. Gideon was not defenceless. He, like the rest of his friends had many weapons hidden about his person. He had merely set down what had been visible to their opponents, and his father had not commanded otherwise, even though he must be aware that this small collection was not all his Guardians carried. Still, Gideon didn't care much for their chances if it came to a fight. He wished now their party was larger, but his father had not wanted to appear threatening.

Their strange entourage led them through the makeshift tents and cooking fires in silence. Gideon looked around guardedly, half expecting the men around them to abandon their apparently innocent tasks and spring into battle. But nothing happened. They were led out of the encampment to a stretch of clear ground where a man sat cross-legged on a blanket, staring fixedly into space.

"The chief of the desert clans," Ibrehem intoned in a voice filled with reverence. The man did not look up or so much as react to their presence. The Guardians looked at one another uncertainly.

"What is he doing?" Carlotta demanded.

Ibrehem gave her a scornful look.

"He is listening to the land, hearing what it would tell him. He hears things that are closed to you and I, in the ground under our feet and the wind in the trees. He has great power and wisdom. You would do well to show him respect. He will attend to you when he has concluded his meditations."

Gideon exchanged a startled look with his father. This man could listen to the land? He had magic? Had the blood of the merpeople really spread so far afield? Gideon had a hundred questions and he waited with mounting impatience for the man's trance to end.

At last the man seemed to become aware of his visitors. His eyes suddenly snapped into focus. Instantly his followers spread out in a protective ring, bowing to their chief. Gideon found himself wondering if they had hidden weapons too.

The chief rose to face them. He was bearded, a turban covering his head. He wore a jerkin over flared baggy trousers.

"I am Sulaiman Muhammed Al-Jaffarin. Called Sulaiman by some." He smiled suddenly as though something amused him. "Will you not sit and drink with us? We mean no harm. In fact, we come to offer you aid in your cause."

As though on cue, several men appeared, carrying wooden cups of some fiery spirit whose aroma hit Gideon long before a cup was put into his hands. He joined his companions on the ground and took a cautious sip. It burned his throat and made his breath catch, but it was deliciously sweet. Sulaiman's men had also come to join them until they all formed a large circle with Sulaiman at its centre, Antonio directly facing him.

"You say you come bringing aid," said Antonio. "But how did you know we were in danger? And who sent you?"

“I have sensed the land’s peril for some time. Where we are is relatively untroubled, but I could feel a faint uneasiness. As we travelled nearer to this city, the feeling grew more acute. The land cries out the pain and suffering of its people. The very air is rife with it.

“As to who sent us, I believe the name of Christophe is not unknown to you, also those of Katie, James and Fiona.”

“The Appointed!” Gideon breathed.

Sulaiman smiled. “Indeed, that is what we also call her. Long ago, my people were given the guardianship of a shrine which warded a strange magic. We were told that one day someone would come with the power to unlock this magic and would use their power to save the people of the land from a grave danger.

“This Fiona was the one. She used a talisman to unlock the shrine and entered it to try and learn its secrets. But before she left she charged us to hurry to your defence so that you might hold out till her return. So in her name we have come to offer whatever help we can, though we do not know the exact nature of what threatens you.”

Gideon could hardly believe what he was hearing. The Appointed had sent these men? But how had she found them. There were at least two hundred men encamped on the plain. Perhaps nearer to three hundred. A small army.

“Anyone who comes in the name of The Appointed is very welcome among us,” Antonio responded. “And there is no doubt that your help is needed, but perhaps you should hear what it is that threatens us before you commit your men to our fight.”

Sulaiman inclined his head.

So Antonio explained about Alfredo’s rise to power and the tyranny they had been forced to live through. He explained the nature of the weapon Alfredo sought and Fiona’s attempts to find and destroy it. He was brief, and when he was done, Gideon found himself watching Sulaiman anxiously. If the chief refused his help, then they were doomed. Alfredo was distracted for a while, but if he were to return with the sceptre, then there would be no hope for any of them.

“Now that I have heard your tale,” Sulaiman said steadily. “I am even more determined to offer all the aid in my power. This weapon is truly a monstrous evil. This man must not be allowed to succeed. We must resist him as long as we can, and hope that our efforts will buy The Appointed the time she needs to complete her task.”

A relieved smile spread across Antonio’s face.

“Come, let us drink to our new alliance.”

As he rose to join in the toast, Gideon felt a trembling in his legs and lightness in his head that he did not think was purely a result of the drink in his cup.

* * *

It was late. The Guardians and their new allies had been busy for most of the day. It had been decided that their best chance of victory was an assault on the prison the following morning, now that there were finally enough men to attempt it. With the fortress taken, the Guardians would be in undisputed control of the city.

A party had left the city in secret to find a tree that could be cut into a suitable ram. Tomorrow would be an important day for all concerned. If the Guardians won, Alfredo would find it hard to regain his hold even with a weapon to aid him. If they lost, they would be annihilated.

Esther tried not to consider this alternative as she made her way through the city streets. She was taking a huge risk. Many of Alfredo's men were still abroad, thirsty for blood. Esther had been hearing horror stories for days about what Alfredo's followers did to any woman caught alone and the wounds she had treated had told grizzly stories of their own. Still, Esther had told no one what she was doing. They would have certainly forbidden it, and with any luck, she would be back before she was missed.

She was no stranger to the city's streets and back alleys. She had got to know them well these last few days since this whole rebellion had begun and she and her fellow healers had combed the city searching for any wounded who were unable to get help for themselves.

It was on Christophe's account that she had ventured out. She had grown used to watching her father and brother going out into the streets each day, while she busied herself with her tasks and tried to drown out the fear that she would never see them alive again. Tomorrow would be no different in that respect. But not knowing what had become of Christophe had nearly been too much for her. As more and more days went by with no news from him or The Appointed, Esther found it increasingly harder to banish images of him lying dead and abandoned to the carrion birds in some lost, remote place, or else in Alfredo's hands, undergoing some unspeakable torment. Now at last here was someone who could give her news of him and with any luck, allay some of her fears.

The encampment appeared silent. It seemed as though everyone was now sleeping, but Esther remembered her brother's story of his welcome and was not surprised therefore when a man suddenly rose up, a spear pointing directly at her chest. Esther immediately froze where she was, palms extended outwards.

"I am unarmed," she said before the sentry could speak. "I intend no threat. I only wish to speak to your chief."

The man lowered his spear, but there was a faint note of disdain in his voice as he answered. "What would a mere city girl want with our chief? He is a great man and not to be bothered by the likes of you. Return to where you belong."

Esther stood her ground, wondering if these next words would be her last. Surely these men would not kill people they were allied with. That was what she had been counting on. She took a deep breath, hoping that her voice did not sound as weak as her knees felt.

"Your chief promised to give whatever aid he could. I come asking his help. Will you refuse me because I am a woman and perhaps beneath his notice? Times are different now. Women fight in this struggle alongside men and it is I and my companions who will tend your wounded tomorrow when the fighting is done. Surely your chief can grant me a few minutes of his time?

"You are very determined," he said grudgingly. "And what you say has some merit. Very well, I will take you to him, but he may well be resting. Our journey has been long and we must recover as much strength as possible if we are to be of any use to your people tomorrow."

"I would not disturb him for the world," Esther replied earnestly. "If he is resting, I will return at once."

He nodded approvingly. "Come then."

Sulaiman was sitting alone on his blanket, very much as Gideon had first seen him. He looked so tranquil that Esther was about to withdraw, when he looked up with a smile.

"You wish to speak with me, child?"

Esther swept the deepest curtsey she could. "Only if I am not disturbing your rest, Sir."

"Of course not," he patted the blanket beside him. "Come, sit by me. I see sorrow in your eyes." To the sentry, "You may return to your post. This woman is to be given safe passage out of this camp whenever she chooses."

The man bowed and left.

Esther approached the chief diffidently and squatted on her heels beside him. He seemed to radiate a strong reassurance that instantly put her at ease. It reminded her of her grandfather. He always had that effect on her, despite his irascibility.

"What do you wish of me, my dear?" Sulaiman prompted gently.

"Nothing," Esther stammered and blushed. "That is… I wish only for news of Christophe. We have heard nothing since he left the city. Was he well when you parted from him? Where was he headed?" In her eagerness for information, she momentarily forgot who she was addressing. She blushed more furiously than ever and hung her head so that her face was hidden by her hair.

"Forgive me!" she murmured.

"This Christophe means a lot to you." It was not a question. Esther nodded, still too embarrassed to lift her eyes.

"He seems a very noble man. High in honour and devoted to his duty. When we first met he was near exhaustion. He and his companions had travelled far and were nearing the end of their strength. His wound still troubles him, more than he will admit. I fear it will never fully heal."

Esther's surprise snapped her head up. "You know about his wound?"

"I could sense it. I can sense many things. Under our care he recovered his strength. We guided them on their journey and when our task was over we saw them on their way with enough food and water for several days. Now that the desert crossing is behind them, they will recover quickly."

Relief swept through Esther. He was alive and well, or as well as could be expected.

"I thank you for telling me this. It is a great relief to me. I will leave you to rest." She made to rise, but Sulaiman's gentle hand on her shoulder prevented her.

"Child, stay a moment." He regarded her sadly. "Christophe may well return to you safely, but he has, I think, long been pledged to another. His coming may not bring you the solace you expect."

Esther felt tears fill her gaze. She knew who he meant of course. She had suspected it before they left. But hearing it confirmed in such a kind voice hit her like a punch in the stomach.

"It is enough to know that he is safe," she said with difficulty. With that, she left him and hurried from the camp. Remarkably, she reached her bed without incident or discovery. It didn't seem as though she had been missed. Despite everything, she slept better that night than she had for a long time.

* * *

The ram was huge. A massive gnarled trunk of elm lopped of all its branches. It took over a dozen men to lift it. They would have to work in relays. Behind them came men carrying ladders and ropes and behind them, the main body of fighters.

Gideon checked the quiver at his waist as he walked. He had waxed his bow and tested the string the previous evening. He supposed he should have been nervous. The future of his people would depend to a large extent on the outcome of their work today. And there was the very likely chance that he would not live to see another sunrise. But adrenalin coursed through him. He could feel it in every nerve and muscle.

He watched the faces of those nearest him. Carlotta was testing her many knives with a thumb. Gideon suspected she had done this repeatedly since waking. He knew better than to try to talk to her now. She would allow no distractions. But he wished there had been a chance to speak before this. He might have missed his only opportunity. This thought sobered him a little. He wished he'd made the time to say a better goodbye to his mother and Esther.

His thoughts turned to Lena and his grandfather Jeremiah, in hiding with the rest of the elderly and younger children. Would he ever see them again? But there was no time to dwell on this. The Guardians were already assuming position, Sulaiman's fighters in their midst.

They had already been spotted. A man appeared on the parapet overlooking the gate.

"What is this?" he sneered. "A motley rabble come to pay us a visit? Or maybe you have come to surrender your heads to the block? There are not enough spikes for all of you, but more could soon be made. Perhaps our master will insist that your women and children help us. A fitting punishment I think."

Antonio stepped forward. He was one of those with the ram.

"Enough of this," he called, his voice strong and clear. "The Appointed has already gone forth on her journey. Your master's time grows short. Release our comrades and leave the city now, and there need be no more bloodshed."

An arrow shot down, narrowly missing Antonio's right cheek and burying itself in the wall at his shoulder.

"Take that for your Appointed. What hope does she have? When our master has crushed her, he will return to grind you all into the dirt where you belong."

"Have it your way." Antonio resumed his hold on the ram, gesturing everyone to their positions. With a mighty heave, the ram swung against the gate. The timbers rang with a hollow thud that seemed to reverberate through the ground at Gideon's feet. The man on the wall ducked out of sight, screaming a warning to his companions. Almost at once a hail of arrows rained down on the men wielding the ram. Three fell at once, but three more rushed in to take their place and the Guardians retaliated with a storm of their own.

Gideon's bow sang with the others, but Alfredo's men had the advantage of height to assist their aim. Every shaft found its mark. Gideon looked around feverishly for anything that would give him some elevation. His eyes fell on an upturned cart. Darting out of the fray, he dragged it over and leaped up on it. This instantly made him more of a target, but it helped his aim by putting him on a better level with his opponents. Guardians were quick to follow his example, jumping onto carts, stone blocks, anything they could find. Now the ladders were in place, and Sulaiman's men swarmed up them. Their spears soon sending men tumbling from the walls. Alfredo's men continued to pour out from every available door and gate in never ending waves. Soon the spearmen were having a hard time keeping them back.

The screams of the wounded were appalling. Gideon seemed to be fighting in something of a daze. Duck and shoot, duck and shoot, while death was dealt out around him. He had no idea how many men he had hit, but he expected any moment to feel the fiery pain of death. He caught a brief glimpse of Carlotta, face grim, eyes blazing as she sent shaft after shaft unerringly to their targets.

Then at last, a portion of the gate's timbers gave. With a roar, the Guardians poured through the breech. Antonio was one of the first. Gideon leaped down from his perch and ran to join him. Hand to hand combat was fierce. The Guardian's first onrush had carried them deep into the courtyard and scores of the enemy were killed in that first charge, but Alfredo's men by sheer numbers drove them towards the wall and the deadly arrow storm. People fell everywhere and were trampled underfoot as the combatants surged back and forth. The ground grew slippery with blood, making footing uncertain. Many a fighter slipped on the treacherous ground and never moved again. The Guardians fought with knife and quarterstaff, but also with their own brand of fighting. Their lightning reflexes enabling them to duck beneath the swing of a club or slash of a blade and deliver punishing kicks and punches to their opponents which crippled without killing, making them helpless. Alfredo's men had no such training, but many were able to pull blades on their attackers even as they were being wrestled to the ground, and inflict terrible damage of their own.

The arrow storm had abated somewhat. Enough of Sulaiman's men had gained the walls now and the archers were forced to turn and fight hand to hand.

Gideon struggled to get out of the press and away from the wall. The Guardians' plan was two fold. Break into the keep and break the prisoners out, while its guards were kept busy. After the first initial charge, Gideon and many of the younger Guardians began fighting to break free of the press and get into the keep. But their progress was hampered as they were constantly forced to turn and fight. More than one fell before they were halfway across the courtyard. Gideon was soon covered in sweat and blood in equal measure, and he wasn't sure how much of it was his own. If he had been hurt, then the pain was swallowed up in the general aching of his muscles. He was exhausted. His reflexes were slowing down.

At last, and somewhat to his surprise, he reached the main entrance. A knot of soldiers held the gate, and Gideon realised he and his companions would have to fight their way through them. There were about twenty with him, men and women, bedraggled and bloodstained and none of them older than he was. Every one of their adversaries was twice their size and their extra weight and strength would act as a decided advantage. But there was no other choice. With a roar of fury he charged the closest man.

The fighting was intense. The din of the larger battle seemed to fade to a meaningless buzz in Gideon's ears, replaced by the cries of his companions and his own laboured breathing. He had managed to dispatch his first opponent. His sudden rush had caught the man off guard and Gideon's blade darted in and out again even as the man crumpled lifeless to the ground. But it was no use. Gideon had seen at least two of his companions fall, and there were simply not enough of them to fight a path through.

Then, as if from nowhere, about two dozen spearmen appeared. The soldiers, caught off guard by their sudden appearance, were momentarily confused. The lightning quick spears dispatched three before they could recover. Gideon saw Ibrehem, bloodied but still on his feet.

"Go!" he growled at Gideon. "We will hold them."

Gideon beckoned frantically to his remaining companions. "We have to move. We need to find the prisoners and get them out of here if we can."

Without waiting for their assent, he set off at a run down the nearest passage.

It was cold in the keep. Water dripped from the walls and torches set in brackets gave off an eerie glow. The air smelled of damp and despair.

Soon he heard the muffled sound of voices, punctuated by weeping. He followed the sound to a fork in the passage where a guard room stood. He cast a quick look inside. The guard was slumped across a table with an empty jug at his elbow. Knives and cudgels lined the walls and a bunch of keys hung on a nail just inside the door. Gideon made a soft noise of contempt as he stole the keys and followed the sound of weeping down the left-hand passage.

The cell was at the far end. Gideon slipped a key into the lock (luckily the first one he tried) and swung the door open.

Several frightened faces blinked in the sudden light. Their fear changed to surprise as they recognized him.

"Gideon!" a woman breathed. "Is it really you?"

Gideon's astonishment was as great as theirs, mingled with an overwhelming sense of relief. It was Bess and her family, crammed into this tiny room. They all looked gaunt and hollow-eyed, and there were cuts and bruises on the faces of Ephrom and his three sons. Bess had an arm round her weeping daughter who had buried her face in her mother's shoulder when the door opened.

"We have no time!" Gideon spoke rapidly. "You must leave now. Are you fit to walk?"

Ephrom nodded.

"Then come!" They staggered out after him, Bess supporting a still tearful Elsa.

By the time they reached the guard room, there were about two dozen prisoners following Gideon. He spoke quickly.

"There is a battle going on outside. Any able-bodied men, who wish to fight, grab whatever weapons you can. The rest of you make for the back streets and you should be safe."

They complied silently, but just as they were creeping away, a drunken voice yelled, "Oy! Whass 'appnin?"

The guard rushed towards them, a vicious club in one hand, a long dagger in the other. Even drunk, he was terrifying, lumbering menacingly at them.

"Run!" Gideon yelled.

"We cannot leave you to face him alone!" one man protested, raising a borrowed stick.

"Never mind that now, get the women and children to safety – move!" They obeyed, and Gideon whirled to meet his opponent's headlong rush.

He was a big man, much stronger than Gideon. Had he been sober, Gideon would have been badly over matched. As it was, he knew it would be his speed and agility that would save him, if anything could. He had not Christophe's skill or Carlotta's luck. He had only his fury to bolster his failing strength. He dodged the first swing, spinning on one foot to kick the dagger from the man's hand. The blade spun away, and the man lunged for it, but he was off balance and Gideon was on him instantly, wrestling him to the ground. He felt a terrific pain in the side of his head as the man's flailing cudgel collided with his skull. Lights exploded behind his eyes as he fought not to pass out. They hit the ground together with a crash, but Gideon was on top. He fought to pin the man as he struggled to reach his knife. He felt a hot, searing pain across his ribs. Either the man had drawn another dagger or he had rolled on it by accident. At last he worked his own blade free and, with the last of his strength, drove it into the man's ribs. Then the world swam before his eyes and he sank down into darkness.

* * *

He woke to the feel of a cool cloth on his forehead. Opening his eyes, he saw Esther bending over him. When she saw that he was awake, she put aside the cloth and lifted a glass to his lips. He tried to sit up, but pain exploded through his head and he fell back with a weak groan. Esther supported him with one arm and helped him take a few swallows. The hot liquid burned his throat and spread warmth through his aching muscles. He lay back.

"Is it over?"

"The Guardians have won," she said, sitting on the floor beside him. "Alfredo's men were routed and the keep taken. Many have fled the city. Now that all the prisoners have been released, the building will be demolished."

Relief washed through Gideon, but already he could feel the desire to sleep gradually stealing over him. He struggled to remain awake. He had so many questions.

"How did I get here?"

"You were discovered when the keep was searched for any remaining prisoners. You were brought in about two hours ago. You received a nasty knock to the head, but there is no damage to the skull. You were lucky. You also took a slash across the ribs but it is shallow and not serious."

"And my father and Carlotta? How are they?"

Esther's face grew grave. "Our father sustained only minor injuries, but Carlotta... she lives, but she was hurt badly. She is being cared for in another part of the city."

Gideon tried to sit up, to scramble out of bed, but the drug Esther had given him was taking effect and she restrained him easily.

"Rest, Gideon, you will be able to see her tomorrow."

Gideon wanted to protest, but his eyes closed of their own accord.

He woke the following morning after a good night's rest, feeling much better. Someone, probably Esther, had laid out clean clothes for him, together with a basin of water. He washed gratefully, cleansing himself of the blood and sweat of the day before. He found numerous cuts and bruises all over his body, but he was careful not to disturb the dressings on his forehead and across his ribs. He dressed as quickly as he could and went in search of Carlotta.

He found her in one of the other infirmaries. One of the women was just applying fresh dressings. Carlotta was a mess. Her face was a mass of cuts and bruises. One arm was in a splint. Her leg was covered in bandages from thigh to knee. Bandages likewise strapped her chest, one shoulder and swathed her forehead. Her eyes were full of pain, but they were alert, and they regarded Gideon warily. The woman finished her task and moved away to the next patient. The pallets were set a good way apart to give the invalids and their visitors some privacy.

Gideon squatted down beside Carlotta. "What happened to you?"

"An arrow in the leg, another in the shoulder. A cudgel broke my arm and caught me across the forehead. Cracked ribs." She listed her hurts matter-of-factly but he could hear the pain in her voice.

"I was worried for you."

She said nothing. Her face was utterly expressionless. Suddenly, before he could stop himself, Gideon burst out, "Carlotta, why have you stayed away from me? You have not looked or spoken to me since the night of the fire. What is wrong?"

She sighed and winced as the movement hurt her ribs. "We want different things, you and I. You want a home and a wife. I knew as much that night when you asked me to marry you."

Incomprehension showed on Gideon's face. "But… but we are betrothed, or as good as. I thought that was what you wanted." He was mystified. She had kissed him, the first joining of a union between a man and a woman. She knew the significance as much as he did. It wanted only the official words to make them man and wife. Why had she entered into this if it was not what she wanted?

"I am a fighter, Gideon. It is what I am. You know as well as I do that no married woman may fight. I will not give up my life for the sake of a husband."

"But what about your brothers and sisters? They need support and protection. We could give them that."

"You mean you could. You would fight the enemies from the door and put food on the table while I made us a comfortable home. I will look after my family as best I can, but I will give up my dreams for no one. I thought you understood that, but that night, I found out I was wrong."

He stared at her, lost for words. He should say something, anything, but the words would not come. He couldn't get anything around the lump in his throat.

Carlotta watched him. It struck him that she looked sad.

"I am sorry," she said more gently. "I never intended to cause you pain."

Gideon nodded. Getting to his feet, he strode as quickly as he could from the infirmary. The city was theirs. The battle was won. But for Gideon, the victory suddenly seemed very hollow indeed.

# Chapter 19

## Jessemine's Story

Esther washed her hands yet again and hurried outside. The fresh air was welcome on her hot face, the stench of blood replaced by the faint smell of the sea. She longed to keep walking until she was far away from the chaos and upheaval of her home. Three days had passed since the Guardians had taken the city and, for Esther, life had not improved greatly. Food and supplies were still as scarce as ever. The streets were no safer to walk alone. Alfredo's men might have been routed, but that did not stop them wandering around the city at night, killing whenever they could. From the moment she woke until the moment she went exhausted to her bed, was toil. The wounds of those involved in the taking of the city were terrible and they lost as many as they saved. She always felt dirty, no matter how many times she washed. She always seemed to see blood on her hands. The cries and groans of the wounded haunted her dreams. More often than not it was Christophe calling for her, wounded and helpless and far beyond her reach. She often woke sobbing from her dreams and then sleep was a long time returning.

Esther felt disillusioned about their entire situation. As far as she could see, taking the city did not guarantee her people freedom. Alfredo would just march back whenever it suited him and reclaim it once more. He was a warlock of incredible power and there was no one to stand against him. His men would come flocking back to him and uncounted numbers of innocent people would pay for their brief taste of freedom with their lives. The Travellers would flee once more and a life of wandering would resume. Yet the Guardians were acting as though they had won a great victory. People were singing in the streets as though all their troubles were at an end. The fools! Didn't anyone realise that their one, their only hope lay in The Appointed, wherever she might be.

It made Esther want to weep. She was tired of travelling, of never being able to settle anywhere, of constantly living in fear for the safety of herself and those she loved. She hated the city with its noise and its violence. She wished more than anything that she could just get away from it all. Settle in a remote little fishing village somewhere with a good husband and a few animals and a large family to raise. It was all she had ever wanted. She was not a fighter or adventurer like her brother was and her sister hoped to become. And there was her final source of grief. The one man who might have made her dreams a reality was lost to her. She had known it, she supposed, from almost the first moment Katie and Christophe laid eyes on each other. No one watching them closely could fail to miss the obvious attraction between them. Yet she had foolishly allowed herself to hope, to believe that one day Christophe would see her as more than the companion he had grown up with for the better part of his childhood. She had been like a sister to him and that was all she would ever be. Sulaiman's words had confirmed as much.

She tried to tell herself that it was for the best; that Christophe would never have been happy leading the kind of life she craved. Christophe was cut from the same cloth as Gideon and Lena and evidently Katie as well. But her heart refused to listen to her head.

A hand on her shoulder startled her. She looked up to find her mother beside her. They had always been close, but their work with the wounded had only strengthened that bond.

Esther was most like her mother, both in looks and in personality. Her mother had not wanted the Traveller's life any more than she did. But she had made the best of it for the man she loved. Esther liked to think that she would have done the same for Christophe if he had asked her. It was, after all, the only life she had known.

"You are unhappy, dear one," her mother said gently.

Esther made no reply. There was no need. Her mother knew everything that was in her heart. Esther had confided in her about the visit she had paid to Sulaiman's camp. She rested her head wearily against her mother's shoulder, needing to feel her closeness. Her mother put her arms around her and stroked her hair as she used to do when Esther was very small. It was all Esther could do to hold back her tears.

"When do you think grandfather and Lena and the others will return?"

"Who knows? A good while longer if they have any sense, but the women will not want to be away from their men-folk much longer."

There was a silence, then, "You miss him don't you?" There was no need to ask who *he* was. Esther nodded into her mother's shoulder.

"Oh, my dear child, I do hate to see you so unhappy."

"I will get over it, Mama," said Esther, more bravely than she felt. "He would never have been right for me. We are too different. Lena is a better match for him and she is just a child."

Her mother sighed regretfully.

"That is true, yet it would have done my heart good to see the two of you wed. It has been my fondest wish ever since you both passed into adulthood."

"And mine," Esther breathed almost inaudibly.

Josephine lifted her daughter's chin and peered with concern into Esther's wan face. "You are worn out, my girl," she said briskly. "You have been overtaxing yourself lately. You will take the rest of the day off. I do not want to set eyes on you before supper time."

Esther tried to protest. "But, Mama, there is so much to do! The wounded—"

"Can be tended by others," was the firm retort. "If you continue like this you will make yourself ill and then you will be of use to nobody. Be off with you!"

Esther gave her a grateful squeeze and set off down the street.

"Do not stray too far," Josephine called after her. "The streets are still not safe. Make sure you stay where the Guardians are patrolling."

Esther waved in response.

She wandered aimlessly, paying little attention to where she was going. The sights around her just washed over her without leaving much impression. She had seen them too many times and was sick of it all. If she looked up she would see the burnt out ruin of Alfredo's former home. She might also see the giant mound of rubble that was now all that remained of the prison keep, and she could stay and watch people fighting over bricks and blocks of stone which they carried away to begin the rebuilding of their houses. She would not have to look far to find any violence. A man perhaps, lying in a gutter while Alfredo's followers kicked and beat him and no one came to his aid because there were no Guardians to hand. Despite their increase in numbers, they were still never able to be everywhere at once and often as not the victims were left where they were for the healers to find if they were lucky. She blotted it all out and kept walking.

Eventually she settled on a broken wall, hands clasped on her drawn up knees. She could see the sea if she strained her eyes. It looked grey and uninviting, rather like her mood, she thought wryly.

For the second time that day, a hand on her shoulder made Esther start violently. She looked up and saw… her mother? But no, it couldn't be. Her mother was at the infirmaries. She had parted from her a few minutes earlier. Yet this woman bore such a striking resemblance to her mother that they could easily have been related, even down to the lines of strain about the eyes. Only their clothes set them apart. The woman wore a plain, shapeless dress that looked as though it had been patched in many places and a threadbare scarf bound up her long hair which was rapidly turning grey.

"My apologies," said the woman. "I did not wish to startle you, but I was wondering if you could help me? There is someone I urgently need to find."

"I will try," said Esther doubtfully. "But this is a large city and many have fled owing to the recent conflicts. Who might you be looking for?"

"I think you will know their names," the woman said a little more confidently. "You wear Traveller's garb, and those I seek are Travellers."

"Very well."

"The people I seek are a husband and wife by the names of Josephine and Antonio."

Esther's mouth fell open. Despite the resemblance, hearing her parents' names uttered shocked her badly. It was with an effort that she regained her composure. Endeavouring to sound merely politely interested, she said, "What do you want with them?"

"Come now," the woman countered. "Did you think I missed your reaction? These names mean something to you, or at the very least you have heard them before. It is imperative that I speak with them!"

There was no point hiding it. Esther took a deep breath. "You are right. I know their names well, but I will tell you nothing unless you first tell me what your business is with them." It was not in Esther's nature to be suspicious, but times like these demanded caution, and the woman's appearance had unsettled her.

The woman struggled to keep the impatience from her voice. "Your caution is admirable, but you really have nothing to fear from me. Josephine is my twin sister, though it is nearly twenty years since we last saw one another."

This was too much for Esther. Twin sister? She had an aunt? Why had her mother never mentioned it? She wanted to doubt the woman's words, but the striking similarity spoke for itself. She slid off the wall.

"Come with me."

Esther hurried back the way she had come, the woman following close on her heels. Esther saw that she glanced continuously up and down the street, as though she expected pursuit. Esther spared no thought for that. She was bent only on reaching a safe place where they could talk in relative privacy. Her head buzzed with questions.

The sleeping quarters were empty at this time of the day. Esther headed for them. It was the only place she could think of where they would not be disturbed.

She dropped onto her straw pallet and motioned the woman to sit across from her. She opened her mouth, but felt suddenly tongue-tied. An aunt? It wasn't possible. Where on earth had she been all these years? Esther was not used to questioning her elders, but she had to know.

Hesitantly she said, "You are right, I do know Josephine and Antonio well. I am their daughter."

Now it was the woman's turn to look surprised.

"Their daughter?"

"Their eldest daughter," Esther amended. "I have a younger sister and a twin brother."

The woman peered at her closely.

"I see the resemblance," she said, smiling for the first time. "I am delighted to meet you…" she hesitated.

"Esther."

"Ah, a pretty name." This time her smile was warmer. "I am Jessemine. This is indeed a glad day!"

Aunt Jessemine. Esther sounded the words in her head. She liked them.

It struck her then how tired her aunt looked. There was a profound sadness about her too. Her manner was controlled, but there was a depth of unhappiness in her eyes that touched Esther.

Casting aside her reservations, she impulsively reached out her hand.

"Will you not tell me what troubles you, Aunt? My mother is busy still tending our wounded and may not be free for a while yet. I would like to help you if I can."

Jessemine took the outstretched hand. "I thank you for your concern. I have kept my council these twenty years. It would do my heart good to speak of it to someone."

"Why have we never heard your name? Mama never spoke of you to any of us."

Jessemine smiled humourlessly. “She probably thought me dead. I wished it myself more than once. Tell me, does my father Jeremiah still live?”

“Yes, though he is no longer in the city. He fled with the elderly and the children when the fighting started. I dare say he will return soon.”

Jessemine’s relief was plain.

“I feared I would never see him again or my sister, though I never stopped thinking of either of them.”

She seemed to deliberate a moment, then taking a deep breath, she began her story.

“I was born and raised in the city. My mother died giving birth to my sister and I. Our father cared for us alone. He was a seer and well respected. As we grew up, he watched us for signs that we had inherited his gift but was not overly concerned when neither of us appeared to have done so. He said that these things were often known to skip generations, and it was far easier being ordinary.

“Those days of my childhood were the happiest of my life. Your mother Josephine and I were inseparable and for most of our growing up years nothing happened to trouble us.

“It was when we were nearing adulthood that Alfredo began his rise to power. He quickly began seeking out all those who had signs of magic. Those who agreed to serve him were sent away somewhere secret to be trained. Those who refused were killed. My father wanted nothing to do with his sorcery, and so was forced to go into hiding. Your mother and I went with him. We sought sanctuary with a group of outlaws who would later become the Travellers. They resisted Alfredo’s rule actively and were persecuted mercilessly. Eventually they were forced to adopt a wandering life in order to survive.

“My sister and father settled among them. Your mother met and fell in love with your father and they were wed a few months after our passage into adulthood. That was when our paths first began to separate. Her place was at her husband’s side, leading the life his people favoured. But I wanted different things for myself. I had been training to become a healer, and it was my wish to remain in the city where I could do some good. I reasoned that I would be in no great danger. I am not sure Alfredo ever learned of my father’s abilities and I had no magic of my own. I was no threat so I felt sure I would be relatively safe.

“I had only been in service a few weeks when word reached me of an outbreak of fever that had ravaged a street community hiding in one of the outlying suburbs. I journeyed there to give what help I could.

“During the night we were attacked. Slave traders slaughtered all those too sick to be of any use and every able-bodied person was taken to market to be sold. I was unable to get word of my plight to my father or sister, and I have not seen them since that day.

“We were duly sold, and it was my ill fortune that I was bought by one of Alfredo’s buyers and sent to be a personal slave in his house.”

Jessemine rolled back the sleeve of her dress to reveal a brand etched into the skin of her forearm. Esther shuddered. She knew it well. A hand upraised as though to hurl down destruction on all who sought to oppose it. It was Alfredo's personal emblem.

Jessemine went on. "For nearly four years I and my fellow slaves cooked Alfredo's meals and kept his house clean. We waited on him and laid out his clothes for him. We helped him to dress every morning and prepare for bed each night.

"I tried to escape more than once, but each time I failed. The brand, you see was more than just a badge showing our station. It was a magical token which Alfredo applied personally. By that means he was able to know where we were at all times no matter where that was. It was a simple matter for him to send his men to hunt me down. The consequences for escape were severe. Punishment greeted any defiance or disobedience but escape was dealt with particularly harshly, and more so with every new attempt. Most slaves never tried it more than once and some did not long survive their punishment."

Jessemine fell silent. A shadow of remembered pain momentarily crossed her face. Esther, horrified, deeply moved, could only wait for her aunt to go on.

At length Jessemine continued. "I believe I intrigued Alfredo. I had a spirit that would not be easily quelled. I think he saw it as a challenge.

"One night I received a message summoning me to his bed chamber. He sent these from time to time to his female slaves, though thankfully they were rare and I had never been called.

"I had no choice but to obey, though I was determined to resist him by whatever means possible. I was at that time untouched by any man and I had no intention of surrendering myself to him.

"But when I entered his room, a wonderful fragrance greeted me. All the things I most loved. The smell of the sea and my father's pipe. There was a wonderful calm presence in the room. It felt peaceful, welcoming, safe. Alfredo was reclining on a couch. He called me to him. His voice was soft and compelling, his expression warm and inviting. I wanted nothing more than to answer his call."

Jessemine's voice grew hard and bitter, her mouth twisting into a self-mocking smile. "It was a spell of course. Alfredo knew I would never willingly give myself to him, so he used magic to seduce me. I was his the moment I opened his door.

"He had two reasons. One, as I have said was that he saw me as a challenge to be bested. The other was that he had no child to carry on his name. I think that troubled him—"

"But Alfredo never had a child!" Esther interrupted, aghast.

Jessemine merely smiled sadly. "From that moment on I lived my life in something of a trance. I was constantly by Alfredo's side. He filled my every waking thought and wandered through my dreams at night.

"Soon enough he got his wish. I became pregnant with his child. Then Alfredo in his twisted cruelty, removed the spell he had laid upon me. He had achieved his desires. There was no further need to play that game."

Esther listened, appalled. She could not believe the matter-of-fact way in which her aunt spoke of what had been done to her. The very thought made her feel ill. Surely anything would be better than being the mother of Alfredo's bastard child. Even death would be preferable to that. But Jessemine was still speaking, and Esther forced herself to give her full attention to her words, while trying to fight the knot of unease forming in her stomach.

"I am sure I do not need to describe my feelings when my eyes were opened once more and the full horror of my situation was revealed. I tried to escape, to end my life, to do anything rather than allow this to happen. But Alfredo thwarted me at every turn. He kept me under guard all day and all night. He personally saw to the preparation of my meals and watched over me as I ate. He allowed me no visitors. He was my only companion. My only consolation was that he made no effort to touch me or violate me any further. My torment was complete enough.

"After a while, my thinking began to alter somewhat. Despite everything, I came to regret my earlier attempts to do away with myself and my child. I expected that Alfredo would have me killed the moment the child was born, as I would have then served my purpose. But I had been taught that all life was precious and should be preserved at all costs. As a healer, I had dedicated myself to that very task. Taking a life went against everything I believed in, particularly that of an innocent child. I formed a new plan. I decided to have one last attempt at escaping with my child as soon as it was born, and try to raise it myself, or else try to find a family who would agree to foster it. I was determined that Alfredo should not have the chance to poison his child's mind.

"So I altered my behaviour. I became docile and compliant. I ate everything that was put in front of me to keep up my strength. Gradually Alfredo relaxed his vigilance. He stopped sitting with me while I ate and reduced the number of guards at my door. He allowed women to attend to me and even to sit with me for short periods. As my time drew nearer, the guards disappeared entirely, Alfredo probably reasoning that a woman in my condition would not be able to run far.

"Several of my fellow slaves were in attendance for the birth. I worried, fearing that Alfredo would strike as soon as the baby was born. I half-expected a man to be placed at my bedside with a dagger. But my fears were needless.

"My daughter arrived safe and strong, and no one came to disturb us. My women left us to rest, and though I knew it was taking a risk, I locked my door on the inside, so I would have some prior warning of anyone attempting to enter. I slept for a time, utterly exhausted. When I awoke it was night time. My daughter was sleeping in a cradle at my bedside. I still felt very weak, but I had to leave now. I wrapped my daughter in my cloak and left my room. There were no guards outside my door, or anywhere in sight. I allowed myself to hope."

Jessemine's voice faltered. A single tear made its way silently down one pale cheek. Angrily she wiped it away. Esther reached out to her, but her aunt leaned away, and resumed her story, her voice filled with bitterness and sorrow.

“I was a fool. I thought I could trick Alfredo, but he was one step ahead of me all along. He let me think I was winning, then proceeded to crush every hope I had.

“I sneaked out of a side door, hoping to attract less attention, just another servant carrying a bundle. My headscarf hid most of my face. But Alfredo was waiting for me, with Miguel, a trusted spy who I had often met when he visited his master’s house to give his reports. Miguel snatched my daughter from me before I could react. I was weak and sore from the birth, I could do nothing. I screamed and that awoke the baby who began crying and crying as though she would never stop. Her father took her from Miguel and unwrapped the cloak to look at her. ‘Did you really think you could trick me?’ he said derisively. ‘Did you really think I would allow my only child to be taken from my grasp?’

“Something like an invisible whip lashed me across my back. My skin seared as though someone had placed a red-hot iron to it. I fell to my knees. It struck again and again. It went on and on until I gave up trying to fight it and lost consciousness.”

She unlaced the back of her dress and Esther saw several long striped scars spread in a complex pattern across her aunt’s back. Esther let out a cry of horror. Jessemine re-tied her dress.

“That should have been the end of me then. I felt certain it was, but once again I had underestimated Alfredo. He never intended to kill me. Instead he arranged that I and his daughter should be given into Miguel’s protection. He wished to keep the identity of his daughter safe, partly so that no one would learn of her existence and try to seek her out to destroy her, and also in case she displayed any signs of magic. He wanted her kept hidden and protected until she was old enough to be given over to him for training as a secret weapon in his rule.

“Miguel and I were forbidden to reveal the identity of her mother. She was to be told that she had been entrusted to the guardianship of Miguel by her father for her own safety. Of course she knew who her father was, but though I raised her, I was only a nurse to her, though the bond of love between us was strong despite that.

“That was perhaps Alfredo’s only mistake. He should never have allowed me to raise her. I could not reveal my true identity to her on pain of death, but I could still be her mother in everything but name. I kept Alfredo’s secret. I would not die and leave my child to the tender care of her father and Miguel.

“From the first, Miguel mistreated her. Alfredo’s personal brand prevented him from doing anything serious to me, beyond striking me sometimes, but my daughter carried no such mark, and Miguel took every opportunity to torment and punish her. He claimed he was fulfilling his duty as guardian.

“My daughter grew up healthy and strong. She was strong-willed and intelligent, though rather quiet and solitary. In one respect my plan had worked. There was no evil or nastiness in her nature, and she hated Miguel with a passion.

"She showed signs of possessing magical abilities early. I was dismayed, but Miguel lost no time in informing Alfredo. He watched me continuously, making sure I did not try to poison my daughter's mind against her father. Because she was clever and quick to learn, she soon mastered her gifts and her control over them. I lived in constant dread of the day when her father would claim her.

"Mostly he was just an occasional visitor in her life. Consequently he became something of a romantic figure for her, and she desperately wanted his approval, to be worthy of his notice.

"Then, a few weeks ago, he came to see her. She had just passed her sixteenth birthday. Her father had a task for her. A chance to try her abilities and test her loyalty to him.

"There was a girl who, according to prophecy, would be Alfredo's downfall. Alfredo charged my daughter to befriend this girl and learn, if she could, how this was to occur. She obeyed willingly. When The Appointed was unexpectedly rescued, my daughter left with her. I am not even sure that she didn't plan the rescue herself. When Miguel was blamed for the escape of The Appointed and arrested, his household were handed over to the slavers. But we were set free by my daughter and a group of friends, including The Appointed. I tried to speak to my daughter, to find out what she intended to do. Now that she was free there was no longer any reason for her to continue carrying out her father's wishes. I would have confessed everything to her then and taken the risks. I could no longer let her continue in ignorance. But she would not stay to listen to me. She disappeared and I have not seen her since.

"I fear the worst. I know that The Appointed has since left the city and I am certain that my daughter has accompanied her. She is nowhere in the city. I fear that she is still working for her father.

"She has the ability to see visions. I fear that he will use her to lead him to The Appointed. This is why I must find my sister. I must know in what direction they went. I have to find my daughter before it is too late. She does not know what she is doing."

Jessemine's urgent voice faded to a distant buzz in Esther's ears. She felt sick. Everything seemed to lurch and swim before her eyes. Horror washed through her in cold, nauseating waves. The girl that had come to them so strangely. The girl who had helped to rescue The Appointed and then volunteered herself as a guide. That girl was Alfredo's daughter. And no one knew. They were walking unknowing into a deadly trap.

She seemed to see again that stranger with her midnight hair blowing in a sea breeze, telling her story. *I am a stranger in Miguel's household. I will offer what help I can.* She had to make certain. Striving to keep her voice steady she said, "I don't think you mentioned your daughter's name."

"Her full name was Katriana, but only her father ever called her that. To the rest of us, she was simply Katie."

Esther bowed her head. It was her. Christophe was in love with Alfredo's daughter. Esther felt cold to her bones. What would happen when he learned the truth? Her heart ached for him and tears pricked her eyes. He probably would not live long enough to find out anything. Alfredo would surely kill him on sight, and The Appointed along with him.

Suddenly galvanised, Esther leaped to her feet.

"Come, I will take you to Mama." She set off at a run, forcing Jessemine to hurry to keep up with her.

"My dear child, whatever is the matter?"

Esther did not spare the breath to answer. She tore along the street and burst through the nearest infirmary door.

"Mama, Mama, where are you?" Her mother came hurrying out of an inner room.

"Esther, what…" her mouth fell open as she saw Jessemine. Her face drained of colour. For a moment she was quite speechless. Finally she whispered, "Jess? Is that really you?"

"Hello, Josie."

Esther barely saw the two women come together. She was already out of the door and running once more. There was only one thought in her head now.

She flung open the door of the tavern so violently that it bounced off the wall. Looking around wildly, she saw Gideon at a table with several other Guardians, taking a brief rest from duty. She made for him at once. He stared at her in amazement and alarm.

"Esther! Has something happened?"

She skidded to a halt, catching at the edge of the table to steady herself. Her knees threatened to collapse under her at any moment. One of the other Guardians solicitously pushed a chair out for her, but she ignored it.

"It's a trap!" she gasped breathlessly. "They are walking into a trap!"

Gideon looked bewildered. "What? Who is walking into a trap? Esther, what are you—"

"The Appointed and Christophe and James, all of them. We have to warn them!" Everyone was staring at her now.

"Esther," Gideon said clearly. "You are not making any sense. What is it you are trying to tell us?"

Tears filled Esther's eyes and this time she could not hold them back. She kept seeing Christophe and The Appointed lying dead from that girl's treachery. Hatred such as she had never felt before flooded her, bringing a feverish flush to her pale cheeks.

"The girl who travels with The Appointed is Alfredo's daughter. She was sent by her father to guide them, and also to lead her father to the sceptre."

There was a ringing silence. Many faces showed shock and anger, others, fear.

Gideon recovered first. "Do not talk nonsense, Esther," he said sharply. "Alfredo has no children."

Her eyes flashed. "You did not know we had an aunt either, but she is with Mama now. I can take you to her if you wish."

Gideon stared at her, completely nonplussed. Finally he said, "You had better tell us everything."

So she did, a condensed version at least. By the time she was done, there was fear and anxiety in every face.

"We have to warn them!" she repeated. "Christophe and The Appointed are walking into a trap and they have no idea of it. Alfredo will take the sceptre and that will be the end for all of us."

"But how can we warn them?" a man at the counter asked shakily. "Nobody knows where they have gone. We would never find them in time."

"We know what direction they took," Esther insisted. "We should be able to find their trail." She thought rapidly. Fiona had told her the cryptic message she had been given as a guide.

"They need to reach the mountains and to do that they would have to cross the desert. After that they were to cross to an island, presumably on the far side of the mountain pass, perhaps over a river. I am sure Sulaiman and his men could guide us. After all, they know the country better than we do."

Gideon got to his feet. "Come, we must find our parents."

As they walked, Esther said worriedly, "What if we are not in time. They have a substantial lead."

Gideon looked at her sharply.

"We? You surely do not think to accompany us? You have no fighting experience. You would only slow us down."

She stopped dead and swung round to face him. There was a hardness and determination in her eyes that Gideon had never seen there before.

"If you think I will just sit at home while the man I love is betrayed to his death, then you do not know me. I will find him by any means possible or alone if need be. I need none of you."

Gideon looked at her for a moment, then drew her close. He could feel her trembling as he held her. Tears coursed silently down her cheeks. He wiped them away with a gentle finger.

"I am sorry. I know how much you care for him."

She lifted her tear-stained face from his shoulder.

"Oh, Gideon, what if Alfredo reaches him first. He will kill him. I could not bear that."

He stroked her hair. "Christophe and his party travelled on foot. It is possible that on horseback we might lessen their lead, though Travellers are not great riders. That is our only hope."

She straightened, stepping out of his embrace. Her tears had stopped, though he could still see them clinging to her eyelashes. But her jaw was set.

"We have to try, for The Appointed!"

# Chapter 20

## Those Within

"Run!" Christophe yelled again.

Fiona stumbled backwards, staring dumbfounded at the cavern ceiling. The rumbling was growing louder every second, punctuated by distant thuds and crashes. Before Fiona's horrified gaze, a fine grey dust began to rain down.

James seized her arm, tugging her backwards.

"Move!" he yelled frantically.

"We'll never get out!" she yelled back. "How can we find our way?"

"We have to try," Christophe's voice was strained. He was poised for flight, but he would not leave her. Katie stood beside him, one arm instinctively lifted to protect her face.

"Are you mad?" Fiona snapped. "We'll be buried alive! There has to be another way." Almost without thinking she lifted out the key. It had been their guide after all. Instantly, bright sparks leapt from the key to dance along the wall. Their direction was purposeful and unmistakable.

"This way!" Fiona yelled and ran after the twinkling lights, the others on her heels. The lights jumped and bounced ahead of them, like tiny fireflies, lighting a clear path. They had barely rounded the first corner when, with a rush and a rumble, a huge section of the ceiling of the cavern they had just left came rushing down in a tumult of falling stone. The sound was deafening.

Fiona screamed and ran flat out, the key's guiding light dancing ahead of her.

It was like some kind of terrible nightmare. Fiona ran with both arms lifted. One to allow the others to see the light, the other to shield her face. At times violent tremors shook the mountain, threatening to fling them off their feet. Yet something protected them. The tunnels caved in around them, the deafening repercussions sounding closer with every blast. Yet still they remained just ahead, though more than once they escaped only barely.

Any moment Fiona expected to fall and be crushed under the immense weight of the rock or else for the key's light to fail, leaving them to wander the passages of their own tomb.

They made it, just. Fiona suddenly became aware of another light besides that given off by the key. It was an odd light, dim, like a half glow. For a moment she panicked. Where was the sunlight they had left behind them? Then her reason caught up with her befuddled senses, and she realised. Twilight! The sun had almost set, giving way to evening. They must have been underground for hours, yet it seemed to have taken no time at all to escape. Did the key know a short cut? There was no time to ponder this.

"We're nearly out!" she shouted over the mountain's continuing destruction. "Keep going!" She thought someone gave a reply, or it might have been a cry of pain.

She burst out into the open air, and instantly turned back, searching for James and the others. They followed seconds later, streaming out in a ragged line.

Fiona swung away and plunged down a rocky trail, her one desire in life to get as far as possible from that death trap, the others right behind her. They careered on downwards, the gentle slope of the land lending extra momentum to their flight. Fiona's lungs burned and her knees began to tremble with exhaustion. But she dared not slow her pace. Not until her foot caught in a tussock and she went tumbling headlong, was her flight checked. She rolled over and over before eventually coming to rest, dizzy and breathless amid a mass of tall waving fronds of heather and swaying dandelions.

She lay where she was, too bruised and dizzy to move. Her chest heaved as her starved lungs gulped thirstily at the cool night air. Her nostrils were full of the loamy scent of grass and earth. She breathed it in, grateful to be alive.

Something was digging into her palm. Looking down, she saw that she still clutched the key. Its light was gone now. It lay cool and quiet in her hand, a dull, harmless piece of metal. She tucked it back inside her tunic, then slowly sat up.

The others came panting up to her, James skidding to a halt at her side.

"Are you alright?" he demanded.

She got to her feet. There was blood on his forehead.

"I could ask you the same thing. What happened?"

James wiped the cut with his sleeve. "It's nothing. A stone hit me, that's all."

Fiona surveyed the others. They appeared to be unhurt, but Katie looked severely shaken, and even Christophe was pale beneath his tan.

As one, they turned to stare back the way they had come. As though on cue, the mountain let out a roar as though in defeat, and with a final rush an entire section sheered away and came clattering and bouncing down in a mass of smashed boulders and loose scree. The air was soon full of the smell of pulverised rock. The way back was blocked. The path nearly obliterated.

"Any closer…" James breathed and left the sentence unfinished. Fiona and Katie reached for each other's hands. Christophe shuddered.

"We should get out of here."

They moved off in silence, following what remained of the path.

No one spoke. Their near brush with death had sobered them all. They were content simply to be alive and to be together. The experience seemed to have drawn them closer somehow.

Not until the terrible landslide was a considerable distance behind them, did they finally give in to their exhaustion and halt for the night and take stock of their surroundings.

They were in a valley, nestled, so it seemed, between the two arms of the mountain. The country was greener than any Fiona had yet seen. Huge trees were dotted everywhere like sentinels, many still bearing blossom. Flowering bushes lent vivid splashes of pink, yellow and purple. Bees flew busily from petal to petal, their droning mingling with the valley's other sounds: the scrape and chatters of insects and the incessant trill of birdsong. It was a tranquil place, far removed from horror and death.

They divided out portions of bread, cheese and fruit, washed down by gulps from their water bottles. Eventually, James broke the silence.

"How could that have happened? Mountains don't just collapse for no reason, and it's a bit of a coincidence that it happened the moment we saw that map or whatever it was. It's almost like it was waiting for us."

"Magic," Katie said softly.

"What?"

"It must have been magic. The merpeople made that map of the island where the sceptre is hidden, and hid it underground so no one would find it. Only the key's magic could lead us to it, and once we had seen it, there was no need to preserve it any longer."

"So the mountain just collapsed?" Fiona said sceptically.

"Maybe there was some sort of warding magic on that map that the key triggered. That was the signal to destroy the map."

"Well, it was a little close for my liking," James muttered.

Christophe nodded. "I know little of magic and how it is used, but we have to remember that this was preordained years ago. The merpeople must have set those precautions in place the moment they knew of the existence of The Appointed."

"So Alfredo could never have got the sceptre anyway?" said Fiona.

Christophe shrugged. "Not unless he was somehow able to break through the disguise on the key. That has proved its nature in every sense of the word."

"What about the island?" James asked. "That map showed a jungle and a bridge and a swamp that we have to cross. Will we be able to pass safely, or will there be things waiting for us?"

"I'd have thought a jungle and a swamp would prove barriers enough," Fiona muttered.

"Surely they won't have made it easy in case the wrong person stumbled across the island," said James.

"Always assuming we can reach the island in the first place," said Christophe.

Fiona frowned irritably. "What are you on about now?"

"Have you forgotten the poem? We have to cross to the island we cannot see. It is hardly likely to be just lying in wait for us. It must be warded somehow and we will have to breach its defences."

"Which is what the key is for." Fiona countered.

"One problem, Fiona," said James. "Look around – do you see any water? We can't cross to an island, visible or otherwise, without water and a boat or something."

He was absolutely right. There was no water in their immediate vicinity, nor could they hear any, no matter how hard they strained to listen. Although, as

Fiona pointed out testily, it was impossible to hear anything over the racket the birds were making.

"I can search for a river," Katie offered.

"You are weary," Christophe protested. "We all are."

She smiled at him. "We have to get out of here. I will tell you my findings in the morning."

This seemed the signal for bed. Katie and Christophe moved a little way from James and Fiona. They lay in each other's arms as always.

By unspoken consent, Fiona and James did the same. They had not done so before, but each needed one another's closeness more than ever after their ordeal. No one mounted a watch. The valley seemed so safe and tranquil. Even Christophe was asleep the moment his head touched the ground.

"You have done well!"

The mocking voice sliced through Fiona's peaceful dreaming like a knife through butter. She knew that voice. It had haunted her ever since the first time it tormented her as she lay buried beneath the sand.

"Get lost," she muttered, fighting the waves of despair and helplessness the voice engendered.

It laughed. Low, mirthless, utterly devoid of emotion. It made Fiona feel cold to her very soul.

An apparition appeared before her. A man, tall, thin, bearded, dressed in black. He seemed to loom over her where she lay, and in his eyes, she saw her death as plainly as if he had held a knife to her throat. She wanted to shrink away, to hide. But the force of his gaze speared her in place where she lay defenceless.

"Such spirit," the voice crooned softly. "I admire it, really I do. It is what has kept you going. It is what has enabled me to track you. Your stubbornness will lead me to my goal and you to your death."

A spark of anger ignited in Fiona's breast. The voice's continual jibes cutting through some of the terror paralysing her. Clenching her teeth to stop them chattering, she snarled, "What makes you think I'll let you have the sceptre? I didn't go through this hell just so you could walk off with it."

This time his laugh was wild, filled with glee.

"What makes you think you could stop me, child! I have power beyond your wildest nightmares. Magic is in my blood. It permeates every fibre of my being. I could crush you into oblivion where you lie, or drag out your torment endlessly as I chose."

Fiona's bravado faded. It was true, she knew it was. In one last desperate effort, she snapped, "Then how about I just turn round right now and head off home? You'd be a bit stuck then, wouldn't you?"

"That would alter nothing. Running like a coward would not save you. I know you more intimately than you know yourself. I could pick out the sound of your heartbeat from a thousand hearts, smell the scent of your skin from a thousand scents, track the pulse of your thoughts. Your face is imprinted on my mind more clearly than my own. There would be nowhere for you to hide. Your memories would be mine, dragged from you one morsel at a time. Your doom is inevitable, Appointed, and your friends as well. Your father's sacrifice was in vain, for it has accomplished nothing. Ponder on that while you can. We will meet soon, One way or another."

"Fiona, wake up!"

Her eyes flew open. James was raised on one elbow, his concerned face bathed in moonlight.

"He's coming!" she whispered hoarsely. "He'll kill us all!"

He reached for her, pulling her close. She clung to him as violent tremors rocked her entire body. He stroked her hair.

"It's alright. You had a nightmare, that's all. It's over now."

"No!" she pulled back from him a little. He looked taken aback by her vehement. She fought to still the trembling of her limbs, to make him understand.

"Alfredo is here."

He started, staring wildly around as if he expected to see Alfredo lurking behind a nearby tree.

She hastened to reassure him. "Sorry, I mean he's following us. He's been tracking us. Even with our short cut through the mountains, he was able to find us. I don't know where he is exactly, but he's out there somewhere."

James opened his mouth as if to deny her words. She forestalled his objections. "It's true, James, I know it is. He spoke to me!"

He found his voice. "How do you mean, he spoke to you?"

"I don't know. I sort of hear his voice in my head. It happened first when I was buried under the sand. Remember? I told you about it afterwards."

"That was just a hallucination or something. You were suffocating!"

"I wasn't suffocating tonight, was I? I saw his face. Oh, James, I've never seen such…" she was trembling again. She hugged herself in a futile effort to bring comfort.

"He's going to kill me. He's going to kill all of us. The only reason he's kept us alive this long is so that we'll lead him to the sceptre. Then that's it. All over. Finished." Her self-restraint broke and she sobbed helplessly in James's embrace.

"Even if we turn round and run and lead him away, he'll find us. He said so! He'll learn what he wants and then he'll kill us anyway, and everyone else too. Either way, we've accomplished nothing." Her sobs re-doubled. Anger and despair filled her. Somewhere at the back of her mind she wondered why Christophe and Katie did not wake, but she was glad of it. She didn't think she could bear it if Christophe saw her like this.

"Why do I have to die? I never asked for any of this. I don't deserve this."

James lifted her chin, forcing her to look at him. She blinked to clear her swimming eyes, while her chest and shoulders still heaved convulsively.

"Don't you think this is what Alfredo wants? He wants us to panic. But he hasn't got the sceptre yet. We've still got time."

She uttered a hysterical laugh that ended in a sob. "Oh really? And how exactly do we destroy this thing? Do you have any bright ideas? I sure as hell don't, and I'm supposed to be The Appointed!"

"The key," James said, grabbing at straws. "It's helped us up to now, and it only answers to you. It'll show you what to do, and it'll help us get by whatever tricks are guarding the sceptre as well. Alfredo won't have that. He'll have to find his own way to the sceptre. I know he's supposed to be all powerful, but the merpeople's magic is bound to slow him a little bit."

She was silent a while.

"You know, when Christophe first brought me here, I didn't give a damn about any of it. These people's problems weren't mine. I just wanted to go home. But after seeing what Alfredo did to his people; those slaves in the market place and especially what happened to the Travellers, I wanted to make a difference. Not because I was The Appointed, but because it was wrong. Finding the key made me believe I could actually do something. I finally accepted the responsibility Christophe and my father gave me. But if I fail, I've condemned them all. What chance do I really have of seeing this through? I haven't the faintest idea what I'm doing!"

James sighed and resumed stroking her hair. "The odds aren't exactly in our favour, I know, but we still have a chance. As long as we can keep ahead of Alfredo, there's a chance we'll win."

"And if we don't? If I can't destroy the sceptre and Alfredo gets it?"

"At least we'll have tried. Better to try our best and fail, than just running away and doing nothing. That's an even bigger failure, isn't it?"

She managed a weak smile. "When did you get so philosophical? It wasn't that long ago you were worried about beating St. Peter's in a friendly."

"Yeah, I wonder how we got on. They'd have been nothing without me, of course."

"Yeah, because your talent is far superior to the rest of the human race." They laughed, glad of the temporary relief. Then James grew serious once more.

"I suppose I've had time to put things in perspective on this mad journey. Nearly dying a few times has made me see things differently. Getting one over on that monster is more important than any football game."

She squeezed his hand. "I know I've said it before, but I'm glad you're here with me. I'd have fallen apart long ago without you."

He squeezed her back. "Let's get some sleep. If we want to stay ahead of Alfredo, we'll have to make an early start. I only hope Katie manages to find out where we have to go."

James's hopes were answered. Over breakfast, Katie explained their new directions.

"We have to cross a river to reach the island. It's not far. We can reach it by midday. We'll have to find our own way across when we get there though."

Fiona looked up in dismay. Alfredo's dire warnings still fresh in her thoughts. "We need to hurry. We have to get to that island today if we can."

Christophe shrugged. "We will do our best, but we have to find our way across first. We may well have to make a raft. Plus we shall have to contend with whatever magic hides the island from sight. That will take some time."

"We have no time!" Fiona snapped. "Alfredo is on our heels!"

Katie went ashen, while for once, Christophe was speechless. Fiona pressed on. "He's been following us ever since we left the city."

"Impossible!" Christophe snapped. "We have kept watch both night and day since we started out. There has been no signs of pursuit."

"Oh, for god's sake. Did you think he was going to stand there with a sign saying *Wait up, I'm on my way?* He's a warlock, Christophe. I'm sure he's more than capable of remaining hidden when he wants to."

There was an uneasy silence. Then Katie spoke, her voice barely more than a croak. "How do you know?"

Fiona sighed heavily. "He spoke to me last night while I was asleep. He's done it twice now."

Katie's face turned, if possible, even paler. "Twice? He spoke to you twice? Why on earth did you not say something?"

Fiona grew angry in her turn. "Because where I'm from, voices in the head usually means you're going round the bend. The first time it happened I was buried under all that sand."

"She told me about it," James admitted. "But I thought it was just a hallucination. I've heard of that sort of thing happening when a person's running out of oxygen."

"I forgot about it, what with meeting Sulaiman's men and finding the map, not to mention that near death experience in the mountain." Fiona shuddered. "But he spoke to me again last night. I saw his face as well. He said... he said he'd kill us all, that we had nowhere to hide. He'd take the sceptre and destroy us all, and if we tried to run, he'd hunt us down wherever we went."

Katie jumped to her feet as though galvanised. She was still chalk white, and she held her composure with an effort.

"We must go now! We have to try to reach that river."

"She's right," said James. "If we can just stay ahead of him, we may still have a chance. He didn't say exactly where he was."

No one argued, but as they set off, Christophe said grimly, "I do not like this. Both contacts have taken place when The Appointed has been close to, or narrowly escaped death. Was it just a coincidence? Or can Alfredo only make contact at such times?"

"Who knows?" Fiona snapped. "I'll try not to die between now and when I've destroyed the sceptre, and perhaps he'll leave me alone."

"I mean," Christophe continued as though there had been no interruption, "That maybe he can see you most clearly at such times. If we can only manage to avoid any danger, it may lessen his lead somewhat."

"Well, that shouldn't be too difficult," Fiona muttered.

Katie took the lead as usual. She set a fast pace, but no one complained. They reached the river a little before midday.

"Now what?" James panted.

The river was fast flowing. Trees reached right down to the water's edge, their low-hung branches swaying a little in the breeze. Logs, dead twigs and other debris were borne along in the swift current, or else lodged in the bank. The water was clear, but deep. Fiona put in a tentative finger. The water was icy. If they fell in, they would surely freeze if they didn't drown.

Christophe pulled some lengths of rope from the bundle on his back. "We must see if we can lash some of these logs together."

Fiona rubbed at her chest. The key was growing warm once more. She could feel it through the fabric of her tunic.

"Wait!" She withdrew the key. Light pulsed strongly from it, warming her cupped hands. The others crowded close.

"What's it up to?" wondered James.

Fiona frowned. "It's trying to tell us something."

She turned her back on the water and took a few steps back the way they had come. Instantly the key's light went out and the heat began to fade. Fiona's puzzlement increased. If the key had meant to find the river for them, then why hadn't it shone on the way down? It had remained cold and dull against her skin. Yet now… she swung back to face the river. The key immediately brightened once more. She faced left and right. The key's light lessened, but did not fade.

"I can't make out what it's saying," she said, frustrated.

"It's clearest when you're facing us," James pointed out.

"Oh, well done, genius." They didn't have time for this. Alfredo could appear any minute.

James's voice was patient. "I mean, it brightens the most when you're standing on the bank. Maybe we've got to look for something there."

"Well what, for god's sake?"

She crouched down, sweeping the muddy ground with the key's light. Nothing! Just dead branches and other flotsam thrown up by the current. Yet the light was blazing fiercely now, almost dazzling her.

Then, as it came to rest on a blackened log partially concealed beneath one of the low-hanging tree branches, the key emitted a flash of brilliant light fiercer than any that had gone before. Fiona blinked to clear the bright spots from her vision. The log still looked the same. Caked in mud and slime with bits of weed clinging to it. With a shudder of revulsion, Fiona reached out and gingerly touched the key to the surface of the log.

Instantly the log shimmered like a mirage, and in its place… "Well, how about that?" James's voice was half incredulous, half admiring. "Those merpeople didn't miss a trick, did they?"

The boat was small, with two pairs of oars and no sail. Her prow had been exquisitely carved in the likeness of a mermaid, poised as though she were about to dive.

"Remarkable!" Christophe breathed. "To think how many years she must have been hidden here."

"It's very convenient if you ask me," Fiona muttered, eyeing the boat as though it were an enemy.

"Not at all," Christophe countered. "Without the key, it would have remained disguised. If we had not possessed it, we would have been stranded. I would wager that this river cannot be crossed by any way other than this boat."

Fiona opened her mouth to argue, but James cut across her.

"It doesn't matter. Christophe's right, this is probably the only way across. We need to go!"

But Fiona was far from happy as she helped drag the boat to the water and launch her. Had the merpeople known she would not refuse them? They had certainly covered every eventuality. Had she never had any say in this at all? She pushed the disquieting thoughts aside. No use dwelling on it now, particularly as it was too late.

The boat was launched. Fiona and Christophe took the oars, while James and Katie settled themselves in the stern with their belongings. They followed the direction of the current for no one doubted now that this was no ordinary river.

For what seemed an age, nothing could be heard but for the oars and the chatter and gurgle of the river as it rushed by.

Then Katie abruptly broke the silence with a cry of alarm. At the same time, James let out a vehement exclamation and pointed ahead.

As one, Fiona and Christophe shipped their oars and turned to stare over their shoulders.

Ahead of them was what appeared to be a solid wall of… nothing. All around them the water was clear and blue and the sun shone down brightly in the sky above, yet ahead of them, a wall of impenetrable darkness loomed. Katie looked desperately for a tiller or some other means of steering the boat, but there wasn't one.

"Turn back!" James yelled. "We're going to crash right into it!"

Fiona and Christophe seized the oars and tried to turn the boat about, but could make no headway against the current.

"No good!" Christophe grunted, his face taut with the strain of wrestling with the boat. "The current is too strong. We are helpless!"

"But we can't just sit here," Fiona snapped. "We'll be smashed to bits!" But even *she* could see that Christophe was right. The boat was racing along at terrific speed, borne along with the river. Fiona reached out to James, just as Katie reached for Christophe. Diving overboard was no use. They would surely drown. Clinging to each other, they awaited the inevitable.

Fiona closed her eyes as the wall of darkness rushed up to meet them. It looked frighteningly solid. She waited for the bone-jarring impact. At least it would be quick. Alfredo would never be able to force her to reveal the whereabouts of the sceptre. She would never know it herself. She would fail everyone. A hysterical sound left her lips, half laugh, half sob.

Silence! Where had the river gone? Were they dead? Yet there hadn't been a crash. She would have remembered, but perhaps she was unconscious. But she could feel James pressed against her. She could feel the material of his tunic beneath her fingers. They didn't seem to be moving either. She decided to risk opening her eyes.

The world was no different than with them closed.

"What happened?" Katie's frightened voice sounded strangely muffled, as though Fiona's ears were stuffed with cotton wool.

Heat flared sharply beneath her tunic. Fiona gasped. The key was burning her skin. Hurriedly she snatched it out.

The key was alight once more. It cast a small sphere of illumination ahead of them, allowing them to see something of their surroundings.

Fiona gasped, and heard it echoed by the others.

They appeared to have left the river behind now. What they floated on now more closely resembled a lake. The surface of the water as far as they could see was glassy smooth. All that moved was the dark. It seemed to swirl and eddy all about them. Not darkness, Fiona realised. Mist. They were cocooned in a blanket of fog.

*"Cross to the island you cannot see,"* Fiona breathed. Without a word, she and Christophe took up their oars, and resumed rowing. The sphere of light moved before their prow, guiding them forward.

It was the strangest sensation Fiona had ever experienced. Rowing through the fog, the sound of the oars unnaturally loud in the eerie gloom. It was almost like they had left the real world behind them. Here, they seemed in a time all their own. Fiona shuddered to think how easily they might have become lost without the key. They would have just drifted aimlessly along for ever, unless they struck the island by chance. She understood now why the boat had no sail. There was no wind to fill it. She began to wonder how she would ever manage without the key to guide her. It hung now outside her tunic, moving with her as she leaned forward and back with each oar stroke.

It was James who broke the silence, though he did not speak above a whisper. "That's all the clues now, isn't it? When we reach the island, that's it?"

Fiona sighed. "I wish! There's still the *path of truth,* whatever that may be, and we have to find the sceptre first. If I remember rightly, we have to cross a bridge and find our way through a jungle and a swamp. No, our troubles are far from over yet."

At last, the mist appeared to be thinning. Chinks of daylight showed through. The key's light dimmed and then faded altogether as the last thin tendrils dispersed. Fiona blinked in the sudden daylight, which seemed unnaturally bright after so long in near darkness.

Before them was a pebble beach with sheer cliffs that rose out of sight. Birds swooped and circled their summits, flying to and from their nests.

"A lonely spot, isn't it?" James commented. They all jumped out and dragged the boat onto dry land. Fiona tucked the key out of sight once more.

“Now what?” Fiona wondered to no one in particular, staring about her with no small amount of misgiving. She was not entirely sure she liked this island. Its very location, so remote and far removed from civilization did not seem very welcoming. She could see no other signs of habitation. No boats drawn up, no fishing nets. The beach was deserted apart from themselves and the birds. Of course, there may well be homes further inland, but the island’s terrain did not sound like an ideal habitat for people to live. How would they be able to grow anything? And surely the merpeople would have wanted an unpopulated island for fear that someone might stumble on the sceptre accidentally.

“We should start at once,” said Christophe. “Who knows how far Alfredo is behind us.”

“That fog’s bound to slow him down a little bit,” said James. “I think we should grab a quick bite to eat first. If we’re going to be wandering about in a swamp and a jungle, I’d rather do it on a full stomach.”

James divided out their rations, but Fiona only picked at hers. The thought that she was so near her goal, robbed her of her appetite. She still didn’t know what she was supposed to do with the sceptre once she found it, and fear of Alfredo loomed like an ever present spectre just out of view.

When it became clear that Fiona could not eat anything and the others had finished their meal, they set off walking inland.

“You should have tried to eat something,” James fretted.

“I can’t!”

James urged her no further, but gave her arm an understanding squeeze.

The pebbles gave way soon enough to short tussocky grass. On the higher slopes they could see wild sheep and goats grazing. Christophe fingered his bow but kept walking.

An unreasoning dread settled over Fiona as they walked, a fear that she could neither identify nor rid herself of. It became a battle of wills just to put one foot before the other. She saw something of her turmoil on the strained faces of the others. Christophe maintained a white-knuckled grip on his dagger and Katie’s eyes darted everywhere like a hunted animal. James strode resolutely forward, only his fists constantly clenching and unclenching betrayed his agitation.

“Is it me,” James ventured at last, “Or is the air different?”

He was right. None of them had noticed at first, the change had been so gradual, but the cool fresh air of the beach was gone. To be replaced by a tropical humidity that made sweat run in rivulets down their backs and under their arms. Their clothes clung to their skin and they breathed with difficulty in the thin air.

“We should go slowly,” Christophe panted. “Conserve our strength.”

“It’s like a tropical rain forest,” James murmured.

“I will die in here,” Katie muttered, half to herself. “The air is suffocating.”

Walls of vines and creepers rose up around them, the foliage growing more dense with every step. Fiona had to fight a growing sense of claustrophobia. Moisture fell from the plants with a steady drip, drip, drip. Shafts of light through the canopy above came more and more sporadically as the gloom closed in.

"I can't stand this," Katie spoke through clenched teeth. "We will never find our way through here without light. We should—" her words ended in a scream as, without warning, a vine slashed at her face. Katie stumbled back just as a second creeper snaked towards James's throat. They were coming thick and fast. Snaking tendrils that curled around their necks and limbs. Thorny fingers that lashed out at their faces with barbs gleaming wetly at their tips. Vines that rose from the ground to trip them. The air was filled with the creaking and groaning of a jungle come to life.

"Do something!" Katie screamed at Fiona.

Fiona plunged her hand down the neck of her tunic, groping wildly. At last her desperate fingers closed on the key and she yanked it out, raising it aloft to challenge their attackers.

Nothing happened. The key lay cold and dull in her cupped hand. A sob of terror rose in her throat.

"It's not working!" She shook the key, pleaded with it mentally, screamed at it aloud, but nothing happened. The key remained inert and useless.

She whirled round, narrowly avoiding a creeper that lunged for her face, meaning to bolt back the way they had come. But the path was gone. A solid wall of creepers blocked their retreat. There was only one way left open to them. Forward.

"Come on!" she screamed and tore off down the path. Instantly limbs reached for her legs and snagged at her clothes, but she plunged on, hearing the others crashing behind her and their cries as the vines tore at them. More than once they stumbled and went down, only to leap up again before the deadly plants could secure a firm enough hold. But their strength was waning. Just when Fiona felt she could run no more, she was forced to an abrupt halt. A low moan escaped her. Her eyes had become attuned to the gloom by this time. Enough to see that a second wall of creepers barred their way, identical to that which cut off their retreat.

Fiona sank to the ground, utterly spent. She raised her head a little and saw James, half dragging, half supporting Katie. They dropped down beside her. They were forced to lie virtually flat to avoid the vicious lunges of the vines. By raising her head the merest fraction, Fiona was able to see that Christophe was still upright, hacking viciously at the vines with his dagger as he vainly sought to clear a path. Sweat ran down his face which was contorted with rage, but he was flagging. He could not keep it up much longer, and his efforts were making no discernible difference.

"Think!" James panted beside her. "We must be missing something. There has to be a way out of here!"

"How? The key doesn't work!"

"James is right," Katie gasped. "There has to be a way, if we can only manage to stay calm and think what it is."

"Oh yeah, let's all stay calm," Fiona snapped. "We're only about to be torn apart, but we won't let that worry us."

Katie's voice held a hysterical note. "We have to try! Christophe cannot keep it up much longer!"

Fiona watched hopelessly as Christophe swung and hacked at the vines. He never even seemed to get near them. The air seemed to shimmer as the knife passed through it. Odd, what did that remind her of? She looked down at her arms. She must be a mass of scratches. But her flesh was smooth. Fiona could hardly believe her eyes. She felt her arms. Not a scratch. And her face likewise, completely unmarked. But that was impossible! In disbelief she examined her clothing. It had snagged several times on the thorns. Yet the fabric was whole. Utterly perplexed, she returned her gaze to Christophe, watching as he slashed at a vine. His dagger seemed to pass straight through it as though it wasn't there. The thought stopped her in her tracks. She watched. Again, that telltale shimmer in the air, just exactly like… "A mirage!"

"What?" said James.

Fiona ignored him. "Christophe!" she yelled at him. "Christophe, stop it! They aren't real!"

He whirled at the sound of her voice. Frantically she beckoned him over. He came, dropping to the ground beside them. His breathing was laboured.

"What is it?" he managed between gasps. James and Katie were looking at Fiona too, though half Katie's attention was on Christophe as she checked for any injuries.

"The vines aren't real," Fiona repeated.

"What are you on about?" said James. "They're all around us."

"I was watching Christophe when he was slashing at the vines. He never seemed to touch them. The air shimmered every time his blade moved through it. And I'm not marked. There's not a scratch on me and my clothes are fine, yet I was caught several times."

James examined himself. "My god, your right!"

Katie looked up, amazed. "There is not a mark on him."

"Nor on you either," said Fiona. Katie nodded.

"This is amazing," said James. "We've been running from something that isn't even there?"

"An illusion," Christophe had got his breath back. "The trick of this magic is in the mind only, which explains why the key failed to work."

"What do you mean?" asked James.

"The key unlocks all doors *except for those within.* That is why it did not work here. The barriers do not exist. There is nothing for it to unlock. If we can keep that in mind, we should be able to pass through."

They got to their feet again. Fiona fixed her eyes on the wall of creepers. They aren't real. They're just an illusion. She concentrated on that with all her might as they began to walk forward. At first the concentration required was fierce, but as her brain got used to the idea, it became easier.

Soon the vines were gone, and a clear path wound ahead of them.

They had walked for several minutes, still deeply shaken by their ordeal, when Fiona suddenly wrinkled her nose. The air had taken on a distinctly stagnant and fetid odour.

"Can you smell that?"

They all nodded.

"We must be approaching the swamp," said Christophe.

"Is that an illusion too?" asked James.

Fiona checked the key. It remained dull.

"Looks like it."

The ground was treacherous and boggy underfoot. It was much harder to concentrate on keeping their minds clear. The stench was nauseating.

"I think this is real, you know," James muttered. He had put a sleeve across his nose and mouth in an effort to block out the foul stench. The others followed suit and breathing grew easier.

Pools bubbled sluggishly. The ground sucked greedily at their feet. The path they trod grew narrower.

Then suddenly, a swarm of midges dived at their faces, buzzing loudly. Fiona swatted at them automatically. Her hand passed straight through them, and again came that telltale shimmer, and a slight tingling in her fingers.

"Here's our illusion," she rasped. "The swamp's real enough."

They were harried constantly after that. More clouds of insects attacked them. Serpentine heads with grinning maws and flailing tentacles lunged at their legs. It was much harder to maintain a relaxed demeanour and keep moving.

At one point, James missed his footing and found himself sinking rapidly. He cried out in alarm, but the others seized him and tugged with all their might, freeing him from the clinging mud.

"Nope, definitely not an illusion," he panted.

But at last the swamp was behind them. The air grew fresher, and they were able to breathe easily once more.

Soon Fiona found that she was shivering. A biting wind had sprung up which she felt keenly through her clothing. Still the key lay dull against her chest. The path ended abruptly, and Fiona froze, her heart in her mouth.

Before her, stretched the biggest chasm she had ever seen. It was so wide that she could not make out its far side. A slender narrow bridge stretched from one side to the other. It looked hardly sturdy enough to support their weight. But that was not the worst of it. When she looked down into its seemingly bottomless depths, she saw a vast lake of molten lava, boiling and churning hungrily.

Fiona's knees trembled. Just the thought of crossing that terrible abyss was more than she felt she could stand. Just one false step and she would fall to a fiery destruction. Yet this had to be an illusion of some sort too, or the key would have warned her. But what was real? The chasm or the lava at the bottom? She hoped it was the latter. There had been a chasm on the map.

She took a tentative step forward onto the bridge. Instantly vertigo took hold and she would have toppled right there and then if James hadn't caught and steadied her.

"I can't!" she panted. "I can't cross that!"

"You must!" James's voice was gentle, but firm. "It's our last obstacle. The sceptre is on the other side of that bridge."

"We will walk in a line and hold hands," said Christophe. "That way if any of us stumble, the others can steady them."

Fiona never knew how she made herself cross that bridge. Christophe went first, with Fiona immediately behind him. James came behind her and Katie brought up the rear. Fiona clung to James and Christophe with hands that were slippery with sweat.

The illusions were cruel. Magic put in place to send people from the bridge. The worst thing was that the same distraction never came twice, so they never knew what to guard against. They could only take one careful step at a time and ignore the dreadful cries of agony that rose up from the pit, or the tremors that shook the bridge, or the freezing gusts of wind that caused them to sway as though they were on the deck of a ship. Each time they had to force the illusion aside and press on, but the urge to over balance was strong.

Fiona knew that it was only the reassuring clasp of her companion's hands that kept her sane. Even so, that crossing pushed them all to the very limits of their endurance.

But at last they made it. They stepped off the bridge and collapsed white and shaking on the ground.

Never again! Fiona vowed silently. Never ever again!

"Welcome, travellers who have come so far."

Fiona's head snapped up. She was kneeling on a flat stone pavement, and before her rose a pair of wrought iron gates, topped with two splendid arches, each crowned by a gigantic statue of a mermaid. There was an ornately carved bench near the gates. More mermaid carvings entwined its legs and arms and snaked along the back. Seated on the bench, was a woman.

Even sitting, Fiona could tell she was tall. She was slender with lustrous silvery-blonde hair that hung down her back to her waist. It was impossible to tell her age. Her face was flawless and unlined. Yet her eyes held the wisdom of uncounted years.

She gestured with one pale hand. "Welcome, Appointed. I have long awaited your coming."

# Chapter 21

## The Path of Truth

"Who… who are you?" The question seemed so inadequate, yet Fiona had never seen anything like this woman. She had been sure the island was uninhabited. Another human presence was the last thing she had expected to encounter. Yet this woman couldn't be human. Fiona was certain of that. The shape of her body and facial features were those of a woman, yet her hair fanned and swirled about her as though tossed in an invisible breeze, and there was a pearly sheen to her skin, as though beads of moisture clung to her.

Her gaze wandered over all of them in turn, but lingered especially on Fiona.

"I am Aqua, the guardian of the sceptre."

The name struck a cord somewhere in Fiona's memory, but she was so exhausted by everything they had gone through since reaching the island that the recollection escaped her. It was all she could do to remain upright.

Aqua seemed to read her thoughts.

"You are welcome to my garden, Appointed. Beyond these gates you will find what you seek and the prophecies will be fulfilled. But not tonight, I think. I see your weariness. Take your ease tonight. On the morrow, you shall complete your quest. Come, eat, and we will talk."

She re-seated herself on the bench and beckoned for Fiona and James to sit on either side of her. James's face wore an openly awestruck expression that at any other time would have made Fiona want to laugh. But she was too busy grappling with her own amazement.

This was the guardian of the sceptre. The one chosen from her people to ward it against danger and await the coming of its destroyer. She remembered what Esther and Gideon had said about merpeople taking human form. She could barely take her eyes off Aqua. Yet why had she taken this form now? Surely there was no need to.

Katie and Christophe settled on the ground at Aqua's feet, and Christophe divided out the last of their rations. Christophe's face wore an expression of delighted wonder that Fiona had only seen once before, when Christophe had been taking her to meet the Travellers and a school of dolphins had swum by.

Katie looked solemn and a little frightened. Fiona wondered if Katie had ever heard the stories of the merpeople, brought up as she had been in Miguel's house. Fiona doubted that such stories would have been told. Miguel and his like had betrayed the ways of the merpeople. They would not wish to remember their treachery.

As for Fiona herself, she felt that here at last was someone who could answer all her questions. Here was someone who could explain what the prophecies really meant and why she had been chosen, and perhaps tell her how to destroy the sceptre. Surely, Aqua, its guardian, would be able to help her. Why else had she remained here all these years? Fiona had so many questions, and no idea where to start.

Aqua saved her the trouble.

"You must have many questions, Appointed. I will answer those that I can."

Fiona's heart sank at those last words. Already half-expecting the answer, she said, "Will you tell me how to destroy the sceptre?"

Aqua looked genuinely sad. "Alas, no. That is something you must discover for yourself."

"Then you do know!"

Aqua made no answer. White hot anger filled Fiona. Before she knew it, she was on her feet, shrugging off James's restraining hand.

"OK, I've had just about enough of this! Ever since I got here, no one's told me anything. You've all just expected me to save the world. Well I'm fed up of it. I'm sick of just blundering along blindly. We all went through hell to get here, and now I want some answers!"

Christophe was on his feet by now. Seizing Fiona roughly by the shoulders, he pushed her none too gently back onto the bench.

"Will you never learn to guard your tongue?"

Fiona shook him off and rounded once more on Aqua. She didn't care who she was, she needed something. Some kind of reassurance. But what she saw in Aqua's eyes froze the words in her throat. Aqua was gazing at her with such naked sorrow and compassion that Fiona felt her blood run cold. Still looking at Fiona, Aqua addressed Christophe.

"Govern your temper, Christophe. The anger of The Appointed is more than justified." Then to Fiona, "What makes you think you are not fit for this task? What makes you feel that you need any help from me?"

Fiona stared at her incredulously. "I haven't got any magical powers. My dad never passed it on to me. How can I destroy anything so powerful without magic? If all it took to destroy the sceptre was to throw it against the wall, you'd have done it long ago."

Aqua laughed. "You have a quick mind. And you are right. It will take enormous power to destroy the sceptre, but not of the kind you think."

Fiona opened her mouth to ask what she meant, but Aqua went on. "When you pass through these gates tomorrow, you will follow The Path of Truth. The last ward I put in place to guard the sceptre. You will travel alone, for the magic was put in place for you only. If anyone else were to go with you or walk the path in your place, they would find it nothing more than a pleasant path through a pretty garden. This path will show you many truths about yourself. You will be forced to confront your deepest fears. Fears you have barely acknowledged to yourself. Yet if you endure, then the answer to your question will lie at the end of the path."

Fiona was silent. She stared at the gates with sick trepidation. The bread in her mouth suddenly felt like ashes. Through the gates lay her answer. The knowledge that would finally enable her to complete her task. But at what price? Was it a price she would be able to pay? And she would be alone. There would be nobody to confide in and ask for advice. No one to protect her. For the first time since her arrival in this world, she would be completely on her own. She saw the same consternation on James and Christophe's faces.

"Please, honoured one," said Christophe. "I swore to protect The Appointed in my father's stead. You surely are not asking me to stand aside and leave her to walk into danger?"

"What kind of friends would we be if we just waved her off and stayed to watch?" James demanded incredulously.

"The very best," Aqua replied seriously. "There are some things that must be faced alone. A true friend knows when to offer friendship and when to step aside. You may well have to follow after The Appointed, but you cannot accompany her. It is hard, I see that, but we all must pay a price in this war."

There was a long silence.

"What price have you paid?" said Katie.

Fiona started. Katie had been quiet for so long. The ordeals of the island seemed to have exhausted her in more ways than one. Her face was haggard and drawn and her voice was brittle and hard. Fiona felt a pang of concern but Katie was not looking at her. She was staring at Aqua, a haunted expression in her eyes. Aqua returned her gaze for long moments before answering. It was as though an invisible current of understanding passed between them.

"I am still paying my price," Aqua said softly. "My torment began years before you were even born and goes on still, though tomorrow it will end one way or the other."

"What do you mean?" said Fiona.

"I committed the worst crime any merman or maid can commit against their people. I betrayed them. Because of my actions, my people were exiled from their ancient halls and persecuted almost to extinction. They were unable to be of use to the land and the humans that they loved, and were forced to cower in hiding like frightened, helpless animals. I did that to them."

Aqua remained utterly calm throughout this confession. Only her eyes betraying her true feelings. But at her last words, a faint note of self-loathing entered her voice and her expression hardened perceptibly.

"What did you do?" James breathed, shocked. But Fiona knew. Memories that had eluded her before, came flooding back, accompanied by her father's voice as she had heard it so many weeks ago.

"You were in love with Alfredo, weren't you? It was you who told him about the sceptre in the first place!" Rage filled her. She had walked into a trap. Alfredo had lured her here with his threats so she would rush to get there ahead of him, only so that Aqua could hold them prisoner until he reached them. All they had gone through had been for nothing. She saw her fury mirrored on James's face, while Christophe looked simply stunned. Katie's face remained expressionless.

“You condemn me, I see,” there was bitter amusement in Aqua’s voice. “Do you not think I have heard everything you can possibly say against me?”

“It was you,” Fiona breathed. “You’re the reason my father sacrificed himself. You’re the reason I’m in this mess in the first place. I’ve been through hell because of you!”

“I do not deny it,” said Aqua. “But you are wrong if you think I have not paid for my folly.”

Fiona snorted.

Aqua’s eyes flashed suddenly. “I speak truly! I have been cut off from my people. Imprisoned alone on this accursed island. I have not seen a living soul in all that time. My powers and identity were all but stripped from me. I was charged with the task of guarding the sceptre until the end of my days, and all because I loved the wrong man.” Her anger subsided as quickly as it had risen. To be replaced by a weary resignation.

“I first met Alfredo when he was very young. He was more powerful than anyone I had ever met. His whole being radiated magic. It defined what he was. It shaped everything around him. I should have seen the signs then. Someone that powerful would have to be very strong-minded indeed to resist its lure. Not to want to draw every drop he could and more. Alfredo lacked that strength. At first he was eager to explore his abilities. He had a hunger to learn which could not fail to delight. I was his tutor. I invested such hopes in him for his people and ours. I thought he might be the one to rid us of the warlock’s threat and that of the sceptre. He was passionate and determined and so vivid with life. I was captivated. I let my hopes and my attraction for him blind me. I was a fool. He charmed me. I never even realised what he was doing, and I, a magic user myself, one of the mergod’s own descendants. But I was young and just discovering the meaning of life. I let him use me. I let him soak me up like a sponge, and when he had drained me dry, he abandoned me. Though not before I had told him everything I knew of the sceptre and the warlocks.”

As Fiona listened, she felt her anger gradually melt away, to be replaced by a grudging sympathy. Aqua had betrayed her people, true, but through no malicious intention.

“What happened after that?” she asked quietly.

“Alfredo disappeared. I never saw him again, though I searched for him in vain. I pined for him, though he did not return. It is obvious now where he went, to give his allegiance to the warlocks and complete his training.

“Then one of our seers had a vision. The vision showed Alfredo with the sceptre, wreaking destruction and misery. It also showed a girl, the one person who could stop him. A child not even born. A child born of a union of a man and a woman from two worlds, whose love defied their differences in culture and upbringing. It was on that girl that all our hopes rested.

“The mergod was furious and demanded to know how Alfredo could have learned of the sceptre’s existence. And then it all came out. I was the youngest of his great-grandchildren and a favourite from birth. The fact that I had betrayed my people hit him hard.

"The sceptre was removed from its place of hiding and taken to this island. The key was created along with the map and the messages to help the one who would one day come to find and destroy it.

"It was to this island I was banished. My powers were stripped from me. I was left with barely enough magic to create the wards that guard this island and the lake that surrounds it. The Path of Truth was to be the final test of course, but I was to provide other smaller tests to measure the determination and endurance of the one who would come. Our only hope was that I had never told Alfredo exactly where the sceptre had previously been hidden. No doubt on his return he hoped to find me and learn where it was, but he found me gone, and so in fury he began persecuting my people. No doubt it was through one of his various interrogations that he was able to learn of the prophecy." She fell silent.

Fiona's emotions were in turmoil. She still could not help but be angry at all the harm Aqua's foolish infatuation had led to, not least that which had affected her and her family directly. But Aqua had been betrayed also, and had been cast out by her own people. She had surely more than paid for her stupidity.

"Why are you in human form?" she said suddenly. "I thought merpeople only took human form when necessary, like when you bred with humans."

Aqua's sigh was bitter. "I was considered no longer worthy to wear the form of my people. When I was banished here, my true form was stripped from me, along with the power to change back. I was trapped in this body as surely as were those first merpeople. The difference being of course, that their transformation was done gladly and of their own free will. I am bound this way for ever unless the sceptre is destroyed or my life is ended."

Fiona stared at Aqua, appalled. "What kind of god would do such a thing? I thought gods were supposed to be forgiving."

"Justice must always be served to those who do wrong, no matter who they are. The god of the sea could hardly make an exception for one of his own kin, or where would it end? He, above all, cannot afford to be seen showing weakness, however much it hurts him. I accept that. I would have done the same in his place."

Fiona had nothing to say to that. She felt in her heart that what Aqua said was wrong, yet there was a hard core to the mermaid's words that brooked no argument. Fiona had no idea how to challenge such convictions, however wrong they felt to her.

She saw the same discomfort on James's face, but before either could say anything, Aqua was speaking once more. "It grows late and you are weary. Tomorrow will see the end of our labours, whatever that end may be."

Fiona yawned. She felt exhausted, but a sudden unpleasant thought struck her. As Aqua rose to leave them, Fiona blurted out, "Do you still love Alfredo?"

They all froze. Aqua turned her gaze on Fiona, and for one awful moment, Fiona was sure she had gone too far.

"No, I do not love Alfredo." It was a simple statement, but spoken with such venom, that Fiona was left utterly speechless as Aqua turned from them and strode away, rapidly disappearing from view.

* * *

"I'll never sleep tonight."

James smiled. "You're exhausted. We all are."

"I'm scared to death and that's the truth. I'm dreading what I'll find on the other side of those gates."

James pulled her close and Fiona rested her head on his shoulder as she had done the night they escaped the mountain. James stroked her hair and his touch soothed her fears a little.

"Just one more day, Fiona, and then we can go home. It'll be over."

"Home," she murmured drowsily, nestling closer. "I've missed it so much."

"I know."

They were silent for a moment.

James wrestled with his emotions. He had kept his feelings for Fiona to himself, partly out of fear of her reaction, but mainly out of guilt over Carolyn. He was still fond of her, but what he and Fiona had been through these past weeks had created a bond between them that he knew transcended anything he had ever felt for Carolyn, or would probably feel for anybody. He had come so close to losing Fiona so many times, that suddenly he did not want to keep silent any longer.

"Fiona, there's something I have to tell you. This is difficult, I mean, we've been friends for ever, but after everything we've been through… well, what I'm trying to say is… I love you!

"Fiona?" But she was already fast asleep.

James sighed, and resumed gently stroking her hair. There was always tomorrow. It was probably better to wait until then. Until all this was over and done with.

Exhaustion claimed him then and he surrendered to it gratefully.

* * *

Katie lay in Christophe's arms as she had done now for many nights. She looked down into his sleeping face and thought her heart would break. When she had first known him, he had slept lightly, and his face had looked strained and troubled. He had tossed in his sleep as he fought his way through whatever bad dreams haunted him, and she had soothed him with little touchings and whisperings as Jessemine had done so often for her when she was little, until his breathing calmed and he grew peaceful once more. Now he always looked contented and at rest at night. She had done that for him. She had brought him that measure of happiness, and she had doomed him. She had become his lover, but she was also his murderer. Oh, she might not be the one wielding the dagger, but she was the cause of Christophe's death as surely as if the blade was in her hand.

The knowledge had threatened to undo her completely. Ever since Fiona had spoken of Alfredo's visitations, and the sick realisation that he had won after all. That despite all her efforts, she had betrayed her friends to their doom.

What a fool she had been. How naïve to think that just by cutting off her father's mental contact with her, she would foil his plans. He had had full access to her mind for days, weeks even, Ample time to sift through her memories, learn all he could of Fiona and accomplish his plan. He had somehow managed to track Fiona without her assistance. But that would not have been the case if she had refused to cooperate with him in the first place. She had been the key. It had been all she could do to hold herself together after Fiona's revelation. She had felt her self-control slipping hour by hour. At times as they crossed the island, she thought it would go altogether.

Aqua knew, she was sure of that. She had seen it in the mermaid's eyes. Felt it in the sudden empathy that had sprung up between them. She did not know if Aqua condemned or pitied her, but she understood. Hadn't she done the same thing, for the same man, albeit for different reasons?

If there was only something she could do to redeem the situation, to save her friends from the doom she had brought about. She could confess everything, try to explain. She quailed inwardly at the thought. Christophe had been shocked to the core by Aqua's betrayal. What would *her* betrayal do to him? There was only one thing she could do.

Very slowly and carefully, she extricated herself from Christophe's embrace. He stirred and she froze, crouched, praying he would not wake. She waited several tense seconds, but he slept on. He would not have done once, she thought, as she got to her feet and tiptoed away.

She passed James and Fiona lying a short way away, fast asleep in each other's arms, but she barely spared them a glance.

She found what she was looking for quickly. Following the garden wall around, she came upon a little bubbling spring that poured into a natural channel it had made for itself. Kneeling in the grass, she cupped some water in her hands and drank. It was sweet and ice-cold and it gave her courage.

In sleep was not the only way to trigger the visionary answers to questions. Though it was by far the easiest, Katie knew that sleep would never find her tonight. There was another way. Katie formed the question in her mind and whispered it to the water.

"Where is Alfredo now, and what does he intend to do? Where is Alfredo now, and what does he intend to do?"

The spring ceased its chattering. The water formed a silent pool. For a moment it was hazy, as though slicked by a layer of oil or filth, but even as Katie watched it was wiped away and the surface of the water became as clear as the finest polished glass. Katie peered into the mirror, and saw her father.

She recognized his surroundings at once. He had reached the island. He had left the beach and was approaching the jungle of vines. They rose to the attack at once but Alfredo did not even check his stride, and they disappeared, leaving his path clear. Alfredo strode along at his ease. He might have been taking a walk in the park. His stride was leisurely, unhurried.

He entered the swamp. There was not a midge in sight. The creatures with tentacles never even showed their heads. Even illusions had no power over him.

Desperately, Katie thrust herself into Alfredo's mind, determined to learn his intentions. To her surprise, his mind opened to her like a flower. There was no resistance at all.

"Hello, Katriana, it is a long time since we spoke like this."

She didn't reply. She had no words.

"You took me by surprise when you forced me from your thoughts. I had no idea you were so powerful. I could certainly use that. Look long. I have nothing to hide from *you.*"

He let her see everything. Alfredo standing on high, the sceptre in his hand. One gesture, and the people cowered at his feet, or else were snuffed out like candles. The other warlocks knelt and paid homage to him and he stripped them of their powers with barely a flick of his wrist.

Alfredo slaughtering the merpeople on the sand, leaving their butchered carcasses out in the sun for all to see and for carrion birds to feast upon. All except the god of the sea himself who knelt at his feet, his powers gone, and worshiped him, a slave to the sceptre's might.

She saw Christophe and Fiona. Heard them screaming in torment as Alfredo leached their lives from them one tiny morsel at a time.

And lastly she saw herself. A prisoner, forced to watch again and again as her father carried out his atrocities, helpless to defy him.

With a wail of despair, Katie pitched forward, breaking the surface of the mirror. The image shattered. Her mind was her own once more.

Katie rolled over onto her side and lay there as the laughing spring once more filled her ears and the scent of grass filled her nostrils. Tears streamed down her face. Gut-wrenching sobs were torn from her one after the other as though they would never stop.

But finally they did stop. Katie lay there, her chest still heaving as an occasional sob racked her, and tried to think what to do. There was no choice now. She had to tell them the truth, whatever the consequences to herself. None of that signified. All that mattered was to save her friends and the world from the imminent disaster threatening them. Katie scrambled to her feet and began to run. She would be in time, she knew it. She *would be in time.*

She threw herself down on her knees beside Christophe and shook him roughly. He woke with a start.

"What is it?" But she was already moving on to James and Fiona.

"Wake up! Oh god, wake up!"

They both sat up, blinking with the heaviness of their sleep.

Christophe hurried over, his knife already half-drawn from its sheath. The sight made Katie want to weep. What use would knives be now?

James had not released Fiona. He was looking at Katie, and she could see by his eyes that he at least, suspected some part of the truth.

"Something's happened, hasn't it?"

"He has come!" They all turned at the new voice. Aqua was running towards them, all dignity forgotten.

“Alfredo is here! He has crossed the swamp, and is even now making his way across the bridge that spans the chasm. My illusions will have no power over him. He will be here within minutes.”

Fiona was fully awake now. She looked at Aqua, the fear evident in her eyes. “How will we stop him? There’s no time!”

“You must go now!” Aqua said brusquely. “You must reach the sceptre ahead of him.”

Fiona stared at the gates. She could see them in the pre-dawn light as the black night sky gave way slowly to the paler hues of morning. They looked forbidding. She wasn’t ready. Aqua had not given her any clear idea of what to expect. Aqua tugged at her arm.

“Come, you must go now!” It took everything Fiona had to tear herself away from James. She cast one last anguished look back at him. Katie and Christophe had moved to stand on either side of him. Katie had an arm round him while Christophe was staring back towards the bridge where Alfredo would soon appear.

Aqua hustled Fiona over to the gates.

“Your key will open these, and any other doors you will find. Otherwise it will not aid you. Find the doors within yourself, open them, and all will be well. The path will lead you to the sceptre. Do not deviate from it. Now go!” She gave Fiona a little push and turned away.

Fiona approached the gates, drawing out the key as she did so. It did not glow or give off any heat. This was just an ordinary garden gate. Fiona shot back the bolts and inserted the key in the sturdy lock. Her hands were slippery with sweat and trembling so badly that it took three attempts before she finally succeeded and the gates swung ponderously open. They made no sound.

Fiona cast one final look back at her friends. Katie and Christophe had their backs to her now, facing the bridge. Aqua was nowhere in sight. Only James was still looking her way. She gave him a small wave and he flipped her a thumbs-up before turning away. She allowed the gates to clang shut behind her and re-locked them, hoping that would at least slow Alfredo down a little.

She gazed around her. She was in a beautiful walled court. Fountains splashed and tinkled musically wherever she looked. The air was heavy with the scent of flowers and fruit from the many large trees that stood around. Honeysuckle climbed up the side of the gate she had come in by.

The path wound ahead of her, flanked on either side by two beautifully kept lawns lined with rows of flower beds alive with colour. She tried to see to the end of it but it stretched away for an immeasurable distance. Clutching the key in her hand for comfort, Fiona began to walk forward.

* * *

Christophe stood with James and Katie, watching the bridge. Somewhere in the back of his mind, the realisation lurked that he was probably going to die, yet he seemed somehow to be outside his emotions and the thought made no impression on him. He was also dimly aware that Aqua was nowhere in sight, but the knowledge flickered in the back of his brain and was instantly dismissed. An odd calm seemed to have settled over him.

This was the day he had been preparing for all his life. This was what all the running and fighting and scheming had been building up to. Against all the odds, he had brought The Appointed to her destiny. This day would either see his people saved or damned.

He should have been terrified, he knew. But he felt nothing. He had no idea how Alfredo had managed to track them, but that was of no real importance. All that mattered now was that The Appointed be given the chance she needed, and he would do his best to make sure she got it. It was his last task. Then the oath that he had sworn would be fulfilled and he could live with his father's memory in peace.

He examined his companions. James looked haunted. His eyes flicked continuously between the bridge and the gates through which The Appointed had disappeared moments before. Christophe could well imagine his feelings of fear and helplessness and he pitied him. This had never been his fight, yet his loyalty and devotion to The Appointed had been unshakeable. Christophe had come to respect him and was glad to have him at his side.

He could have wished Katie elsewhere. If she came to harm, he would never be able to live with himself, yet he knew she would never leave him. She stood a little apart from him now, her body tense, her face white and strained. She was trembling a little. He could see the brief tremors that shook her from time to time. He took a step forward, meaning to go to her, and Alfredo stepped off the bridge.

Alfredo's gaze took in each of them as they stood ranged before the gates. The force of his stare seemed to strike like an invisible whip crack and both James and Katie flinched, though neither looked away.

Christophe too stood his ground. Here he was at last, face-to-face with his enemy. The man who had murdered his family and slaughtered his people and taken everything he had a right to expect. His way of life, his freedom, and branded him a criminal. There was no room in Christophe's heart for fear.

Alfredo seemed to register this. Though he spoke to all of them, it was to Christophe that he principally addressed himself.

"Well, I am surprised to see you here. I did not expect a welcoming committee." His eyes wandered lazily over them once more. "I see The Appointed is not with you. Perhaps she has already passed through these gates, and you are the *defence* set to guard against anyone following her? Or was she only ever a tool? Sent to do the work you were too cowardly to attempt?"

Christophe returned his gaze steadily. "She is the one who will see your tyranny ended and your ambitions destroyed and she will watch with us when you die."

Alfredo smiled, though his eyes remained as cold and merciless as winter. "You always did have spirit, Christophe. A trait I usually admire. You would have made a loyal servant, were you not so stubborn."

"I would die first!" Christophe spat the words through clenched teeth.

Alfredo's smile broadened. "Oh, you will die. You, your friend and your Appointed. Do you really think that the moment I have built up to all my life will be thwarted by her? A mere child. Too choked by fear of her own weaknesses and inadequacies to threaten anyone's life but her own. Your Appointed has no power. There is nothing special or different about her."

"Then what are you waiting for?"

Christophe's eyes flicked to James, as did Alfredo. His voice was quiet, but his body was taut and his eyes smouldered with suppressed rage. He seemed ready to fly at Alfredo at any moment. Katie saw it too. She stared at James, pleading mutely with him, but James went right on. "If she's so helpless, what are you hanging around here talking to us for? We can't stop you. You could have caught up to her by now. But she's still one step ahead of you, as she's been all along."

Alfredo's face darkened. At that moment he looked truly terrifying.

"You dare to taunt me, you worthless cur?" Alfredo flung out his arm in a sweeping gesture. James was picked up and hurled backwards twenty feet to fall to the ground in a lifeless heap. A trickle of blood ran slowly down his right temple.

"No!" Katie screamed. "You do not need to do this. You are right, they cannot stop you. You have what you came for, just leave them alone!"

Alfredo shot her one contemptuous glance before turning back to Christophe, a gleam of triumph flickering in his merciless eyes.

"Is not my daughter fickle? One moment she is swearing undying loyalty to me, the next she is begging me to spare the lives of my enemies. She is growing tender-hearted, a common trait in the young."

The words were a meaningless buzz in Christophe's ears. He heard, but it took several seconds before his brain could compute the sounds Alfredo was making into recognizable language.

"What… what do you mean?"

This time Alfredo's smile did touch his eyes. It was terrible to see.

"Poor Christophe, you understand so little. I see you were never aware of your companion's true identity. A costly mistake. She played her part well, did she not? It was through my mental link with her that I was able to track you. It was through my access to her memories that I was able to scry your precious Appointed and follow her wherever she went."

"No," Katie gasped, barely able to get out the words. "Christophe, it was not like that! I did not—"

Alfredo rode ruthlessly over her. "Oh come now, Katriana, all traitors are unmasked eventually. Do you deny that you befriended The Appointed when she was a prisoner in Miguel's house? That you used your knowledge of the old smuggler's passages to plan her rescue? That you ingratiated yourself with the travellers and made yourself invaluable to them so that Christophe would take you along as guide? That we spoke on the journey and that you knew I followed behind? Do you deny all this?"

There was a terrible silence. Christophe stared at Katie. His lover, his friend, willing her to refute the accusations, to stop the fall into the abyss of horror that was threatening to swallow him whole.

She stared back at him, her eyes full of despair. When she spoke, the words were barely a whisper. “He speaks the truth.”

Christophe sagged. Something hurt deep in his chest. It felt as though his heart had been torn out and thrown still beating at his feet. He could barely keep upright.

“No!” he mouthed the word soundlessly. He wanted to scream, but his throat seemed to have sealed shut on his pain.

“Ah, Christophe,” Alfredo’s voice came from a long way off. “You have learned a hard lesson. I am glad I was able to teach you. Love has always been the undoing of *decent* people. It allows them to be manipulated so easily. I am glad you should know this before you die.”

Somewhere even further away, he seemed to hear Katie sobbing.

Alfredo made another sweeping gesture, this time including both Christophe and Katie. Instantly they were frozen in place, unable to move anything except their eyes and mouths.

“I have wasted too much time already, and you too I am sure have much to discuss. Take heart, Christophe. Your Appointed will soon cease to suffer. Her cares will be over. She will never see my conquest of human kind, or live to know the truth. That at least, you *have* managed to protect her from.” With that, he laid a hand on the gates. They trembled a moment as though in a high wind, then crumbled to dust, statues and all. Alfredo stepped through the revealed opening without a backwards look.

Christophe stood listening as Alfredo’s footsteps faded away. Then Aqua appeared as though from out of the earth. She dropped to her knees at James’s side and bent low over him.

Christophe could not see what she was doing, but James suddenly rolled over and opened his eyes. Christophe watched with a kind of numb detachment as Aqua lifted James into a sitting position. He groaned as Aqua placed her fingers over the wound on his temple and shuddered once. Then slowly, with Aqua’s help, he regained his feet and saw Christophe and Katie.

“What happened to you?”

“There is no time!” Aqua gasped. She was still on her hands and knees on the ground, her head bowed as though with exhaustion.

“Katie and Christophe are trapped and I have neither the strength nor the power to free them. The spell will wear off, but by then it will be too late. The Appointed will be dead and Alfredo will have his prize. You must go after her. Do everything you can to protect her.”

“Where were you when Alfredo was here?” James demanded angrily. “You were quick to come out of hiding when he was gone.”

“I have no way to resist him. He would have killed me on sight. What use would I have been to you then? Go, if you value your friend’s life at all.”

James wavered, cast one regretful glance at Katie and Christophe's motionless forms. Christophe held his gaze, saying with his eyes what he could not put into words.

It is up to you now. Do what you can. James nodded once, then turned and sprinted off down the winding path. He was soon lost from view, and Aqua had also vanished, fading away into the air. Christophe and Katie were alone.

* * *

He stood, unable to move, cramps stabbing through his arms and legs from being held rigid so long in one position. He wanted to close his eyes, shut out Katie's face, and lock away his grief, but he knew it would do no good. Her face was etched on his mind and there was no escape. He forced a word out through the tightness in his throat. "Why?"

Her voice was flat and empty. "He was my father. I lived with Miguel but Alfredo was my real father. I rarely saw him. I was so happy when he asked me to help him. I thought at last he had noticed me. That I could be of use to him. I wanted his approval. I wanted him to love me."

"So it was all a lie? Everything between us was a lie?"

"No! How can you believe that? I befriended you at first because I needed to get close to you and Fiona, but I meant every word I ever said to you. I love you!"

"And you expect me to believe you? You have lied from the moment we met. How can I trust you now? How can I believe anything that comes out of your mouth?" His voice broke.

"I loved you so much. I would have done anything for you, given my life for you, and all the time…" he broke off, unable to continue.

Katie's eyes pleaded with him.

"I tried to stop him. When I realised what he was really like, I shut him out. But it was too late. He already knew what Fiona looked like by then, and could scry her whenever he needed to."

Christophe uttered a choked laugh. "So you betrayed your father too? Your conscience really is a law unto itself."

"That is cruel," she whispered, tears filling her eyes.

"You accuse me of cruelty? You served the most evil man in the land!"

"I didn't know!" she screamed. "I didn't know what he was like. I never knew him. I wanted to tell you so many times but—"

"But what?" he shouted back, voice cracking. "What stopped you, another rush of conscience?"

"I was afraid," she said softly. "Afraid you would never forgive me. Afraid I would never see you again." She strained against the invisible bonds holding her, trying to reach out to him.

"Please, Christophe, it does not have to be like this. We can get out of here, start our lives afresh. We can still be together."

His voice was drained of emotion. “What do you think my people would do to you once they learned who you were? It would mean your death and mine as well.”

“Then we will not return to them.” Her voice was desperate now. “We can go somewhere they would never find us. I cannot live without you.”

He felt something inside him break. He could go with her. He was tempted. Despite everything, he knew he still loved her, but he couldn’t trust her. He would never be able to do so again. What sort of life would they have with no trust? A life without that was no existence at all, and all other feelings would quickly die. His duty was here with The Appointed and with his people.

Though every word seemed to kill him over and over again, he said, “It is too late for that, Katie. When I get free of this magic, I will go after The Appointed. You had better flee while you have the chance.”

She stared at him, tears streaming down her cheeks, her rigid body trembling with the force of her grief. He closed his eyes so he wouldn’t have to see.

Alfredo’s spell seemed to take an agonising amount of time to wear off, but finally they could move again. Katie reached out to him but he pushed her away. If he embraced her now, he would be lost. He would abandon all reason and The Appointed would be doomed. He turned and stumbled off down the path. It cost everything he had not to look back, but he knew he had left half his soul behind with the figure kneeling bowed and crumpled among the paradise of Aqua’s garden.

* * *

Fiona followed the path as it wound its way through the flower beds and fountains. The air was sweet and fresh and the rising sun warmed the back of her neck pleasantly.

At any other time she might have enjoyed this walk, but she barely noticed the beauty all around her. She was alone with only her own thoughts for company.

Soon, with any luck, she would find what she searched for. And then what? She was still none the wiser about how the sceptre could actually be destroyed. Yet if Aqua was to be believed, the answers were waiting for her. She shuddered inwardly. Another test. Didn’t the merpeople ever trust anyone? What more did she have to prove? She had obtained the key, after all. It had responded to her and enabled her to pass the various wards and solve the clues that had led her here. She had even figured out how to combat the magic that Aqua had placed over the island. What more could they ask of her?

Despite what Aqua had said, she still could not fight off the fear that it would take magic of some kind to destroy the sceptre. Power she didn’t have. She had said as much to Aqua, but did Aqua believe her? Surely anyone who could use the key and survive so many dangers must have some power. Fiona wished it was true.

She pulled out the key, half hoping to see its glow and feel its comforting warmth, but it was cold and lifeless. She sighed heavily and tucked it away once more.

She wished James was with her. It seemed too much to expect her to save the world alone. She was only now coming to realise just how much she had come to rely on James's strength since her arrival in this strange land. And how reassuring it was to have him near her. Sleeping close to him made her feel safe. Being without him made her feel vulnerable.

Fiona stopped abruptly. Lost in her thoughts, she had paid no attention to where her feet were carrying her. The path ended abruptly in a high brick wall into which was set another gate.

Fiona looked around uncertainly. Aqua had specifically instructed her to follow the path. She scanned her immediate surroundings quickly. Nothing but lawns to either side. The wall before her was sheer and so high that she could not see over it. It seemed her only way forward was through the gate. Praying that the path would continue on the other side, Fiona took out the key and inserted it into the lock. The gate swung open soundlessly.

A shrieking blast of wind struck her like a hammer blow. Simultaneously, a brilliant shaft of light slanted through the opening. Fiona flung up a hand to shield her eyes, reaching out with the other for something to grasp on to. The wind was a tornado of fearsome strength and ferocity, plucking at her with powerful, icy fingers. Unable to prevent it, Fiona felt her balance shifting. She dug in her heels, grabbing futilely for the gate post. She opened her mouth to scream and was picked up and hurled forward into a whirling vortex of bright colours and changing images.

She hit the ground hard, her momentum causing her to skid several yards on her back before coming to a stop. Bruised and aching, she got unsteadily to her feet, looked around and saw… her mother!

Fiona stared in disbelief. It couldn't be! She squeezed her eyes shut for a count of five, then opened them again. Her mother was still there, further away now, but unmistakeably real. Fiona stared wildly around her. Somehow, impossibly, she was back on Earth. More than that, this was the town where she'd grown up. She recognized the street, and could even catch a distant glimpse of the building where she went to school. This made no sense. How had she managed to step from one world into another? Was she dreaming? Had she been knocked out when she was hurled through the air? She pinched herself hard. It hurt, so she supposed that meant she was awake.

Her mother was nearly out of sight now around a corner. Suddenly frightened that she would lose her altogether, Fiona hurried after her.

"Hey, Mum, wait up!" Mrs Armstrong did not look back. She kept walking, head tucked low into her collar for warmth. It was a blustery, overcast day. Fiona felt cold in her leggings and tunic.

She ran after her mother, weaving and dodging through the busy street. No one glanced at her as they hurried past. Fiona had the uncomfortable feeling they were staring right through her, as though she were transparent, or not really there at all. That thought sent a twinge of fear down her spine, but she quelled it at once. Of course she was here. She could hear the traffic rushing by on the main road on her left. She could feel the solidity of the ground beneath her feet, and she could see her mother, solid and alive. She was here, but she had no idea how it had happened. What had become of the world she had left? What had happened to the sceptre? Where were her companions?

Then a truly horrible thought struck her. James was still there! He hadn't come back with her, unless he had somehow managed to find his own way. But she knew he would never willingly have gone without her. That meant he was probably still there. She would have to go back for him but not just yet. The lure of her mother's face was too much to resist.

She longed to run to her, to hear her voice once more. The longing was an ache deep in her chest that would not be denied.

Her mother was entering the supermarket where they had always shopped for groceries as long as she could remember. Fiona watched as she selected a trolley and set off down the first aisle, the fruit and vegetables.

Fiona hurried after her.

"Mum, Mum, stop! It's me! It's Fiona!" Her mother did not even turn her head, though she must have heard.

Fiona was hurt. Why was her mother ignoring her?

She stopped where she was, looking around. A man was coming towards her with a loaded trolley. Fiona stuck out her foot. Instead of the violent swerve and accompanying oath, the man simply walked through her foot as though it was nothing but thin air.

Fiona was more confused than ever. She was back on Earth, yet for some reason, nobody could either see or hear her. Was this another illusion? Like those on the island? She stood where she was, eyes squeezed tightly shut, concentrating with all her might on the garden and the path she had been following.

*I'm still there. Nothing is real. I'm still there.* But when she opened her eyes, she was still in the supermarket.

Not knowing what else to do, Fiona hurried to catch up with her mother once more. She had stopped and was filling a carrier bag with apples. Close to, Fiona saw that she looked pale and drawn. There were dark circles beneath her eyes, which wore a look of such infinite sadness that it wrung Fiona's heart.

A woman accosted her.

"Liz! How are you?"

Fiona remembered this woman vaguely. She had been a neighbour of theirs when Fiona was very small. She had moved away to the other side of town.

Mrs Armstrong looked up from the apples and gave a wan smile. "Oh, bearing up you know, Carol. Just taking each day as it comes. Not much else I can do really."

The other woman clucked with sympathy. "I read about it in the papers. I'm so sorry, Liz. I can't imagine what you must be going through."

Mrs Armstrong nodded. "Thank you."

"How's Michael taking it?"

"He moved out about three months ago. He just couldn't cope. Fiona's death, it broke his heart. He'd go out every day looking for her. He refused to give up. Then one day he just stopped. He spent hours shut up by himself in his study. He barely talked any more. I tried everything I could to reach him. To make him talk about it. But he just locked it all up inside and that was the end. The divorce should come through early next year."

Fiona stared at her mother in horrified disbelief. Her parents were getting divorced? No! I'm still alive! But it was no good saying it aloud. She knew her mother wouldn't hear. She was forced to stand there helplessly and listen to the conversation.

"Her room is still just as she left it," Mrs Armstrong was saying in a brittle voice. "I just haven't been able to bring myself to clear it out. Somehow, I still keep expecting her to walk through the door any day. Silly, I know."

Carol put an arm round Mrs Armstrong's shoulders.

"It's not silly at all. I was the same way when my Robert died. Even now I think of things I want to tell him, and it's always a shock when I remember he's not there."

"The worst thing," said Mrs Armstrong, starting to sob, "is that we'll never know what really happened to her. She just disappeared near the lake, but her body was never found. She just vanished without a trace. She had no reason to run away. She'd just won a swimming scholarship."

"Wasn't there a boy involved? I understood the police were looking for him?"

"There's no trace of him. The police are not even sure he even existed. Even the lifeguards at the pool never saw him. They were all told that they weren't needed on the day of the swimming gala, though no one seems to know who sent the message. The police are saying it was a tragic accident, or worse. But I can't believe it. She had no reason to take her own life. Someone must have…"

Fiona couldn't stand to hear any more. The idea that her mother could even think that she would run away, let alone commit suicide was more than she could bear. She reached frantically for her mother's hand.

"Mum, I'm here! Mum, for god's sake, look at me!" But it was no good. Her mother made no response. Carol made no response. She just patted her mother's back as she continued to cry into her friend's shoulder. Shoppers were looking over, staring right through Fiona, intent on the scene playing out in front of them.

Sobbing herself, Fiona blundered towards the exit.

"I'll kill you, Christophe," she said between her teeth.

She flung open the door. A blast of wind hit her, caught her up. There was another moment of swirling colour, and she was back in the garden once more. The gate clanged shut behind her.

Then, before her eyes, the gate began to melt into the wall, taking the way back to Earth with it. Fiona stared a moment, transfixed, then hurled herself at the gate, but it was already too late. There was nothing but hard, unforgiving stone. She struck the key against it repeatedly, beat the stone with her fists until her knuckles bled, but the gate did not return. The wall itself began to fade before her eyes until the path stretched unbroken before her once more.

She stood there, hands hanging limply at her sides, head bowed, face hidden by her hair. Her way back, possibly her only way home, gone. She felt an indescribable sense of loss. Her mother's face seemed to swim before her eyes. She heard her voice, sad and bewildered. *"She had no reason to take her own life."* She didn't think she would ever forget it. But gradually, her shocked senses reasserted themselves and she began to puzzle it through.

She had arrived on what she thought was Earth, yet she hadn't really been there. She had just been a wraith. A spectre of her past. She drew a sharp breath. Was that the test? To choose between the people of her past and those in her present? The way she saw it, she had two choices. She could either stay here and wait for the gate to reappear or go searching for it, or she could do what she had been given to do and find her way back later. Somehow she knew that whatever she decided, it would come to pass. If she wanted to return now, she could. As though to verify this, an outline of the gate shimmered before her. It was hazy and distorted, awaiting her decision. With a deep groan, Fiona forced herself to resume walking, but with every step it felt like she was deserting her parents all over again. *I'll come back, she vowed silently. When this is finished, I swear I'll come back, whatever it takes!*

She approached the next gate warily. It appeared just as suddenly as the first. A solid brick wall barring her path with a gate set into it. Fiona stopped and looked around. As before, there was no way forward except through the gate. She took out the key once more and unlocked it.

This time, she was a little more prepared for the whirling vortex and bright flashes of colour, but the sensation was equally unpleasant. Fiona squeezed her eyes shut and waited for it to stop. When at last the world stopped spinning, she opened her eyes, and found herself staring at a scene of slaughter.

She recognised where she was. The city port where all her troubles had really begun. Where Christophe had brought her, what now seemed a lifetime ago.

The scene was one of total devastation. The few buildings still standing were little more than gutted, blackened ruins. Mounds of rubble as high as houses blocked the streets and alleys. But that was not the worst of it.

Bodies lay everywhere. Some still recognisable, others mutilated past identifying. Some people lay where they had fallen. Others were piled in mounds. The ghastly stench of death made Fiona gag. As she picked her way gingerly forward, rodents darted out from under her feet, and a carrion bird with a cruel, curved beak and malevolent eyes, suddenly soared into the air with an angry screech.

Fiona fought hard not to vomit. What on earth had happened here? Had all this happened since she'd been gone? Who was responsible? Not Alfredo, surely! He had been busy tracking her.

She caught a flicker of movement out of the corner of one eye. Turning, she saw a hand protruding from a mound of bricks. It twitched feebly. Fiona could hardly believe it. Someone was still alive. She hurried over.

"Hang on!" She heaved frantically at the brick pile. The bricks proved remarkably easy to dislodge. Many crumbling into dust at her touch. The figure was quickly revealed. Fiona went cold.

It was Christophe. He lay on his side, his head cradled in the crook of one arm. His face and arms had been cruelly lacerated and his hair was matted with blood. His tunic too was soaked with it. His breathing came in laboured gasps.

An image rushed into Fiona's head. Christophe lying in the street after the beating he'd received from Miguel's men. His own blood pooling around him.

"No!" Fiona whispered. "This can't be real! You're not dead; you're on the island with James and Katie." She crouched at Christophe's side. His eyes had flickered open at the sound of her voice, and their expression made Fiona rear back. There was such concentrated hatred in his gaze that it struck Fiona like a physical blow.

"So," he rasped. "Are you satisfied with what you have done?"

"What *I've…*" Fiona stared in confusion. "I haven't done anything! What's happened?"

"What do you think?" He spat out the words. Flecks of blood appeared on his lips. "Alfredo took the sceptre. While you were safe and sound in your cosy world, Alfredo used the sceptre to turn this city to rubble. While you hid like a coward, your people were butchered and left like carrion for the rats!"

Fiona hid her face in her hands, trying desperately to blot out Christophe's words and the burning accusation in his eyes.

"This isn't real, it can't be! I left you in Aqua's garden. This can't be true!"

"Ah, yes, deception. You deceived your own people; I never thought you would deceive yourself. Is that how you live with your treachery? Is that how you sleep at night?"

"Shut up!" Fiona was nearly in tears. "I don't know what you're talking about! I haven't returned to Earth. I'm going to get the sceptre right now. You're hurt, delirious or something."

Christophe tried to laugh, but it came out as a wheezing cough. "Look around you!"

Fiona did, and saw Esther and Gideon lying a short way off. Lena lay between them. They each had an arm out flung towards her as though to protect her. Antonio and Josephine were also there, and Jeremiah, and Bess and her family.

"Do you deny it now?" the voice was a harsh croak as Christophe fought for breath. "While you ran and hid, people who loved you and believed in you died! You abandoned them." He fell back, his breathing rattling his chest. A sudden spasm of pain racked him. He convulsed once, then lay still.

Fiona ran. Blindly she fled through the ruins and the dead. Fleeing the spectres that chased her. The ghosts of her guilt and remorse and the faces of those she had betrayed. Christophe's final words seemed to echo in her head to the frantic beat of her heart. The sound of her own pounding footsteps was all that she could hear in a silence loud with accusation.

A building appeared on her left. A yawning well of blackness. She dived towards it, seeking somewhere, anywhere to escape her demons. It swallowed her up like a hungry mouth, and spat her out once more into Aqua's garden. The gate and wall shrank instantly into nothingness.

Fiona lay where she was, trembling and sobbing, so relieved to be free at last of that hideous nightmare.

It took many minutes before she had calmed down sufficiently to think through what had happened and determine the purpose of that horrific ordeal.

It couldn't have been real. Though it had seemed so, none of that could have actually happened. The sceptre had not even been found. And she had never returned to Earth at all.

But she had wanted to. When she had seen her mother's face, hadn't she wanted nothing more than to abandon everything and go to her? She had been plagued with fears and doubts ever since she had first learned what was expected of her. She had nearly given in to them on more than one occasion. A warning then? Of what would happen if she were to succumb to her fears? Fiona shuddered. No, it would not happen. She would do everything in her power to prevent the horrors she had just witnessed from becoming a reality. It was this determination that eventually gave Fiona the strength to climb to her feet and continue on, but she wondered, with something very close to panic, what other torments lay in store for her before this was over.

When she saw the third gate, Fiona almost turned and fled there and then. She stood motionless, staring at the gate for several seconds before mustering the courage to approach. The key shook slightly in her hand as, with a deep sense of dread, she inserted it into the lock. For the third time she was engulfed and spun into the void, to land… Fiona opened her eyes.

The hall was magnificent. Tall, elaborately carved pillars rose to support a ceiling too high to make out. Richly beautiful tapestries decorated the walls, depicting ships riding at anchor and mermaids reclining languidly on rocks.

In stark contrast to the hall's grandeur, the walls were lined, not with rows of richly carved chairs, but plain, ordinary wooden benches. These were arranged in rows down both ends of the room, and they were packed.

The very centre of the hall was a dais, on which stood a high-backed gilt chair that bore greater resemblance to a throne. Fiona sat in this chair.

She stared around her in disbelief. Where on earth was this place? It was nowhere she had ever been, she was certain of it.

Directly before her stood a small round table on which rested a velvet cushion. Something lay on the cushion, but it was covered by a strip of cloth. Yet Fiona could feel it calling to her. Something deep inside her seemed to respond to whatever was concealed there. She had an almost overwhelming urge to twitch the cloth aside and take it. She didn't know what it was, but she knew it belonged to her.

While she still wrestled with these confusing thoughts, a door at the back of the room opened and a small procession entered. The hall instantly fell silent as everyone leaned forward to watch. Fiona also craned her neck, her preoccupation momentarily forgotten. What she saw made her mouth fall open in shock.

About half a dozen men were making their way towards her. They were of all ages and dressed in the typical clothing of the Guardians. She recognised none of them, except the boy leading.

It was Christophe. He was armed, as were the others, as though for battle. His quiver hung at his waist and his bow rested across his back. His usual array of knives hung at his belt. But his eyes had a quality that Fiona had never seen there before. Merciless was the word that jumped to her mind as she watched him. There was no forgiveness there, no shred of compassion.

The men were leading two captives with them. Heavy manacles shackled their wrists and ankles so that they could only shuffle awkwardly along. Jewelled collars with leashes attached were fastened to their necks and held by their captors. They wore long hooded robes that obscured their faces. Fiona stared in mounting astonishment as the procession approached. What was going on? She watched with some anxiety as the prisoners were forced to their knees before her. Those holding the leashes maintained their grip, while Christophe stepped forward and whisked off the men's hoods.

Fiona gave an audible gasp and an angry hiss rippled through the spectators. The two prisoners were Alfredo and Miguel. They knelt before her, their captors standing menacingly over them. Fiona gaped from them to Christophe, utterly bewildered.

Miguel's face was chalk white. A sheen of sweat dampened his forehead and his eyes darted constantly around the room like those of a hunted animal. Fiona could hear his laboured panting. He was terrified.

Alfredo on the other hand, stared up at Fiona with a look of disdain on his face. Even shackled and on his knees, he still maintained an air of authority.

What was she expected to do? Fiona looked appealingly at Christophe.

As though in answer to her unspoken question, Christophe announced in a ringing voice that all could hear, "My people! The accused have been brought before you today, so that you may witness with your own eyes, the fate of these men whose heinous deeds are known to all here.

"The charges are: The slaughter of their fellow citizens, the rape and assault of our women, the torture and imprisonment of all free-thinking beings and the trafficking of their fellow citizens into slavery. These crimes deserve the severest penalty, and by the grace of our Appointed saviour, who has delivered us all from their tyranny, we will see justice served." Turning to Fiona, "We call upon you now, Appointed, to carry out the sentence of your people. That for their evil, these men shall suffer instant and immediate death."

A roar of agreement filled the hall as every person gathered leaped to their feet to shout their approval. Several leaped onto the benches and began to clap and stamp in rhythm. Soon others joined in until the walls rang.

Fiona turned to Christophe, intending to demand if he and his people had taken leave of their senses. How on earth was she expected to kill Alfredo? And why was it up to her?

Then she remembered the cushion on the table before her, and the mysterious object that had seemed to reach out to her. Suddenly, she knew what she would find beneath the cloth. It must be the sceptre. Somehow, this was a future time, in which the sceptre had been found and Alfredo deposed. Was this where she would find the sceptre at last? She twitched aside the cloth.

Instantly the room was silent once more. All eyes were fixed on her. Miguel began struggling futilely against his bonds, but Alfredo's eyes were riveted on the sceptre, now revealed for all to see.

As Fiona gingerly picked it up, a tremendous heat seemed to rush through her veins. Anger such as she had never felt before coursed through her. She surged to her feet. The power was awesome, intoxicating. She felt exhilarated, invincible. All these people gathered here were nothing, insignificant compared with the power she wielded.

For the first time, she saw real fear on Alfredo's face, and the sight was like the sweetest honey to her. Now she would have her revenge. She would obliterate these two men who had caused her so much torment. Snuff them out of existence. Exultantly she raised the sceptre above her head.

"No! Fiona, stop!" She whirled around, furious. Who dared to interrupt her moment of triumph?

A boy stood leaning against the door that the prisoners had entered by, his back pressed firmly against the rough wood, his gaze fixed squarely on her.

Fiona lowered the sceptre. She remembered this boy. It was her friend James. The one who had been with her when all this began, and who she had feared she would never see again.

"James! What are you doing here?"

"Put it down, Fiona. Put the sceptre down. This is not who you are."

She stared at him, perplexed. "What do you mean? Now's my chance. I can get rid of these men once and for all, and then the people will be safe. I am The Appointed."

"You aren't a killer. If you kill them now, what makes you think you'll be any better than them? That's exactly what they would do. Attack someone who can't fight back."

Fiona felt confused. The power still coursed through her, and the sense of invincibility, but doubts wormed their way into her mind. Doubts that she couldn't ignore.

"They're evil," she said uncertainly. "Surely they should be punished?"

"Two wrongs don't make a right. The Fiona I know would never take another person's life, whatever the reason."

"But—"

"Make up your mind, Fiona. Who do you want to be? The Appointed? Or yourself? There will be no turning back once you decide."

His words echoed in Fiona's head. Everything else around her seemed out of focus. Even James was blurred, as though she only saw a hazy reflection rather than a real person.

She had a choice. The sceptre still called to her, with a voice as sweet as a melody, enticing her with promises. But James's voice was strong and discordant with the seductive music of power.

Fiona pressed her free hand to her throbbing temples. Why destroy the sceptre? Why not use it to put an end to Alfredo and Miguel, an end to the suffering her people had endured for so many years. Wasn't she the Appointed? Saviour of her people? What better way to save them?

Memories of her father's voice joined the discordant racket inside her head. His description of the sceptre as a weapon of evil. Created by evil and used for evil. Embedded with the magic of twisted souls that in turn fed on the emotions of the wielder and allowed that person to enforce their will. Such a weapon as that could never be used for good. The sceptre would always find a way to feed on the corrupt nature of humans and overcome them in the end. Some minds would be stronger than others, more able to resist, but none would be impervious. Their very humanity would prove their undoing. Fiona might be able to save her people from Alfredo, but she would not be able to save them from herself. The one, the only way to guarantee their salvation was to destroy the sceptre and its foul magic for ever.

Fiona opened her hand. Her movements were slow and jerky, each costing a tremendous effort. The sweet music rose to a desperate shriek as one by one she uncurled her fingers and let the sceptre fall. Then she turned and flung herself through the door at her back, to arrive a few seconds later in the peace of Aqua's garden.

She knelt on the path for a time, watching as the gate faded to nothing and her breathing slowed to normal. Then she climbed to her feet once more.

"Thank you, James," she whispered under her breath, wondering if he'd really been there at all.

* * *

Christophe stumbled blindly forward, not caring about anything except putting as much distance between himself and Katie's desperate face as he could. But it wasn't long before he was forced to stop, unable to go on. He needed release or he would go mad. He chanced one glance back over his shoulder. Katie was nowhere in sight, nor was the ruined entrance he'd come in by.

Christophe let his grief overcome him then. Sinking down with his back against a tree, he put his head in his hands and let himself cry. It seemed to take several minutes, but finally his shoulders ceased shaking and he was able to look up. He scrubbed the wetness from his cheeks with a sleeve. He could not remember the last time he had broken down completely like that.

He had learned early on how to govern his feelings. Emotions clouded your judgement. They got in the way of your duty. He uttered a sound halfway between a laugh and a sob. He had failed completely in his duty to The

Appointed. In his promise to guide and protect her. He had failed his people, his father's memory, and most especially himself. He had never tried to help her. He had just expected her to take up her father's crusade, regardless of what she wanted. He had dismissed her concerns, been impatient with her doubts and fears. And all the time he had been falling hopelessly in love with the person who would doom his people and lead The Appointed to her death. Some protector he had turned out to be.

Christophe scrambled up, ignoring the protestations of his still cramped muscles. Perhaps there was still time to reach her. Perhaps he could still fulfil the task he had sworn to carry out all those years ago, and thereby live with himself. He set off at a brisk walk. He did not allow himself to think about the possibility that he was already too late.

* * *

James's lungs were bursting for air and a sharp stitch twisted like a knife in his side. His head still throbbed from the blow he had received, and every now and then, waves of dizziness made him stumble, but he didn't dare slacken his pace. He had to reach Fiona. If Alfredo found her first, then she would surely die. He had no idea how he would protect Fiona from Alfredo. He only knew he had to try.

* * *

Fiona felt oddly cleansed as she continued to follow the path. She sensed somehow that this was the final stretch; that her goal waited at the end of it. There was nothing left to show her. As Aqua had promised, she had discovered the truth about herself. She had confronted her deepest fears and survived. She had faced temptation and resisted. She still had no idea how the sceptre was to be finally destroyed, but she was now firmly convinced that this was the only course of action, and she had the strength and determination, if not the knowledge, to see it through. She strode ahead, quickly, confidently, anxious to end this, completely unaware of the invisible presence which stalked her.

# Chapter 22

## The Price

The path ended in a short flight of steps. Fiona descended these quickly, sure now that the sceptre waited for her at the bottom.

She found herself on a small lawn, wild in comparison with those that had bordered the path. The lawn was dotted all around with various garden statues not dissimilar to those she might find back on Earth. She made her way through them, barely giving them a passing glance. The entire focus of her attention was fixed on a large pedestal in the very centre of the lawn. She wanted to run to it, but the long grass hindered her. Hurrying as fast as she could, she crossed the lawn, and beheld the sceptre at last.

When she had glimpsed it in that other future, Fiona had paid little attention to its appearance. All that had mattered then was the power it would give her. Now she eyed it closely, taking in every bit of it.

It was a flexible rod made of some kind of metal that Fiona did not recognise, though it gave off a dull sheen as though of bronze. One end was fashioned into a claw-like hand, making for a firm grip. The other was set with two rubies the size of coins. It was hard to believe, looking at it, that it held such formidable power. Fiona thought of the souls trapped within the metal. Men who had given up their lives willingly in order to create a weapon that had the power to alter the world irrevocably. What was it her father had said? Its power was limited only by the wielder's imagination.

Fiona had hoped, when she finally clapped eyes on the sceptre, that she would somehow know how to destroy it. Aqua had told her she would find all her answers here, at the end of the path of truth. Yet as she gazed upon it now, no insight came to her. No sudden flash of understanding. The sceptre rested on its pedestal, looking harmless and fairly nondescript. But she had to think of something. She must have been gone some time. The others would be anxious for her, and there was the very real possibility that Alfredo might appear any second. He'd had no trouble tracking her this far.

Fiona looked around anxiously, but there was no sign of anyone. The garden was utterly silent. No bird calls, not even a breath of wind. It was as though the garden were holding its breath, waiting to see what she would do.

Perhaps she should just take the sceptre and run. Get out of here while she still had time and find the others. They needed to leave this island and head back to the city. That was where she was needed. Hopefully between them, they would be able to figure out what to do.

Her decision made, Fiona leaned forward and picked up the sceptre. The moment it was in her hand, the two rubies blinked open, revealing themselves to be two glowing red eyes. Fiona cried out in shock and dropped the sceptre. It fell with a loud clang back onto its pedestal. Behind her, Fiona heard a slow handclap.

* * *

James nearly tumbled headlong down the steps. He had been running flat out, desperate to reach the end of this infernal path. Fiona was alone, in danger. Any moment might be her last. James had seen no sign of Alfredo. He had more than half expected to run into him, though he had no idea what he would do if he did, except try and stall him somehow. Alfredo had already proved that he would have little trouble disposing of James or anyone else who got in his way.

Yet there had been no sign of him. That meant one of two things. Either he was lost, which was wishful thinking at best, or he had reached Fiona already.

James did not even want to consider that possibility. Their one chance was for James to reach Fiona first, to get her away, and to hell with the sceptre.

But he was tiring. His legs felt like jelly and his lungs were bursting for air.

He only just managed to apply the brakes in time, but even so his momentum caused him to skid several paces.

He stood where he was, bent over as he gasped for breath. The stitch in his side made every breath stab through him. His chest burned.

Fiona was at the bottom of those steps he knew; along with the sceptre. Fiona, and more than likely Alfredo, as well.

James descended the steps quickly, looking around guardedly for some sign of either Alfredo or Fiona. When he reached the bottom, he ducked quickly behind the railing and peered out.

There they were, in the middle of the lawn. Even from a distance he had no difficulty recognising them. He could see the telltale gleam of Fiona's hair as the sun caught it, and there was no mistaking Alfredo's tall, gaunt figure. He was too late.

They seemed to be speaking together, which surprised James, but he was grateful for it. Perhaps, like any typical villain, Alfredo wished to savour his triumph, knowing Fiona was helpless. What was the hurry? He had won.

James ground his teeth. He longed to charge at Alfredo and pound him into the dirt, but he knew from painful experience how that would turn out. Surprise was his only weapon. Now, while Alfredo was in the throes of his victory and would believe himself safe. He wished Christophe was here. There would be no better person to have at his side at a time like this. He glanced hastily back the way he had come, half hoping to see a sign of the other boy. But he was alone. It was up to him. Even if Christophe was on his way he would never reach them in time.

Drawing his knife, James dropped into a crouch and began to move as stealthily as he could through the tall grass.

* * *

"Bravo, *Appointed!*" The name was spoken with scorn and derision. Fiona turned slowly, knowing whom she would see.

There he was, the living, breathing counterpart of the face that had tormented her dreams. His face might have been carved from weathered granite. His black robes hung loosely off his gaunt frame. But it was his eyes that froze Fiona to her marrow. They were flat, utterly without mercy, and they held a fanatical gleam that made Fiona feel sick to her stomach. It was all she could do to hold up her head and return that cold, pitiless gaze.

"At last we meet," said Alfredo. His voice was soft, and as cold as his eyes. "You have led me on quite a chase these past weeks. But it is over now. At last, I shall claim my prize. My birthright."

Fiona forced her legs to move, round to the other side of the pedestal so that it was between her and Alfredo. There was only one idea in her numb brain. Keep him talking. Divert his attention somehow. Perhaps, if she could distract him long enough, help would come. Surely the merpeople would not leave her here to die? Surely that hadn't been part of their prophecy? Or perhaps she could distract his attention enough to enable her to snatch the sceptre and run. Though at the moment her legs felt about as substantial as rubber.

"Your birthright?" she said, with a bravado she was far from feeling. "I don't see your name on it."

"Foolish child. This day and this claiming have been written in time long before you were even born. When the idea for the sceptre was first conceived, it was known that it would take someone of immense power to wield it. Perhaps the most powerful of all.

"When the sceptre was stolen, the warlocks simply bided their time, waiting until such a one was revealed to them. Then they took and trained him and when he was ready, they unleashed him on their enemies and set him on the path to claim what is rightfully his."

"And that man was you, I suppose?"

Alfredo shot her a look of contempt but she rushed on. "There's a prophecy about me too, you know. That one's also been around for quite a while. I am The Appointed. The one chosen to destroy the sceptre. Don't you think I was chosen for a reason? Such a task wouldn't be trusted to just anybody."

"You are forgetting that I have been inside your mind. I have felt your despair. I have smelled the fear leaching through the pores of your skin. Do not try to bluff me! You are as significant as…" he raised his foot, and very slowly and deliberately, brought it down on an ant that was crawling up a blade of grass. "I will dispose of you with no more effort than it took to kill that insect, and you are powerless to prevent it."

Sudden anger flared in Fiona, momentarily blotting out fear. This man was a bully. Strip away his power, and that was all that would be left. A common thug who liked to torment smaller children in the playground just because they could.

"If you're so powerful, then how come Christophe has managed to run rings round you for years? I don't see you squashing *him* like a bug. It must be really frustrating for someone of your *skill*," she invested the word with as much sarcasm as she could muster, "to have your ass beaten time and again by a boy."

Alfredo was furious. He seemed to grow taller before Fiona's eyes. His eyes blazed with fire as red as the sceptre's rubies.

"Your so-called protector fell to pieces the moment he realised that the girl he had fallen hopelessly in love with had betrayed him. His failure broke him like a knife would an egg. He will not be coming to save you now. You are alone, and now, you will die."

Before Fiona could even absorb Alfredo's words, he was lunging for the sceptre that lay between them. Fiona reflexively grabbed for it too. Their hands closed on either end. Alfredo surged upright, trying to wrench the sceptre from Fiona's grip. Fiona hung on like grim death, using both hands. She was pulled backwards and forwards as Alfredo sought to wrest it from her.

Alfredo was snarling, his lips peeled back from his teeth like a rabid dog. His eyes were twin points to the sceptre, whose red glare grew brighter and brighter.

Fiona dug her feet into the soft ground, fighting with all her might to end their tug of war.

Then from nowhere, James exploded up out of the grass and, with a wordless yell, threw himself at Alfredo.

Both Alfredo and Fiona were caught utterly by surprise at the ferocity of James's attack. James's knife flashed. Bright blood appeared from somewhere. Then they all crashed over together, James somehow ending up on top of Fiona. The sceptre let off a blinding flash, and was wrenched from her grasp as Alfredo rolled clear.

A searing, burning pain lanced across Fiona's palm. It felt as though someone had pressed a red-hot branding iron to her skin. She screamed once, then blacked out.

She must have been unconscious for only a few seconds. When she opened her eyes, all was silent. Her hand smarted and stung. She tried to lift her arm to look at it, but she couldn't move. James was still lying across her, his weight pinning her to the ground.

"James," she whispered hoarsely, "Let me up!" No answer. James didn't move.

With great difficulty, Fiona managed to roll free. She ached all over. Sitting up cautiously, she hugged her wounded hand to her chest and looked around.

James lay beside her, face-down, unmoving.

Alfredo lay a short way off, blood soaking the left shoulder of his robes. He was hurt, perhaps stunned. The sceptre had fallen from his hand and rolled away. It lay in the grass, the rubies still pulsing faintly with their internal light.

Fiona turned her attention back to James. With her good hand, she shook his shoulder gently.

"James, wake up!" No response. She shook him again, more roughly. "James, wake up! We have to get out of here now, while he's out of it!" Still nothing.

Fiona frowned, puzzled. There was no blood on him that she could see. Why then wouldn't he wake up? She tried to think back to just before she had passed out. There had been the pain of her hand, and… the flash! The sceptre had done something when they were all on the ground.

Sick dread washed over Fiona. Scrambling to her knees, she began feeling over James's body. It was difficult. Her left hand was sore and clumsy. She pressed her fingers to James's wrist, feeling for a pulse. There was none. She seized his other wrist with the same result. She tried again and again, alternately trying his wrist and his neck. Praying for just the slightest flutter. But both fingers and ears alike gave her nothing.

She felt a rising panic. James couldn't be dead, *he couldn't be dead*. It wasn't possible. She would not allow it to be possible. In desperation she seized his shoulders, meaning to turn him over to get a look at his face.

A sudden movement made her freeze where she was, crouched over James's body. Her head whipped around.

Alfredo was on his knees. He looked a little dazed. Blood still streaked one arm. But his eyes were alive with malice.

Fiona met his gaze, still crouched protectively over James.

"You killed him!"

"He was a fool," Alfredo sneered. "He should not have interfered. Now, he has paid the price. There is only you and I."

Fiona drew her knife, but she knew already that it was too late. Alfredo had already picked up the sceptre. She would never reach him in time. Alfredo rose to his feet, the sceptre held aloft. Fiona lunged forward.

Alfredo's body seemed to go rigid. For a second he froze in place, like a puppet whose strings have just been cut, a look of utter astonishment on his gaunt face. Then he pitched forward onto his face, the sceptre falling from lifeless fingers. Fiona looked down in complete bewilderment, and saw an arrow protruding from Alfredo's back, buried up to the shaft.

For a moment, Fiona stared, quite unable to believe her eyes. Then she looked up and saw Christophe coming towards her, replacing an arrow in his quiver as he did so.

* * *

Christophe saw the flash from the top of the steps. It lit up everything, forcing him to throw an arm across his eyes.

The brightness diminished quickly. Christophe blinked a few times to clear the spots from his vision. He craned his neck, trying to discover the source of the light. He had a nasty feeling that he knew exactly what it had been.

He heard Fiona scream and panic gripped him. Was he too late?

He leaped down the steps and dived behind the railing. He waited a moment, but nothing happened. Everything was still and silent. Too silent.

Dreading what he would see, Christophe got to his knees and peered guardedly out from his hiding place. He saw the prone figures on the lawn. One of them seemed to be stirring. He watched as Fiona disentangled herself from another. Christophe could not tell who. Whoever it was, they were lying face-down.

He saw Fiona leaning over the motionless form, apparently checking them for injuries. James then.

Christophe's eyes snapped back to the other figure. It was stirring, getting to its knees. Alfredo! Christophe did not need to be up close to know it was him.

His mind flicked through his options. He would have no time to run across the lawn to Fiona. He would have to act from where he was. He thought of his knives, but even with his considerable skill, he would be lucky to hit Alfredo at this range. And he would only get one chance. If he missed, it was all up.

Christophe strung his bow with a sure, practised motion. Alfredo had picked something up from the grass.

Fiona was aware of him. She had drawn her knife, still shielding James with her body.

Christophe selected an arrow from his quiver and nocked.

Alfredo was standing up now, raising something above his head that gleamed as the sun caught it.

Christophe drew the arrow to his cheek and loosed. He felt it whiz past, snatching off a lock of his hair as it went. Christophe was on his feet, already taking another arrow from his quiver. His eyes followed the arrow's flight. It sped true. Christophe saw it strike Alfredo in the middle of his back, punching through clothing and flesh and bone. He watched as Alfredo slowly toppled forward.

Then he was moving, setting off across the lawn to where Fiona waited, replacing his arrow in his quiver as he came.

When they met, neither said anything for a moment. Christophe's eyes wandered between the two motionless figures on the ground. Alfredo lying in a spreading pool of blood, the sceptre lying near an outstretched hand, almost as though inviting Alfredo to reach down and pick it up. But Alfredo would never wield the sceptre or anything else. Christophe did not need to see the man's face to know that he was dead. The arrow had lodged itself so deeply in his back that there was no way he would have survived.

Christophe's gaze strayed to James. He seemed unmarked, yet he lay seemingly where he had fallen, as motionless as Alfredo.

Christophe turned then to Fiona. She was still kneeling in the grass. Her face was white and frightened. It struck Christophe, perhaps for the first time, how vulnerable she looked. Her eyes looked unnaturally large. Her clothes were streaked with mud and grass stains. Her hair was tangled and her face scratched and dirty.

"Are you hurt?" Christophe asked gently.

She shook her head, not in denial, so much as an inability to really answer.

"James," she whispered. "I… I couldn't feel a pulse."

Cold with foreboding, Christophe took James gently by the shoulders and turned him over.

James's eyes stared sightlessly back at them, as blank as an empty page. Other than that he looked peaceful, as though death had come too suddenly and unexpectedly for him to feel fear. If it were not for his open eyes, he might have been merely sleeping.

Christophe bent and placed an ear to James's chest, but he already knew what he would find.

He lifted his head, his look telling Fiona all that she needed to know.

Fiona shifted into a sitting position beside James. She took his head and cradled it in her lap. Then she reached for one of his hands and clung on tightly. Her expression was vacant, as though she was not really seeing Christophe or anything of the world around her.

Christophe sat down close by her. "What happened?" he asked.

For a while he thought she wasn't going to answer him. He wasn't even sure if she had heard him.

Then, "He saved my life." Her voice was flat and distant, as though she had removed herself from what she was saying.

"Alfredo tried to grab the sceptre but I got to it at the same time. We struggled, then James appeared from nowhere. He leaped on Alfredo and we all fell, but the sceptre went off and…" she stopped, unable to go on.

Then at last she said, "What happened to you?"

"Alfredo happened upon us a moment after you had gone through the gates. He stunned James and imprisoned Katie and I with magic. Then he left us to follow you. James came to and went after you. I had to wait until the magic wore off. I came as swiftly as I could. I was too late!"

His last words were little more than a whisper. He looked down once more at James. Fiona was gently lifting a lock of hair away from his face with her free hand.

Christophe gasped. "What happened to your hand?"

She held out her hand mutely for his inspection. He leaned over it, concerned, and saw that her palm was burned. Three angry red welts lined her palm, already starting to blister.

"How did this happen?"

"It was the sceptre," she said indifferently. "It happened when he tore it out of my grip."

Christophe tore some strips of cloth from his tunic and bound up the hand. Fiona submitted to his treatment wordlessly, barely even wincing, though he knew he must have hurt her, however much care he took.

When he was done, she went back to stroking James's face, his hand still tightly clenched in her good one.

Looking Christophe in the eye, she said, "Is it true what Alfredo told me? Did Katie betray us?"

Christophe bowed his head, unable to meet her gaze. "It is true. She is his daughter. She was sent as a spy to guide us, and by doing so, her father, to the sceptre. It was through her memories of you that Alfredo was able to discover what you looked like and track you personally. That was also how he was able to torment you with those visions."

Fiona made no answer. Letting James gently down to the ground once more, she got to her feet and walked away. Christophe let her go, knowing she wanted to be alone.

He looked down at James again. It was his fault. He knew that. It was no use blaming Alfredo or even Katie, though they had been both instrumental in causing James's death. The blame lay at his door. If he had not taken Fiona in the first place, James would not have come after her.

He remembered the first day they had met, when he had saved James's life. But he hadn't saved it, not really. He'd just bought James a little more time.

James had been Fiona's true protector. He had even given his life for her, the ultimate sacrifice a Guardian could make for his charge.

It should have been him lying there. And would have been, if he had done his duty correctly.

* * *

Once she was a good distance from Christophe and James's body, Fiona sat down with her back against a tree and waited for some release. But none came. The tears gathering behind her eyes remained unshed. The scream of despair she longed to utter remained lodged in her throat.

James was dead. Her friend and companion since she was old enough to walk. The one who had been with her through everything, both good times and bad, gone for ever. And he had taken the better part of herself with him. How would she get through life without him by her side, as he had always been? And how would she ever explain to his father or Carolyn? She knew she wouldn't. She could never tell anyone the truth, and she would not insult James's memory by lying.

She wished she had her time over to do things differently, to stop James from dying. Or better still, the power to bring him back.

She started. The sceptre! Would it work? It was a weapon of evil, but could it be used for good? It depended largely on the will of the one who held it. Could she make James live again? Laugh again?

Before she could think better of it, she was running back to Christophe.

He looked startled as she came panting up to him, and downright alarmed as she swooped down on the sceptre and snatched it up.

"What are you doing?" he said sharply.

"I'm going to try to bring James back."

"But that is impossible! You know it is! Nothing can bring back the dead."

"Maybe this can," she hefted the sceptre. Its eyes had blinked open again.

Christophe surged to his feet. "No, Fiona, you must not do this!"

It was the first time he had ever used her name. The sound of it reached her. For the first time she really focused on him, seeing him.

"That weapon is evil," he said earnestly. "It cannot be used for good."

"We don't know that, not until we try."

"And suppose James comes back as a warlock? A monster like Alfredo?"

Fiona took a deep breath. "Then we'll just have to kill him again, for... for his own sake."

Christophe hesitated a minute, then nodded. "Alright. Try it."

Fiona knelt beside James once more, grasping the sceptre firmly in both hands. She concentrated every particle of her mind on what she desired, willing her determination to travel down the sceptre and into James's heart.

The sceptre began to judder violently in her grip, but she pushed harder, willing life back into James, willing him to breathe, to live, to return to the life that had been so cruelly snatched from him.

The sceptre began to emit a high-pitched keening that made Christophe cover his ears, but Fiona didn't notice. Her eyes remained fixated, sweat trickling down her forehead.

Then with a sound like a thunder clap, the sceptre shattered. It didn't just crack in two. It splintered into a myriad minute fragments that lay twinkling in the grass.

Fiona came back to herself. She stared from her empty hands to James. There was no change. She bowed her head in defeat.

"You destroyed it!" Christophe breathed, but Fiona didn't care. As far as she was concerned, she had made no difference at all.

* * *

The Guardians leapt lightly ashore, dragging their rafts up on to the banks. There were at least twenty of them, accompanied by two dozen of Sulaiman's men, which also included the chief himself.

They looked around warily, scanning the terrain with practised eyes. The beach seemed to be deserted, but there was a small boat drawn up on the bank.

Esther felt tension knot her stomach.

They had reached the island in record time thanks to the superb tracking of Sulaiman's men. They had picked up the trail easily and they followed it with little rest. Now it had brought them to this island.

Esther wondered what they would find here. Were they too late to save Christophe and Fiona and James? Was Alfredo here also? There was no other boat, but that meant nothing. Alfredo was a warlock, he could easily have used magic to cross the river.

"Fan out, everyone," Antonio ordered, keeping his voice low. "And search for a trail."

It didn't take long to find.

A brief whistle from Gideon brought everyone clustering around him. He indicated four sets of footprints, obvious even to Esther's inexperienced eye, and all clearly heading in one direction. A fifth fresher set of footprints led in the same direction. The sight of them made Esther's heart quail. Alfredo was also on the island. Please let them not be too late.

The Guardians formed up with Esther in their midst and began to follow the prints. No one spoke, but everyone had a hand within easy reach of his or her weapons. Even Esther gripped the haft of a long hunting knife her father had insisted she carry.

They had been walking for several minutes in silence when Sulaiman, who was on point, suddenly froze and held up a hand for them all to stop.

"There is something moving within those trees," he murmured, pointing.

Esther followed the direction of his finger, and sure enough, it looked as though someone was pushing their way through the dense branches. They were moving slowly. Esther gripped her knife more tightly. Alfredo. It had to be. She held her breath.

"Who is there?" Antonio demanded, his voice loud and strong. "Show yourselves!"

The branches were thrust aside and two figures emerged, carrying a third between them on a litter.

"Well met, my friends," Christophe said.

* * *

Esther stood by the river bank, head bowed with the others as the bearers laid James on the funeral pyre and one of them struck a light to the freshly gathered wood. The blaze caught immediately. The summer drought had ensured that the tinder was dry.

Tears rolled ceaselessly down Esther's face as she watched. She had liked James in the little time she had known him.

As he had taken the rite of adulthood, he was accorded the same funeral rites as the Travellers. His ashes would be scattered into the river by the breeze, to eventually be carried down to the sea.

They had shared each other's stories, which had taken most of the day. Christophe had told of their journey to the island and the many trials they had faced, Fiona only speaking to describe James's death.

Gideon told of the battle to regain the city and Esther spoke of Jessemine's revelation and their subsequent flight.

No one mentioned Katie. She had been nowhere in sight all day and Esther was glad of it. She did not know what she would have done if she had clapped eyes on the girl. Her cousin! The relationship made her feel sick to her stomach.

Looking at Christophe where he stood on her right, Esther saw the deep sorrow in his pale face. His eyes were haunted, as though they did not see the world around him. She longed to reach out to him, to give him some comfort, but she didn't dare. She didn't think anything she could do would lessen Christophe's grief and the knowledge saddened her almost as much as James's death. He seemed more lost to her than ever.

As much for comfort as to give it, Esther turned to Fiona, standing on her other side, and put her arms around her.

Fiona hadn't cried. She didn't seem able to. Her face was wooden, her eyes dry and blank, locking away her grief. But she returned Esther's embrace and they watched together as the pyre burned.

* * *

The journey back to the city passed in something of a haze for Fiona. She could recall nothing of it clearly, even many years later.

She seemed to be sleepwalking most of the time, eating and drinking when she had to. Speaking when she was spoken to, but otherwise remaining silent.

The days were not so bad, the constant movement seemed to provide some obscure comfort.

But at night, alone in her blankets, it would wash over her. The realisation that James was dead. What hurt her the most was that she seemed unable to grieve for him. It was all pent-up inside her and she could find no release. She had not shed a single tear since James's death. Though she often awoke at night, sweating and shaking after some nameless nightmare that she could never afterwards recall. At those times, she would sit up to find Christophe, wide awake, sitting gazing into the fire.

She never spoke to him on those occasions. In fact she never conversed with him at all. She actively avoided him, and Christophe, for his part, never sought her company. She was glad of that.

Predictably, their welcoming committee was loud and joyous. The news had travelled ahead, and the travellers found that a parade had been arranged in their honour.

Fiona was hoisted onto the shoulders of the crowd as, with Christophe at her side, the procession made its laughing noisy way through the streets to the main square.

Children ran behind and before them, strewing the ground they walked with petals. The air was filled with music and singing.

At one point, a small girl exploded out of the crowd and threw herself at Christophe, nearly sending him sprawling.

"Oh, Christophe, I missed you so much! I thought I would never see you again!"

His face breaking into the first smile he had worn for days, Christophe swept the little girl up in his arms and kissed her.

Esther, watching, was glad to see this momentary show of happiness, but she felt a tiny stab of envy that it was Lena, not she, who was able to give Christophe the comfort he needed. She squashed the feeling at once, ashamed. Lena was only a child.

After that, Lena joined the parade, clinging to Christophe's hand until it finally stopped.

A hush fell as Jeremiah stepped forward, lifting up his voice so all could hear.

"My people. As prophecy foretold, The Appointed has saved our world from a great evil. Through her courage and sacrifice, Alfredo was destroyed and his power with him, thereby removing the greatest threat this land has ever known. Through the valour of our Guardians, the city has been reclaimed, and you may all live once again as free men and women. Give thanks, all!"

Everyone bowed or sank to one knee, hands across their hearts, including the Guardians.

Fiona watched. She was glad that the people were saved, but their thanks meant nothing to her. Didn't these people understand that James was dead? Killed in the struggle for their safety. It had not been her sacrifice, it had been his. He should be here, receiving the thanks of these people.

The rest of the day was taken up with feasting and dancing, the celebrations lasting well into the night. But as soon as she could, Fiona broke away, wandering alone down to the deserted beach. The tide was out, the waves lapping gently on the shore.

Fiona sat a while, listening to the sea, waiting. At last, as she had felt sure she would, she heard the distant sound of singing.

The heavenly music rose and fell on the clear night air. At any other time it would have delighted her, but now she just watched and waited.

A mermaid appeared, swimming towards the shore with powerful strokes of her fish's tail. She settled in the shallows and turned to regard Fiona, her eyes sad and full of compassion.

"You got your form back then?" Fiona said.

Aqua smiled. "With the death of Alfredo and the destruction of the sceptre, I was freed from my service and allowed to return to my people."

"Good for you."

"It was your doing, Fiona. You gave me back my life. I will never be able to repay you."

"Why?" said Fiona. She did not elaborate. Aqua knew what she meant.

"It was necessary," Aqua said gently.

"Necessary? James had to die? There was no other way?"

"The prophecy told of a girl of two worlds who would one day set her people and ours free. For this to come to pass, the sceptre had to be destroyed. To do that, a sacrifice was needed. You were the one appointed to bring the one who would be the sacrifice to the place the sceptre was hidden, for only by a sacrifice, could the sceptre be destroyed. It was by your desire that the sceptre was finally broken. The sceptre fed off the corrupt emotions of human kind. It was how the captive souls maintained their existence. Like any captive spirit, they needed something to prey upon. When you wielded the sceptre, it was with the sole desire of restoring the life of your friend, to give him back what had been taken from him. This emotion, so pure, unable to be corrupted was too much. The souls could not feed on it. It was like poison to them and so the sceptre broke."

"Tell me this," said Fiona. "When the sceptre flashed, was that my fault? Did I kill James?"

"You were holding the sceptre, but it was Alfredo's will guiding it. The sceptre could only ever work the will of its wielder, and it would never have been your will to kill your friend."

Relief washed through Fiona. She had been wrestling on and off with that fear ever since James's death. She did not know what she would have done if

Aqua's answer had been the opposite. The dam that had previously locked away her emotions broke and she wept.

She cried until she had no strength left. Relieved at last to be able to mourn James. In the days since his death, she had come to realise just how much James had meant to her. He had been her friend and her conscience, but she had never told him how important he was to her. What an integral part of her life he was. Now she grieved for that loss.

At last, utterly exhausted, she curled up and went to sleep.

It was there that Christophe found her the following morning when he came to look for her. Aqua was still watching over her.

"You must take her home, Christophe," she said sombrely.

Christophe looked from the mermaid to the sleeping girl. "This is her home."

"It is her world, but not her home. It never will be until she is healed of the hurts she has suffered here. For that she needs time and those she loves around her."

Christophe nodded. "I always intended to take her home when this was over."

Aqua smiled. "You have become wise, Christophe. Though you hurt now, you will learn from your mistakes and be a better person because of them. Now wake her. We held back the tide to await your coming, but it will now be released. Just let it carry you both where it will."

Christophe nodded once more and Aqua sank beneath the waves.

Christophe bent to rouse Fiona.

"What is it?" she mumbled, blinking sleepily at him.

"It is time for you to return home. The merpeople have prepared a portal for you."

She was fully awake now, looking towards the sea, which was now a foaming whirlpool. Then she turned to Christophe. Her face disbelieving.

"You're really letting me go?"

Christophe felt a wave of sadness. "Yes," he said gently. "You have done what we asked of you. It is only fitting that you should go now where you wish. Come, do not fight the current. Let it take you where it will."

They dived into the boiling surf together and were instantly swept away.

Fiona went under, the force of the water hammering the air from her lungs. She spun helplessly, unable to fight, unable to breathe. Then, just when she was sure she was drowned, the spinning stopped. Her head broke the surface of the lake, Christophe rising up beside her.

Wordlessly they swam to shore and scrambled, dripping and shivering out on to the bank.

For a moment they just looked at each other, not saying anything.

"I suppose I had better go," Christophe said finally. "I will be missed, and you should be getting home."

Fiona nodded.

"Farewell, Fiona. I can never thank you enough for all you have done and sacrificed for my people."

She nodded again.

Christophe prepared to enter the lake, but Fiona calling his name stopped him. He turned back to her.

"I want you to know," she said without a trace of emotion in her voice. "That I hold you responsible for James's death. If you hadn't taken me, he would not have followed, and someone else would have been sacrificed."

He lowered his eyes, unable to meet her gaze.

"Goodbye, Christophe."

He made no answer, but flung himself into the lake and was swallowed up at once.

Fiona watched him go. The waters of the lake gradually quietened until only tiny ripples marked its surface. Then even they were still.

Fiona looked around her, taking in the familiar park where she had so often played as a child, dreaming of exploring the mysteries of the lake.

It was a mild, sunny morning, very like the one on which she had left. It was almost possible to believe that nothing had changed. And yet it had. The girl who was returning home bore little resemblance to the one who had left it what seemed a lifetime ago.

She sighed. She supposed she would have to think up some suitable explanation for where she had been. Explaining what had become of James would be harder still. She got to her feet.

Something bounced against her chest. She reached inside her clothing and drew out the key on its leather cord. She stared at it a moment. She had completely forgotten it was there. Then she tucked it away again. She would decide what to do with it later.

Turning her back on the world of her birth, Fiona set off for home.

* * *

The house was just as she remembered it. Nothing had changed. A row of milk bottles leant against the step, waiting to be collected. Fiona pushed open the gate and was about to walk up the drive when the front door opened and her mother appeared. Fiona watched as she stooped to gather up the milk bottles.

She felt suddenly anxious, vividly remembering how she had last seen her mother. She had been just a wraith then, not even visible. Was she so still? Was this a last cruel trick?

Her mother started to straighten. Fiona hurried forward, her feet crunching on gravel.

Her mother looked up at the sound and their eyes met.

Mrs Armstrong dropped the milk bottles. "My god, Fiona, is that really you?"

"Hello, Mum."

Mrs Armstrong seized her daughter in a tight embrace, crushing her so hard against her chest that Fiona could hardly breathe.

"Your dad and I thought you were … Where have you been?"

"That doesn't matter. I'm home."

# Epilogue

Katie crouched alone and desolate on the river bank. She had witnessed James's funeral and watched from hiding as Christophe and the others had left aboard their rafts. She had also searched the island and found her father's body.

They were all gone now. She had no one. She was marooned on this deserted island with no prospect of rescue, but what did she care? Christophe was gone. She would never see him again. What else did she have to live for?

A movement caught her eye. A raft was approaching, towed through the water by someone swimming alongside it.

Aqua's face met Katie's startled gaze.

"Come, Katie, climb on. You must leave this place. There is work to be done."

"What work?" said Katie distantly. "Leave me alone. There is nothing left in this world for me."

"You are mistaken. You have merely begun to walk your life's path. There is so much for you still to do."

Katie's mouth fell open. "What do you mean?"

"There is power in you, child. Power you have barely begun to discover. Your ability to see visions, your skills in telepathy and mind protection are but a small portion of the legacy inherited from your father. You could use that power."

Katie's voice was bitter. "I want nothing of my father's magic. It has destroyed my life."

"You do not have to use it as he did," Aqua said gently. "The merpeople are offering you the chance to train with us. To learn to use your magic for the good of the land as we intended your father to do. That, after all, is the true reason why magic was given to your race."

"I am a traitor. No one would ever accept help from Alfredo's daughter."

"I know, it will be difficult, but you have the power to alter your life if you wish. You proved that when you chose to defy your father; Alfredo's daughter died that day. You have shown yourself willing to fight for what is right. Use such courage and strength as you have for the benefit of the people. Their attitude would change given time."

Katie gazed out to sea, at the tranquil waters which only a few moments ago she had thought to surrender herself to. Christophe was gone. Nothing could make up for his loss. But here was an opportunity to try and make amends for what her father had done, a chance to help rebuild the land he had worked so hard to destroy.

She turned to Aqua, and the mermaid could read the decision in her eyes.

"Come," she said quietly.

Katie stepped down onto the raft and immediately it began to glide smoothly forward. She looked back once, in time to see the island sink beneath the waves. Soon it was as if it had never been.